FOOD FOR
THOUGHT

NEW SOUTHERN CLASSICS ~BLENDED~ WITH
STORIES FROM CELEBRATED BIRMINGHAM AUTHORS

The Junior League of Birmingham, Alabama

First Printing   30,000 copies
August 1995

Printed in the United States of America
by EBSCO Media

To obtain additional copies of
Food for Thought,
use the order forms at the back of this book or contact:

JLB Publications
Junior League of Birmingham
2212 20th Avenue, South
Birmingham, Alabama 35223
(205) 879-9861

Purpose

The Junior League of Birmingham, Inc. is an organization of women committed to promoting voluntarism and to improving the community through the effective action and leadership of trained volunteers. Its purpose is exclusively educational and charitable.

The Junior League of Birmingham, Inc. reaches out to women of all races, religions and national origins who demonstrate an interest in and commitment to voluntarism.

On the Cover:
Shrimp and Grits Boursin, page 224

FOOD FOR THOUGHT

came to be through the selfless efforts of many individuals who joined in this project.
Thousands of volunteer hours brought this publication from vision to fruition.
Each has volunteered from the heart.

STEERING COMMITTEE:

Editors	*Molly Pearce Clark*
	Jean Kinnett Oliver
Editorial Assistant	*Elizabeth McDonald Dunn*
Business Managers	*Cameron Daley Crowe*
	Susan Lindley Jackson
Food Editors	*Mary Reid Reynolds Fisher*
	Melanie Berry McCraney
	Spence Lee Stallworth
Testing Chairman	*Kelly Scott Styslinger*
Testing Co-chairman	*Elisabeth Crow Branch*
Community Editor	*Sandy Jenkins Bowron*
Marketing Director	*Jann Turner Blitz*
Public Relations	*Melanie Berry McCraney*
Art	*Kitty Caddell White*
Production Manager	*Ashley Carr Smith*
Copy Editor	*Peggy Shook Zeiger*

Community Advisor:	*Southern Progress Corporation*
Original Concept:	*SlaughterHanson Advertising*
Creative Direction & Graphic Design:	*Alyce Heggeman Head*
Assistant Graphic Design:	*Peggie Faulkner Hodges*
Copy Chief:	*Susan Emack Alison*
Photography:	*Ralph Anderson*
Photo Stylist:	*Virginia Ravenel Cravens*
Food Stylist:	*Julia Dowling*
Promotions:	*Davis Denny Advertising*

[Handwritten annotations:]
Happy 50th! Nancy Patsy Jan ♪ ♪ ♪

Happy Cookin"! Ann

Much Love, Sylvia

What a wonderful 50th! You've celebrated for two weeks! Love ya! Regina

Sorry I missed the party — Hope you had a happy day Love Vickie

THE JUNIOR LEAGUE OF BIRMINGHAM

THE ORGANIZATION

The Junior League of Birmingham is an organization of women committed to improving the Birmingham community. Each year, the League contributes over 45,000 volunteer hours and over $200,000 in funds to a variety of projects in such areas as education, child safety and wellness, and transitional services to the homeless. Proceeds from this book will open the door for many—serving the community and transforming dreams into reality.

BIRMINGHAM, ALABAMA

Birmingham became known as the Magic City over a century ago, as it grew "like magic" from a sleepy valley town to a large, thriving industrial complex.

Today, the metropolitan area covers five counties and is home to over a million people. As the state's largest city, Birmingham is now a center for business and finance, manufacturing and distribution. A mecca for education, insurance, healthcare, and banking, the city also encompasses a wealth of arts, sports, and recreational activities.

However, it's the combination of natural beauty, resources, and people that makes Birmingham the city it has become. It's rich in culture, filled with creativity and diversity. Most of all, it's Southern—remembering its heritage, yet planning for progressive tomorrows. This, then, is the home of the Junior League of Birmingham—the heart of the South.

INTRODUCTION

A cookbook for all the senses, FOOD FOR THOUGHT is full of the flavor of the South. More than just a taste of what we eat—it is a sampling of how we think, create, and live. As you read through its pages, listen to the Southern voices woven throughout. You'll remember your grandmother's soft reply when you asked if the cookies were cool yet. A son's quiet pride as you serve the fish that he and his dad caught early that morning. Remember the wonderful aroma of the warm pound cake your neighbor brought over the day you moved in.

You'll detect the Southern accent in such traditional favorites as "buttermilk fried chicken," and in newer fare such as "lamb chops stuffed with feta" or "curry-crusted oysters." You'll hear the exalted tenor of a new restaurant whose young chef creates a surprising new take on foods Southerners hold dear.

Yet, FOOD FOR THOUGHT is a book not just to prop on the counter, but to cuddle up with on the couch. It stirs the imagination while filling the mind. Within you'll hear the voices of Birmingham's celebrated authors as they open each chapter with their own interpretation of "a taste of the South." Their words will give you a unique perspective on the simple joys of our Southern culture.

A collection of more than 450 recipes, FOOD FOR THOUGHT captures the best of what are sure to become new Southern classics: recipes rich in tradition, inspired by many ethnic influences and a colorful history, yet expressing the changing taste of the Southern palate and lifestyle.

Come join us, as FOOD FOR THOUGHT celebrates the warmth and comfort of Southern cuisine and the heritage of our Southern hospitality.

~ AUTHORS ~

CATHY CRISS ADAMS

MARGARET WALKER ALEXANDER

FRED BONNIE

LOIS TRIGG CHAPLIN

MARK CHILDRESS

VICKI COVINGTON

ELIZABETH DEWBERRY

FANNIE FLAGG

JOHN FORNEY

CHARLES GAINES

CHARLES GHIGNA

PAUL HEMPHILL

JOHN LOGUE

ROBERT REEVES

ELLEN TARRY

Of Grits and Greens

-FANNIE FLAGG-

HAVING BEEN BORN AND RAISED IN ALABAMA I am convinced that most Southerners tend at times to become highly emotional and completely irrational over five things in life: Mother...The South...Football...Manners...and Barbecue. Thus explaining why we are so misunderstood.

I personally have seen the shock and horror on the faces of my Northern friends when I brought them home to Birmingham with me, after they have had a taste of grits or turnip greens—two things a true Southerner will crave on his deathbed. Their usual reply is (in a loud voice, I might add), "How can you eat this stuff... you don't really like this do you?" Which brings me back to manners. I will never forget my first California dinner party when I was served vegetables that were practically raw, and a salad piled full of some sort of odd green things that were similar if not identical to things my father used to pull out of the front lawn every Saturday afternoon. I of course was perfectly charming and lied like a good Southern lady so as not to hurt their feelings. "My, how fresh and crisp the broccoli is. I can just taste how healthy it must be for you!" But in my heart I was convinced I was being poisoned and feared for every capped tooth in my mouth.

That meal turned out not to be unusual. That's just the way they eat out here. I quickly found myself surrounded by health freaks. You would be hard put to find a spot of grease on anything except on the underside of a car out here. Honestly, it makes you want to eat a tablespoon full of Crisco just for spite.

Californians are so health food conscious, that one time ·CONTINUED·

FANNIE FLAGG

FANNIE FLAGG WAS BORN IN
BIRMINGHAM AND ATTENDED
THE UNIVERSITY OF ALABAMA.
WELL-KNOWN FOR HER CAREER
AS AN ACTRESS AND COMEDIENNE,
SHE ACHIEVED NATIONAL
RECOGNITION AS A WRITER
WITH HER FIRST NOVEL,
DAISY FAY AND THE MIRACLE MAN.
HER SCREENPLAY OF *FRIED GREEN
TOMATOES AT THE WHISTLE STOP
CAFE,* HER SECOND NOVEL, WAS
NOMINATED FOR AN ACADEMY
AWARD. SHE PUBLISHED THE
WHISTLE STOP CAFE COOKBOOK
IN 1993 AND IS CURRENTLY
WORKING ON A PLAY,
THE MAUDE NOEL SECRET SOCIETY.
FANNIE FLAGG LIVES IN SANTA
BARBARA AND BIRMINGHAM.

I went to church with a friend and even the Communion they gave out to the congregation was made out of organic whole wheat bread.

After I've given you some idea about what sort of people I am dealing with you can well imagine the looks of terror and the sheer hysteria I encounter when sometimes at dinner parties, while poking around on my plate of Nouvelle Cuisine of undercooked everything and not enough of whatever it is, I have been known to stare wistfully off into space and murmur..."I'd kill for a good ole greasy barbecue right now!" After my dinner partners have moved three seats away from me, they proceed to lecture me in loud voices about the dangers of barbecue. First of all, it's MEAT!!! They can hardly get the word out, and second of all it's not only meat, but PORK!!! That stuff will kill you. I have to smile as I think of all the eighty and ninety-year-old men and women I know at home sitting around enjoying a good ole barbecue with that wonderful smoky flavor served with creamy coleslaw and finished off with a slice of homemade lemon icebox pie. They just don't understand us at all. Why they actually think they won the Civil War. They don't understand that when General Lee went into that room in Appomattox he saw Grant standing there at the door and thought he was the butler and just naturally handed him his sword! But we were just too courteous to point that out. THE END

Table of Contents

EXTRA THOUGHTS

Lobster Beggar's Purses, page 39

Southern Medley

·Elizabeth Dewberry·

MY MOTHER AND I HAVE A FAVORITE ANTIQUES SHOP for winding up our Saturday browsing. We like to start out at Rich's, getting doused with whatever scents the ladies in hats and high heels have to offer that day, then move out into the mall for lunch, pausing to look at window displays or rummage through a sale rack. But by early afternoon the serious shoppers have arrived, and we head for the relative tranquility of yellowing Battenburg tablecloths and mahogany clocks that don't work.

Although I can't usually remember from week to week the difference between colognes at the perfume counter, I can always tell which potpourri the shop's owner has set out in the back of the store. As we move through her tapestries and candlesticks, we are embraced by the warm aromas of Autumn, Springtime, Country Morning. I love to open the canisters of dried flowers and spices and close my eyes, breathing in those essences.

The last time we visited there, the proprietor mentioned that she was expecting a new variety of potpourri, Southern Medley. It piqued my curiosity to wonder what scents could suggest the essence of the South and how they would do together in one bowl. I think a Southern medley of scents should include the warm, lemony breeze you get on the back porch in August when you're sipping iced tea, and the crisp excitement of those little brown paper bags of hot roasted peanuts you can buy at cold football games. The intoxicating smell of a peach orchard with just a hint of over-ripeness at your feet, and peach cobbler with cinnamon. The tense, stuffy sogginess of a black morning that erupts into thunderstorm by lunch and disintegrates into steamy ·CONTINUED·

ELIZABETH DEWBERRY

A NATIVE OF BIRMINGHAM,
ELIZABETH IS THE AUTHOR
OF THREE NOVELS,
*MANY THINGS HAVE
HAPPENED SINCE HE DIED*,
BREAK THE HEART OF ME,
AND *TOUCH ME*, *TOUCH ONLY
ME (FORTHCOMING)*.
SHE HOLDS A B.S. IN
ENGLISH AND CREATIVE
WRITING FROM VANDERBILT
UNIVERSITY AND A PH.D.
IN AMERICAN LITERATURE
FROM EMORY UNIVERSITY.
SHE LIVES IN
LAKE CHARLES, LOUISIANA,
WITH HER HUSBAND,
ROBERT OLEN BUTLER.
A VERSION OF "SOUTHERN
MEDLEY" FIRST APPEARED
IN *SOUTHERN LIVING*
MAGAZINE.

sunshine before dusk.

I hope it would suggest the warm chocolate aroma of brownies baking and the sweet dirty-sweaty smell of children who've played outside in the grass from the time school let out until darkness set in, calling them to supper. And pine cones, and rain so fine you can't see it until you feel it on your face, and the lipstick-and-powder fragrance of grandmothers.

If Southern Medley wants to evoke the idea of Southern hospitality, it should also smell like coffee brewing and strawberries with a faint hint of silver polish. Or aftershave and hairspray with a touch of the stale heaviness of mothballs. When I was a child and my parents had guests, I would pile their coats on my bed, and when dinner was served, I would throw myself on those coats and bury myself in them, so wet wool mingled with English Leather and Aqua Net always evoke memories of laughter and music and tinkling glasses for me.

A real Southern medley would also suggest a touch of the masculine scent of leather—leather books, leather footballs, leather upholstery in dark, pine-paneled dens with big, stone fireplaces. And bread baking, because everybody loves the smell, though few of us have time to bake it anymore. And the smoky, almost-tangible tanginess of barbecue.

When I smell a cedar closet, it reminds me of the hamsters who used to live in my bedroom, and for me that is also a Southern smell. Maybe not. I'm also wavering on paper mills. But definitely the fecund smell of the Georgia and South Carolina marshlands—death rotting into life—mixed with wet salt air from the coast, and dirt, preferably dirt from your own backyard, the clean, brown, gritty way it smells to plant flowers. Freshly plowed fields. Jambalaya, which smells like jazz, and Coca-Cola, which feels like jazz when you try to smell the bubbles. The crunchy, leafy smell of the Tennessee Smokies when you're near a waterfall. Something that would make you think of Spanish moss dripping from Mississippi live oaks. And of course, magnolias and gardenias and oranges, with a sprig of mint.

For Southerners, the smell of the South is whatever holds our memories of the past and suggests promises of a future that will somehow be connected to that past. Some of it really does smell wonderful, and some of it, we love the way it smells because that's the nature of love— it encompasses everything about the thing that is loved. Some of it is indigenous to the South, and some of it we call Southern because we like to think of anything that reminds us of home as Southern. It's a term of affection.

So my mother and I will go buy Southern Medley when it comes in, and we'll both put some in our living rooms and bedrooms and kitchens. But we're skeptical. We figure they'll get the magnolias and the gardenias, and we won't be surprised if they get oranges and mint. As for the rest, they can't possibly do it justice. THE END

COMPANY'S COMING through the front door—no time to prepare?
Here are some quick-fix appetizers...

- Stir 2 tablespoons pesto into 1 (8-ounce) carton of sour cream. Serve with assorted raw vegetables.

- Sprinkle shredded Cheddar cheese over individual tortilla chips. Top with one sliced jalepeño, sliced black olive or pimiento. Microwave to melt cheese—the assortment looks great.

- Combine equal parts cream cheese and cottage cheese. Fold in equal parts red and black caviar or lumpfish roe. Fill drained artichoke hearts. (It may be necessary to enlarge artichoke cavity by removing inner leaves.) Remove narrow slice from bottom of artichoke to level.

- Fill drained and scooped-out cherry tomatoes with commercially prepared guacamole, a mixture of cream cheese and chopped olives, or chicken salad.

- Spread olive oil on thin slices of party-sized French bread. Top with slice of grilled Italian sausage, slice of roasted red pepper, and mozzarella cheese. Bake at 375° for 15 minutes or until cheese melts.

- Skewer cooked tortellini and serve with a mixture of olive oil and melted butter as a dip.

- Slice top off entire head of garlic. Place in shallow pan; drizzle with olive oil. Cover and bake 45 minutes or until tender. Cool slightly. Squeeze out and spread on toasted bread rounds.

- Combine 3 to 4 ounces cream cheese with 1 teaspoon lemon juice, 1 teaspoon capers, and 1 teaspoon chives. Spread on thin wheat bread and cut into fourths. Top each with slice of smoked salmon and dash of black pepper.

- Wrap sesame bread sticks with thin strip of bacon. Roll in mixture of Parmesan cheese and a dash of garlic salt. Microwave until bacon is crisp.

- Halve and seed cucumbers. Fill with baby shrimp mixed with herb mayonnaise and white pepper or canned salmon mixed with cream, lemon juice, dill, and black pepper.

- Keep tubes of commercial polenta on hand. Slice, top with a pungent cheese, bake, and garnish with fresh herbs.

- Add 1 jar dried beef, torn into bite-size pieces, to 1 carton sour cream. Serve with assorted crackers.

A P P E T I Z E R S

C H E E S E

Basil Pesto Cheesecake 21

Blue Cheese Tarts 16

Blue Cheese Wafers 18

Brie & Chutney Tartlets 19

Cheese Pastries Supreme 23

Goat Cheese Spread With
    Roasted Red Peppers 18

Greek-Style Cheese Ball 23

Ham Cheese Ball 17

Mexican Cheesecake 20

Roasted Red
    Pepper Spread 19

Sun-Dried Tomato and Herb
    Cheese Strudels 22

Sun-Dried Tomato Spread . . . 17

Tomato Toasties 17

D I P S / S A L S A S

Avocado-Corn
    Confetti Salsa 26

Basil Dip 24

Black-eyed Pea Dip 25

Green Chile Dip 24

Hot Bacon and Swiss Dip . . .25

Just Good Salsa 26

Southwestern Chile Dip 25

Spicy Black Bean Salsa 27

Vidalia Onion Dip 21

V E G E T A B L E S

Asparagus Spears With Prosciutto
    and Parmesan 31

Cocktail Tarts 29

Cucumber Salad 30

Forest Mushroom
    Fior Di Latte 16

Fresh Mushroom Pâté 27

Grilled Quesadillas 28

Phil's Fantastico Olivata. 32

Pickled Okra-Ham Rolls. . . .30

Polenta Circles 41

Quesadillas With Goat Cheese and
    Garden Vegetables 28

Stuffed Mushrooms 31

M E A T / P O U L T R Y

Chicken Curry Balls 40

Chicken Pâté 39

Phyllo Triangles With Rosemary
    and Prosciutto 40

Trio Meat Skewers 44

S A N D W I C H E S /
T O A S T S

Bruschetta Romano 44

Ladies Day BLT's 41

Pita Chips 42

Southern Tea Sandwiches 42

Tomato Basil Crostini 43

Italian Toast 43

Watercress Sandwich
    Spread 42

Arman's Pizza 45

S E A F O O D

Avocado Crabmeat Spread . . .36

Bebla's Shrimp Bits 33

Caviar Mousse 38

Crabmeat Mousse 35

Crawfish Canapés 37

Hot Crab Dip 34

Lobster Beggar's Purses 39

Mindy's Crawfish Dip 37

Shrimp Butter 33

Shrimp Extravaganza 34

Smoked Oyster Pâté 36

Smoked Salmon Canapés 38

Spicy Cocktail Shrimp 32

"That Crab Thing" 35

SERVES 4

1/2 cup butter
1 large portabello mushroom
6 large fresh Cremini mushrooms
6 large fresh shiitake mushrooms
   Salt and pepper
1/4 cup balsamic vinegar
1/4 cup beef stock
1 small can veal demiglace*
4 balls fresh milk mozzarella,
   sliced (no substitute)
   Garnishes: julienned sweet red
   peppers, artichoke hearts,
   fresh basil

*Available at specialty food stores

FOREST MUSHROOM FIOR DI LATTE

Melt butter in a large skillet over medium-high heat. Add mushrooms. Season to taste. Add vinegar, stock, and demiglace. Sauté until mushrooms are tender. ✐ Arrange mushrooms on plates. Top with slices of fresh milk mozzarella, and garnish as desired. Serve warm.

[BONGIORNO ITALIAN RESTAURANT]

MAKES 40

1 package frozen puff pastry
1 (8-ounce) package cream cheese,
   softened
1 (4-ounce) package blue cheese,
   softened
1/4 cup sun-dried tomatoes,
   finely chopped
1/4 cup commercial pesto sauce
1/4 cup chopped walnuts
1/4 cup freshly grated
   Parmesan cheese

BLUE CHEESE TARTS

Thaw puff pastry for 1 hour. Unfold onto a cutting board, and cut into 1-inch squares. Bake at 350° until browned (about 10 minutes). Remove top half of squares, and discard. ✐ Thoroughly mix cream cheese, blue cheese, and sun-dried tomatoes. ✐ Spread each pastry square with about 1/4 teaspoon cheese mixture. Top each with a dab of pesto. Sprinkle with walnuts and Parmesan cheese. Put on an ungreased cookie sheet, and broil until cheese melts, (about 3 to 4 minutes). Serve immediately.

[LYDIA LONGSHORE SLAUGHTER]

S U N - D R I E D   T O M A T O   S P R E A D

Chop tomatoes in food processor, and set chopped tomatoes aside. Combine cream cheese and next 3 ingredients in food processor, and process until smooth. Spread mixture in a circle on a platter. Cover with chopped tomatoes, and chill for 4 to 24 hours. Serve with baguette slices.

[T O O K I E   D A U G H E R T Y   H A Z E L R I G]

SERVES 15

7 ounces sun-dried tomatoes in oil, drained
2 (8-ounce) packages cream cheese, softened
4 green onions
12 fresh basil leaves
Dash Worcestershire sauce
Baguette slices

H A M   C H E E S E   B A L L

Combine first 5 ingredients in medium mixing bowl. Cover and chill for 30 minutes to 1 hour. Shape mixture into a large ball, and coat with chopped nuts. Wrap with plastic wrap and refrigerate. Serve chilled with assorted crackers.

[C A R O L Y N   H I L L]

Hint: This may be frozen before adding nuts. Add nuts after thawing.

SERVES 12 TO 15

2 (8-ounce) packages cream cheese, softened
1 cup ground smoked ham
1 tablespoon grated onion
2 teaspoons dried parsley flakes
1/2 teaspoon seasoned pepper
1/2 cup finely chopped pecans

T O M A T O   T O A S T I E S

Cut rounds the size of a cherry tomato from bread. Crisp lightly in oven. Top each with a tomato half. Combine next 3 ingredients, and season with salt and pepper to taste. Top tomato with dab of cheese mixture. Broil until mixture bubbles. Top with crumbled bacon. Serve hot.

[B E T T Y   B L A C K M O N   K I N N E T T]

MAKES 2 DOZEN

1 loaf thinly sliced white bread
1 pint cherry tomatoes, halved
1/3 cup chopped green onions
3/4 cup mayonnaise
3/4 cup grated Cheddar or Swiss cheese
Salt and pepper
8 slices of bacon, cooked and crumbled

MAKES 7 DOZEN

6 ounces grated sharp
   Cheddar cheese
1/2 cup butter, softened
4 ounces blue cheese, crumbled
1 1/2 teaspoons seasoned salt
1/8 teaspoon cayenne pepper
2 3/4 cups all-purpose flour
1 cup chopped pecans

BLUE CHEESE WAFERS

Combine first 5 ingredients in a food processor. Add flour, and process until dough is smooth. Add pecans. Shape dough into 2 logs, and wrap in wax paper; refrigerate overnight. Slice into 1/4-inch-thick slices, and place on a cookie sheet coated with cooking spray. Bake at 375° for 10 to 12 minutes or until lightly browned.

[GRACE BRADY BENTLEY]

*To vary, use 8 ounces Cheddar, 1 1/2 cups flour, and
2 tablespoons chopped fresh chives; omit blue cheese and pecans.
These are so easy to make and keep on hand. They freeze well.*

MAKES 2 CUPS

1 (8-ounce) package cream
   cheese, softened
8 ounces goat cheese, crumbled
1 teaspoon olive oil
2 teaspoons fresh thyme leaves
3 sweet red peppers

GOAT CHEESE SPREAD WITH ROASTED RED PEPPERS

Combine first 4 ingredients in a food processor, and blend until smooth. Press mixture into a ramekin or mold lined with plastic wrap, and chill. Roast peppers over gas flame or under broiler, turning until the skins are charred all over. Place peppers in a bowl, cover tightly with plastic wrap, and set aside for 20 minutes. Halve the peppers and remove the cores; peel off skin. Cut peppers into 1-inch strips, and place strips in food processor; pulse 3 or 4 times. Unmold chilled cheese mixture; top with red pepper puree. Serve with crostini or melba toast.

[KIMBERLY JUSTICE ROGERS]

ROASTED RED PEPPER SPREAD

Low Fat

MAKES 2 CUPS

14 ounces chopped roasted
   sweet red pepper
2 tablespoons olive oil
2 tablespoons minced
   Italian parsley leaves
1 tablespoon lemon juice
2 teaspoons capers, drained
1 medium clove garlic, crushed
1/4 teaspoon salt

Arrange peppers on layer of paper towels, and let dry. ✍ Combine remaining ingredients in food processor; process until capers and parsley are finely chopped. Add red pepper and pulse several times, stopping occasionally to scrape sides of bowl to ensure mixture is evenly chopped. Check seasonings, and adjust as necessary. Store spread in container in refrigerator. Let stand at room temperature 30 minutes before serving. Serve on toasted baguette slices.

[MEADOWLARK RESTAURANT]

BRIE AND CHUTNEY TARTLETS

MAKES 7 DOZEN

1 loaf thin white bread
1/4 cup melted butter
7 to 8 ounces Brie
6 to 8 ounces commercial
   chutney

Remove crusts from bread. Roll trimmed bread out flat with rolling pin. Using small biscuit cutter, cut 4 circles out of each slice. ✍ Lightly butter miniature muffin pans. Place 1 bread round in each muffin cup. Dab each with melted butter. ✍ Bake at 375° for 4 to 8 minutes or until bread is lightly toasted. (These may be made ahead and frozen.) ✍ Remove shells and place on a baking sheet. ✍ To prepare tartlets, place a small piece of Brie in each tartlet shell. Put a dab of chutney on top. Bake at 350° for 7 to 10 minutes or until cheese melts.

[JOAN BROCK]

MEXICAN CHEESECAKE

SERVES 12 TO 15

2/3 cup finely crushed tortilla chips

2 tablespoons melted butter

1 cup cottage cheese

3 (8-ounce) packages cream cheese, softened

4 eggs

10 ounces grated sharp Cheddar cheese

1 (4½-ounce) can chopped green chilies, drained

¼ teaspoon Tabasco Sauce

1 (8-ounce) carton sour cream

1 (8-ounce) container jalapeño Cheddar cheese gourmet dip

Garnishes: 1 ounce chopped tomatoes, ½ cup chopped green onions, ¼ cup pitted sliced ripe olives

Combine tortilla chips and butter. Press mixture into bottom of 9-inch springform pan. Bake at 350° for 15 minutes. ✒ Process cottage cheese in blender or food processor on high until smooth. Transfer to large bowl and add cream cheese; beat at medium speed with an electric mixer until well blended. ✒ Add eggs, one at a time, mixing well after each addition. Blend in Cheddar cheese, chilies, and Tabasco Sauce. ✒ Pour the mixture over the baked crust, and bake at 350° for 1 hour. ✒ Combine sour cream and jalapeño Cheddar gourmet dip. Spread sour cream mixture over the hot cheesecake, and bake 10 additional minutes. Remove from oven, and let cool slightly. Loosen the cake from the rim of the pan. Cool completely before removing the rim. ✒ Refrigerate cheese-cake until ready to serve. ✒ Garnish with tomatoes, green onions, and olives, if desired, before serving. Serve with tortilla chips.

[SUSAN SMITH ELLARD]

Just a Thought

Cheesecake needs to be thoroughly cooled before serving, preferably for 12 hours. For safe storage, keep refrigerated, lightly covered.

Seasoned hostesses choose cheesecakes for entertaining, as they can be prepared and easily stored for days in advance.

V I D A L I A   O N I O N   D I P

Combine all ingredients in a greased round 2-quart baking dish. Bake at 350° for 30 minutes. Serve with melba rounds or other firm crackers.

[B R I G H T   K I N N E T T   W R I G H T]

MAKES 1 1/2 QUARTS

2 cups mayonnaise
2 cups grated Swiss cheese
2 to 4 cups chopped Vidalia onions or other sweet onion
1 (8-ounce) can sliced water chestnuts, drained

B A S I L   P E S T O   C H E E S E C A K E

Butter bottom and sides of 9-inch springform pan. Combine breadcrumbs and 1/4 cup Parmesan cheese. Sprinkle mixture into pan, turning to coat completely. Refrigerate.   Combine basil and next 4 ingredients in blender or food processor, and process until a smooth paste forms (about 2 minutes), stopping occasionally to scrape down sides. Transfer mixture to a large bowl.   Combine ricotta cheese, cream cheese, and Parmesan cheese in blender or food processor, and mix until smooth (about 2 minutes). Mix in eggs. Pour basil mixture back into processor with cheese mixture and process together until combined. Pour into prepared pan. Sprinkle top with pine nuts. Place pan on a baking sheet.   Bake at 325° for 1 1/4 hours. Turn oven off, and cool cheesecake in oven about 1 hour with door ajar. Transfer to a wire rack. Remove sides from springform pan. Garnish with basil leaves and serve at room temperature with crackers.

[C A R O L I N E   S T E V E N S   B O L V I G]

SERVES 15 TO 20

1 1/2 teaspoons butter
1/4 cup fine breadcrumbs, lightly toasted
1/4 cup grated Parmesan cheese
2 1/2 cups fresh basil
1/2 cup parsley sprigs, stemmed
1/4 cup olive oil
1/2 teaspoon salt
1 clove garlic
16 ounces fresh whole milk ricotta cheese (room temperature)
2 (8-ounce) packages cream cheese
8 ounces grated Parmesan cheese
4 eggs
1/3 cup pine nuts, lightly toasted
Garnish: basil leaves

S U N - D R I E D   T O M A T O   A N D   H E R B   C H E E S E   S T R U D E L S

MAKES 60 SLICES

9 ounces soft fresh goat cheese, room temperature

9 ounces cream cheese, room temperature

1/4 cup plus 2 tablespoons minced, sun-dried tomatoes packed in oil, drained

2 tablespoons minced fresh parsley

2 tablespoons fresh minced oregano or 1 1/2 teaspoons dried, crumbled

12 frozen phyllo pastry sheets, thawed

1/3 cup olive oil

Pepper

1 large plum tomato, seeded and diced

Fresh oregano sprigs

Combine first 5 ingredients in bowl; mix until smooth. Add pepper. Set aside. Place 1 phyllo sheet on work surface (keep remainder covered with damp towel). Brush lightly with olive oil, and season with pepper. Top with one more phyllo sheet. Brush lightly with oil, and season with pepper. Repeat with one more sheet. Fold stacked phyllo in half lengthwise. Brush top with oil. Spoon one-fourth of filling in 1-inch-wide log down long side of sheet, leaving 1-inch borders. Fold each short end over filling. Brush edges with oil. Roll up into log, starting at long side. Brush strudel lightly with oil. Press seam to seal. Wrap strudel tightly in plastic. Refrigerate seam side down. Repeat with remaining phyllo and filling, forming 4 strudels total. (Can be prepared 2 days ahead or frozen up to 2 months.) Lightly oil cookie sheet. Place strudels seam side down on cookie sheet. Using serrated knife, score each strudel (cutting through phyllo only), making 14 diagonal cuts in each. Brush strudels with oil. Bake at 375° about 15 minutes or until golden. Cool on cookie sheet 10 minutes. Cut through score lines, forming slices. Arrange slices cut side up, on platter. Garnish slices with tomato and oregano.

[CAROLINE McDONNELL FARWELL]

CHEESE PASTRIES SUPREME

Cream butter and cheese; gradually add flour and salt. ✒ Roll dates in sugar. Add dates, pecans, and red pepper to butter mixture. ✒ Roll dough into balls, and place on an ungreased cookie sheet. ✒ Bake at 300° for 20 to 25 minutes. (Make sure they do not get too brown on the bottom.) ✒ Cool and serve, or keep in tins for up to 1 week. Dust with powdered sugar to use as a dessert.

[MELANIE DRAKE PARKER]

MAKES 4 TO 5 DOZEN

1 cup butter, softened
1 pound grated sharp Cheddar cheese
2 cups sifted all-purpose flour
1 teaspoon salt
3/4 pound pitted chopped dates
1 1/2 teaspoons sugar
1 1/2 cups chopped pecans
3/4 to 1 teaspoon ground red pepper
Powdered sugar (optional)

GREEK–STYLE CHEESE BALL

Cut both cheeses into chunks. Process in a food processor until smooth. ✒ Reserve 1 tablespoon olives and 1 tablespoon thinly sliced green onions. Stir in remaining olives and green onions, and shape mixture into a ball. Cover and chill. ✒ Sprinkle with basil and reserved olives and green onions. Serve with toasted pita bread wedges, mild crackers, or thinly sliced French bread.

[PEGGY LANNING BYRD]

MAKES 1 BALL

4 ounces dry packed feta cheese
8 ounces cream cheese, softened
1/3 cup ripe olives, chopped, divided
2 tablespoons thinly sliced green onions, divided
1 tablespoon chopped fresh basil or 1 teaspoon dried basil

MAKES 1 1/2 CUPS

1 (8-ounce) package light cream
   cheese
20 basil leaves, chopped
   Dash of garlic powder
   Dash of Worcestershire sauce
   Dash of hot sauce
1 small package of sun-dried
   tomatoes
   Fresh basil leaves

BASIL DIP

Process first 5 ingredients in a food processor until smooth. Mold in a small, round plastic bowl, and chill. Unmold onto a serving plate, and top with chopped sun-dried tomatoes, reconstituted according to package, and basil leaves. Serve with assorted crackers.

[MARION HUNT NEWTON]

MAKES 1 1/2 CUPS

1 (6-ounce) can chopped green
   chilies
1 (2 1/2-ounce) can chopped
   ripe olives
2 to 3 tomatoes, diced
3 green onions, chopped
3 tablespoons vegetable oil
1 1/2 tablespoons vinegar
   Garlic salt
   Pepper

GREEN CHILE DIP

In a large bowl, combine green chilies, olives, tomatoes, and onions. Combine oil, vinegar, and garlic salt and pepper to taste. Pour over chili mixture. Chill 24 hours. Serve with corn chips.

[LAURI GASKELL JORDAN]

Just a Thought

*Be creative when serving dips. Try carving out the center
of a cantaloupe, pineapple, grapefruit, large cucumber,
or colored peppers for serving containers.
Be sure to cut a thin strip off bottom to level.*

H O T   B A C O N   A N D   S W I S S   D I P

Soften cream cheese in a mixing bowl. Add mayonnaise, Swiss cheese, and green onions; mix well. Transfer to a baking dish. Top with bacon and crackers. Bake at 350° for 15 to 20 minutes or until bubbly.

[P E G G Y   B E R N H A R D   M c D U F F I E]

SERVES 8 TO 10

1 (8-ounce) package cream cheese

1/2 cup mayonnaise

1 cup grated Swiss cheese

2 tablespoons chopped green onions

8 slices bacon, cooked and crumbled

1/2 cup crushed Ritz crackers

S O U T H W E S T E R N   C H I L E   D I P

Combine cheese, mayonnaise, half the olives, chilies, garlic powder, and Tabasco Sauce in a large bowl. Stir until well combined. Spread mixture into a 9-inch pieplate or quiche dish. (At this point, the mixture may be covered with plastic wrap and chilled up to 4 hours. Bake as directed, increasing baking time).   Bake at 350° for 20 minutes or until thoroughly heated.   Sprinkle with tomato, remaining olives, and green onions.   Serve warm with chips.

[C A T H Y   C R I S S   A D A M S]

SERVES 8 TO 10

2 cups grated Cheddar cheese

1 cup mayonnaise

1 (4 1/2-ounce) can chopped ripe olives, drained

1 (4 1/2-ounce) can chopped green chilies, drained

1/4 teaspoon garlic powder
Dash of Tabasco Sauce

1 medium tomato, chopped

1/4 cup sliced green onions

B L A C K – E Y E D   P E A   D I P

Cook peas 2 minutes, and drain. Lightly mash peas, and mix with salt and next 6 ingredients. Pour into a 9-inch round baking dish, and top with mozzarella cheese.   Bake at 350° for 25 minutes. Serve warm.

[C A R L A   K N I G H T   N E S B I T T]

SERVES 12

1 (15-ounce) can black-eyed peas

1 teaspoon seasoned salt

2 tablespoons minced onion

1 tablespoon diced jalapeño pepper

1 tablespoon jalapeño juice

1 1/2 cups grated sharp Cheddar cheese

1/4 cup butter

1 (3-ounce) can deviled ham

3 ounces grated mozzarella cheese

MAKES 4 CUPS

3 ears fresh corn

2 ripe avocados, peeled, seeded, and diced

1 purple onion, finely diced

1 sweet red pepper, finely diced

2 tablespoons olive oil

1/3 cup red wine vinegar

1 teaspoon dried crushed red pepper

1 teaspoon dried oregano

Juice of 2 limes

Salt and coarsely ground black pepper

AVOCADO CORN CONFETTI SALSA

Blanch corn in boiling water for 2 to 3 minutes. Rinse in cold water, and drain. Scrape kernels from the cob, and place in a medium-size bowl. Add avocado and next 7 ingredients to corn; mix well. Add salt and pepper to taste. Cover and chill up to 4 hours. Serve with chips.

[ELIZABETH HAMES HESTER]

MAKES 4 CUPS

4 tomatoes, chopped

4 pickled jalapeño peppers, chopped

2 teaspoons jalapeño pepper juice

1/2 cup minced onion

1/3 cup finely chopped green pepper

2 teaspoons olive oil

1 tablespoon fresh lime juice

1/2 teaspoon dried oregano, crumbled

4 small cloves garlic

1/4 cup minced fresh cilantro

Salt

JUST GOOD SALSA

Low Fat

Stir all ingredients together in a bowl. Cover and chill for 2 hours. Serve with chips.

[CAROL S. RICHARD]

Just a Thought

Cilantro, actually leaves of the coriander plant resembling a flat-leafed parsley, is used widely in many Latin, Mediterranean, and some Indian dishes.

SPICY BLACK BEAN SALSA

Low Fat

Combine first 10 ingredients in a large bowl. Season with salt and pepper. Cover and refrigerate 24 hours, stirring occasionally. Serve with tortilla chips or as a side portion to any Mexican or Southwestern dish.

[BETH OLIVER LEHNER]

SERVES 8

2 (15-ounce) cans black beans, drained

1 (16-ounce) can whole kernel corn, drained

1/2 cup chopped fresh cilantro

6 tablespoons lime juice

6 tablespoons vegetable oil

1/2 cup finely chopped purple onion

1 1/2 teaspoons ground cumin

1/2 (16-ounce) can tomatoes, chopped

1/2 (10-ounce) can Rotel tomatoes, pureed

1/2 to 3/4 cup medium picante sauce

Salt and pepper

FRESH MUSHROOM PÂTÉ

Cook mushrooms in butter in a large skillet over medium to high heat for 10 minutes or until liquids have evaporated. Drain and set aside. Combine cream cheese and next 4 ingredients in a large bowl; blend until smooth. Add mushrooms, and mix well. Chill at least 4 hours. Mold half of mixture and top with half of chopped parsley. Add remaining mixture, and garnish with remaining parsley and a few sliced mushrooms. Serve with assorted crackers.

[GERRY PALFERY GILLESPY]

MAKES 1 1/2 CUPS

12 ounces fresh mushrooms, chopped

2 tablespoons butter

8 ounces cream cheese, softened

1 tablespoon lemon juice

1/4 teaspoon ground white pepper

1/4 teaspoon garlic powder

2 to 3 drops Tabasco Sauce

Chopped parsley, divided

Sliced fresh mushrooms

SERVES 4

10 ounces fresh spinach
(do not substitute)

2 tablespoons olive oil

5 to 6 green onions, chopped

2 ears fresh corn, cooked and
cut from cob (may substitute
1 cup frozen or canned corn
kernels)

4 roasted sweet red peppers,
peeled, seeded, and chopped

3 ounces goat cheese

8 large flour tortillas

Quesadillas With Goat Cheese And Garden Vegetables

Wash and remove stems from spinach. Tear into pieces. Heat olive oil in a large skillet over medium heat. Stir in spinach and green onions. Sauté until spinach begins to wilt. Transfer to a large bowl, and stir in corn, roasted red pepper, and goat cheese. Spread mixture evenly over 4 tortillas, and top with remaining tortillas. Place quesadillas on foil-lined baking sheets. Bake at 375° for 7 to 10 minutes or until thoroughly heated. Slice into wedges and serve hot.

[MIKE McCRANEY]

Just a Thought

To roast peppers: Preheat oven to broil. Place peppers on baking sheet several inches below heat. Roast until charred on all sides, turning as needed. (Peppers will be black when ready.) Remove from oven, and place in plastic bag; seal and let stand 15 minutes. (Peppers will have steamed.) Remove from bag, peel, seed, and slice or chop.

Grilled Quesadillas

Toss first 5 ingredients together until well mixed. Spread one-fifth of cheese mixture on tortilla, and top with another tortilla. Repeat process until you have 5 quesadillas. Heat grill to medium-high. Grill quesadillas until cheese begins to melt. Turn quesadillas, and grill until cheese is melted. Remove from grill, and let stand a minute to make cutting easier. Use scissors to cut them neatly. Cut into wedges, and garnish each serving with sour cream and chopped fresh cilantro. Serve with salsa for dipping.

MAKES 20

8 ounces grated Monterey Jack
cheese

4 ounces grated Cheddar cheese

1/4 cup chopped green chilies

1/4 cup sliced ripe olives

4 green onions, chopped

10 (6 to 7-inch) flour tortillas
Salsa
Garnishes: sour cream,
chopped fresh cilantro

C O C K T A I L   T A R T S

S H E L L S :

¹/₂ cup butter, softened
4 ounces cream cheese, softened
1 cup all-purpose flour

To prepare shells, combine butter and cream cheese in large bowl. Add flour and mix well. Roll dough into a ball. Chill for 1 hour. Divide dough into 24 pieces. Press into lightly greased miniature muffin pans. For each tart, divide solid filling ingredients among shells. Mix egg(s), milk, and salt. Pour evenly over shells. Bake at 350° for 25 to 30 minutes.

F I L L I N G S :

M A K E S   2   D O Z E N
A S P A R A G U S   B A C O N

¹/₄ pound fresh asparagus,
  steamed, trimmed, and chopped
5 slices bacon, cooked and
  crumbled
3 scallions, chopped
1 large egg, beaten
¹/₂ cup milk
1 teaspoon salt
¹/₂ teaspoon dry mustard
¹/₂ teaspoon garlic salt

M A K E S   4   D O Z E N
M U S H R O O M   P A R M E S A N

¹/₂ pound mushrooms, diced,
  sautéed in 3 tablespoons butter
1 cup grated Parmesan cheese
2 large eggs, beaten
1 cup milk
¹/₂ teaspoon salt

M A K E S   2   D O Z E N
C H I C K E N   C U R R Y

1 tablespoon butter, softened
¹/₂ cup golden raisins
¹/₂ cup chopped walnuts
¹/₂ cup chopped, cooked chicken
1 teaspoon curry powder
1 egg, beaten
¹/₂ cup milk
¹/₂ teaspoon salt

Easy to prepare ahead and offers great versatility.
Be creative! Make up your own fillings
from ingredients on hand.

MAKES 50

1/2 pound thinly sliced Virginia
    ham
1 (8-ounce) container whipped
    cream cheese with chives
1 (12-ounce) jar pickled okra

PICKLED OKRA-HAM ROLLS

Lay ham pieces out flat. Spread cream cheese onto ham. Trim ends of okra. Lay okra end to end across one side of ham. Roll up so there will be several layers of ham. ✎ Chill until ingredients are firm. Slice into 1/2-inch pieces, and serve. ✎ Looks best on green leaf lettuce.

[LANDON ALFORD STIVENDER]

SERVES 12

3 tablespoons white wine vinegar
    or balsamic vinegar
1/4 cup extra-virgin olive oil
1/4 teaspoon salt
1/4 teaspoon pepper
2 tablespoons grated onion
1 clove garlic, finely minced
3 cucumbers, peeled and sliced
2 tablespoons fresh chives, finely
    chopped
2 tablespoons fresh chervil,
    finely chopped
    goat cheese (optional)

CUCUMBER SALAD

Low Fat

Combine first 6 ingredients, and toss well with sliced cucumbers. Keep chilled. ✎ Sprinkle with chives and chervil. Serve on toasted pita wedges, and sprinkle with goat cheese, if desired.

[LAURA SAMMIS PEARCE]

*For a light summer meal, serve with grilled chicken
and sliced fresh tomatoes.*

ASPARAGUS SPEARS WITH PROSCIUTTO AND PARMESAN

Trim off about 1 inch from ends of asparagus. Wash, and cook asparagus in a small amount of boiling water until soft (2 to 3 minutes). Submerge into cold water; drain. ✎ Cut each slice of prosciutto in half. Wrap each asparagus spear with a piece of prosciutto. Place on a cookie sheet. Brush each roll with olive oil, and sprinkle with cheese. Broil until cheese melts. Serve immediately.

MAKES 24

1 bunch asparagus (24 spears)
12 large slices Swiss prosciutto
Olive oil
Grated Parmesan cheese

STUFFED MUSHROOMS

Heat olive oil and butter in a large skillet over medium heat. Sauté onions and garlic until translucent. Add walnuts and green onions. Cool. Stir in cheeses and spices. ✎ Fill mushroom caps with cheese mixture, and place on broiler pan. Bake at 400° for 3 to 5 minutes, just until cheeses melt.

MAKES 24

1 teaspoon olive oil
2 teaspoons butter
1 small onion, minced
1 clove garlic, minced
3 tablespoons chopped walnuts
2 green onions, minced
1 1/2 ounces feta cheese, crumbled
2 ounces Gruyère cheese, shredded
Salt and pepper
24 large mushroom caps

Just a Thought

Never soak mushrooms. Rinse quickly and pat dry with paper towels.

MAKES 12

2 (6-ounce) cans pitted ripe
  olives
2 anchovy fillets
3 cloves fresh garlic
1 to 2 tablespoons sun-dried
  tomatoes packed in oil
1/8 teaspoon salt
  Freshly ground pepper
  Ground bay leaf
  Baguette slices
  Olive oil

PHIL'S FANTASTICO OLIVATA

Combine first 5 ingredients in a food processor, and pulse gently several times to a textured paste or spread. Remove from processor, and put in a bowl. Let stand overnight, or at least 4 to 6 hours for flavors to blend. Season with pepper and ground bay leaf to taste. Dip baguette slices in olive oil, and toast. ✍ Serve olive mixture on baguette slices. Wonderful as an appetizer or to accompany soup and a salad.

[RHODA WATKINS]

Just a Thought

Sweet Bay, or Laurus nobilis, leaves are slightly bitter when fresh, so they are usually dried for use in cooking. The leaves release flavor slowly, so are most often used whole in soups and stews. They are less frequently ground, but impart its true flavor even in this form.

MAKES 40

1 quart apple cider vinegar
2 (12-ounce) cans beer
1/2 cup salt
1/4 cup ground black pepper
1/8 cup ground red pepper
5 pounds fresh shrimp, peeled
  Melted butter

SPICY COCKTAIL SHRIMP

Combine cider vinegar and next 4 ingredients in a large stockpot, and bring to a boil. Add shrimp, and boil in mixture until done (about 5 minutes). ✍ Dip in melted butter. Delicious and spicy!

[JANET LINTON WRIGHT]

Shrimp that has been peeled cooks much faster than unpeeled. Cook only until it turns pink.

S H R I M P   B U T T E R

Cook shrimp in water; peel shrimp, and devein, if desired. Reserve a few shrimp for garnish. Chop remaining shrimp. Beat butter and next 4 ingredients. Add lemon juice, chopped shrimp, and onion, and mix well. Chill and serve with assorted crackers.   Garnish with reserved fresh shrimp, chopped fresh parsley, and lemon slices.

[A N N I S   I R A   D A L E Y   ]

MAKES 1 PINT

1 pound unpeeled fresh shrimp
1/4 cup butter
1 (8-ounce) package cream cheese, softened
4 tablespoons mayonnaise
1/2 teaspoon garlic salt
1 teaspoon paprika
Juice of 1 lemon
1/4 cup minced onion
Garnishes: chopped fresh parsley, lemon slices

B E B L A ' S   S H R I M P   B I T S

Cut shrimp into small pieces. Combine shrimp and 5 tablespoons hollandaise, cheese, and pimientos, if desired. Spread on toasted rounds. Top each with a dab of remaining 2 tablespoons hollandaise sauce, and sprinkle with paprika.   Bake at 350° for 10 to 12 minutes. For quick blender hollandaise, see page 276.

MAKES 30

1/2 pound medium-size fresh shrimp, boiled, peeled, and deveined
7 tablespoons hollandaise sauce, divided
1/2 cup grated Swiss cheese
2 tablespoons chopped pimientos (optional)
Toasted thin bread rounds or melba toast
Paprika

SERVES 50

12 *pounds unpeeled, medium-size fresh shrimp*
3 *quarts water*
3 *cups celery tops*
2 *cups pickling spice*
4 *tablespoons salt*
6 *cups sliced white onions*
40 *bay leaves*
4 *heaping tablespoons seafood seasoning*
6 *tablespoons capers with juice*
4 *tablespoons celery seed*
8 *teaspoons salt*
8 *drops Tabasco Sauce*
 Juice of 2 lemons
1 *cup rice vinegar*
3 *cups olive oil*

SERVES 10 TO 12

2 *(8-ounce) packages cream cheese, softened*
2 *pounds fresh lump crabmeat or 1 (7½-ounce) can crabmeat, undrained and flaked*
 Lemon juice
¾ *teaspoon seasoned salt*
¾ *teaspoon Accent*
 Tabasco Sauce
 Seasoned salt
 Paprika

SHRIMP EXTRAVAGANZA

Cook shrimp in 3 quarts water with next 3 ingredients, just until shrimp turn pink. Immediately drain, and cool with ice cubes. Peel shrimp, and devein, if desired. Combine onions and remaining ingredients in a 2-gallon jar; add shrimp, and shake well to combine with seasonings. Refrigerate up to 4 days, and serve.

[MELANIE DRAKE PARKER]

HOT CRAB DIP

Combine cream cheese, crabmeat, in its liquid, and lemon juice. Mix until dip consistency. Sprinkle in seasoned salt, Accent, and Tabasco Sauce to taste; mix well. Spoon into a 1-quart round baking dish, coated with vegetable cooking spray. Sprinkle with seasoned salt and paprika. Bake at 350° for 25 to 30 minutes or until bubbly. Broil 30 seconds to 1 minute to brown slightly. Serve with assorted crackers.

[MARY O. ROEBUCK]

" T H A T   C R A B   T H I N G "

Sauté green pepper in oil. Add artichoke hearts and next 9 ingredients. Put in an ovenproof chafing dish. Sprinkle almonds over top. 🖉 Bake at 375° for 25 to 30 minutes. Serve with pita chips, bagel chips, or crackers.

[T O O K I E   D A U G H E R T Y   H A Z E L R I G]

Just a Thought

To liven up the flavor of canned crabmeat,
soak in ice water for a few minutes; drain well and blot dry.

C R A B M E A T   M O U S S E

Sauté red pepper in butter until crisp-tender; set aside. 🖉 Heat cream cheese, cream of celery soup, and onion in the top of a double boiler, mixing well, until thoroughly heated. 🖉 Dissolve gelatin in boiling water, and add to soup mixture. Transfer mixture to mixing bowl. On lowest speed of electric mixer, mix in remaining ingredients (except lettuce) and sautéed red peppers until well blended. 🖉 Pour mixture into an oiled copper fish mold. Chill at least 3 hours. Unmold onto lettuce-lined platter, and serve with thin wheat crackers.

[E L L E N   M A C E L V A I N   R H E T T]

SERVES 12

1 large green pepper, chopped
1 tablespoon vegetable oil
2 (14-ounce) cans artichoke hearts, drained and chopped
2 cups mayonnaise
1/2 cup chopped green onions
1/2 cup pimientos
1 cup freshly grated Parmesan cheese
1 1/2 tablespoons lemon juice
4 teaspoons Worcestershire sauce
3 jalapeño peppers, chopped or 1 (4.5-ounce) can chopped green chilies, drained
1 teaspoon celery salt
1 pound crabmeat (either fresh or canned), drained and flaked
1/3 cup sliced almonds

MAKES 4 1/2 CUPS

1/4 cup finely chopped sweet red pepper
1 tablespoon butter
8 ounces cream cheese, softened
1 (10-3/4-ounce) can cream of celery soup
1 medium onion, finely chopped
2 tablespoons unflavored gelatin
1/4 cup boiling water
1 (4 to 6-ounce) can fancy white crabmeat, rinsed and drained
1 cup finely chopped celery
1 cup mayonnaise
1/4 teaspoon Worcestershire sauce
1/4 to 1/2 teaspoon hot sauce
1/2 teaspoon dry mustard
Lettuce leaves

SERVES 6 TO 8

1 ripe avocado, peeled, seeded, and mashed
1 tablespoon lemon juice
2 tablespoons mayonnaise
2 tablespoons sour cream
2 tablespoons instant minced onion
1½ teaspoons lemon pepper
2 teaspoons dill
1 teaspoon prepared mustard
¼ teaspoon salt
¼ teaspoon Tabasco Sauce
6 ounces fresh crabmeat or 3 ounces canned
4 ounces cream cheese, softened
Garnishes: 2 halved cherry tomatoes, chopped purple onion

AVOCADO CRABMEAT SPREAD

Combine avocado and lemon juice in a large bowl. Add mayonnaise and next 7 ingredients. 🖋 Drain crabmeat thoroughly. Combine with cream cheese, and then fold into avocado mixture. 🖋 Place in a decorative container. Garnish with halved cherry tomatoes or chopped purple onion, if desired. Chill at least 2 hours prior to serving.

[ALISON BERRY]

SERVES 10

16 ounces cream cheese, softened
½ cup sliced ripe olives
½ cup chopped celery
1 tablespoon finely chopped onion
¼ teaspoon onion salt
1 (4-ounce) can smoked oysters, drained
½ cup chopped pecans or walnuts

SMOKED OYSTER PÂTÉ

Combine first 5 ingredients, and mix well. 🖋 Chop oysters into small pieces, and add to cream cheese mixture. Shape into mound; and cover with chopped nuts. Chill. Serve with plain crackers.

[CAROLYN SHANKS]

MINDY'S CRAWFISH DIP

SERVES 8 TO 10

1 pound crawfish tails
2 ounces cream cheese
1/2 cup butter
2 to 3 green onions
  Dry Creole seasoning

Clean crawfish, or buy frozen packages, which are already clean. Rinse crawfish tails to remove fat. ✎ Place in microwave-safe bowl with remaining ingredients. Microwave on HIGH for 1½ minutes, and stir well. Repeat microwave procedure 3 more times. Refrigerate overnight. ✎ Serve with Ritz or other crackers.

[KELLI NELSON JETMUNDSEN]

CRAWFISH CANAPÉS

MAKES 30

1/2 cup chopped celery
1/2 cup chopped spring onions
1/2 cup butter
2 tablespoons all-purpose flour
1 cup milk
1/2 (10½-ounce) can cream of
  mushroom soup
1 teaspoon Worcestershire sauce
1 teaspoon salt
  Dash of pepper
1/4 cup dry vermouth
2 pounds crawfish meat
1 (16-ounce) package wonton
  papers

Sauté vegetables in a large skillet coated with vegetable cooking spray. Remove vegetables and set aside. ✎ Melt butter in same skillet; stir in flour to make a thick paste. Warm milk, and gradually add to flour mixture, using a whisk to smooth any lumps. Once sauce is smooth, add cream of mushroom soup, next 4 ingredients, and sautéed vegetables. Stir in crawfish meat. ✎ Crisp wonton papers by placing each one in a cup of a miniature muffin pan (trim edges if necessary). Spray with vegetable cooking spray. Bake at 325° for 8 to 10 minutes or until lightly browned. ✎ Fill browned wonton papers with crawfish mixture, and bake at 325° for 10 minutes. Serve immediately.

[NATALIE HICKS LEE]

C A V I A R   M O U S S E

SERVES 20

1¼ envelopes unflavored gelatin
¼ cup cold water
6 ounces black caviar
2 tablespoons grated onion
1 tablespoon lemon juice
½ teaspoon salt
1 cup sour cream
1 cup whipping cream, whipped
Fresh parsley

Soften gelatin in cold water for 5 minutes. Dissolve over low heat, and cool slightly. Rinse caviar through a fine wire-mesh strainer; drain well. Combine gelatin, caviar, and next 4 ingredients in a bowl, and blend well. Stir in whipped cream gently. Turn mixture into oiled 3 to 4-cup mold. Chill until firm. (This may be frozen.) Unmold and garnish with a wreath of parsley. Serve with melba or water crackers.

[M E L A N I E   D R A K E   P A R K E R]

S M O K E D   S A L M O N   C A N A P É S

MAKES 24

8 ounces cream cheese, softened
2 teaspoons fresh lemon juice
½ teaspoon grated onion
   Several grinds black pepper
4 (7-inch) flour tortillas
1 tablespoon plus 1 teaspoon
   capers (nonpareil size)
½ pound smoked salmon,
   thinly sliced
   Garnish: fresh dill

Combine cream cheese with lemon juice, onion, and pepper. Spread cream cheese mixture evenly over tortillas. Sprinkle evenly with capers. Add a layer of smoked salmon to each. Roll each tortilla jellyroll fashion. Slice each roll into 6 pinwheels and serve immediately, or chill and slice into pinwheels at serving time. Top each pinwheel with a sprig of dill.

[M E L A N I E   B E R R Y   M C C R A N E Y]

An easy and elegant way to serve smoked salmon.

L O B S T E R B E G G A R ' S P U R S E S

SERVES 8

To prepare crêpes: Combine first 5 ingredients and, if desired, dill; mixing well. Refrigerate batter 1 hour. Place a crêpe pan over medium-high heat, and brush with oil or melted butter. Add about ¼ cup of the batter, and swirl it around to cover the bottom of the pan. Cook for about 30 seconds; turn and cook for about 15 seconds. Remove and put on a sheet of wax paper. To prepare filling: Combine all ingredients, and chill for about 1 hour. Place a heaping tablespoon of filling in the center of each crêpe, and gather the edges up into a little "purse" or drawstring bag. Tie each with a whole chive or green onion. (Blanch chives or green onions for 5 seconds, then immerse in cold water. This makes them pliable and easy to tie.)

[LYDIA LONGSHORE SLAUGHTER]

Crêpes:
- 1 cup all-purpose flour
- ¼ teaspoon salt
- 1¼ cups milk
- 2 eggs
- 2 tablespoons melted butter
- ½ to 1 teaspoon chopped fresh dill (optional)
- 1 tablespoon vegetable oil or melted butter

Filling:
- 2 cups diced cooked lobster meat
- ½ cup chopped celery
- ¼ cup chopped onion
- 4 tablespoons mayonnaise
- 1 teaspoon lime juice
- ½ teaspoon salt
- ⅛ teaspoon freshly ground black pepper
- ⅛ teaspoon ground red pepper
- Whole chives or green onions

C H I C K E N P Â T É

SERVES 8

Blend chicken, nuts, and garlic in food processor until smooth. Add basil leaves and salt; blend again until well blended. Adjust seasonings to taste. Stir in mayonnaise to desired consistency (½ cup to mold or ¾ cup to make a dip). If making a mold, coat a 1½ to 2-cup mold with vegetable cooking spray. Flavor improves with time. Best if prepared 24 hours ahead. Serve with French bread slices or assorted crackers. Great use for leftover turkey or chicken.

[LINDA JOHNSON STONE]

- 3 boneless, skinless chicken breast halves, cooked
- 1 (3½-ounce) jar macadamia nuts
- 2 large cloves garlic, peeled
- 15 to 20 fresh basil leaves
- ½ teaspoon salt
- ½ to ¾ cup mayonnaise

MAKES 2 TO 3 DOZEN

4 ounces cream cheese, softened
2 tablespoons mayonnaise
1 cup chopped cooked chicken
1 cup sliced almonds, blanched
1 tablespoon curry powder
1 tablespoon chutney
1/2 teaspoon salt
1 scallion, minced (optional)
1/2 cup flaked coconut, toasted

MAKES 60

2 egg yolks
1 cup ricotta cheese
1/4 pound finely chopped prosciutto
1/4 cup grated Parmesan cheese
1 1/2 teaspoons dried rosemary,
 crumbled
Salt and pepper
Phyllo pastry, thawed
1 cup melted butter

CHICKEN CURRY BALLS

Blend cream cheese and mayonnaise in a large bowl. Add chicken and next 5 ingredients. Mix well. Chill 4 hours.   Shape into 1-inch balls, and roll in coconut. Serve chilled.   (To toast coconut, spread on baking sheet; bake at 325° for 2 to 3 minutes.)

[JOAN BROCK]

For a colorful variation, fill scooped-out cherry tomatoes with chicken-curry mixture.

PHYLLO TRIANGLES WITH ROSEMARY AND PROSCIUTTO

Beat egg yolks into ricotta. Stir in next 3 ingredients and season with salt and pepper to taste.   Brush 1 phyllo sheet with butter. Stack second sheet on top, and brush with butter. Cut crosswise into fifths.   Place 1 teaspoon filling in center of strip 1 inch from top. Fold like a flag into a triangle.   Place on buttered cookie sheet, and brush triangle with butter. (Can chill or freeze at this point.)   Bake at 350° for 25 minutes or golden brown. Serve warm.

[CINDY SMITH SPEAKE]

Just a Thought

When using phyllo, keep sheets covered with a damp towel until needed. Brush edges with butter to keep from breaking.

LADIES DAY BLT's

Cut bread into rounds with small (2^{1}/2-inch or 1^{3}/4-inch) biscuit cutter. Lightly toast rounds on each side. ✤ Combine mayonnaise and next 4 ingredients. Spread mixture on bread rounds. Top with crumbled bacon and tomato slices. ✤ (To make bite-size cocktail sandwiches, use 1^{3}/4-inch biscuit cutter.)

[SARAH DRUHAN DAVIS]

Makes 32 (2^{1}/2-inch) or 96 (1^{3}/4-inch) sandwiches.

MAKES 32 OR 96

1 *loaf light wheat bread*
1 *cup mayonnaise*
1^{1}/2 *teaspoons sweet brown mustard*
1^{1}/2 *teaspoons lemon juice*
    Pinch of sugar
1 *tablespoon chopped fresh parsley*
^{1}/2 *to* ^{3}/4 *pound bacon, cooked and crumbled*
1 *pint Roma or cherry tomatoes, sliced*

POLENTA CIRCLES

Cook polenta, or buy commercial blocks and cut in half to ½-inch-thick slices. Cut out circles. Top with pancetta (an Italian bacon). Sprinkle with cheeses. Broil. ✤ Garnish with fresh herbs, if desired.

[CAMERON DALEY CROWE]

MAKES 2 DOZEN

Polenta (6.6-ounce box commercial or fresh)
3 *ounces pancetta*
3 *ounces Emmental cheese, grated*
3 *ounces fontina cheese, grated*
4 *ounces grated Parmesan cheese*
    Fresh herbs (optional)

Just a Thought

Three types of cornmeal are commercially available: fine, medium, and coarse (also known as polenta).

S O U T H E R N T E A S A N D W I C H E S

MAKES 3^1/2
TO 4 DOZEN

1/2 cup finely chopped ham
1 (8-ounce) can crushed
 pineapple, drained
1 (8-ounce) package
 cream cheese, softened
1/2 cup chopped pecans
1 to 2 tablespoons mayonnaise
1 loaf white sandwich bread

Combine ham and pineapple; stir in cream cheese and pecans. Add enough mayonnaise to moisten. Spread on half of bread slices; top with remaining bread slices. Trim crusts and cut into small finger sandwiches.

[JANE ESTES]

W A T E R C R E S S S A N D W I C H S P R E A D

MAKES 1^1/2 CUPS

1 (8-ounce) package cream
 cheese, softened
1 bunch watercress leaves,
 washed and dried
1/4 to 1/3 cup horseradish,
 drained and squeezed dry
1/2 teaspoon ground white pepper
1 green onion, thinly sliced
Thinly sliced white bread

Process first 5 ingredients in a food processor. Chill mixture for 2 hours. Spread mixture onto bread, and serve.

P I T A C H I P S

MAKES 24

6 large pita bread rounds
8 tablespoons butter, melted
1/4 cup grated Parmesan cheese
1/2 teaspoon garlic salt
1/4 teaspoon ground red pepper

Divide pita rounds into 2 circles; cut each in half. Cut each in half again. Place pita wedges on baking sheets, rough side up. Brush with melted butter. Mix cheese, salt, and red pepper; sprinkle over pita wedges. Bake at 350° for 20 minutes or until lightly browned.

[LAURI GASKELL JORDAN]

*For a lower fat chip, omit butter and
spray wedges with butter-flavored vegetable cooking spray.*

TOMATO-BASIL CROSTINI

Combine first 11 ingredients, and mix well. Top with feta cheese, and serve on toasted French bread rounds.

[HEIDI CONN]

10 Roma tomatoes, chopped
3 to 6 green onions, chopped
1/2 cup chopped purple or Vidalia onion
1/4 to 1/2 cup chopped fresh basil
2 teaspoons minced garlic
1 tablespoon olive oil
2 tablespoons balsamic vinegar
2 tablespoons white wine vinegar
1 tablespoon sugar
1/4 teaspoon salt
1/4 teaspoon pepper
1 (4-ounce) package feta cheese
French bread rounds, toasted

ITALIAN TOAST

Slice French bread thinly, slightly diagonal. Brush each slice with olive oil. ✐ Arrange bread slices, oil side up, on an ungreased cookie sheet. Bake at 250° about 10 minutes or until crisp. Cool slightly, and top each slice with 2 or 3 tomato slices. Sprinkle evenly with basil, cheese, and pine nuts. ✐ Increase heat to 375°, and toast again until cheese melts. Serve immediately.

[BETH WALKER WILLIAMS]

1 loaf French bread
Olive oil
8 to 10 fresh Roma tomatoes, thinly sliced (may substitute cherry or any fresh tomato)
2 tablespoons chopped fresh basil leaves
4 ounces grated fontina cheese
1/3 cup coarsely chopped pine nuts

SERVES 8

8 (1-inch-thick) slices French
bread

6 tablespoons extra-virgin
olive oil

8 to 10 scallions, thinly sliced

1/2 cup grated fresh Romano cheese
Freshly ground black pepper

SERVES 10 TO 12

2 pounds boneless lamb,
cut in chunks

2 cups pearl onions

2 medium green peppers,
cut in chunks

2 pounds boneless beef,
cut in chunks

1 pound fresh mushrooms

1 pint cherry tomatoes

2 pounds boneless, skinless
chicken, cut in chunks
(approximately 6 chicken
breasts)

2 cups pineapple chunks

1/2 pound snow pea pods

BRUSCHETTA ROMANO

Broil bread slices on one side for about 1 minute, just until lightly toasted. Remove from oven, and set aside. In a heavy skillet, cook olive oil over medium heat. Add scallions; sauté, stirring often, 4 to 6 minutes or until scallions are tender. Turn bread slices so that toasted side is down. Spread scallion mixture over top. Sprinkle evenly with cheese. Top with black pepper to taste. Broil 1 to 2 minutes or until lightly browned.

TRIO MEAT SKEWERS

Marinate lamb, pearl onions, and green pepper chunks in lamb marinade. Marinate beef, mushrooms, and cherry tomatoes in beef marinade. Marinate chicken, pineapple chunks, and snow peas in chicken marinade. Marinate all meat and vegetables at least 4 hours or overnight. Drain meat and vegetable mixtures. Place each mixture on skewers, and grill until done. Serve lamb with mint sauce, pg. 276, beef with béarnaise sauce, pg. 278, and chicken with peanut sauce, pg. 198.

LAMB MARINADE	CHICKEN MARINADE	BEEF MARINADE
1 1/2 cups olive oil	1 3/4 cups pineapple juice	1/2 cup butter, melted
3/4 cup soy sauce	1/2 cup soy sauce	1/2 teaspoon dried parsley flakes
1/4 cup Worcestershire sauce	1 cup Sauterne	1 1/2 tablespoons lemon juice
2 tablespoons dry mustard	1/2 teaspoon garlic salt	3 tablespoons sherry
2 1/4 teaspoons salt	1/4 cup sugar	1 tablespoon soy sauce
1 tablespoon pepper		1 teaspoon mixed dried herbs
1/4 cup red wine vinegar		2 teaspoons salt
1 1/2 teaspoons dried parsley flakes		1/2 teaspoon coarsely ground pepper
2 cloves garlic, minced		

ARMAN'S PIZZA

Mix yeast with water and sugar until dissolved. In a large bowl, stir together oil, salt, 1 cup flour, and yeast mixture. Add remaining flour $1/2$ cup at a time until incorporated. Dough should be smooth and a little sticky. ✐ Place bowl covered with towel in warm area and let rise by 50% again. Shape dough by hand or with rolling pin to form crust. Brush with olive oil or any of the oils listed below. Add toppings desired, and bake at 350° for 15 to 20 minutes.

[CHEF ARMAN DeLORENZ]
ARMAN'S AT PARKLANE

MAKES
1 (16-18") CRUST OR
2 (10-12") CRUSTS OR
3 (8") CRUSTS

Pizza dough:
  2 teaspoons dry yeast
  1 cup warm water (105°-115°)
    Pinch of sugar
  2 tablespoons olive oil
  1/2 teaspoon salt
  2 1/2 - 3 cups unbleached all-purpose flour

Suggested Toppings

Oils:
  Extra-Virgin olive oil
  Pure olive oil
  Walnut oil
  Corn oil
Tomatoes:
  Fresh or canned tomatoes, seasoned with salt, pepper, chopped garlic, and basil
Olives:
  black, purple, green, oil cured, Italian, Greek

Peppers:
  Roasted or sautéed, green, yellow, or red, dried or fresh chiles
Cheeses:
  Shredded mozzarella
  Buffalo mozzarella
  Smoked mozzarella
  Fontina
  Provolone
  Romano
  Ricotta
  Montrachet goat cheese
  Dry Jack
  Cheddar

Gorgonzola
Meats:
  Cooked pancetta, sweet or hot sausage, bacon, salami, pepperoni, or prosciutto
Herbs and Spices:
  Onions, shallots, chives, scallions, garlic, any dried or fresh herbs
Other:
  Capers, fresh vegetables, grilled or roasted, such as spinach, eggplant, artichokes, etc.

Just a Thought

Have your next dinner party in the kitchen. Your guests can create "designer pizzas" while you toss a big green salad. Casual and fun!

Egg Roulade, page 55

Eggs and Cheese

-CATHY CRISS ADAMS-

EGGS AND CHEESE. THE SIMPLE STAPLES the British call nursery food connote for me the infancy of my adulthood.

Fresh out of college I came to Birmingham as *Southern Living*'s assistant foods editor. Having lied that I could cook, I attempted to make a lemon pie the first day on the job and blew egg whites in my boss's face. I still tremble at the mention of meringue.

Eggs almost cost me my job, but on a limited and mismanaged budget they became indispensable allies. My roommate and I lived, as only the young can do, for the moment's gratification, usually from payday on, impoverished but marching around downtown in designer shoes. Chronically broke, we lived on eggs—scrambled for breakfast, hard boiled to munch as lunch as we made our way from the office to Loveman's, Pizitz, and Burger Phillips, and as something approximating cheese omelets for dinner. An extravagant occasional dinner out was macaroni and cheese at Britling's.

Recalling the wonder years of my newfound independence, I see a summer Sunday afternoon when, down to our last egg, we scoured our purse linings and pockets and came up with a handful of change—just enough to make a run to Browdy's for a tiny jar of caviar to be garnished with that egg. We considered ourselves rich in sophistication.

I didn't stay long at *Southern Living*, but I will always be grateful to them for giving me the city which I came to call home. The downtown department stores are gone now, and Britling's has sadly long since served their CONTINUED

CATHY CRISS ADAMS

A GRADUATE OF THE
UNIVERSITY OF MISSISSIPPI,
WITH DEGREES IN ENGLISH
AND JOURNALISM,
CATHY CRISS ADAMS CAME
TO BIRMINGHAM IN 1972,
AS AN ASSISTANT EDITOR AT
SOUTHERN LIVING MAGAZINE.
HER FIRST NOVEL,
OTHER AUTUMNS,
WAS PUBLISHED IN 1994
BY ATTICUS PRESS.
IT DEPICTS THE VARIETY
AND ECCENTRICITIES
OF PERSONALITIES FOUND IN
ANY SMALL SOUTHERN TOWN.
AT HOME WORKING
ON A SECOND NOVEL, CATHY
CRISS ADAMS LIVES WITH HER
HUSBAND AND TWO CHILDREN.

last heaping helping of incomparably crusted macaroni and cheese. I cried when Browdy's closed the little grocery store which made a kid from the country buying caviar feel like a Parisian parading Fauchon's.

From a small Southern town via Oxford, Mississippi, I was frequently lost as well as undercapitalized as I explored a big, Magic City after work. Living on Valley Avenue, I had, like a friendly lighthouse, Vulcan's torch for orientation. I still live within the shadow of that city symbol and know my way around, but late on a winter afternoon, 280 traffic reminding me of how this city has grown as I have grown to love it, I catch sight of that green beacon in the distance, and it tugs on my heart with a memory as it points me home.

I keep a dusty pair of Burger-Phillips shoes in the back of my closet for old times sake and never get down to just one egg without having the impulse to collect the pocket change that accumulates on the top of the dryer and go out to purchase caviar, paying in pennies.

Eggs and cheese, nursery foods, simple and basic and infinitely comforting, as sustaining as well-worn memories.

THE END

B R U N C H

K's Oatmeal Pancakes

MAKES 1 1/2 DOZEN

2 cups uncooked oats
1 cup raisins or chopped prunes
2 1/2 cups buttermilk, divided
1/2 cup all-purpose flour
2 tablespoons sugar
1 teaspoon baking powder
1 teaspoon baking soda
1/2 teaspoon ground cinnamon
1/4 teaspoon salt

Soak the oats and raisins in 2 cups buttermilk overnight. Combine flour and remaining ingredients, and add to soaked oat mixture. (Stir in up to 1/2 cup buttermilk if mixture is too dry.) Pour batter onto a hot greased skillet or griddle and cook until done. (Pancakes will cook more slowly than regular pancakes.) Serve with real maple syrup.

[SALLY SCHROEDER PRICE]

Incredible Waffles

MAKES 3 TO 4
BELGIAN WAFFLES OR
10 TO 12 REGULAR

2 cups biscuit mix
1/2 cup vegetable oil
1 egg
1 1/3 cups club soda
(1 [10-ounce] bottle)
3/4 cup fresh or frozen blueberries
(optional)

Combine biscuit mix, oil, and egg. Stir well. Add club soda, and mix well. Pour batter onto a preheated, greased waffle iron, and add blueberries to each waffle if desired. Cook 4 to 5 minutes or until done.

[CAROLINE McDONNELL FARWELL]

Just a Thought

For a new twist on an old favorite, substitute a waffle as the base for Eggs Benedict.

D E C A D E N T F R E N C H T O A S T

Combine corn syrup, brown sugar, and butter in a saucepan. Heat until bubbly. Pour into a 13 x 9 x 2-inch baking pan. Place bread slices in pan, making 2 layers. ✍ In a separate bowl, combine the eggs, milk and vanilla. Pour over bread. Cover and refrigerate overnight. ✍ Bake at 350° for 45 minutes. ✍ Spread sour cream over French toast; top with sliced strawberries. Serve hot.

SERVES 6

2 tablespoons light corn syrup
3/4 to 1 cup light brown sugar
5 tablespoons butter
12 slices wheat bread (crusts removed)
5 eggs
1 1/2 cups milk
1 teaspoon vanilla extract
1/2 cup sour cream
1 1/2 cups sliced strawberries

D U T C H B A B Y

Melt butter in a 12-inch iron skillet. ✍ In a mixing bowl, beat eggs for 1 minute. Add milk, flour, and almond extract. Pour batter slowly into hot skillet. ✍ Bake at 425° for 20 to 25 minutes (pancake will fall). Remove pancake to a serving platter. Top with fresh fruit or berries, and cut into wedges. Serve with Custard Sauce, syrup, cinnamon, or powdered sugar.

[M A R G A R E T M c W H O R T E R K I N G]

Beautiful for guests, this is a colorful, elegant dish.

SERVES 4

1/4 cup butter
4 eggs
1 cup milk
1 cup all-purpose flour
1 teaspoon almond extract
Sliced fresh fruit or seasonal berries
Custard Sauce
Maple syrup
Ground cinnamon
Powdered sugar

C U S T A R D S A U C E

Beat egg yolks. Add sugar and salt. Scald milk; add slowly to egg mixture. Cook in top of double boiler over hot water, stirring constantly until it thickens. Cool slightly and add vanilla. Chill.

SERVES 4

3 egg yolks
1/4 cup sugar
1/8 teaspoon salt
1/2 cup milk
1 teaspoon vanilla extract

G R U Y È R E   E G G S

Cook bacon until crisp. Drain. Crumble bacon into a 6-ounce ramekin. Add cream and 1 tablespoon grated Gruyère. Break an egg into the ramekin, and sprinkle with salt. Set ramekin in a shallow baking pan filled with water. Bake at 350° for 15 minutes. Sprinkle with chopped chives and remaining cheese. Bake about 5 additional minutes or until egg is set.

[B O B B I E   H U R L E Y   H A R P E R]

T H E   P L O W M A N ' S   O M E L E T T E

Cook bacon in a skillet until crisp. Crumble bacon, and set aside; reserve drippings in skillet. In 2 to 3 tablespoons bacon drippings, sauté onion and green pepper until tender (1 to 2 minutes). Add potatoes and cook 5 more minutes. Combine eggs, milk, thyme, basil, and salt and pepper to taste. Place bacon and potato mixture in an omelette pan or skillet, lightly coated with vegetable cooking spray. Pour in eggs. Cook 2 to 3 minutes over medium heat. Add tomato, cheese, and crumbled bacon. Allow cheese to melt, then fold omelette. Serve immediately.

SAVORY EGGS WITH MUSHROOM CREAM SAUCE

SERVES 8 TO 10

Remove egg shells, and cut eggs in half lengthwise. Remove yolks and mash yolks well. Season with salt and pepper to taste, and stir in 2 tablespoons softened butter to bind the mixture. Add the mushroom stems and pieces, if desired. ✐ Stuff the egg whites with the egg yolk mixture. Place eggs, yolk side up, in a single layer in a greased 2-quart casserole dish. Brown green onions in 2 tablespoons melted butter. Add the diced tomatoes. Cook until thick. ✐ Combine 1 tablespoon butter, flour, and milk. Cook over low heat until white sauce is thickened. Season with salt, pepper, and Worcestershire to taste. Add sauce to tomato mixture. Pour over stuffed eggs. ✐ Bake at 350° for 20 minutes.

6 hard-cooked eggs
  Salt and pepper
2 tablespoons butter, softened
1 (2-ounce) can mushroom stems and pieces, drained (optional)
1 cup chopped green onions
2 tablespoons butter, melted
1 (14½-ounce) can diced tomatoes, drained
1 tablespoon butter
1 tablespoon all-purpose flour
1 cup milk
  Salt and pepper
  Worcestershire sauce

COOCHIE'S MEXICAN QUICHE

SERVES 6

Sauté onion in butter until tender. Place in bottom of 9-inch pastry shell. Add tomato slices. Beat eggs and cream together. Add remaining ingredients. Pour over tomato slices. ✐ Bake at 375° for 30 minutes. Let cool 15 minutes, and serve.

[REBECCA OLIVER HAINES]

½ cup chopped onion
2 tablespoons butter
1 (9-inch) baked pastry shell
1 to 2 tomatoes, sliced
5 eggs
1 cup whipping cream
1½ cup grated Monterey Jack or Colby cheese
1 teaspoon salt
¼ teaspoon pepper
¼ cup chopped jalapeño peppers

O M E L E T T E G R A N D E B R E T A G N E

SERVES 6 TO 8

1 (28-ounce) can chopped
 tomatoes, undrained
1 tablespoon dried basil
1 tablespoon dried oregano
1 clove garlic, minced
1 teaspoon salt
1 teaspoon pepper
1 medium-size green pepper,
 seeded and chopped
1 large white onion, chopped
1 stalk celery, chopped

1 pound fresh crabmeat, drained
 and flaked
2 tablespoons butter, melted
1 tablespoon Worcestershire sauce
1 pound fresh medium-size
 shrimp, cooked, peeled, and
 deveined
1/2 pound sea scallops, quartered
2 tablespoons butter
2 tablespoons olive oil, divided
2 dozen eggs
3 to 4 ounces feta cheese,
 crumbled

To prepare tomato sauce, combine first 9 ingredients in a saucepan, and cook over low heat 15 minutes. Keep warm. Toss crabmeat in 2 tablespoons butter and Worcestershire sauce. Set aside. Bring shrimp to room temperature. Sauté scallops in 2 tablespoons butter and 1 tablespoon olive oil. Heat a large skillet with remaining 1 tablespoon olive oil. Beat eggs with a rotary beater or an electric mixer until light. Pour beaten eggs into hot skillet (can also use a broiler pan and bake in an oven). When eggs are set, put a thin coating of tomato sauce (1/3 cup) on top of eggs. Spoon seafood over eggs, and fold omelette in half. Slide onto a warm platter. Pour remaining tomato sauce over omelette, and sprinkle with feta cheese. Serve immediately.

[CARL MARTIN HAMES]

H A M A N D S W I S S T A R T

SERVES 6

2 cups cooked and cubed ham
1 cup grated Swiss cheese
1/4 cup finely chopped celery
1/4 cup finely chopped green pepper
2 tablespoons minced onion
1 teaspoon dry mustard
1 tablespoon lemon juice
1/3 cup mayonnaise
1 (9-inch) frozen pastry shell

Combine first 8 ingredients, and pour into pastry shell. Bake uncovered at 375° for 25 to 35 minutes or until golden brown.

[CATHY CRISS ADAMS]

BRUNCH ROULADE

SERVES 6

5 eggs, separated
$1/2$ teaspoon salt
$1/4$ teaspoon ground white pepper
Paprika
1 cup warm milk

Filling:
1 (10-ounce) package frozen chopped spinach
1 cup grated fresh Parmesan cheese
6 slices bacon, cooked and crumbled

To prepare the egg portion: Line a jellyroll pan with parchment or wax paper, and spray well with cooking spray. In a small bowl, combine egg yolks, salt, and pepper, beating well. Using an electric mixer, beat egg whites in a large bowl until stiff. Fold egg yolk mixture into beaten egg whites. Do not over-stir. Using a rubber spatula, spread the egg mixture evenly into prepared pan. Sprinkle with paprika. Bake at 375° for 10 minutes (or until the top is brown). Cut around the edges of the egg to loosen. Turn the baked egg onto another piece of parchment paper coated with cooking spray, and peel off first sheet. Pour warm milk over the egg layer; make certain to cover the edges. Let the milk soak in. (Do this step in a pan or tray with a rim to avoid milk running everywhere.) To prepare the filling, cook spinach according to package directions. Let cool, then squeeze all of the moisture out of spinach. Sprinkle cheese onto the egg layer. Then distribute the spinach evenly over the cheese. Finally, top with crumbled bacon. Roll egg jellyroll fashion from one long side to form a long roll and enclose filling. Place seam side down on a cookie sheet. (Can prepare to this point the night before; cover and refrigerate. Let the roulade come to room temperature again before baking). Bake at 350° for 15 minutes or until hot. Place on a serving tray; cut into $1^1/2$-inch slices to serve.

*Let this versatile new Southern classic inspire you!
Experiment with a variety of fillings.*

ARTICHOKE QUICHE

Heat olive oil and butter in a skillet. Sauté onion, celery, garlic, and parsley. Add artichokes, and mix well. Place artichoke mixture in bottom of a round casserole dish. Top with mushrooms. Blend milk, eggs, biscuit mix, cheeses, garlic powder, and pepper for 10 seconds or until well blended. Pour over artichoke mixture and mushrooms. Bake at 350° for 30 to 35 minutes.

[MRS. CLIFFORD EMOND]

SERVES 8

1½ tablespoons olive oil
1 tablespoon butter
½ cup chopped onion
1 tablespoon diced celery
2 cloves garlic, minced
2 teaspoons chopped fresh parsley
2 (14-ounce) cans artichoke hearts, drained and chopped
1 (4-ounce) can sliced mushrooms, drained
1¼ cups milk
4 eggs
⅔ cup biscuit mix
⅓ cup grated Swiss cheese
¼ cup grated fresh Parmesan cheese
¼ teaspoon garlic powder
¼ teaspoon pepper

MEXICAN CHEESE STRATA

Sprinkle broken chips in bottom of a lightly greased 2-quart casserole dish. Cover with grated cheese. ✑ Combine eggs and next 7 ingredients, and pour over cheese. Cover and refrigerate several hours or overnight. ✑ Bake, uncovered, at 325° for 1 hour. ✑ Garnish with tortilla chips and tomato, if desired.

[CINDY SMITH SPEAKE]

Great meatless meal.

SERVES 6

4 cups cheese-flavored tortilla chips, broken and crushed
2 cups grated Monterey Jack cheese (with peppers optional)
6 eggs, beaten
2½ cups milk
1 (4½-ounce) can chopped green chilies, drained
¼ cup finely chopped onion
3 tablespoons ketchup
¼ teaspoon Tabasco Sauce
¼ cup chopped green pepper (optional)
½ teaspoon salt
Garnishes: whole tortilla chips, tomato slices, or salsa

BLUEBERRY WHEATCAKES

MAKES 1 1/2 DOZEN

Combine eggs and milk in medium bowl. Add syrup and stir. Combine dry ingredients. Add to egg mixture. Add melted butter and stir again. Fold in blueberries. Cook on a greased griddle or in a skillet, turning once.

2 eggs, beaten
1 3/4 cups milk
2 tablespoons pure maple syrup
1 cup whole wheat flour
1 cup all-purpose flour
1 tablespoon wheat germ
1 1/2 teaspoons baking powder
1 teaspoon baking soda
1 teaspoon salt
4 tablespoons butter, melted
2 cups fresh blueberries

POACHED EGGS WITH MUSHROOMS

SERVES 8

Sauté mushrooms and green onions in butter in a skillet for 5 minutes. Remove mushrooms and green onions, reserving butter in skillet. Place mushrooms and onions in a bowl. Add flour to the reserved butter, and stir well to remove lumps. Add wine, half-and-half and seasonings. Simmer until thickened. Return mushrooms and onions to sauce, and keep warm. Warm the puff pastry shells. Poach eggs and make hollandaise sauce (see page 276 for recipe). Place about 3 tablespoons mushroom sauce in each pastry shell. Top with an egg and hollandaise sauce. Serve with a slice of ham, if desired.

1 pound fresh mushrooms, chopped
3 tablespoons chopped green onions
3 tablespoons butter
1 1/2 tablespoons all-purpose flour
1/4 cup port wine
1/2 cup half-and-half
1/2 teaspoon salt
Dash of pepper
8 baked puff pastry shells
8 eggs
1 recipe hollandaise sauce

3 to 4 tablespoons butter, softened and divided

8 slices dry bread with crust

6 ounces sharp Cheddar cheese, grated

5 eggs, beaten

2½ cups milk

¼ teaspoon Tabasco Sauce

⅛ teaspoon ground white pepper

½ teaspoon salt

1½ tablespoons basil pesto

4 sun-dried tomatoes packed in oil, drained and chopped

MAKES 2
(13 x 9 x 2-INCH)
CASSEROLES

1 large loaf day-old French bread

6 tablespoons butter, melted

Ham slices (to cover 2 [9 x 13-inch] casseroles)

½ cup chopped green onion

8 ounces grated Swiss cheese

8 ounces Monterey Jack cheese, grated

16 eggs

3¼ cups milk

½ cup white wine

1 tablespoon Dijon mustard

¼ teaspoon ground black pepper

⅛ teaspoon ground red pepper

1½ cup sour cream

⅔ cup grated Parmesan cheese

BASIL CHEESE STRATA

Butter an 8-inch square baking pan. Spread remaining butter on bread slices. Put one layer of bread in pan, buttered side up. Top with half of cheese. Repeat layers. Whisk together eggs and remaining ingredients, and pour over layers. Cover and refrigerate overnight. ✿ Bake casserole at 350° in the upper one-third of the oven 30 to 40 minutes or until puffy and brown.

[KELLI NELSON JETMUNDSEN]

EGG STRATA WITH DIJON WINE SAUCE

Cut bread into ½-inch slices. Arrange bread on the bottom of 2 13 x 9 x 2-inch baking dishes. Drizzle evenly with melted butter. ✿ Layer ham, green onions, and cheeses. ✿ Combine eggs, milk, wine, mustard, and peppers. Pour over cheese. ✿ Spread sour cream over top. Cover and refrigerate overnight. ✿ Bake, covered, at 325° for 1 hour. Uncover and sprinkle with Parmesan cheese. Bake 10 additional minutes.

[FLETCHER HANSON CHAMBLISS]

S H R I M P & G R I T S

Cook bacon until crisp. Drain, reserving drippings in skillet. Crumble bacon, and set aside. ✒ Sauté green pepper, mushrooms, and garlic in bacon drippings. Sprinkle flour over vegetables, and cook, stirring constantly, about 2 minutes. Add broth and next 7 ingredients. Cook 5 minutes or until heated thoroughly. Keep warm. ✒ For grits, bring water and margarine to a boil in a heavy saucepan. Stir in grits, and return to a boil over medium heat. Reduce heat, and cook, stirring occasionally, for 10 minutes or until thick, continuing to stir. Stir in 1/4 cup milk; simmer 10 minutes. Salt. Add remaining 1/4 cup milk; simmer 10 minutes. ✒ Serve shrimp mixture over cooked grits. Top with crumbled bacon and parsley.

[J A N E G L E N N O N F E A G I N]

G O U R M E T
C H E E S E G R I T S

Bring milk to a boil over medium heat, stirring often. Add 1/2 cup butter and grits. Cook, stirring constantly, until mixture is the consistency of oatmeal (about 5 minutes). ✒ Remove grits from heat. Add salt, pepper, and egg, beating until well combined. ✒ Add 1/3 cup butter and Gruyère cheese. Pour into a greased 2-quart casserole dish. Sprinkle with Parmesan cheese. ✒ Bake at 350° for 1 hour.

[A N G E L I A P I T T S B R A D Y]

Can be made the day before and cooked just before serving.

SERVES 2 TO 4

6 slices bacon
1/3 cup chopped green pepper
1 cup sliced fresh mushrooms
1 clove garlic, minced
2 tablespoons all-purpose flour
3/8 cup chicken broth
2 tablespoons lemon juice
1 pound fresh shrimp, peeled
1 cup chopped green onion
1/4 teaspoon salt
1/8 teaspoon ground red pepper
  Dash Creole seasoning
  Dash Tabasco Sauce
2 tablespoons chopped fresh
  parsley

2 cups water
2 tablespoons margarine
1/2 cup grits, uncooked
1/2 cup milk, divided
1/4 teaspoon salt

SERVES 10

1 quart milk
1/2 cup butter
1 cup uncooked grits
1 teaspoon salt
1/2 teaspoon ground white pepper
1 egg
1/3 cup butter
4 ounces Gruyère cheese, grated
1/2 cup grated fresh Parmesan
  cheese

SERVES 8

Batter:
- 2 eggs, well beaten
- 1 cup all-purpose flour
- 1/2 teaspoon salt
- 1 cup skim milk
- 1/2 teaspoon sugar

Filling:
- 1 (8 ounce) carton small curd cottage cheese
- 1 egg yolk
- Pinch of salt
- 1 tablespoon sugar
- 1 tablespoon butter
- 1/2 teaspoon ground cinnamon

SERVES 6

- 1 pound ground pork sausage
- 1/2 cup finely chopped onion
- 1/4 cup grated Parmesan cheese
- 1/2 cup grated Swiss cheese
- 1 egg, beaten
- 1/2 teaspoon Tabasco Sauce
- 1/2 teaspoon salt
- 2 tablespoons chopped fresh parsley
- 1 cup biscuit mix (or 1 cup all-purpose flour, 1 teaspoon baking powder, and 1/2 teaspoon baking soda)
- 3/4 cup milk
- 1/4 cup mayonnaise
- 1 egg yolk
- 1 tablespoon water

CHEESE BLINTZES

For batter, mix ingredients in blender. Chill 30 minutes. Add water, if necessary; batter should be thin. Lightly grease a 7-inch or 8-inch crêpe pan with butter, and place over medium-high heat. Add 1 large tablespoon batter. As soon as it sets, flip it, and cook an additional 30 seconds. Turn out onto dry towel. Repeat procedure with remaining batter. Crêpes may be stacked as they cool. Add additional butter to pan as needed. For filling, combine all filling ingredients. Add a teaspoonful of filling to each blintz; fold ends and roll up. To serve, place blintzes in a greased casserole dish, and bake for 2 to 3 minutes on each side. Serve with sour cream and fresh strawberries or strawberry preserves.

[CAROLYN TURNER]

SAUSAGE COFFEE CAKE

Cook sausage and onion until sausage is browned. Drain well. Add cheeses, egg, Tabasco Sauce, salt, and parsley. Set aside. Combine biscuit mix, milk, and mayonnaise to make a batter. Spread half of batter into a greased 9-inch square baking pan. Spread sausage mixture over batter. Pour remaining batter over top. Combine egg yolk and water, and brush over batter. Bake at 400° for 25 to 30 minutes. Serve warm.

[RAMONA S. MELTON]

SOUR CREAM COFFEE CAKE

Cream butter, sugar, eggs, and vanilla. Combine flour, baking powder, and salt. Add to creamed mixture. Fold in sour cream. Pour half mixture into greased and floured Bundt pan. Top with half mixture of nuts, cinnamon, brown sugar, and sugar. Repeat these layers. Swirl the batter with knife. Bake at 350° for 50 to 60 minutes.

[BECKY HERREN BASHINSKY]

SERVES 16

2 sticks butter or margarine

2 cups sugar

2 eggs

1/2 teaspoon vanilla

2 cups flour

1 teaspoon baking powder

1/2 teaspoon salt

1 cup sour cream

1/2 cup chopped pecans

3 tablespoons cinnamon

4 tablespoons brown sugar

3 tablespoons sugar

GRANOLA

Combine first 8 ingredients. Place in a large jellyroll pan, and bake at 300° for 40 to 50 minutes or until golden brown, stirring frequently. Stir in raisins or other fruit. Cool. ✧ Store in an airtight container in refrigerator. ✧ Add chocolate pieces to make a great trail mix or snack. Delicious as is or with yogurt and fresh fruit.

[SUSAN NABERS HASKELL]
PAST PRESIDENT

MAKES 5 CUPS

2 1/4 cups quick-cooking or regular oats, uncooked

1/2 cup instant nonfat dry milk powder

1/2 cup sunflower seeds

1/2 to 1 cup chopped nuts (almonds, pecans, or walnuts)

1/2 cup wheat germ

1/2 cup firmly packed brown sugar

1/2 cup butter, melted

1/4 cup honey

1/2 cup raisins, chopped prunes, or chopped apricots

Candy-coated chocolate pieces (optional)

Just a Thought

Make a quick breakfast parfait. In a tall stemmed glass, layer fresh berries with lemon yogurt, and sprinkle with granola.

SERVES 2 TO 4

1 cup any flavor yogurt

1 ripe banana

1 cup fruit (cantaloupe, honeydew, strawberries, pineapple, or combination)

1½ cups orange juice

1 tablespoon honey (optional)

3 tablespoons wheat germ (optional)

1 to 2 cups ice cubes

MAKES 3 QUARTS

1 (46-ounce) can tomato juice

1 (46-ounce) can V-8 juice

½ cup fresh lemon juice

¼ cup fresh lime juice

1 teaspoon salt

1 teaspoon black pepper

2 teaspoons celery seeds

1 tablespoon prepared horseradish

5 tablespoons Worcestershire sauce

8 to 10 drops Tabasco Sauce (optional)

Vodka, to taste (optional)

Celery stalks with leaves (optional)

SERVES 4

1 (6-ounce) can lemonade concentrate, thawed

1 (6-ounce) can pineapple juice

½ quart orange juice

Garnish: fresh mint sprigs

BREAKFAST SHAKE

Low Fat

Combine first 4 ingredients in blender. Add honey and wheat germ, if desired. Process until smooth. Add ice, and blend until mixture reaches desired consistency. Great with muffins or bagels for a nutritious breakfast.

[LEE STYSLINGER]

TAILGATE BLOODY MARYS

Combine first 9 ingredients. Add Tabasco Sauce, if desired. Refrigerate up to 48 hours. If desired, pour vodka into individual glasses, or mix in just before serving. Garnish each glass with a celery stalk.

[CINDY COMPTON TAYLOR]

CITRUS COOLER

In a quart jar, combine lemonade and pineapple juice. Fill remainder of jar with orange juice. Garnish with fresh mint.

M A G N O L I A   F A R M ' S   S W E E T   M I N T   T E A

Place tea bags, sugar, and mint into a 2-quart container. (If using fresh mint, twist leaves but not stems.) Pour boiling water over. Cover; let steep 15 minutes. Discard mint and tea bags. Cool; add lemon juice, if desired. Pour through a wire-mesh strainer. Refrigerate.

[B E T T Y   B L A C K M O N   K I N N E T T   ]

C O F F E E   P U N C H

Prepare coffee, and place in a 5-quart container. Add salt, cinnamon, sugar, and chocolate syrup; mix well. Cover and chill. ✒ To serve, place ice cream in a punch bowl, and pour coffee mixture over it. Garnish, if desired.

[C A R O L Y N   R I T C H E Y   K I N G   ]

S P I C E D   T E A

Boil water in a large saucepan and add teabags. Steep for 10 minutes. Remove teabags. Add all other ingredients and simmer slowly. Serve hot in winter or chilled in summer.

[T O O K I E   D A U G H E R T Y   H A Z E L R I G   ]

MAKES 2 QUARTS

1 *family-size tea bag*
1 *cup sugar*
5 *to 10 sprigs fresh mint or*
  1/8 teaspoon mint extract
  (not peppermint)
2 *quarts boiling water*
1/8 *cup lemon juice (optional)*

SERVES 25

1 *gallon strong coffee*
  Pinch of salt
1/2 *teaspoon ground cinnamon*
1 *cup sugar*
1/2 *cup chocolate syrup*
1/2 *gallon vanilla ice cream*
  Garnish: chocolate shavings

MAKES 6 1/2 QUARTS

6 *quarts water*
4 *family-size tea bags*
3 *cups sugar*
3 *teaspoons whole cloves*
1 *(6-ounce) can frozen*
  lemonade concentrate
1 *(6-ounce) can frozen orange*
  juice concentrate
12 *ounces pineapple juice*

Sun-dried Tomato Bread, page 84, Praline Muffins, page 82, and Pumpkin Bread/Muffins, page 81

True Biscuit

-MARK CHILDRESS-

YOU WON'T FIND IN THESE PAGES A RECIPE for my grandmother's biscuit. Notice I use the singular form of the word. Outside the cities of Alabama, biscuits have always been referred to as "biscuit," as in: "Lord, don't that girl know how to make good biscuit," or "We'll be eatin' just soon as the biscuit's done." I believe this linguistic curiosity arises from the fact that, in the country places, biscuit has always constituted its own separate food group.

We ate biscuit with breakfast, dinner, and supper. Alone or with butter or fig preserves or scuppernong jelly. Stuffed with salty-sweet country ham or peppery patty sausage from Conecuh County. When a finger-hole was poked in the side and filled with sorghum syrup, a biscuit became a "boley holey," a kind of portable dessert, the Alabama equivalent of a Twinkie. Sometimes biscuit was crumbled in milk, and eaten with a spoon. Sometimes on a Sunday the biscuit dough was rolled out flat, cut into little crinkle-edged strips, and lodged deep inside a chicken pie, where it magically transformed itself into a dumpling.

The reason you won't find my grandmother's recipe for biscuit is that she never worked from a recipe. She just knew how to do it. She began with a handful of "sarmilk starter" from the large white bowl at the back of the refrigerator, threw in flour and baking powder and salt and lard and buttermilk in quantities sufficient to make it come out right. She kneaded the dough, patted it out, cut out rounds with a tin can that had been sawed in half to make a sharp edge, and baked the .CONTINUED.

MARK CHILDRESS

BORN IN ALABAMA IN 1957,
MARK CHILDRESS GRADUATED
FROM THE UNIVERSITY OF
ALABAMA AND WENT ON
TO SERVE ON THE
EDITORIAL STAFFS OF
THE BIRMINGHAM NEWS,
*THE ATLANTA JOURNAL-
CONSTITUTION*, AND
SOUTHERN LIVING MAGAZINE.
HE IS AUTHOR OF
A WORLD MADE OF FIRE,
V FOR VICTOR, *TENDER*,
AND *CRAZY IN ALABAMA*.
HE NOW LIVES IN
COSTA RICA AND
IS WORKING
ON HIS FIFTH NOVEL.

biscuit on an old black cookie sheet in a hot oven until they were done.

My mother and various members of the family have been trying for twenty-five years to reproduce these biscuit, with some success. I've tasted some mighty fine biscuit in that time, but there's an airiness, a certain sharp, subtle tang that remains elusive. The secret seems to have resided in that mysterious white bowl on the top shelf of Grandmother's Frigidaire: a sour-milk culture which for all I know may have originated with the ancient Egyptians. That starter was the primal ingredient. When Grandmother died, somebody washed out the bowl, and the secret was lost forever.

I think most folks' grandmothers must have had a bowl like that at the back of the fridge. As these ladies passed on, they have taken the secret of the true biscuit with them. Our collective longing for biscuit is reflected in the fast-food joints, which crank out millions of neo-biscuits every morning, stuffed with sausage or ham, or with things that have no business being inside a biscuit, such as "chopped steak" and American cheese. Some of these imitations are quite tasty, but they bear the same relation to a true biscuit that looking at an old photograph bears to having lived through the old times yourself: it gives you the general idea, but it's not quite the same as having been there. THE END

B R E A D S

WHOLE WHEAT BISCUITS

Combine flours in bowl. Remove 1 to 2 tablespoons flour, and sprinkle on rolling surface. To flour in bowl, add baking powder and salt. Cut in shortening. Stir in half-and-half. Roll dough out to $1/2$-inch thickness, and cut in desired shape. Place biscuits on lightly greased baking sheet. Bake at 450° for 10 minutes.

[HATTIE MAE REED]

BUTTERMILK BISCUITS

Combine first 5 ingredients. Cut in butter until mixture resembles coarse crumbs. Add buttermilk; stir until well mixed. Turn dough out onto floured surface; knead lightly 3 or 4 times. Roll dough out to $1/2$-inch thickness. Cut into rounds or desired shapes. Bake at 475° for 10 minutes.

[PATTY GAFFNEY GILBERT]

CRANBERRY SCONES

Combine first 4 ingredients. Cut in butter until well blended. Add buttermilk, egg, and cranberries. Mix well. Knead lightly, 3 to 4 times, and roll out. Form into a circle. Place on a lightly greased cookie sheet. Dust with cinnamon sugar. Bake at 400° for 15 minutes or until golden. Slice into wedges.

[JEAN KINNETT OLIVER]

MAKES 1$1/2$ DOZEN

1 cup all-purpose whole wheat flour
1 cup all-purpose white flour
2 teaspoons baking powder
$1/4$ teaspoon salt
3 tablespoons shortening
$1/2$ to $3/4$ cup half-and-half

MAKES 12 TO 14

2 cups all-purpose flour
2 teaspoons baking powder
$3/4$ teaspoon salt
$1/4$ teaspoon baking soda
2 tablespoons sugar
$1/4$ cup butter
1 cup nonfat buttermilk

SERVES 8

3 cups all-purpose flour
2 teaspoons baking powder
$1/2$ teaspoon salt
$1/4$ cup sugar
6 tablespoons butter, softened
$3/4$ cup buttermilk
1 egg, beaten
1 cup coarsely chopped cranberries
Cinnamon sugar

TOMATO-BASIL BISCUITS

Combine first 4 ingredients in a large bowl. Cut butter into dry mixture until it resembles coarse crumbs. Add half-and-half, tomatoes, and basil. Stir well. Transfer dough to floured surface; knead 30 seconds. Roll out to 1-inch thickness, and cut into desired shapes. Bake at 425° for 15 minutes or until golden.

[STEPHANIE DESPINAKIS BOSTWICK]

MAKES 2½ DOZEN

1 cup all-purpose flour
2 teaspoons baking powder
½ teaspoon salt
¼ teaspoon sugar
4 tablespoons unsalted butter
¼ cup half-and-half
2 ripe tomatoes, peeled, seeded, drained, and chopped
⅓ cup chopped fresh basil

HATTIE'S CHEESE BISCUITS

Combine first 4 ingredients. Cut in shortening until mixture resembles crumbs. Stir in cheese and milk. Knead lightly. Roll out to ½-inch thickness, and cut or drop onto a lightly greased baking sheet. Bake at 400° for 20 minutes.

[BETTY BLACKMON KINNETT]

MAKES 2 DOZEN

2 cups all-purpose flour
½ teaspoon salt
1 tablespoon baking powder
⅛ teaspoon cayenne pepper
¼ cup shortening
1 cup grated extra-sharp Cheddar cheese
¾ cup milk or buttermilk

SWEET POTATO BISCUITS

Combine first 7 ingredients in a mixing bowl. Cut shortening into mixture. Fold in sweet potatoes. Combine egg and buttermilk; add to flour-potato mixture, and mix well. Drop 12 (2-ounce) dollops onto greased cookie sheet, spacing evenly. Bake at 350° for 12 to 15 minutes. Leftover batter may be stored in refrigerator.

[JIM MUIR]
CRAPE MYRTLE AND WILD ROOT CAFE

MAKES 1½ TO 2 DOZEN

4 cups flour
½ cup sugar
1½ tablespoons baking powder
1 scant teaspoon baking soda
½ teaspoon cinnamon
Pinch nutmeg
Pinch salt
1 cup shortening
⅔ cup sweet potatoes, cooked and chopped
1 egg
3¼ cups buttermilk

MAKES 2 LOAVES

Starter:
- 2 packages active dry yeast
- 1/2 cup warm water (105° to 115°)
- 2 cups warm water, divided
- 1 1/3 cups sugar, divided
- 6 tablespoons instant potato flakes, divided

Sourdough bread:
- 1 cup starter
- 1/2 cup vegetable shortening, melted
- 1 1/2 cups warm water (not hot)
- 1 teaspoon salt
- 6 cups flour
- 3 tablespoons butter, melted

SISTER SCHUBERT'S SOURDOUGH BREAD

STARTER:

Dissolve yeast in 1/2 cup warm water. To this, "feed" 1 cup warm water, 2/3 cup sugar, 3 tablespoons instant potato flakes. Let sit out all day or overnight. Refrigerate 2 to 5 days. Feed again with same water, sugar, potato flake combination. Let sit out all day or overnight. Use 1 cup of starter to make bread. Refrigerate remainder; feed starter once a week.

BREAD:

Mix all ingredients in a large bowl. Batter will be stiff. Cover and let rise in a warm place all day or overnight. Punch down; knead a few times. Turn out onto a floured surface. Divide dough into 2 equal parts; knead a few more minutes. ✐ Place each loaf in a well-greased loafpan. Brush tops with melted butter. Cover and let rise 6 hours or until dough rises above pan. ✐ Bake at 325° for 45 minutes. Cool on wire rack.

[PATRICIA W. "SISTER" SCHUBERT]

Sister Schubert built a baking empire on the tried-and-true notion that the Southern table is not complete without fresh-baked breads and rolls. The business that started out of her kitchen in Troy, Alabama, now sells millions of rolls and specialty breads throughout the South.

FILLINGS FOR YEAST ROLLS

HAM SPREAD:

Combine first 5 ingredients. Stir in ham and cheeses. Place 1 teaspoon filling in center of each roll. Place back in pan. Cover until ready to heat. Cover rolls with aluminum foil, and heat at 375° for 15 to 20 minutes.

TENDERLOIN:

Combine first 4 ingredients. Spread small amount in center of roll, and place slice of tenderloin on top. Cover until ready to heat. Bake, covered, at 350° for 15 to 20 minutes.

TURKEY:

Spread small amount of orange marmalade on center of rolls and place slice of turkey on top. Cover until ready to serve. Bake, covered, at 350° for 15 to 20 minutes.

[PATRICIA W. "SISTER" SCHUBERT]

MAKES 2 TO 3 DOZEN

Ham Spread:
- *1/2 cup butter, softened*
- *2 tablespoons prepared mustard*
- *1/2 teaspoon Worcestershire sauce*
- *1 tablespoon poppy seeds*
- *3 green onions, chopped*
- *1 pound honey ham, chopped*
- *6 ounces grated Swiss cheese*
- *4 ounces grated Parmesan cheese*
- *6 ounces grated sharp Cheddar cheese*

MAKES 2 DOZEN

Tenderloin:
- *1 cup sour cream*
- *1/3 to 1/4 cup horseradish*
- *1/4 teaspoon salt*
- *1 tablespoon lemon juice*
- *24 slices beef tenderloin*

MAKES 1 DOZEN

Turkey:
- *4 ounces orange marmalade*
- *12 slices roasted or smoked turkey*

Just a Thought

For a cocktail buffet, fill our Tomato-Basil Biscuits with beef tenderloin, Hattie's Cheese Biscuits with sliced ham, or Sweet Potato Biscuits with smoked ham.

G I A N T   P E C A N   P O P O V E R S

MAKES 6

2 eggs
1 cup milk
1 cup all-purpose flour
1/4 teaspoon salt
1/4 cup chopped pecans

Bring eggs and milk to room temperature; beat together for 5 seconds. Add flour and salt, and beat again for 10 seconds. Stir in pecans. ✑ Spoon into well-greased custard cups, filling half full. ✑ Bake at 475° for 15 minutes. Reduce heat to 350° and bake for 25 to 30 additional minutes.

[V A L   G A Y D E N   H O L M A N]

*For rave reviews, serve with Maple Butter:
Combine 1/2 cup softened butter and 3/4 cup pure
maple syrup, and mix until fluffy.*

L I L I E ' S   N O - C O R N   B R E A D

SERVES 6 TO 8

1 cup uncooked Cream of Wheat
1 cup self-rising flour
1 egg, beaten
5 tablespoons vegetable oil, divided
3/4 cup water

Combine Cream of Wheat and flour. Stir in egg, 3 tablespoons oil, and water to make soft dough. ✑ In a cast-iron skillet or cornbread pan, heat remaining 2 tablespoons oil. When hot, pour batter into pan. Bake at 425° for 45 minutes.

[M A R T H A   S U L Z B Y   C L A R K]

BUTTERMILK-SAGE CORN MUFFINS

Combine first 5 ingredients; set aside. Combine buttermilk and eggs; whisk lightly. Add to dry ingredients. Add oil, mixing until just moistened. Spoon into a greased muffin pan. ✒ Bake at 400° for 15 to 20 minutes.

MAKES 1 DOZEN

1 cup self-rising cornmeal
1 cup all-purpose flour
1/2 cup grated sharp Cheddar cheese
1/4 teaspoon dried sage
1/8 teaspoon cayenne pepper
1 1/4 cups buttermilk
3 eggs
1/4 cup vegetable oil

SAUSAGE-APPLE CORNBREAD

Brown sausage in a large skillet; drain, reserving 2 tablespoons drippings. ✒ Arrange apple slices in bottom of greased 10-inch pieplate. Cover with half of sausage and 1/2 cup cheese. Combine flour and next 4 ingredients. Set dry ingredients aside. ✒ In large bowl, combine milk, egg, and reserved drippings. Add dry ingredients and remaining sausage and cheese; stir well. Pour into pieplate. Bake at 425° for 30 minutes.

[B A R B A R A   B A N K H E A D   O L I V E R]

SERVES 6

1 pound ground pork sausage
2 large tart apples, cored and sliced
1 1/2 cups grated Cheddar cheese, divided
1 cup all-purpose flour
1 cup yellow cornmeal
2 tablespoons sugar
1 tablespoon plus 1 teaspoon baking powder
1/2 teaspoon salt
1 1/4 cups milk
1 egg, beaten

Just a Thought

All true Southerners know that the secret to great cornbread is a well-seasoned heavy iron skillet. If you didn't inherit Grandmother's, hit the local flea markets to find one.

MAKES 4

1 package rapid-rise yeast
4½ to 5 cups bread flour
1 tablespoon sugar
2 teaspoons salt
2 cups warm water
1 tablespoon vegetable oil
  cornmeal
1 egg, beaten
1 teaspoon cold water

FRENCH BREAD   *Low Fat*

Mix yeast and next 3 ingredients in large bowl. Add warm water all at once, and stir until it forms a ball. Turn out onto floured surface. Knead until the dough is soft. ✍ Oil same large bowl, and return dough to it. Cover and let rise 15 to 20 minutes. Grease 2 jellyroll pans, and sprinkle with cornmeal. ✍ Divide dough into 4 equal parts. Roll out each piece; roll up jellyroll fashion, forming long loaf. Place loaves seam side down on prepared pans. Make 2 to 3 lengthwise slits across top of each loaf. Combine egg and cold water; brush loaves with egg mixture. Let rise 2 to 3 hours or until doubled in bulk. ✍ Bake at 425° for 10 to 15 minutes. Cool on wire rack. Serve warm, or wrap tightly to freeze.

For regular loaf bread: Divide dough into 2 portions. Roll out and roll up into 2 loaves. Place in 9 x 5 x 3-inch loafpans. Brush tops, and let rise again. Bake at 425° for 20 to 40 minutes. Slice for sandwiches.

MAKES 4 DOZEN

1 cup butter, softened
2 cups sugar
2 eggs
3 tablespoons ground cinnamon
1 teaspoon ground allspice
2 teaspoons baking soda
½ teaspoon salt
4 cups all-purpose flour
2 cups applesauce
1 cup raisins (optional)
½ cup chopped walnuts
  (optional)

APPLESAUCE MUFFINS

Cream butter and sugar. Add next 5 ingredients. Mix well. ✍ Add flour and applesauce; blend well. Add raisins and walnuts, if desired. ✍ Pour into lightly greased muffin pans. Bake at 350° for 25 to 30 minutes.

[MANDY HAMEL ROGERS]

HERB BREAD

Sprinkle yeast and sugar over warm water in a small bowl. Stir to dissolve; let stand until foamy, about 10 minutes. ✍ Combine milk, brown sugar, salt, herbs, and if desired, walnuts. Add yeast mixture. Add flours gradually, kneading until dough is smooth. Cover and let rise until doubled in bulk, about 45 to 60 minutes. Punch down and divide in half. ✍ Place dough into 2 (9 x 5-inch) or (8$\frac{1}{2}$ x 4$\frac{1}{2}$-inch) loafpans. Let rise until barely doubled. Bake at 375° for 35 to 45 minutes or until bread sounds hollow when tapped on bottom.

[DR. HAROLD CANNON]

PECAN WHOLE WHEAT BREAD

Proof yeast in warm milk in large bowl.* Add next 6 ingredients. Mix together. Add bread flour, $\frac{1}{2}$ cup at a time; mix until dough is stiff. ✍ Remove to well-floured surface. Knead in enough remaining flour to make a soft dough. Place in lightly oiled bowl, and let rise until doubled in bulk. Punch down and divide in half. ✍ Place dough into 2 (9 x 5-inch) or (8$\frac{1}{2}$ x 4$\frac{1}{2}$-inch) loafpans. Let rise until doubled. Bake at 350° for 35 minutes. Remove from pans. Cool on wire rack. (May need to cover tops with foil for final 10 to 15 minutes of baking if tops of loaves brown too quickly.)

[DR. HAROLD CANNON]

*Refer to "Just a Thought," page 78, for tip on working with yeast.

MAKES 2 LOAVES

1$\frac{1}{2}$ packages (1$\frac{1}{2}$ tablespoons) active dry yeast
Pinch of sugar
$\frac{1}{4}$ cup warm water (105–115°F)
1$\frac{1}{2}$ cups warm milk (105–115°F)
3 tablespoons brown sugar
4 teaspoons salt
$\frac{1}{2}$ to $\frac{2}{3}$ cup any fresh chopped herb (or 3 tablespoons dried)
1 cup walnuts, coarsely chopped (optional)
4 cups unbleached white flour
2 cups whole wheat flour

MAKES 2 LOAVES

2 tablespoons active dry yeast
2$\frac{1}{2}$ cups warm milk (105-115°F)
$\frac{1}{3}$ cup molasses
3 tablespoons vegetable oil
2 teaspoons salt
2 cups toasted pecans, chopped
2 cups whole wheat flour
1 cup rye flour
3 to 4 cups bread or all-purpose flour

SERVES 10 TO 12

Dough:

1 cup sour cream
1/2 cup sugar
1 teaspoon salt
1/2 cup melted butter
2 packages active dry yeast
1/2 cup warm water
2 eggs, beaten
4 cups all-purpose flour

Cheese Filling:

2 (8-ounce) packages cream
    cheese, softened
3/4 cup sugar
1 egg, beaten
3/8 teaspoon salt
2 teaspoons vanilla extract

Glaze:

2 cups powdered sugar
1/4 cup milk
2 teaspoons vanilla extract

CREAM CHEESE BRAIDS

Heat sour cream over low heat in medium saucepan. Stir in sugar, salt, and butter. Cool to lukewarm. Sprinkle yeast over warm water in large mixing bowl, stirring until yeast dissolves. Add sour cream mixture, eggs, and flour to yeast mixture. Mix well. Cover tightly and chill dough overnight. Combine cream cheese and remaining filling ingredients. Set filling aside. Divide dough into 4 equal parts. Roll out each part onto a well-floured surface, forming an 8 x 12-inch rectangle. Spread each with one-fourth of the cheese filling. Roll, jellyroll fashion, beginning at one long side. Pinch seam to seal, and fold ends under. Place rolls, seam side down, on a greased 15 x 10 x 1-inch jellyroll pan. Cut dough at 2-inch intervals, slicing about two-thirds of the way through the dough, to resemble a braid. Cover and let rise in a warm place (85°), free from drafts, until doubled in bulk (about 1 hour). Bake at 375° for 12 to 15 minutes. Combine glaze ingredients, and spread over rolls while warm.

[CAROLYN RITCHEY KING]

Just a Thought

Great to make ahead–freezes well. After baking, wrap tightly and freeze. Thaw before reheating. For a dessert with a twist, add chopped tart apple and blueberries into filling.

S C H N E C K E N

Dissolve yeast in milk, and set aside. Cream butter and ½ cup sugar. Add eggs, salt, flour, sour cream, and yeast mixture. Mix well. Chill dough overnight or at least 6 hours. ❧ Roll out dough into an 18 x 10-inch rectangle on a well-floured surface. Sprinkle with ¼ cup sugar and cinnamon; add raisins, if desired. Roll up jellyroll fashion. Cut into ½-inch-thick slices, and place into well-greased muffin pans. ❧ Cover loosely with wax paper; let rise in warm place (85°), free from drafts, for 2 to 3 hours or until doubled in bulk. Bake at 350° for 10 to 15 minutes or until light brown. Combine powdered sugar and milk, and drizzle icing over top while warm.

[M A R G A R E T   S .   D E R R I C K]

MAKES 2 DOZEN

2 packages active dry yeast
½ cup lukewarm milk
1½ cups unsalted butter, softened
½ cup granulated sugar
3 eggs
⅛ teaspoon salt
5 cups all-purpose flour
1 cup sour cream
¼ cup granulated sugar
1 tablespoon ground cinnamon
½ cup chopped raisins (optional)

Icing:
1 (1-pound) box powdered sugar
¼ to ½ cup milk

F R E N C H   P U F F S

Cream butter and sugar. Add egg, and blend well. ❧ Combine flour and next 3 ingredients. Add to batter alternately with milk. ❧ Spoon into greased muffin pans, filling two-thirds full. ❧ Bake at 350° for 20 to 25 minutes for regular muffins, 10 to 12 minutes for miniature muffins. ❧ Remove muffins from pan. ❧ Combine sugar, cinnamon, and nutmeg. Dip top of warm muffins in melted butter and then in sugar mixture.

[M A R Y   Z E I G E R   S T A G G S]

MAKES 1 DOZEN REGULAR OR 3 DOZEN MINIATURE

⅓ cup butter, softened
½ cup sugar
1 egg
1½ cups all-purpose flour
1½ teaspoons baking powder
¼ teaspoon ground nutmeg
¼ teaspoon salt
½ cup milk

Topping:
½ cup sugar
2 teaspoons ground cinnamon
½ teaspoon ground nutmeg
¼ cup butter, melted

GIGI'S CHRISTMAS STOLLEN

MAKES 3 LARGE
LOAVES

12 ounces golden raisins

1/4 cup rum (optional)

3 tablespoons active dry yeast

3 cups warm milk, divided

2/3 cup plus 1 tablespoon granulated sugar, divided

3 eggs

1/2 cup butter, melted

8 to 10 cups all-purpose flour, divided

1 1/4 teaspoons salt

3/4 teaspoon ground nutmeg

3/4 teaspoon ground cinnamon

Grated rind of 1 orange or 1 tablespoon candied orange peel

Grated rind of 2 lemons or 3 tablespoons candied lemon peel

1 1/2 cups chopped or sliced almonds

3 cups various chopped dried fruits: apples, peaches, apricots, pears, prunes, pineapple, cut up

1/2 cup glacé cherries, quartered

1/4 cup butter, melted

1/2 cup powdered sugar

Soak raisins in rum, or plump in boiling water to cover. Combine yeast, 1 cup warm milk, and 1 tablespoon sugar. Stir until dissolved. Mix eggs and remaining 2 cups milk. Add to yeast mixture. In large bowl, combine yeast mixture, remaining sugar, butter, 2 cups flour and next 8 ingredients. Stir in remaining 6 cups flour. Turn out and knead 5 to 10 minutes, adding flour as needed (up to 1 1/2 cups). If kneading in mixer, knead until dough clings to hook. Wash, dry, and lightly grease bowl. Return dough to bowl, cover and let rise in a warm place until doubled in bulk (1 to 2 hours). Punch dough down. Knead 3 additional minutes. Divide and shape into free-form loaves on greased baking sheets. Let rise again (approximately 45 minutes). Bake at 350° for 30 to 45 minutes. Cool on wire rack. Brush tops of warm loaves with melted butter, then powdered sugar.

[ANNE THIELE BLACKERBY]

Just a Thought

*When working with yeast breads it's essential to "proof" the yeast.
If it doesn't get frothy when combined with the liquid,
toss it out and start over with fresh yeast.*

GREEK EASTER BREAD

Combine yeast, warm milk, and 1 teaspoon sugar. When frothy , add remaining sugar, salt, butter, vanilla, lemon rind, and 2 cups flour. Mix well.   Add eggs, and gradually add remaining flour. Knead well. Dough should be elastic.   Lightly grease dough, cover and let rise in a warm place (85°), free from drafts, until doubled in bulk. Punch down. Divide into halves, and divide each half into thirds. Roll each piece into a long strand. Braid 3 strands to form each loaf, and form into desired shapes.   Let rise again until doubled in bulk. Combine egg white and water. Brush surface of loaves with egg white mixture. Place on greased baking sheets.   Bake at 350° for 25 to 30 minutes. Cool on wire racks.

[ANNE THIELE BLACKERBY]

For a traditional Greek Easter,
tuck colored eggs into the folds of the braid.

MAKES 2 LARGE
BRAIDED LOAVES

2 tablespoons active dry yeast
1 cup warm milk (105°)
2/3 cup sugar, divided
1/2 teaspoon salt
1/2 cup melted butter
1 teaspoon vanilla
1 tablespoon grated lemon rind
5 1/2 cups flour, divided
4 eggs, lightly beaten
1 egg white
2 tablespoons water

CURRANT SCONES

Combine first 4 ingredients. Cut in butter until mixture resembles coarse crumbs. Stir in cream, and mix until dough holds together.   Soak currants in 3 tablespoons brandy or sherry until plump. Drain currants and add to dough. Wrap dough in plastic wrap and chill.   Roll dough out onto a lightly floured surface to 1/2-inch thickness for small or 3/4-inch for larger scones. Brush top with whipping cream for a glazed finish. Bake at 375° for 13 to 15 minutes.

[SUE FISHER]

MAKES 1 DOZEN

4 1/2 cups all-purpose flour
2 teaspoons baking powder
1/2 teaspoon baking soda
2 tablespoons sugar
1/2 pound butter
1/2 pint whipping cream
1 cup dried currants
3 tablespoons brandy or sherry
Whipping cream

MAKES 1 DOZEN

1 package active dry yeast
1¼ cups warm water
2 cups all-purpose flour
2 tablespoons butter, melted
2 tablespoons honey
2 tablespoons syrup
½ teaspoon salt
1 cup whole wheat flour

QUICK & EASY WHOLE WHEAT ROLLS

Dissolve yeast in warm water. Add flour and next 4 ingredients; mix well. Stir in whole wheat flour. ✿ Place dough in greased bowl. Cover; let rise in a warm place (85°), free from drafts, for 30 minutes. Punch down dough. Place balls of dough into greased muffin pans, filling two-thirds full. ✿ Bake at 375° for 10 to 15 minutes.

[DONNA ROBUCK SEIBELS]

For a different twist, roll dough into "ropes" and tie in a knot, folding ends under. Place on a greased baking sheet.

MAKES 4 DOZEN

1 (¼ ounce) package active dry yeast
1½ cups warm water
⅔ cup sugar
1½ teaspoons salt
⅔ cup shortening, melted
2 eggs, lightly beaten
1 cup warm mashed potatoes
5 cups all-purpose flour
½ cup butter, melted

REFRIGERATOR ROLLS

Dissolve yeast in warm water in a large bowl. Add sugar and next 4 ingredients. Mix well. ✿ Sift flour; add to potato mixture. Beat well. ✿ Knead 5 to 10 times on well-floured surface, until smooth and elastic. ✿ Place in a greased bowl and cover with damp cloth. Chill at least 8 hours. About 2 hours before baking, roll out dough, and cut into circles. Fold circles in half to form rolls. Place rolls close together in a greased 13 x 9 x 2-inch pan. Brush tops with melted butter. ✿ Cover pan with towel, and let rise in a warm place (85°), free from drafts, 1 to 2 hours or until doubled in bulk. ✿ Bake at 375° for 12 to 15 minutes.

[ELIZABETH CARPER HOFFMAN]

PUMPKIN BREAD / MUFFINS

Combine first 8 ingredients in a large mixing bowl. Add eggs, oil, pumpkin, and water; beat well. Fold in nuts and dates, if desired. Pour into a greased loafpan or muffin pans. Bake at 350° for 1 hour for loaf or 15 minutes for muffins.

[CAROLINE McDONNELL FARWELL]

MAKES 2 LOAVES OR
2 DOZEN REGULAR
OR 4 DOZEN
MINIATURE MUFFINS

1²⁄₃ cups all-purpose flour
1½ cups sugar
¾ teaspoon salt
1 teaspoon baking soda
½ teaspoon ground cloves
½ teaspoon ground nutmeg
½ teaspoon ground cinnamon
¼ teaspoon baking powder
2 eggs
½ cup vegetable oil
1¼ cups mashed cooked pumpkin
½ cup water
½ cup chopped nuts (optional)
½ cup chopped dates (optional)

RAISIN BRAN MUFFINS

Combine first 8 ingredients. Add eggs and next 3 ingredients. Blend well. Add raisins, if desired. Spoon into muffin pans, filling two-thirds full. Bake at 375° for 15 to 20 minutes.

[CYPRESS INN,
TUSCALOOSA, ALABAMA]

MAKES 2 DOZEN

15 ounces Raisin Bran cereal
3 cups sugar
5 cups all-purpose flour
5 teaspoons baking soda
2 teaspoons salt
1 teaspoon ground cinnamon
1 teaspoon ground cloves
1 teaspoon ground nutmeg
4 eggs
1 cup vegetable oil
1 quart buttermilk
2 teaspoons vanilla extract
1 cup raisins (optional)

P R A L I N E   M U F F I N S

MAKES 1 DOZEN
REGULAR OR 2 DOZEN
MINIATURE

1 cup coarsely chopped pecans
1 cup light brown sugar
1/2 cup all-purpose flour
1/4 teaspoon baking powder
1/4 teaspoon salt
2 eggs
1/2 teaspoon vanilla extract
2 tablespoons butter, melted

Combine first 5 ingredients; mix well. Add eggs, vanilla, and butter. Stir well. 🖉 Spoon into greased muffin pans, filling half full. 🖉 Bake at 300° for 20 to 30 minutes.

[P O L L Y   J O R D A N   P O W E L L]

G I N G E R E D   P E A R   M U F F I N S

Low Fat

MAKES 1 DOZEN

1 cup All-Bran cereal
1 cup buttermilk
2 egg whites or 1 whole egg
1 teaspoon vanilla extract
2 tablespoons vegetable oil
3 tablespoons molasses
1/2 cup sugar
1 1/2 cups all-purpose flour
2 teaspoons ground ginger
1 teaspoon baking powder
1 teaspoon baking soda
1 teaspoon ground cinnamon
1/8 teaspoon ground nutmeg
1/8 teaspoon ground cloves
1 cup peeled and chopped ripe pear
1/2 cup raisins

Combine first 6 ingredients in a large bowl. Let stand 5 to 10 minutes. 🖉 Combine sugar and next 7 ingredients. Add to cereal mixture. Stir in pear and raisins. 🖉 Pour into greased muffin pans. Bake at 400° for 20 minutes.

[S A L L Y   S C H R O E D E R   P R I C E]

ORANGE BLOSSOM MUFFINS

Combine first 4 ingredients; add biscuit mix and stir 30 seconds. Stir in marmalade and pecans.   Grease muffin pans and fill two-thirds full. Combine sugar, cinnamon, flour, and nutmeg; cut in margarine until crumbly, and sprinkle over batter. Bake at 350° for about 20 minutes.

[BOBBIE HURLEY HARPER]

MAKES 1 DOZEN

1 egg, slightly beaten
1/4 cup sugar
1/2 cup orange juice
2 tablespoons salad oil
2 cups packaged biscuit mix
1/2 cup orange marmalade
1/2 cup chopped pecans
1/2 cup sugar
1/2 teaspoon cinnamon
1 1/2 tablespoons flour
1/4 teaspoon nutmeg
1 tablespoon margarine

SNAPPY GINGER MUFFINS

Combine first 8 ingredients. In a large bowl, beat eggs, oil, sugar, and molasses. Add dry ingredients and buttermilk. Fold in chopped nuts, if desired.   Pour into greased muffin pans. Bake at 400° for 12 to 15 minutes.

[SALLY SCHROEDER PRICE]

MAKES 1 1/2 DOZEN

2 cups all-purpose flour
1 teaspoon baking powder
1/2 teaspoon baking soda
1/2 teaspoon ground ginger
1/2 teaspoon ground cloves
1/2 teaspoon ground cinnamon
1/2 teaspoon salt
1/2 teaspoon ground white pepper
2 eggs, beaten
3 tablespoons vegetable oil
3/4 cup sugar
1/3 cup molasses
1/4 cup buttermilk
1/2 cup chopped nuts (optional)

MAKES 1 LOAF

2 large ripe bananas
2/3 cup sugar
2 eggs, beaten
1/3 cup buttermilk
1/2 teaspoon salt
3/4 cup regular uncooked oats
1 1/2 cups all-purpose flour
2 teaspoons baking powder
1 teaspoon baking soda
1/4 cup vegetable oil
3/4 cup fresh blueberries

MAKES 3 LOAVES

2 1/2 cups all-purpose flour
2 teaspoons baking powder
1 1/4 teaspoons salt
1/2 teaspoon baking soda
1 cup grated Muenster or
   provolone cheese
1/2 cup chopped scallions
2 tablespoons minced fresh
   parsley
3/4 tablespoon dried rosemary,
   crumbled
3/4 teaspoon fresh ground pepper
1/3 cup sun-dried tomatoes packed
   in oil, drained and chopped,
   reserving 2 tablespoons oil
2 tablespoons shortening
2 tablespoons sugar
2 cloves garlic, minced
2 large eggs
1 1/4 cups buttermilk
1/3 cup toasted pine nuts
   (optional)

BLUEBERRY BANANA BREAD

Mash bananas in a large bowl. Add sugar and next 4 ingredients. Let stand 5 minutes, until oats soften. ✍ Combine flour, baking powder, and baking soda. Add to banana mixture alternately with oil, stirring just to incorporate. Fold in blueberries. Pour into a greased 9 x 5 x 3-inch loafpan. ✍ Bake at 350° for 50 to 55 minutes or until tester comes out clean.

[ALYSON LUTZ BUTTS]

SUN-DRIED TOMATO BREAD

Combine first 4 ingredients in a large bowl. Add cheese and next 5 ingredients. ✍ In a medium bowl, whisk shortening, sugar, and 2 tablespoons reserved oil until smooth. Add garlic, eggs, and buttermilk, mixing until blended. ✍ Combine liquid and flour mixtures; stir just to incorporate flour. Fold in pine nuts, if desired. ✍ Pour into 3 well-greased 5 x 3 x 2-inch loafpans. Bake at 350° for 50 minutes or until tester comes out clean. Cool in pans on rack for 5 minutes before turning out.

[ALYSON LUTZ BUTTS]

S T R A W B E R R Y   B R E A D

Combine first 5 ingredients in a large bowl. Add eggs and vegetable oil; mix. Stir in strawberries.   Pour batter into 2 greased 8$\frac{1}{2}$ x 4$\frac{1}{2}$ x 3-inch loafpans. Bake at 350° for 1 hour or until tester inserted in center comes out clean.   (Freezes well.) Combine cream cheese, reserved strawberry juice, and powdered sugar to make a spreadable mixture.   Slice loaves thin, and spread slices with cream cheese mixture.

[D A W N   L A N E   T U C K E R   ]

Just a Thought

To vary this recipe, use raspberries and
add 1 teaspoon vanilla extract and $\frac{1}{2}$ cup chopped pecans.

P O P P Y   S E E D   B R E A D

Combine bread ingredients and stir until smooth. Pour into 2 prepared (9x5x3-inch) loafpans and bake at 350° for 45 to 50 minutes.   Test middle.   While bread is baking, mix glaze ingredients in a small bowl. Let bread cool 10 minutes; remove from pan, and glaze while warm.

Great for gifts or to have in the refrigerator when company's coming.

MAKES 2 LOAVES

3 cups all-purpose flour
2 cups sugar
1 teaspoon baking soda
1 teaspoon salt
1 teaspoon ground cinnamon
4 eggs, beaten
1 cup vegetable oil
2 (10-ounce) packages frozen strawberries, thawed and drained, reserving $\frac{1}{2}$ cup of juice
1 (8-ounce) package cream cheese, softened
$\frac{1}{4}$ cup powdered sugar

MAKES 2 LOAVES

3 cups all-purpose flour
2$\frac{1}{2}$ cups sugar
1$\frac{1}{2}$ teaspoons baking powder
1$\frac{1}{2}$ teaspoons salt
3 eggs
1$\frac{1}{2}$ cups of milk
1$\frac{1}{8}$ cups vegetable oil
2 tablespoons poppy seeds
1$\frac{1}{2}$ teaspoons vanilla extract
1$\frac{1}{2}$ teaspoons almond extract
1$\frac{1}{2}$ teaspoons butter extract

Glaze:
1$\frac{1}{4}$ cups sugar
$\frac{1}{2}$ cup orange juice
$\frac{1}{2}$ teaspoon vanilla extract

Tomato Tortellini Soup, page 99, and Quick & Easy Whole Wheat Rolls, page 80

The Power of Persuasion

-FRED BONNIE-

ONCE I MET THE KIM FAMILY, we spent a lot of time together. Mrs. Kim, a tall, ceremonious woman in her fifties, had come to the United States convinced that there was a fortune to be made here in the restaurant business. Perhaps she was right, in Atlanta or New Orleans. In Birmingham, people were still more interested in barbeque than bul kogi and kimchee. Mrs. Kim's daughter, Hyang Shim, was twenty-six, petite, utterly radiant in her white, cotton summer dress. She had smooth, golden skin and laughing eyes, and her thick, blue-black ponytail hung halfway down her back.

I first saw her in a used car lot. "No, I'm not a salesman," I told them. "I'm trying to find a car to buy. Just like you."

Mama spoke no English, so Hyang Shim translated.

I spent the next two days helping them find a car, and the next week after that teaching Hyang Shim how to drive. Her driving skills were, at best, hazardous to the public, but she learned quickly. I sat in the front seat, rigid with terror whenever a car approached from the opposite direction, ready to thank her for saving my life each time she managed to swerve back into her own lane and avoid a head-on collision. Mama, aloof and fearless in the backseat, seemed oblivious to the danger she was in.

The Kims were hoarding their money for their restaurant-to-be. As a result, their apartment was sparsely furnished, with only a few folding chairs, a dining table, four scrolled Korean landscape paintings for the walls, and an enormous TV console. They were very quality conscious, and Hyang Shim proudly pointed out that the TV had cost nearly a thousand dollars, and that these were ·CONTINUED·

FRED BONNIE

FRED, A NATIVE OF
MAINE, LIVED IN
BIRMINGHAM FROM
1974 TO 1992.
HE NOW LIVES
IN MOBILE.
A FORMER GARDEN
EDITOR OF
SOUTHERN LIVING,
HE HAS PUBLISHED
SIX BOOKS
ON GARDENING AND
FOUR COLLECTIONS
OF SHORT STORIES.

excellent folding chairs, made of wood, not metal.

What they lacked in furniture they made up for in food. Their refrigerator was always overflowing with vegetables they bought at the farmers market, where they went daily, once Hyang Shim got her driver's license. An enormous jar of spicy pickled cabbage, called kimchee, took up most of one shelf in the refrigerator. They had every kind of leek, radish, and squash I'd ever seen, and many more that I hadn't. They always insisted that I eat with them. They were curious and asked many questions, even personal ones. Mama sensed that I was attracted to Hyang Shim, so she wanted to know how much money I made. And did I plan to make more at some time in the future? Did I go to church? When would I quit smoking?

Hyang Shim would glance at me with a pleasant tolerance, but never a sustained gaze. I knew she was shy, but I also suspected she had no interest in me beyond my role as driving instructor and city guide. And Mama always came along whenever I took Hyang Shim out to eat or to a movie. Hyang Shim translated less and less for me, and I would sit for five minutes at a time as she and mama bantered back and forth, their version of my name (hu-RED-duh) popping up often. We were an odd and constant trio.

So it was a rare moment when I found myself alone with Hyang Shim as she showed me how to make cabbage soup. Mama was in the bedroom, talking on the phone with some Korean people she'd met at church. We cut chunks of stew beef into small pieces, chopped up green onions, potatoes, zucchini, a head of cabbage, and some baby carrots. When all the ingredients were ready, she directed me to sauté the beef and half the chopped green onions in sesame oil. The meat sizzled with a nutty aroma.

"Smell so good, isn't it?" she said.

She touched my arm, her face serious. "Ah, I almost forget. Very important. We put in the MSG." She reached into a cupboard above the stove for a shaker of Accent.

"I don't like MSG," I said.

"You allergy, something like that...?"

"No, I just don't like to use chemicals in my food."

She picked up the salt shaker. "You think this not chemical?"

I shook my head. "We don't need MSG."

Her stare was both playful and wilting. I turned back to the meat and started to stir again. She suddenly and silently hovered close to me and her lips brushed my cheek, pausing for an instant.

She withdrew with a nervous laugh and studied me from a step away. We could hear Mama coming out of the bedroom.

"Now you put in MSG?" Her smile vanished, as if she had done nothing more than flick a piece of lint from my shirt.

My fingers quivered as I took the shaker from her outstretched hand. "You ask so irresistibly. How much?"

We laughed. Mama looked from me to Hyang Shim, her expression grave as she recognized that something important had changed while she was out of the room. THE END

THE VARIETY OF FRESH LETTUCES, vegetables and herbs now readily available prompts these innovative suggestions for tossing a salad. Armed with one of these suggestions, you can breeze right through the produce section knowing just what you're looking for. The following vinaigrette recipe will adapt to any of the ideas.

• Basic Vinaigrette: Mix $2/3$ cup extra-virgin olive oil, $1/4$ cup white wine, red wine or balsamic vinegar, $1/2$ teaspoon salt, and $1/2$ teaspoon freshly ground pepper in a jar; cover tightly, and shake to blend.

• Arrange torn romaine lettuce, julienned smoked turkey or ham, sliced red onion, pear slices, and chopped walnuts on serving plates; add 2 ounces crumbled blue cheese to Basic Vinaigrette.

• Mix watercress leaves, torn red leaf and Boston or Bibb lettuce, toasted pecans, orange sections; add 1 teaspoon grated orange rind to Basic Vinaigrette, and toss with greens. Sprinkle with crumbled goat cheese.

• Add 2 cloves crushed garlic and 2 tablespoons minced fresh mint to Basic Vinaigrette made with white wine vinegar, and let stand 1 hour. Toss spinach, thinly sliced red onion, imported ripe olives, crumbled feta cheese, toasted pine nuts, and salad dressing.

• Add 2 tablespoons Dijon mustard to Basic Vinaigrette, and omit salt. Mix blanched green beans, minced shallots, boiled and sliced new potatoes, and diced tomatoes with salad dressing; marinate, then serve on red lettuce leaves. Garnish with sliced hard-cooked eggs, if desired.

• Add 1 to 1 and $1/2$ teaspoons ground cumin and crushed garlic to Basic Vinaigrette, and substitute fresh lime juice for part of vinegar. Toss rinsed and drained black beans, corn, diced tomato, green chilies and cilantro with dressing.

• Mix 1 cup thinly sliced fresh basil, 1 pound plum tomato wedges, sliced fresh mozzarella cheese, drained capers, and Basic Vinaigrette. Cover and refrigerate overnight, stirring gently and occasionally. Serve on romaine lettuce or radicchio leaves.

• Add 3 tablespoons soy or teriyaki sauce and 1 tablespoon sesame oil to Basic Vinaigrette, and omit salt. Mix blanched sugar snap peas or snow peas, thinly sliced sweet red pepper, julienned yellow squash and julienned carrots with salad dressing; marinate 1 to 2 hours. Serve on Bibb lettuce leaves; sprinkle with toasted sesame seeds.

• Add 2 tablespoons minced fresh dill to Basic Vinaigrette. Toss blanched fresh asparagus spears and thinly sliced sweet yellow pepper with some of vinaigrette; marinate. Serve on radicchio leaves, and sprinkle with toasted slivered almonds.

• Add 3 tablespoons minced fresh herbs (thyme, basil, oregano, rosemary) to Basic Vinaigrette. Toss diced eggplant, thickly sliced shiitake mushrooms, and sliced carrots with a little olive oil; roast at 450° until lightly browned, stirring occasionally. Cool; toss with assorted torn greens and salad dressing.

• Arrange mixture of torn arugula and red leaf lettuce on salad plates. Toss sliced ripe avocado and thinly sliced red onion with some of Basic Vinaigrette; arrange avocado mixture, fresh pink grapefruit sections or sliced mango or papaya, and imported ripe olives on lettuce; drizzle with Basic Vinaigrette.

SOUPS & STEWS

SERVES 4 TO 5

2 cups fresh strawberries
1/2 cup sugar, approximately (to taste and based on natural sweetness of fruit)
1/2 cup sour cream
2 1/2 cups half-and-half

SERVES 4 TO 6

1 clove garlic, pressed
1/2 teaspoon salt
4 medium cucumbers, peeled
2 (14 1/2-ounce) cans chicken broth
4 tablespoons white vinegar
1 (16-ounce) carton nonfat sour cream
2 drops Tabasco Sauce (optional)
1 tomato, chopped
1 medium cucumber, peeled and chopped
1 onion, chopped

SERVES 4

2 large or 4 small zucchini, sliced
1 medium onion, chopped
1 tablespoon chopped fresh parsley
1 tablespoon chopped fresh dill
3 cups chicken broth
1 cup sour cream
1 teaspoon fresh lemon juice
Salt and pepper
Garnishes: fresh chopped parsley or chives

CHILLED STRAWBERRY SOUP

Rub the berries through a fine sieve. Add sugar to taste and sour cream. Mix. Add half-and-half and correct sweetening. Chill.

[CHEF BERNARD AXEL]
CHRISTIAN'S AT THE TUTWILER

CUCUMBER GAZPACHO

Low Fat

Place first 5 ingredients in blender or food processor. Puree mixture. Stir in sour cream and Tabasco Sauce, if desired. Chill soup mixture. Spoon equal amounts of chopped tomato, cucumber, and onion in the bottom of individual serving bowls. Top evenly with chilled soup, and serve.

[BRIGHT KINNETT WRIGHT]

COLD ZUCCHINI SOUP

Bring first 5 ingredients to a boil, and cook until tender. Cool. Put vegetables, broth, and sour cream in blender; blend until smooth. Add lemon juice and salt and pepper to taste. Chill 24 hours. Serve cold, and garnish with fresh parsley or chives, if desired.

[MRS. WILLIAM N. McQUEEN]

L O W C O U N T R Y   G U M B O

Cook sausage; drain and set aside. To make roux, heat oil in a heavy stockpot over medium heat. Add flour slowly, stirring constantly, 30 to 40 minutes or until medium brown. Add celery and next 4 ingredients. Cook 45 minutes, stirring often. To the roux, add chicken broth, water, Worcestershire, Tabasco Sauce to taste, tomato sauce, tomato, bacon, seasonings, and sausage. Simmer 2 to 3 hours, stirring occasionally. (Prepare fish while tomato mixture is simmering.) About 30 minutes before serving, add seafood, brown sugar and lemon juice to tomato mixture. Serve mixture over hot cooked rice, with French bread. Freezes well. (Do not add oysters if freezing.)

[S A N D Y   R E E V E R   K I L L I O N]
P A S T   P R E S I D E N T

3 links andouille sausage, sliced and browned
1 cup vegetable oil
1 cup all-purpose flour
6 stalks celery, chopped
2 onions, chopped
1 green pepper, chopped
2 cloves garlic, minced
1/2 cup chopped fresh parsley
2 quarts chicken broth
2 quarts water
1/2 cup Worcestershire sauce
  Tabasco Sauce
1/2 cup tomato sauce
1 large tomato, chopped, or 1 (16-ounce) can tomatoes, drained and chopped
4 slices bacon, cooked and crumbled
2 tablespoons salt
2 bay leaves
1/4 teaspoon dried rosemary
1/4 teaspoon dried thyme
1/8 teaspoon cayenne pepper
2 cups fresh fish, poached and diced or 2 cups chopped cooked chicken
2 pounds crabmeat, flaked
4 pounds medium fresh shrimp, peeled
2 pints oysters, drained
1 teaspoon brown sugar
  Juice of 1 lemon
  Hot cooked rice

SERVES 12

1 pound bacon

1 medium onion

2 (16-ounce) cans solid pack
 pumpkin

2 cups half-and-half

4 cups milk

2 teaspoons ground cumin

2 teaspoons salt

1/2 teaspoon ground white pepper

1/4 cup chopped fresh parsley
 Garnish: grated Swiss cheese,
 chopped fresh cilantro, toasted
 pine nuts

AUTUMN PUMPKIN BISQUE

Dice bacon and fry in a 6-quart stockpot until done. Drain; add chopped onion to same pan. Continue to sauté until onion is clear. Add pumpkin and 2 cups cream; blend well. Add milk until desired consistency is reached. Add cumin, salt, pepper, and parsley. Heat thoroughly but do not boil. Garnish individual servings with grated Swiss cheese, chopped cilantro, and pine nuts. For a wonderful warm winter lunch, serve in a small, hollowed-out pumpkin, with a toasted Swiss cheese sandwich.

[SHIRLEY ANNE STRINGFELLOW]

MAKES 1 1/2 QUARTS

1 lobster, steamed

1/4 to 1/2 cup sherry

2 (14 1/2-ounce) cans chicken
 broth

1/2 cup water (optional)

1/2 cup chopped onion

1 stalk celery, chopped

1 carrot, finely chopped

1 (10 3/4-ounce) can condensed
 tomato soup
 Whipping cream or milk

LOBSTER BISQUE

Remove lobster meat from shell, and marinate meat in sherry. Bring chicken broth and water to a boil. Reduce heat and add vegetables. Cook until vegetables are tender. Cool vegetable mixture, and puree. Add tomato soup; whisk in cream until you get the salmon color you desire. Add lobster meat. Serve immediately.

[MARION HUNT NEWTON]

C R A B C H O W D E R

Melt butter in a large saucepan. Sauté onion until translucent. Add celery, and cook for 1 to 2 minutes; add milk and next 6 ingredients, and stir well. Add sherry, parsley, crabmeat; cook over low heat approximately 30 minutes, stirring frequently to avoid burning soup in bottom of pan.

*Homemade Potato Soup: *peel and dice 2 baking potatoes. Cook in water to cover for 15 to 20 minutes. Combine 1 cup milk and 1 tablespoon cornstarch. Add to potatoes and cook to desired consistency.*

[A S H L E Y C A R R S M I T H & C A N D Y A B N E Y W H I T A K E R]

MAKES 1 1/2 QUARTS

3 tablespoons butter
1/2 cup chopped onion
1/2 cup chopped celery
3 cups milk
1 (10 3/4-ounce) can condensed cream of potato soup or homemade*
1 (15-ounce) can cream-style corn
1/4 teaspoon salt
1/4 teaspoon dried thyme
1/2 teaspoon cracked pepper
1 bay leaf
1/4 cup sherry
1/4 cup chopped fresh parsley
1/2 pound lump crabmeat

O Y S T E R   A R T I C H O K E   S O U P

Drain juice from oysters to make 3 cups (adding water, if necessary). Set oysters aside. 🖉 Bring oyster juice and chicken broth to a boil in a medium saucepan; reduce heat and simmer 8 to 10 minutes. Set aside. 🖉 Melt butter in a large iron skillet. Whisk in flour, stirring constantly, and cook 2 to 3 minutes. Stir in green onions, parsley, salt, thyme, and cayenne. Gradually whisk in reserved oyster liquid and whipping cream until smooth. Bring to high temperature (do not boil); decrease heat and add oysters and artichokes. Garnish with green onion tops or parsley.

[M A U B Y ' S R E S T A U R A N T]

SERVES 6

2 dozen oysters, shucked and retain juice
1 teaspoon chicken broth
4 tablespoons butter
4 tablespoons flour
1/2 cup green onions, sliced
2 teaspoons parsley, chopped
1/2 teaspoon salt
1/2 teaspoon thyme
1/2 teaspoon cayenne pepper
1 cup whipping cream
1 (14-ounce) can artichoke hearts

B R A N D I E D
S H R I M P   B I S Q U E

Sauté celery and onion in butter over medium heat in large saucepan. Sauté until opaque. Remove vegetables, and reserve butter in pan. ✒ In food processor, blend vegetables with 1 cup half-and-half. Add shrimp and process a few more seconds. ✒ Reheat butter in saucepan over medium heat. Whisk in flour until smooth. Gradually stir in remaining 1 cup half-and-half, milk, and chicken broth to make a light white sauce. When sauce thickens, add pureed shrimp and vegetable mixture. Add brandy, ketchup, and salt and pepper to taste. Serve hot. ✒ Garnish, and pass a small pitcher of sherry when serving.

[L A U R A   W O R T H I N G T O N   B E R R Y   ]

M U S H R O O M   B I S Q U E

Melt butter in a large saucepan. Add flour; cook, stirring constantly, over medium heat. Add chicken broth; whisk constantly 2 to 3 minutes. Add mushrooms and onion. Simmer 20 minutes, stirring occasionally. ✒ Gradually stir in milk and cream. Simmer 10 minutes. Add salt and peppers. Stir in wine and parsley just before serving.

½ cup chopped celery

½ cup chopped onion

½ cup butter

2 cups half-and-half, divided

1 pound fresh shrimp, cooked and peeled

6 tablespoons all-purpose flour

2 cups whole milk

2 cups chicken broth

2 tablespoons brandy

3 tablespoons ketchup (optional)

Salt and white pepper to taste

¼ cup sherry (optional; if used, omit salt)

Garnish: sliced shrimp and lemon zest

MAKES 3 QUARTS

4 tablespoons butter

4 tablespoons all-purpose flour

3 cups chicken broth

1 pound fresh mushrooms, stemmed and sliced

1 cup finely chopped onion

2 cups milk

1 cup whipping cream or half-and-half

½ teaspoon salt

¼ teaspoon white pepper

¼ teaspoon ground red pepper

3 tablespoons Madeira or sherry

¼ cup chopped fresh parsley

B R O C C O L I   S O U P

Cook broccoli in chicken broth about 6 minutes or until tender; set aside. In a large saucepan, melt butter; add flour to make a roux. Add half-and-half and cook slowly until mixture thickens. Add salt and next 3 ingredients. Pour broccoli mixture into blender or food processor, and puree. Add to half-and-half mixture, and cook until thoroughly heated. Garnish with thin slice of lemon and broccoli floret.

[A L I C E   C A R T E R   K E N O N]

SERVES 4

2 (10-ounce) packages frozen chopped broccoli

2 cups chicken broth

1½ tablespoons butter

3 tablespoons all-purpose flour

2 cups half-and-half

½ teaspoon salt

½ teaspoon grated lemon rind

1 teaspoon grated onion

¼ teaspoon Tabasco Sauce
   Garnishes: lemon slices and broccoli florets

C R E A M   O F   B L U E
C H E E S E   S O U P

Sauté onion, celery, and carrot in butter in a large saucepan for 5 minutes or until vegetables are tender. Add potatoes and chicken broth. Cover and simmer 15 minutes. Puree soup in batches in blender or food processor until smooth. Return soup to saucepan, and stir in half-and-half. Cook until thoroughly heated. Add blue cheese, stirring until melted and soup is smooth. Stir in sherry, and serve immediately. Garnish individual bowls with freshly cracked pepper or a dash of paprika.

[A N N E   T E R R Y   J O H N S O N]

SERVES 6

½ cup chopped onion or leek

½ cup chopped celery

½ cup chopped carrot

3 tablespoons unsalted butter

1½ pounds baking potatoes, peeled and thinly sliced

3 cups chicken broth

1 cup half-and-half

3 to 4 ounces premium brand blue cheese (preferably Maytag)

3 tablespoons sherry (optional)
   Garnish: freshly cracked pepper or paprika

BAKED POTATO SOUP

MAKES 2 QUARTS

8 slices bacon

1 cup diced yellow onion

2/3 cup all-purpose flour

6 cups hot chicken broth

4 to 5 cups peeled and sliced
   baked potatoes
   (5 medium-large)

2 cups half-and -half

1/4 cup chopped fresh parsley

1 1/2 teaspoons minced garlic

1 1/2 teaspoons dried basil

1 teaspoon salt

1 teaspoon coarsely ground
   black pepper

1/2 teaspoon Tabasco Sauce

1 cup grated Cheddar cheese

1/4 cup sliced scallions

Garnishes: cooked, crumbled
   bacon; grated Cheddar cheese;
   chopped fresh parsley

Cook bacon until crisp; remove bacon, reserving drippings. Crumble bacon, and set aside. Cook onion in reserved drippings over medium-high heat about 3 minutes or until transparent. Add flour, whisking until smooth or until mixture just begins to turn golden. Add chicken broth gradually, whisking until liquid thickens. Add potatoes and next 7 ingredients. Reduce heat, and simmer 10 minutes. (Do not allow soup to boil.) Add grated cheese and scallions. Heat until cheese melts completely. Garnish each serving with bacon, Cheddar cheese, and parsley.

[LEE FOSTER NIX]

POTATO AND LEEK SOUP

MAKES 3 QUARTS

3 to 4 cups peeled, thinly sliced
   potatoes

3 to 4 cups thinly sliced leeks

2 1/2 cups water

5 chicken-flavored bouillon
   cubes

Garnishes: coarsely ground
   pepper, chopped chives,
   chopped fresh parsley,
   diced sweet red pepper,
   carrot curls

Combine potatoes and next 3 ingredients. Simmer about 1 hour or until vegetables are very tender. Puree mixture in food processor until smooth. Serve hot or cold. Garnish as desired.

Use two-thirds of leek stalk, white bulb through pale green.

[ANNE THIELE BLACKERBY]

A S P A R A G U S A N D T O M A T O S O U P

1½ cups cooked asparagus spears
5 cups chicken broth
1 medium onion, chopped
1 carrot, chopped
1 tablespoon chopped fresh parsley
1 bay leaf
2 cups canned tomatoes
⅛ teaspoon freshly ground pepper
1 teaspoon salt
½ teaspoon thyme
½ teaspoon sugar
2 tablespoons butter, melted
2 tablespoons all-purpose flour
Garnishes: sour cream and chopped fresh or frozen chives

Combine first 11 ingredients in a stockpot. Cover and simmer for 45 minutes.   Remove bay leaf. Blend soup mixture in food processor in 2 to 3 batches until smooth.   Return mixture to stockpot, and cook over low heat. Combine butter and flour together. Stir into soup. Simmer 20 to 30 minutes.   Garnish each serving with 1 tablespoon sour cream and ½ teaspoon chopped fresh or frozen chives.

[P A T M C C A B E F O R M A N]
P A S T P R E S I D E N T

T O M A T O T O R T E L L I N I S O U P

MAKES 2 QUARTS

1 tablespoon plus 1 teaspoon olive oil
½ cup chopped onion
1 cup chopped carrot
½ cup chopped fennel (optional)
2 cloves garlic, minced
1 teaspoon dried basil
1 teaspoon dried oregano
1 bay leaf
4 cups canned whole tomatoes in thick puree, chopped
2 cups water
2 cups chicken broth
1 package dried cheese tortellini
2 cups escarole or spinach, shredded
Garnish: Italian parsley

Heat olive oil in large stockpot; sauté onion, carrot, fennel (if desired), and garlic. Cook until vegetables are limp; stir in herbs, and cook 1 minute. Stir in chopped tomatoes, 2 cups water, and chicken broth, and cook 15 minutes. Add pasta, and cook until tortellini is tender, adding additional water, if necessary. Add escarole or spinach, and cook 6 minutes.   Garnish with Italian parsley.

[M A R I O N H U N T N E W T O N]

MAKES 2 QUARTS

1/4 cup butter

1 large onion, chopped
   (about 1 1/4 cups)

3 pounds ripe tomatoes or 2
   (16-ounce) cans whole
   tomatoes, undrained

3 tablespoons tomato paste

1 tablespoon finely
   chopped fresh thyme

3 tablespoons finely
   chopped fresh basil

1 teaspoon sugar

1/4 teaspoon pepper

1 teaspoon salt

3 cups chicken broth, divided

3/4 cup whipping cream

2 ounces vermouth

TOMATO SOUP WITH BASIL AND VERMOUTH

Melt butter in a large saucepan. Add onion. Sauté 7 to 8 minutes over medium heat. Chop tomatoes, reserving juice. Add tomatoes and juice to onion mixture. Stir in tomato paste and next 5 ingredients. Reduce heat. Cover and simmer 10 minutes. Add 2 cups broth. Cover and simmer 30 additional minutes. Remove from heat. Puree in batches in electric blender or food processor, adding remaining 1 cup chicken broth. Return soup to pan. Reheat, stirring in cream and vermouth. (Do not boil.)

[LEE WILSON MARKS]

MAKES 1 1/2 QUARTS

4 boneless, skinless chicken
   breasts

4 cups water

1/2 teaspoon salt

2 baking potatoes, peeled, cubed,
   and cooked

3 carrots, peeled and sliced

1 medium onion, chopped

1 medium green pepper, chopped

2 stalks celery, chopped

1 (17-ounce) can creamed corn

1 (16-ounce) can tomatoes,
   undrained

1 (15-ounce) can tomato sauce

Salt and pepper

CHICKEN CHOWDER

Boil chicken in 4 cups water and 1/2 teaspoon salt for 30 minutes over medium heat. Reserve 3 cups chicken broth. Shred chicken when cool. Place reserved broth in a large Dutch oven; add potatoes, carrots, onion, green pepper, and celery. Simmer 10 minutes. Add corn, tomatoes, tomato sauce, and shredded chicken. Simmer 15 minutes. Add salt and pepper or other favorite seasonings to taste. Serve with corn muffins.

[SALLIE HARRIS PRADAT]

S A N T A   F E   S O U P

Cook meat and onion together until meat is browned. Stir Ranch-style dressing mix and taco seasoning mix into meat. Add remaining ingredients with juices from all. Add water. Simmer for 2 hours. (If mixture is too thick, add additional water.) Garnish each serving with sour cream, shredded Cheddar cheese,and sliced green onions, if desired. Serve with tortilla chips.

[M A R I O N   H U N T   N E W T O N]

C H I C K E N
N O O D L E   S O U P

Sauté carrots, celery, onion, garlic, and marjoram in butter until vegetables are crisp-tender. Add chicken broth and chicken. Cook over medium heat for 20 minutes. Add egg noodles, and cook 10 to 15 additional minutes. Season to taste. Mix milk and flour or cornstarch in separate bowl. Add to soup to thicken, stirring until well blended. Wonderful home-style flavor and so easy!

[M A R Y   S U L L I V A N   S A N D E R S]

MAKES 4 QUARTS

2 pounds ground turkey or beef
1 onion, chopped
2 (.5-ounce) packages Ranch-style dressing mix
2 (1¼-ounce) packages taco seasoning mix
1 (16-ounce) can black beans, undrained
1 (16-ounce) can kidney beans, undrained
1 (16-ounce) can pinto beans, undrained
1 (16-ounce) can diced tomatoes with chilies, undrained
1 (16-ounce) can tomato wedges, undrained
2 (16-ounce) cans white corn, undrained
2 cups water
Garnish: sour cream, shredded Cheddar cheese, sliced green onions

MAKES 3 QUARTS

1 cup sliced carrots
1 cup chopped celery
1 small onion, chopped
2 cloves garlic, minced
1 tablespoon chopped fresh or 1 teaspoon dried marjoram
3 tablespoons butter, melted
8 cups chicken broth
2 cups chopped cooked chicken
1 (8-ounce) package small egg noodles
Salt and pepper
½ cup milk
½ cup all-purpose flour
Salt and pepper

SERVES 8 TO 10

SERVES 8 TO 10

1 cup olive oil

3 cups yellow onion, diced

8 cloves garlic, pressed

2 pounds dried black beans,
    soaked overnight

1 to 2 smoked ham hocks or
    1 ham bone

4 quarts water

2 tablespoons plus 1 teaspoon
    ground cumin, divided

1 tablespoon dried oregano

3 bay leaves

1 tablespoon plus 2 teaspoons salt

2 teaspoons black pepper

1/4 teaspoon cayenne pepper

6 tablespoons chopped
    fresh parsley, divided

1 medium sweet red pepper, diced

1/4 cup dry sherry

1 tablespoon brown sugar

1 tablespoon lemon juice
    Sour cream or Crème Fraîche

SERVES 6 TO 8

1/4 cup olive oil

3 pounds lean lamb stew meat

2 cups chopped onion

2 cloves garlic, minced

1 cup red wine

3 cups water

2 beef bouillon cubes

1/2 cup fresh chopped parsley

2 bay leaves

1 tablespoon salt

1/2 teaspoon pepper
    Assorted vegetables: small new
    potatoes, carrots, fresh pearl onions

1/4 cup cornstarch

1/2 cup cold water

BEST BLACK BEAN SOUP

Heat oil in stockpot. Add onion and garlic, and cook over low heat about 10 minutes or until tender. ✿ Drain soaked beans and add to pot. Add ham hocks and water. Stir in 2 tablespoons cumin and next 5 ingredients. Add 2 tablespoons parsley. ✿ Bring to boil; reduce heat, and simmer about $1\frac{1}{2}$ to 2 hours or until beans are tender. Transfer ham hocks to plate, and cool. Shred any meat, and return into soup. Stir in remaining parsley, remaining cumin, red pepper, and next 3 ingredients. Simmer an additional 30 minutes, stirring frequently. ✿ Serve hot with sour cream.

[ELLISON JONES GRAY]

Just a Thought

*To thicken soup slightly, puree 4 cups of soaked black beans,
then return to soup.*

HEARTY IRISH STEW

Heat oil in a Dutch oven. Add meat, and brown on all sides. Add onion and garlic; cook until onion is soft and golden. Add wine and next 6 ingredients. Bring to a boil; reduce heat. Cover and simmer for $1\frac{1}{2}$ hours. ✿ Add vegetables as desired; simmer until tender (about 1 hour). ✿ Mix cornstarch and cold water; stir into stew. Simmer over low heat, stirring constantly until thickened.

[LINDA McMEANS BYRNE]

Just a Thought

This is also excellent with beef tips or stew meat.

MULLIGATAWNY SOUP

Wash chicken and dry with paper towels. Combine flour and next 3 ingredients, and rub well into chicken. ✦ Heat butter in 6-quart stockpot, and lightly brown chicken on all sides. Add cloves and next 3 ingredients. Bring to a boil; reduce heat, and simmer, covered, for 1 hour. Remove chicken pieces, discarding peppercorns and cloves. ✦ Skin and bone chicken, and cut meat into small pieces. Return to soup with lemon juice and cream. Simmer soup, and add salt to taste. Serve in heated bowls with hot cooked rice, and pass garnishes separately. (Soup may be mixed in blender for a smoother texture.)

[NEILL ROSS]

SERVES 6

2 pounds chicken pieces
2 tablespoons all-purpose flour
2 teaspoons curry powder
1 teaspoon turmeric
½ teaspoon ground ginger
4 tablespoons butter
6 whole cloves
12 peppercorns
1 large apple, peeled and sliced
6 cups chicken broth
2 tablespoons lemon juice
½ cup whipping cream
  Salt
  Hot cooked rice
  Garnishes: commercial chutney, coconut, sultanas, chopped peanuts, crumbled bacon, chopped green onions

BRUNSWICK STEW

Cook chicken and ham hock in 6 cups water until tender. Drain, reserving broth. Discard ham hock. Skin and bone chicken. ✦ Place reserved 6 cups broth in large stockpot. Add onions, tomatoes, tomato paste, and next 3 ingredients. ✦ Simmer 3 hours. Add chicken during last hour of cooking. Season with butter and remaining ingredients.

[LUCIE HOWISON MILLER]

SERVES 20

1 (6-pound) hen
1 ham bone or hock
6 cups water
2 large onions, diced
2 quarts canned tomatoes, cut in pieces
1 (6-ounce) can tomato paste
10 ounces frozen chopped okra
10 ounces frozen baby limas
10 ounces frozen shoepeg corn
½ cup butter, melted
1 teaspoon Tabasco Sauce
1 teaspoon Worcestershire sauce
½ teaspoon salt
½ teaspoon pepper
¼ cup sherry

SERVES 8

1 pound dried Northern beans
   or 3 (16-ounce) cans
2 medium white onions, chopped
1 clove garlic, minced
1 tablespoon vegetable oil
4 cups diced cooked chicken
   (approximately 5 medium
   breasts)
5 cups chicken broth
2 (4 1/2-ounce) cans green chilies
   drained, peeled and chopped
2 tablespoons ground cumin
1/4 teaspoon cayenne pepper
1/4 teaspoon dried oregano
1/4 teaspoon ground cloves
1/2 tablespoon chili powder
1/8 teaspoon hot paprika
   (optional)
1/8 teaspoon ground cardamom
   (optional)
Grated Monterey Jack cheese
Sour cream
Commercial salsa

SERVES 8

6 hot Italian sausages, chopped
1 1/2 pounds beef tips
1 large yellow onion, sliced
2 cloves garlic, minced
1 medium green pepper, chopped
1 medium sweet red pepper,
   chopped
2 (16-ounce) cans kidney beans,
   drained
2 medium potatoes, chopped
1 tablespoon chopped fresh basil
1/2 teaspoon salt
1/4 teaspoon pepper
2 beef bouillon cubes
1 cup hot water

W H I T E   B E A N   C H I L I

Cook beans according to package directions. Sauté onion and garlic in oil until tender. Combine beans, onion mixture, chicken, and next 9 ingredients in a 5-quart stockpot, and bring to boil. Reduce heat to low, and simmer for 1 hour. Add additional seasonings to taste. Serve with grated Monterey Jack cheese, sour cream, and salsa. Best prepared one day in advance.

[W E N D Y J O H N S O N R O D D E]

S A U S A G E A N D   B E E F   S T E W

Brown sausage in ovenproof Dutch oven; remove and set aside. Brown beef tips in Dutch oven; remove and set aside. Sauté onion and garlic, and add peppers, beans, potatoes, and seasonings. Dissolve bouillon in 1 cup hot water, and add to mixture. Stir in sausage and beef tips. Cover and bake in Dutch oven at 350° for 1 hour and 15 minutes.

[L O U I S E R H E T T O R E M]

BLACK BEAN AND VEGETABLE CHILI

Cook onion and, if desired, sausage in oil in a large saucepan. Add tomatoes, picante sauce, and seasonings. Cover and simmer 5 minutes. ✒ Stir in beans, peppers, and squash. Cover and simmer about 15 minutes or until vegetables are crisp-tender. ✒ Serve over rice. ✒ Garnish each serving with sour cream, chopped fresh cilantro, shredded cheese, and hot picante sauce.

[LISA CHEATHAM WARNOCK]

TOMATO BISQUE

Combine first 6 ingredients in 2-gallon pot; sauté until brown. Add chicken broth and bring to a boil. ✒ Add half-and-half and whipping cream, and bring to low boil. Make a roux; stir into soup until consistency is even throughout. Add wine, salt, and pepper to taste. ✒ Remove pot from heat, and add tomatoes and basil.

[JIM MUIR]
CRAPE MYRTLE AND WILD ROOT CAFÉ

To make roux, put 1 1/2 cups flour in a large saucepan.
On low heat, gradually whisk in butter a little at a time.
Keep whisking until color of peanut butter.

SERVES 8

1 large onion, coarsely chopped

1 pound Kielbasa sausage, sliced (optional)

1 tablespoon vegetable oil

1 (28-ounce) can whole tomatoes, undrained and coarsely chopped

2/3 cup picante sauce

1 1/2 teaspoons each: dried rosemary, oregano, chili powder, cumin

1 teaspoon dried basil

2 (16-ounce) cans black beans, rinsed and drained

1 green pepper, cut into 3/4-inch pieces

1 red pepper, cut into 3/4-inch pieces

1 large yellow squash and/or zucchini, cut into 1/2-inch chunks

Hot rice

Garnishes: Sour cream, chopped fresh cilantro, shredded cheese, and hot picante sauce

SERVES 12

1 red pepper, seeded and diced

1 green pepper, seeded and diced

4 stems celery, diced

1/2 yellow onion, diced

1 teaspoon garlic

1/2 cup butter

1 quart chicken broth

1 quart half-and-half

1 pint heavy whipping cream

1/2 cup white wine

Salt and pepper

1 pint diced tomatoes

1/2 cup dried basil or chopped fresh basil

MAKES 1 QUART

1/2 cup all-purpose flour
Salt and pepper
1 pound cubed veal
1/4 cup vegetable oil
1/2 cup chopped onion
8 ounces fresh mushrooms, sliced
1/4 sweet red pepper, chopped
1 (14 1/2-ounce) can chicken broth
1/4 to 1/2 cup red wine
2 tablespoons tomato paste
1/2 teaspoon dried parsley
1/4 teaspoon fines herbes
1/2 (10-ounce) package frozen
    artichoke hearts
1/2 (10-ounce) package frozen
    green peas
12 fingerling carrots (optional)
Hot cooked rice

SERVES 2

2 tablespoons olive oil
    (less if desired)
1 sweet red pepper, julienned
1/2 medium onion, thinly sliced
6 to 8 ounces grilled or roasted
    beef, lamb, or chicken
2 (6-inch) submarine rolls, split
2 slices provolone cheese
Additional melted butter
    or olive oil

RAGOUT OF VEAL AND ARTICHOKES

Combine flour and salt and pepper to taste. Dredge veal in flour mixture. Lightly brown veal in oil. Add onion; sauté until soft. Add mushrooms and red pepper; sauté until juices release. Add chicken broth, wine, tomato paste, and seasonings. Simmer, covered, for 10 minutes. Adjust seasonings. Simmer over low heat, approximately 1 hour, or until meat is tender. Add artichoke hearts and peas or carrots, if desired, and cook until thoroughly heated. Serve with hot cooked rice.

[TRICIA JENKINS NOBLE]
PAST PRESIDENT

THE "HALF-TIME SPECIAL"

Heat olive oil in a large skillet over medium-high heat. Add red peppers and onions. Sauté, stirring occasionally, until vegetables are crisp-tender. Add meat; sauté until heated. Drain. Place rolls, cut side up, on baking sheet. Arrange meat and vegetables on one side of bun. Cover with cheese. Brush other bun halves with butter or olive oil. Broil until buns begin to brown and cheese melts. Serve immediately.

[MIKE McCRANEY]

G R I L L E D   V E G E T A B L E   S A N D W I C H   W I T H   L I G H T   A I O L I

Process first 3 ingredients in food processor to make aioli; set aside. ✎ Slice baguette in half lengthwise, removing some of inside bread. Toast baguette lightly. ✎ Slice squash, eggplant, zucchini, and red pepper lengthwise; place on baking sheet coated with cooking spray. Spray vegetables with cooking spray, and broil until blackened, turning as necessary. Peel red pepper when cooled. Salt and drain eggplant. ✎ Spread bread with aioli, and layer vegetables evenly over. Top with fresh basil or cheese, if desired. Cut into fourths.

[M A R I O N   H U N T   N E W T O N]

SERVES 4

1 cup fat-free mayonnaise
1 tablespoon olive oil
4 to 5 cloves garlic
  Baguette
2 to 3 medium yellow squash
1 small eggplant
1 small zucchini
1 medium sweet red pepper
  Chopped fresh basil (optional)
  Cheese of choice (optional)

G R E E K   S A L A D   S A N D W I C H

Cook bread dough according to directions. Cut bread loaves or round in half horizontally, and scoop out some of inside from top half. Brush bottom half with 1/2 cup vinaigrette. ✎ Arrange lettuce on bottom half; top with cheese. Layer cucumber slices in overlapping rows. Repeat with chopped tomato. Layer onion over tomatoes. ✎ Sprinkle with olives and oregano. Add pepper to taste. ✎ Brush inside of top half of bread with remaining vinaigrette. Put top and bottom pieces together. (To compress ingredients, place several dinner plates on top of loaf for about an hour before serving.) Wrap in plastic wrap. To serve, unwrap and cut into wedges.

[V I C K I E   W A L T O N   R A D E R]

SERVES 4

2 packages frozen French bread dough or 1 (10-inch) round loaf
1/2 cup oregano lemon vinaigrette (page 204)
1/2 head romaine lettuce
1 pound feta cheese, cut into 1/4-inch thick slices
1 cucumber, peeled and thinly sliced
12 slices sun-dried tomatoes packed in oil, chopped
1 small purple onion, thinly sliced
1/2 cup ripe oil-cured olives, pitted and coarsely chopped
1/2 cup chopped fresh oregano
  Freshly ground pepper

Caribbean Salad With Mango Salsa, page 126

My Grandma's Potato Salad Recipe

ˉM A R G A R E T W A L K E R A L E X A N D E Rˉ

6 to 8 medium-sized white potatoes

1 small red onion

5 or 6 stalks of celery

2 or 3 hard-boiled eggs

pickles

homemade mayonnaise, using 1 to 2 egg yolks

1 cup unsaturated oil, such as Wesson or olive oil

$\frac{1}{2}$ teaspoon mustard, dash of salt

liquid pepper if desired (Never use black pepper in potato salad)

White pepper or liquid red pepper may be used

MOST PEOPLE REMEMBER ALWAYS having chicken in every pot on every Sunday. I can remember having chicken every Sunday, but I also had potato salad every Sunday. My grandmother's potato salad was special but I didn't know that then. I found out much later that her potato salad was different ˉC O N T I N U E Dˉ

MARGARET WALKER

MARGARET WALKER'S CAREER
AS A PUBLISHED WRITER SPANS
MORE THAN SIXTY YEARS SINCE
1934. SHE HAS WRITTEN FIVE
BOOKS OF POETRY (INCLUDING
THE BESTSELLER *FOR MY PEOPLE*),
SEVERAL NONFICTION BOOKS
AND THE HIGHLY ACCLAIMED
NOVEL *JUBILEE*. SHE GRADUATED
FROM NORTHWESTERN
UNIVERSITY IN 1935. SHE
RECEIVED A MASTER OF ARTS
DEGREE AND A PH.D.
IN ENGLISH, BOTH
FROM THE UNIVERSITY
OF IOWA. IN 1954, SHE WAS
A FORD FELLOW AT YALE
UNIVERSITY. A WIDOW,
MARGARET WALKER WAS MARRIED
FOR 37 YEARS TO THE LATE MR.
FIRNEST JAMES ALEXANDER, SR.

from everybody else's. I remember as early as ten years of age I was making the mayonnaise for Grandma's potato salad. She had explicit directions for every step of the process, using 6 to 8 medium-size white potatoes. First, boil the white potatoes slowly and simmer them a long time but do not let the skin burst. Do not prick the potatoes in the pot and make holes while they are cooking. Then mash them gently to make sure they are thoroughly done. Overcooking the potatoes would make them mealy and they should stay waxy—but done, nevertheless. Cool them carefully and prepare strips of celery without the strings. Chop them finely until you have a cup of chopped celery. Grandma used red onions but she used small ones. And one small onion was generally enough. If you have pickles and hard-boiled eggs—they add color and texture to the salad. I don't recall my grandmother ever having pimiento or stuffed olives in her salad. That is my addition.

The mayonnaise was always homemade. I don't recall using bought mayonnaise until after I was an adult. I separated one to two egg yolks from the white and used only the yolk, a dash of salt and a small cup of Wesson oil and dribbled slowly while I beat the eggs furiously. This made a large cup of mayonnaise—just enough for the potato salad. Add lemon juice or a tablespoonful of vinegar and one-half teaspoon of cream-style mustard. Then the mayonnaise before mixing it in the salad.

And that is all. But, oh, so good! THE END

S A L A D S

C O N G E A L E D

Cranberry Salad 131
Holiday Mold 132
Mama Bright's Tomato Aspic 131

F R U I T / G R E E N

An Autumn Dinner Salad . . .119
Apple-Celery-Swiss Salad . . .119
Baja Salad 116
Bibb Salad With Maple
    Vinaigrette 115
Boston and Watercress With
    Lemon-Dijon Vinaigrette .117
Fresh Fruit Salad With Orange
    Liqueur Dressing 118
Green Salad With Fruit 118
Romaine With Roasted Peppers
    and Goat Cheese 115
Spinach Salad With Feta, Mint,
    and Olives 116
Spinach Salad With Tarragon
    Vinaigrette 117

R I C E

Black Bean and Rice Salad .129
Saffron Rice Salad 130
Mama Nim's Tabbouleh 130
Seafood Rice Salad 129

P A S T A

Chicken Fettucine Salad 114
Grilled Chicken Pasta Salad .112
Summer Shells With Shrimp
    and Cucumber 113
Tortellini With Pesto
    Vinaigrette 112
Tortellini and Sun-Dried
    Tomato Salad 113
Tri-Color Rotini Tossed With
    Chicken and Vegetables . . .114

P O U L T R Y

Caribbean Salad With Mango
    Salsa 126
Grilled Chicken Salad 124
Chicken Salad With Warm Purple
    Onion Vinaigrette 126
Chinese Chicken Salad 124
Jack Daniels Smoked Turkey
    Salad 125
Spring Garden Chicken 125

S E A F O O D

Shrimp, Mango, and Avocado
    Salad 127
Shrimp and Spinach Toss . . .128
West Indies Salad 128
Zesty Creole Shrimp Salad . .127

V E G E T A B L E

Artichoke-Tomato Salad 120
Asparagus With Olives in Red
    Wine Vinegar 120
Dill-Artichoke Potato
    Salad 121
Corn and Arugula Salad . . .132
Finley Avenue Summer
    Salad 123
Greek Salad With Lemon-Herb
    Dressing 121
Green Bean Salad With Dill and
    Roquefort 122
Marinated Slaw 123
Marinated Winter Salad 122

D R E S S I N G S

Balsamic Vinaigrette 135
Blue Cheese Vinaigrette 135
Birmingham's Favorite Slaw
    Dressing 134
Celery Seed Dressing 133
Green Goddess Mayonnaise . .135
Louis Dressing 134
Poppy Seed Dressing 133
Roquefort Dressing 133
Spinach Salad Dressing 134

SERVES 4 TO 6

6 *skinless, boneless chicken breast halves, cut into ¹/2-inch-wide strips*
³/4 *cup soy sauce*
¹/3 *cup balsamic vinegar*
¹/3 *cup cider vinegar*
¹/2 *cup olive oil*
1 *tablespoon Dijon mustard*
  Salt and pepper
3 *green onions, chopped*
1 *small red pepper, cut into strips*
1 *carrot, scraped and cut into strips*
  Angel hair pasta, cooked

GRILLED CHICKEN PASTA SALAD

Low Fat

Marinate chicken breasts in soy sauce in refrigerator 2 to 3 hours. Grill chicken over medium heat 10 minutes. Combine balsamic vinegar and next 3 ingredients. Whisk or shake until well blended. Add salt and pepper to taste, whisking until blended. Set dressing aside. Toss chicken, green onions, red pepper, and carrots with dressing. Refrigerate overnight, tossing occasionally. Serve salad on beds of cold angel hair pasta. Spoon additional dressing over salad when serving.

[GINI MCCORMICK WILLIAMS]

SERVES 8 TO 10

Pesto Vinaigrette:
1¹/2 *teaspoons minced garlic*
  ¹/3 *cup white wine vinegar*
  2 *teaspoons Dijon mustard*
  2 *teaspoons minced fresh basil*
  2 *tablespoons minced fresh parsley*
  ¹/4 *teaspoon dried thyme, crushed*
  ¹/2 *teaspoon salt*
  1 *tablespoon pesto*
  ¹/2 *cup olive oil*

  1 *pound fresh meat-filled tortellini*
  1 *teaspoon vegetable oil*
  2 *cups broccoli florets*
1¹/2 *cups finely julienned carrots*
  ¹/2 *cup thinly sliced green onions*

TORTELLINI WITH PESTO VINAIGRETTE

Whisk together first 8 ingredients until blended. Whisk in olive oil. Set dressing aside. Cook tortellini in 8 cups boiling salted water with oil 5 to 7 minutes or until done. Drain tortellini and rinse under cold water. Transfer to large mixing bowl. Steam broccoli 3 to 5 minutes. Rinse under cold water, and drain well. Add broccoli, carrots and green onions to tortellini. Toss with Pesto Vinaigrette Dressing.

[KATHY G. MEZRANO]
KATHY G'S CATERING, INC.

T O R T E L L I N I A N D S U N - D R I E D T O M A T O S A L A D

SERVES 8

Drain tomatoes, reserving 1 tablespoon oil. Chop tomatoes, and set aside. ✒ Combine reserved oil, olive oil, and next 4 ingredients. Stir in chopped tomatoes, artichoke hearts, and cashews. Add tortellini, tossing to combine. ✒ Let salad stand at room temperature for 1 hour for flavors to blend, or chill overnight. Serve with grilled chicken.

[ALYSON LUTZ BUTTS]

8 ounces sun-dried tomatoes packed in oil, undrained
1/3 cup olive oil
1 tablespoon fresh lemon juice
2 cloves garlic, minced
1 teaspoon freshly ground pepper
1/2 teaspoon salt
8 ounces marinated artichoke hearts drained
4 ounces whole cashews
1 pound dried cheese-filled tortellini, cooked, drained, and cooled

S U M M E R S H E L L S W I T H S H R I M P A N D C U C U M B E R

SERVES 8 TO 10

Chop shrimp coarsely, add cucumbers, and toss. ✒ In a separate bowl, combine cream, lemon juice, and mustard. Add salt and pepper to taste. Gradually add oil in a slow, steady stream, whisking constantly until blended. Set dressing aside. ✒ Toss shrimp and cucumbers with half of the dressing. Fill shells with mixture and refrigerate. ✒ Pour remaining dressing over shells just before serving.

[SARA JANE BALL]

Serve on cups of baby lettuce leaves.
Beautiful for a summer luncheon, served with a chilled soup.

1 pound medium fresh shrimp, cooked, peeled, and deveined
2 small cucumbers, peeled, seeded, and chopped
1/2 cup whipping cream
2 tablespoons lemon juice
1 tablespoon Dijon mustard
Salt and pepper
1/2 cup vegetable oil
15 to 20 jumbo pasta shells, cooked and drained

SERVES 8 TO 10

Dressing:
- 1 cup mayonnaise
- 1 teaspoon dried dillweed
- 1/4 teaspoon Cajun seasoning
- 1/4 teaspoon pepper

- 8 ounces fettuccine noodles
- 3 tablespoons olive oil
- 4 skinless, boneless chicken breast halves
- 1/4 cup wine vinegar
- 1 teaspoon salt
- 1 cup chopped celery
- 1/2 cup chopped fresh parsley
- 1/4 cup chopped green onions
- 1 cup chopped pecans
  Red leaf lettuce

SERVES 10

- 2 pounds cooked chicken, chopped
- 6 cups tri-color rotini pasta, cooked and drained
- 2 1/2 teaspoons salt
- 1 cup chopped celery
- 2 tablespoons Creole seasoning
- 1 cup chopped green peppers
- 4 ounces chopped pimiento, drained
- 2 cups fresh broccoli florets

Dressing:
- 1 cup olive oil
- 1/2 cup red wine vinegar
- 1 cup mayonnaise
- 2 tablespoons lemon juice
- 2 tablespoons dried dillweed

CHICKEN FETTUCCINE SALAD

Combine all dressing ingredients and set aside. Cook and drain fettuccine. Toss fettuccine with olive oil. Cook and chop chicken. Toss chicken with wine vinegar and salt. Combine fettuccine, chicken mixture, and next 4 ingredients; toss all with dressing. Serve on a bed of red leaf lettuce.

[JEAN SYLVERT WELCH]

TRI-COLOR ROTINI TOSSED WITH CHICKEN AND VEGETABLES

Toss chicken with next 7 ingredients. To prepare dressing, combine all dressing ingredients in a medium bowl. Toss chicken mixture with desired amount of dressing. Marinate in refrigerator at least 6 hours before serving.

[FLETCHER HANSON CHAMBLISS]

Just a Thought

Put the broccoli florets into the colander before draining the pasta. The hot water will steam the broccoli.

BIBB SALAD WITH MAPLE-RASPBERRY VINAIGRETTE

Combine first 3 ingredients, whisking until blended. Set dressing aside. ✦ Arrange Bibb lettuce and onion rings on individual salad plates. Sprinkle evenly with blue cheese and pine nuts. Drizzle with dressing.

[MOLLY PEARCE CLARK]

SERVES 6

1/4 cup raspberry vinegar
2 1/2 tablespoons maple syrup
2/3 cup vegetable oil
2 heads Bibb lettuce, torn
1 small purple onion, sliced into rings
4 ounces crumbled blue cheese
1/4 cup toasted pine nuts

ROMAINE WITH ROASTED PEPPERS AND GOAT CHEESE

Whisk together first 3 ingredients. Gradually add olive oil in a slow, steady stream, whisking constantly until blended. Set White Wine Vinaigrette aside. ✦ Preheat broiler. Place peppers on a broiler pan. Broil close to heat source, turning occasionally until all sides are charred. They are done when black on all sides. Remove from oven, and place peppers in an airtight bag or covered bowl. Steam at least 15 minutes. Remove peppers, and slip off skins. Remove and discard stem and seeds. Slice peppers. ✦ Arrange sliced peppers on romaine lettuce on salad plates. Sprinkle goat cheese evenly over peppers. Drizzle desired amount of White Wine Vinaigrette over salad. Reserve any leftover vinaigrette for future use.

[MELANIE BERRY McCRANEY]

This colorful salad goes well with grilled lamb or veal chops.

SERVES 4

White Wine Vinaigrette:
1/4 cup white wine vinegar
1 teaspoon Dijon mustard
1 clove garlic, minced
1/2 cup extra-virgin olive oil

2 large sweet red peppers
1 head romaine lettuce, washed and torn into bite-size pieces
4 ounces goat cheese, crumbled

B A J A   S A L A D

SERVES 6

3 ripe avocados, peeled, seeded, and cubed

1/3 cup plus 2 tablespoons fresh lime juice, divided

6 ripe plum or Roma tomatoes, chopped

3 tablespoons purple onion, chopped

1 tablespoon Dijon mustard

1 teaspoon garlic, minced

1/2 cup olive oil
Salt and pepper

1 tablespoon chopped fresh cilantro

1 tablespoon chopped fresh oregano

1 tablespoon chopped fresh parsley
Bibb or leaf lettuce

Place cubed avocados in a large bowl and sprinkle with 2 tablespoons lime juice. Toss in tomatoes and purple onion. In a separate bowl, whisk together 1/3 cup lime juice, mustard, and garlic. Slowly drizzle in olive oil, whisking constantly. Add salt and pepper to taste. Pour about 1/3 cup of the dressing over salad. Toss. Save additional dressing for another use. Just before serving, toss with fresh herbs. Adjust seasonings to taste. Serve on bed of Bibb or leaf lettuce.

[ALISON BERRY]

S P I N A C H   S A L A D   W I T H   F E T A ,   M I N T ,   A N D   O L I V E S

SERVES 6

1/3 cup extra-virgin olive oil

2 large cloves garlic, minced

2 tablespoons rice wine vinegar

1/8 teaspoon salt

1/4 teaspoon freshly ground black pepper

6 cups fresh spinach leaves, torn

1/3 cup thinly sliced purple onion

2 ounces feta cheese, crumbled

6 Calamata olives

1/2 teaspoon finely chopped fresh mint
Croutons

Whisk together first 5 ingredients. Toss dressing with spinach and next 4 ingredients. Garnish with croutons, if desired.

[SALLY PELTON MATHIS]

SPINACH SALAD WITH TARRAGON VINAIGRETTE

SERVES 6 TO 8

To prepare Tarragon Vinaigrette, whisk together vinaigrette ingredients. Refrigerate. Dressing is more flavorful if made several hours in advance. (May be made up to 2 days ahead.) Wash and stem spinach. Tear into bite-size pieces. Cook bacon; drain and crumble. To assemble salad, toss spinach, eggs, mushrooms, and onions rings with desired amount of dressing. Toss in bacon and sesame seeds. Serve immediately.

[LAURA BERRY]

*Tarragon and sesame seeds give
a classic spinach salad a whole new flavor.*

Tarragon Vinaigrette:
 3/4 cup vegetable oil
 1/2 cup red wine vinegar
 2 tablespoons sugar
 1 clove garlic, crushed
 1 teaspoon Worcestershire sauce
 2 drops Tabasco Sauce
 1/2 teaspoon salt
 1/4 teaspoon freshly ground pepper
 1/2 teaspoon dried tarragon
 1/2 teaspoon dry mustard

 10 ounces fresh spinach leaves
 8 slices bacon
 3 hard-cooked eggs, chopped
 1/2 pound fresh mushrooms, sliced
 1/3 small purple onion,
   thinly sliced
 1/4 cup sesame seeds, toasted

BOSTON AND WATERCRESS WITH LEMON-DIJON VINAIGRETTE

SERVES 6

To prepare dressing, combine first 5 ingredients. Add salt and pepper to taste, mixing well to blend. To prepare salad, wash and dry lettuce and watercress. Tear Boston into small pieces. Combine greens in large bowl. Layer with cucumber and sliced onion. Sprinkle with sesame seeds. Pour vinaigrette over salad and toss.

Lemon-Dijon Vinaigrette:
 6 tablespoons vegetable oil
 3 tablespoons olive oil
 3 tablespoons white wine
   vinegar
 3 tablespoons lemon juice
 1 tablespoon Dijon mustard
   Salt and pepper

 1 head Boston lettuce
 1 large bunch watercress
 1 cucumber, peeled and sliced
 1 small purple onion, thinly
   sliced
 1 tablespoon sesame seeds,
   toasted

SERVES 6 TO 8

Dressing:
- ½ cup vegetable oil
- ¼ cup tarragon vinegar
- 3 tablespoons sugar
- ½ teaspoon Tabasco Sauce
  Salt and pepper

- 1 large head red or green
  leaf lettuce
- 1 (11-ounce) can mandarin
  oranges, drained
- 1 cup strawberries, sliced
- 1 kiwifruit, peeled and sliced
- 1 cup blueberries
- ½ cup chopped celery
- 1 (3¾-ounce) package slivered
  almonds, toasted

SERVES 6

- 2 fresh peaches, peeled and
  sliced
- 1 to 2 fresh mangoes, peeled
  and chopped
- 1 cup fresh blueberries
- 1 cup cantaloupe balls
- 1 cup sliced fresh strawberries
- 1 cup seedless green grapes
- 3 to 4 kiwifruit, peeled
  and sliced
- 3 tablespoons orange-flavored
  liqueur
- ⅔ cup sour cream
- 4 tablespoons packed brown
  sugar, divided

GREEN SALAD WITH FRUIT

To prepare dressing, combine first 4 ingredients. Add salt and pepper to taste, mixing well to blend. 🌿 Tear lettuce into bite-size pieces, and place in a large salad bowl. Add fruit, celery, and almonds. Toss with desired amount of dressing. (Use leftover dressing for any green salad.)

[JANET SMITH LUCAS]

Just a Thought

These colorful salads can be enjoyed with any fresh fruits in season and may accompany almost any entree.

FRESH FRUIT SALAD WITH ORANGE LIQUEUR DRESSING

Combine fruit, and toss gently with liqueur. 🌿 Combine sour cream and 3 tablespoons brown sugar. Set dressing aside. 🌿 Serve fruit mixture with sour cream dressing. Sprinkle with 1 tablespoon brown sugar.

[CATHY CRISS ADAMS]

An Autumn Dinner Salad

To prepare Balsamic Vinaigrette, combine dry mustard, seasoned salt, and pepper. Stir in vinegar, onion juice, and garlic. Let stand 1 hour. Just before serving, pour through a wire-mesh strainer to remove garlic. Beat in olive oil with a wire whisk, and serve with salad. ✐ To prepare salad, melt butter in a heavy skillet over medium heat. Add walnuts and brown sugar, and sauté until nuts begin to soften. Remove from pan to cool. ✐ Wash and drain lettuce. Tear into bite-size pieces, and place in a large bowl. ✐ At serving time, core fruit and cut into pieces. Toss lettuce, fruit, sprouts, scallions, and half the nuts and cheese with Balsamic Vinaigrette. Sprinkle remaining nuts and cheese over top. Serve immediately.

[BETSY BARNUM]

SERVES 4 TO 6

Balsamic Vinaigrette:
- 1 teaspoon dry mustard
- 1/2 teaspoon seasoned salt
- 1/4 teaspoon freshly ground pepper
- 3 tablespoons balsamic vinegar
- 1/2 teaspoon onion juice
- 1 clove garlic, crushed
- 3/4 cup olive oil

- 2 tablespoons butter
- 1/2 cup chopped walnuts
- 3 tablespoons brown sugar
  Mixed salad greens – romaine, leaf lettuce, Boston lettuce, radicchio
- 1 firm pear or apple
  Alfalfa sprouts (optional)
- 3 scallions, chopped
- 3 to 4 ounces crumbled blue cheese

Apple-Celery-Swiss Salad

Whisk together first 5 ingredients. Set dressing aside. ✐ Cut cheese and celery into strips the size of matchsticks. Toss together cheese, celery, and apples. Whisk dressing, pour over salad, and toss again. Garnish with celery leaves, if desired.

[CAROLINE STEVENS BOLVIG]

SERVES 4

- 1/2 cup vegetable oil
- 2 tablespoons apple cider vinegar
- 2 tablespoons chopped fresh parsley
- 2 teaspoons Dijon mustard
- 1 teaspoon caraway seeds
- 4 ounces Swiss cheese
- 4 stalks celery
- 2 Granny Smith apples, cored and chopped
  Celery leaves

SERVES 6 TO 8

1/2 cup tarragon vinegar

1 cup olive oil

2 tablespoons chopped fresh chives

1 tablespoon chopped tarragon leaves

1 tablespoon chopped fresh basil leaves

1 teaspoon salt

2 (10-ounce) packages frozen artichoke hearts, cooked and drained

4 ripe tomatoes

8 pitted ripe olives

SERVES 6

2 pounds fresh asparagus

1/3 cup chopped fresh parsley

1/2 cup sliced ripe olives

1/2 cup sliced pimiento-stuffed olives

1 (2-ounce) jar pimientos, drained

2 tablespoons chopped green onions

1 1/2 cups vegetable oil

1/2 cup red wine vinegar

2 teaspoons lemon juice

1 teaspoon Worcestershire sauce

1 tablespoon dried basil

2 teaspoons coarsely ground pepper

1 teaspoon dried oregano

1/2 teaspoon garlic powder

1/2 teaspoon salt

1/4 teaspoon sugar

Bibb lettuce

12 Roma tomatoes, sliced

ARTICHOKE-TOMATO SALAD

Combine first 6 ingredients. Shake well. Pour two-thirds of dressing over artichokes. Cover and chill. ✒ Just before serving, cut tomatoes into wedges. Toss tomatoes with artichokes, olives, and remaining dressing.

[SUSAN NABERS HASKELL
PAST PRESIDENT]

ASPARAGUS WITH OLIVES IN RED WINE VINAIGRETTE

Low Fat*

Trim and blanch asparagus. Arrange parsley and next 4 ingredients over asparagus. Set aside. ✒ Combine oil and next 9 ingredients in a 1-quart jar. Cover and shake; pour over asparagus. Cover asparagus and chill 8 hours. ✒ To serve, line plates with lettuce. Remove asparagus and olives from marinade, and arrange on lettuce leaves. Place tomatoes on lettuce beside asparagus.

[SUE ELLEN GERMANY LUCAS]

*Low fat if olives are omitted

DILL-ARTICHOKE POTATO SALAD

Cook unpeeled potatoes, covered, in boiling salted water about 20 minutes or just until tender. Drain and cool potatoes. Cut into bite-size pieces. ✒ Stir together mayonnaise and next 4 ingredients in a large bowl. Gently fold in cooked potatoes, eggs and next 3 ingredients. ✒ Cover and chill at least 4 hours. Stir gently before serving. Garnish with dill sprigs, if desired.

[CAROLYN RITCHEY KING]

GREEK SALAD WITH LEMON-HERB DRESSING

Whisk together first 5 ingredients. Add salt and pepper to taste. Set Lemon-Herb Dressing aside. ✒ Toss lettuce and remaining ingredients in a large salad bowl. Add dressing, and toss gently. Serve immediately.

[ANNALISA THOMPSON JAGER]

SERVES 8 TO 10

3 pounds tiny new potatoes
1 cup mayonnaise
2 tablespoons red wine vinegar
2 tablespoons Dijon mustard
1 tablespoon lemon-pepper seasoning
1 tablespoon chopped fresh dill or 2 to 3 teaspoons dried dillweed, crushed
4 hard-cooked eggs, chopped
2 (6-ounce) jars marinated artichoke hearts, drained and sliced
3/4 cup chopped onion
2 tablespoons chopped dill pickle
Fresh dill sprigs

SERVES 4

Lemon-Herb Dressing:
3 tablespoons olive oil
3 tablespoons lemon juice
1 teaspoon Dijon mustard
1 clove garlic, crushed
1/4 teaspoon dried oregano
Salt and pepper

1 head Boston lettuce, torn into bite-size pieces
1/2 cucumber, sliced
1 small purple onion, thinly sliced
1 green pepper, sliced
1 pint cherry tomatoes, cut in half
4 fresh basil leaves, julienned
8 sun-dried tomatoes packed in oil, drained and sliced
1/2 cup pitted ripe olives
2 ounces feta cheese, crumbled

SERVES 8 TO 10

Dressing:
   1 cup vegetable oil
   ¼ cup white vinegar
   3 tablespoons lemon juice
   ½ tablespoon cracked black pepper
   1 tablespoon dried dillweed
   ¼ teaspoon paprika
   ½ teaspoon dry mustard
   1 clove garlic, minced

   2 pounds whole green beans, trimmed
   1 teaspoon seasoned salt
   1 clove garlic, minced
   1 slice onion
   ½ pound bacon, cooked and crumbled
   1 bunch green onions, chopped
   4 ounces Roquefort cheese
   ¼ cup mayonnaise
   2 tablespoons sour cream

SERVES 8

   1 (16-ounce) jar whole baby carrots, drained
   2 cups sliced zucchini (about 1 medium)
   1 (14-ounce) can hearts of palm, drained and sliced
   1 (7-ounce) jar pickled baby corn, drained (optional)
   ⅔ cup vegetable oil
   ¼ cup vinegar
   1 clove garlic, minced
   1 teaspoon sugar
   ¾ teaspoon salt
   ¾ teaspoon dry mustard
   2 ounces crumbled blue cheese

GREEN BEAN SALAD WITH DILL AND ROQUEFORT

Combine first 8 ingredients. Shake well. Refrigerate dressing. Bring a large pot of water to a boil. Add green beans, seasoned salt, garlic, and onion slice. Reduce heat. Cook until tender. Drain and cool. Toss beans with bacon, green onions, Roquefort cheese, ¼ cup dressing, mayonnaise, and sour cream. Chill well before serving. Serve in a tomato cup or on a bed of red leaf lettuce.

[PEGGY LANNING BYRD]

MARINATED WINTER SALAD

Combine carrots, zucchini, and hearts of palm. Add pickled baby corn, if desired. Combine oil and next 5 ingredients in a jar. Pour over vegetables. Marinate in refrigerator several hours or overnight. To serve, drain vegetables. Serve on Boston or Bibb lettuce leaves. Sprinkle with blue cheese.

[TOOKIE DAUGHERTY HAZELRIG]

FINLEY AVENUE SUMMER SALAD

Low Fat

Steam corn 1 minute. Cut kernels from cob. Steam okra 1 minute; slice. ✿ Combine corn kernels, sliced okra, onion, red pepper, and basil. Toss with vinegar to taste. Season with salt and pepper to taste. Chill.

[ANNE THIELE BLACKERBY]

(Finley Avenue is Birmingham's largest farmers market.)

2 ears fresh corn

2 cups fresh baby okra

1/2 cup chopped sweet onion

1/2 to 1 cup chopped sweet red pepper

1/4 cup chopped fresh basil

White wine vinegar or herb vinegar

Salt and pepper

MARINATED SLAW

Combine first 7 ingredients in a saucepan. Bring mixture to a boil. ✿ Layer cabbage, onions, and peppers in a large salad bowl. Pour dressing over vegetables. Chill overnight.

[CAROLINE MONTGOMERY BROWN]

1 cup vinegar

1 cup sugar

1 cup vegetable oil

2 tablespoons salt

3 tablespoons prepared mustard

2 teaspoons celery seeds

1/4 cup chopped pimiento, drained

3 pounds cabbage, shredded

2 medium onions, chopped

2 medium green peppers, chopped

SERVES 8

5 to 6 skinless, boneless chicken breast halves
1/4 cup Worcestershire sauce
1/4 cup soy sauce
1/3 cup mayonnaise
1/2 cup honey mustard
2 stalks celery, finely chopped
3/4 cup seedless red grapes, cut in half
1 cup chopped pecans
Salt and pepper

GRILLED CHICKEN SALAD

Marinate chicken in Worcestershire and soy sauces for 20 minutes. Grill chicken over medium heat 15 minutes or until done. Cut chicken into chunks. Whisk together mayonnaise and mustard in a small bowl; set aside. Combine chicken, celery, grapes, and pecans in a large bowl. Add mayonnaise mixture, tossing until blended. Season to taste. Serve chilled.

[KELLY SCOTT STYSLINGER]

SERVES 2 TO 4

Dressing:
2 tablespoons sesame oil
1/4 cup plus 2 tablespoons vinegar
1/4 cup sugar
1 teaspoon salt
1/2 teaspoon pepper

2 skinless, boneless, chicken breasts
1 head iceberg lettuce, torn
4 green onions, chopped
1 (6-ounce) package slivered almonds, toasted
1/4 cup sesame seeds, toasted
Chow Mein noodles, toasted

CHINESE CHICKEN SALAD

Whisk together sesame oil, vinegar, sugar, salt and pepper. Chill overnight. Cook chicken breasts; cool and cut into chunks. Set aside. Arrange lettuce in a large salad bowl. Add chicken, onions, almonds, and sesame seeds. At serving time, toss with dressing. Top with Chow Mein noodles.

[REBECCA OLIVER HAINES]

SPRING GARDEN CHICKEN

Whisk together first 7 dressing ingredients until blended; set aside. ✒ Cook asparagus and carrots separately in a small amount of boiling water until crisp-tender. Drain asparagus and carrots. Plunge vegetables into cold water to stop cooking process. Toss asparagus, carrots, chicken, peas, and onion with Mustard-Dill Vinaigrette. Chill at least 4 hours.

[DIANE COPELAND NORTH]

JACK DANIELS SMOKED TURKEY SALAD

Whisk together first 4 ingredients. Set dressing aside. ✒ Toss turkey and next 5 ingredients with dressing. Season with salt and pepper. Chill. ✒ Serve in a cantaloupe for a pretty luncheon dish.

[CHEF SCOTT BERG]
VINCENT'S

SERVES 2 TO 4

Mustard-Dill Vinaigrette:
1/2 cup olive oil
1/4 cup white wine vinegar
2 teaspoon Dijon mustard
2 cloves garlic, minced
1 teaspoon dried dillweed
1 teaspoon salt
1/4 teaspoon pepper

5 cups fresh asparagus, cut into 1-inch pieces
3 cups carrots, scraped and sliced
4 skinless, boneless chicken breasts, cooked and chopped
2 1/2 cups frozen baby English peas, thawed and drained
2 tablespoons sliced green onions

SERVES 8

3/4 cup mayonnaise
1/3 cup honey mustard
1 ounce Jack Daniels whiskey
2 tablespoons chopped fresh basil

2 pounds fresh smoked turkey breast, cubed
2 stalks celery, diced
1 1/2 bunches green onions, thinly sliced
1 sweet red pepper, julienned
1 sweet yellow pepper, julienned
4 slices bacon, cooked and crumbled
1 teaspoon salt
1 teaspoon freshly ground black pepper

SERVES 6

3 skinless, boneless whole chicken breasts
1 (8-ounce) bottle Jamaican jerk sauce
2 heads romaine lettuce
1 large sweet red pepper
1/2 purple onion, chopped
1 (15-ounce) can black beans, drained
1 ripe mango, peeled and chopped
1 (10 to 12-ounce) bottle raspberry vinaigrette
1 (10 to 12-ounce) bottle honey-Dijon salad dressing
Garnishes: 3 ripe avocados, peeled and sliced, 6 tablespoons pumpkin seeds

CARIBBEAN SALAD WITH MANGO SALSA

Cut chicken breasts in half; marinate in jerk sauce. ✒ Tear lettuce into bite-size pieces; set aside. ✒ Roast red pepper, then peel, seed, and chop. ✒ Combine red pepper, onion, black beans, and mango. Add raspberry vinaigrette, and chill several hours. ✒ Grill chicken over medium coals until done. Toss romaine with honey-Dijon dressing. Place on individual plates. Slice chicken lengthwise, and fan onto lettuce. Using slotted spoon, serve salsa on top. Garnish each with sliced avocado and pumpkin seeds, if desired.

[CAMERON DALEY CROWE]

SERVES 2 TO 4

1 small purple onion
4 large or 6 small skinless, boneless chicken breasts
1 tablespoon minced fresh thyme
Salt and pepper
1/4 cup vegetable oil
3 tablespoons balsamic or red wine vinegar (more, if desired)
1/2 head romaine lettuce
1/2 head red leaf lettuce

CHICKEN SALAD WITH WARM PURPLE ONION VINAIGRETTE

Cut onion into paper-thin slices; separate rings. ✒ Chop chicken into 1-inch cubes. Sprinkle with thyme and salt and pepper to taste. ✒ Heat oil in large skillet over medium-high heat until hot but not smoking. Add chicken, and sauté 5 minutes, stirring frequently, until cooked through. Add vinegar; stir with a wooden spoon to deglaze. Remove from heat; stir in onion. ✒ Arrange lettuces on plates, and top with chicken-onion mixture. Spoon remaining oil and vinegar over top. Serve warm.

[KATE GILMER PHILLIPS]

ZESTY CREOLE SHRIMP SALAD

Whisk oils, vinegar, and mustard together in a large bowl. Add capers and next 7 ingredients, and stir well. Set marinade aside. Boil shrimp in salted water until pink. Drain. Combine shrimp and marinade, and chill overnight. Drain and serve over a bed of assorted lettuces or cold pasta.

[NATALIE HICKS LEE]

SERVES 10

½ cup olive oil
½ cup vegetable oil
1 cup cider vinegar
4 tablespoons Creole mustard
2 tablespoons capers
2 tablespoons caper liquid
1 medium onion, grated
  Juice of 1 lemon
¼ teaspoon ground red pepper
2 ounces prepared horseradish
3 large cloves garlic, crushed
2 bay leaves
2 pounds fresh shrimp, peeled
  and deveined

SHRIMP, MANGO, AND AVOCADO SALAD

Combine first 8 ingredients in a mixing bowl. Whisk well to blend. Set dressing aside. Cut avocados in half lengthwise. Remove seeds. Spoon avocado flesh out of shells. Reserve shells. Dice avocado flesh into medium-size pieces. Lightly toss avocado pieces, mangoes, shrimp, and mushrooms in dressing. Serve in avocado shells or on a bed of lettuce.

[MIMI McCAULEY RENNEKER]

SERVES 6

1 teaspoon freshly grated ginger
½ cup salad oil
2 tablespoons white vinegar
1 teaspoon honey
1 teaspoon coarsely ground
  mustard
1 tablespoon lemon juice
1 tablespoon freshly chopped
  chives
1 tablespoon freshly chopped dill

3 medium avocados
2 medium mangoes, peeled and
  diced
1½ pounds fresh shrimp, cooked,
  peeled, and deveined
4 ounces fresh mushrooms, sliced

- S A L A D S -

3 tablespoons soy sauce
2 tablespoons red wine vinegar
3 tablespoons vegetable oil
1 teaspoon sugar
1/2 teaspoon garlic salt
1 teaspoon minced onion
1/4 teaspoon pepper
1/2 pound fresh spinach, torn into
    bite-size pieces
2 cups fresh shrimp (about 1
    pound unpeeled shrimp),
    cooked, peeled, and deveined
2 cups fresh broccoli florets
1 (8-ounce) can sliced water
    chestnuts, drained
1 cup fresh or canned bean
    sprouts
1/4 cup grated fresh Parmesan
    cheese
4 slices bacon, cooked and
    crumbled

1 medium onion, finely chopped
1 pound fresh lump crabmeat,
    drained
Salt and pepper
Ripe olives, sliced (optional)
Chopped celery (optional)
Chopped artichoke hearts
    (optional)
1/2 cup vegetable oil
1/3 cup cider vinegar
1/2 cup ice water
Lettuce leaves
Garnish: lemon or lime slices

SHRIMP AND SPINACH TOSS

Combine first 7 ingredients in tightly covered jar, and shake well. Set dressing aside. Toss spinach and next 4 ingredients with dressing. Sprinkle with Parmesan cheese and bacon. Serve immediately.

[HELEN MORRIS CAMP]

WEST INDIES SALAD

Assemble in large glass salad bowl. Arrange half of the onion in bottom of bowl. Cover with crabmeat. Top with remaining onion. Add salt and pepper to taste. Add olives, celery, and artichoke hearts, if desired. Combine oil, vinegar and water. Pour over salad. Marinate 2 to 12 hours in refrigerator. Toss lightly before serving. Serve on a lettuce leaf. Garnish with a thin slice of lemon or lime.

S E A F O O D   R I C E   S A L A D

SERVES 6 TO 8

Combine first 5 ingredients. Toss and refrigerate. ✻ Cook shrimp: peel, devein, and chop. Blanch green pepper. Cook and chop lobster tails. ✻ Gently toss shrimp, lobster, and crabmeat together with pimiento and next 4 ingredients. ✻ At serving time toss all ingredients together with mayonnaise and lemon juice. Garnish and serve immediately.

[T E A C E   M A R K W A L T E R   S A N D E R S]

Excellent as a main dish at a summer luncheon.
Also works well at brunch. Serve with ham and biscuits.

SERVES 6 TO 8

2 cups cooked white rice
1 tablespoon vinegar
1/4 cup vegetable oil
1 1/2 teaspoons salt
1/2 teaspoon pepper

1 pound fresh shrimp
2 tablespoons chopped green pepper
1 cup lobster (2 lobster tails)
1/4 cup chopped pimiento
1/4 cup chopped onion
1/4 cup chopped fresh parsley
1/2 cup frozen baby green peas, thawed
Sliced ripe olives
1 cup fresh lump crabmeat, drained
2/3 cup mayonnaise
1 tablespoon lemon juice
Garnishes: lemon slices, lobster claws

B L A C K   B E A N
A N D   R I C E   S A L A D

Low Fat

Combine first 5 ingredients. Shake or whisk until well blended. Set dressing aside ✻ Combine beans and next 6 ingredients in a large bowl. Add dressing, and toss lightly. Chill at least 1 hour before serving.

SERVES 6

1 tablespoon white wine vinegar
2 tablespoons olive oil
1/4 cup chopped fresh cilantro
1/2 teaspoon salt
1 tablespoon lime juice
1 (16-ounce) can black beans, rinsed and drained
1 cup cooked white rice
1 cup fresh tomatoes, chopped
1/2 cup green pepper, chopped
1/2 cup sweet red pepper, chopped
1/2 cup sweet yellow pepper, chopped
1/4 cup purple onion, chopped

SAFFRON RICE SALAD

SERVES 8 TO 10

3 cups water
1½ cups uncooked long-grain rice
½ teaspoon saffron
4 tablespoons red wine vinegar
½ teaspoon salt
¼ cup olive oil
2 tablespoons vegetable oil
¼ teaspoon black pepper
½ sweet red pepper, diced
½ green pepper, diced
½ medium tomato, chopped
⅓ cup ripe olives, chopped

Bring 3 cups water to a boil in a large saucepan. Stir in rice and saffron. Cover and simmer 20 minutes or until rice is tender and water is absorbed. Transfer rice to a large bowl. ✐ Whisk together vinegar and next 4 ingredients. Pour over warm rice. ✐ Add red and green peppers, tomato, and olives. Toss well to blend. Serve at room temperature or slightly chilled.

[BESSIE VERNEN MCGUIRE]

A colorful side dish for grilled chicken or fish.

MAMA NIM'S TABBOULEH

SERVES 6

⅓ cup bulgar wheat
1 head iceberg lettuce, finely chopped
3 ripe tomatoes, finely chopped
3 to 4 green onions, finely chopped
1 cup finely chopped fresh parsley
⅓ cup lemon juice
1 teaspoon salt
2 teaspoons black pepper
⅓ cup olive oil

Soak wheat in hot water to cover for about 20 minutes or until soft. Drain well. ✐ Toss wheat, lettuce, and next 3 ingredients in a large bowl. Add lemon juice, salt, pepper, and oil, one at a time. Toss well and chill.

[NIM SMITH]

MAMA BRIGHT'S TOMATO ASPIC

Low Fat

SERVES 4 TO 6

24 ounces tomato juice
$\frac{1}{2}$ cup chopped green pepper
1 small onion, chopped
2 stalks celery, chopped
3 drops Tabasco Sauce
1 tablespoon Worcestershire sauce
1 teaspoon salt
$1\frac{1}{2}$ envelopes unflavored gelatin
$\frac{1}{4}$ cup cold water
3 to 4 tablespoons lemon juice
Garnish: homemade mayonnaise

Grease a glass dish or individual gelatin molds. ✒ Combine first 7 ingredients in a medium saucepan over medium heat. Simmer 10 minutes. Pour through a wire-mesh strainer, discarding solids. ✒ Dissolve gelatin in cold water. Add to tomato mixture. Add lemon juice, and stir. Pour into glass dish or molds. Chill until set. ✒ Garnish with homemade mayonnaise, if desired.

[BETTY BLACKMON KINNETT]

Variation: Add sliced green olives or artichoke hearts to salad before congealing.

CRANBERRY SALAD

SERVES 12

1 pint fresh cranberries
1 cup sugar
1 (8-ounce) can pineapple chunks, undrained
Orange or pineapple juice
1 (3-ounce) package cherry or raspberry-flavored gelatin powder
1 envelope unflavored gelatin
4 oranges, peeled, seeded, and chopped
1 cup chopped pecans
Lettuce leaves
Garnishes: mayonnaise, paprika

Finely chop cranberries. Add sugar. Refrigerate $\frac{1}{2}$ hour. ✒ Drain pineapple, reserving juice. Set pineapple aside. Add water or other additional orange or pineapple juice to reserved pineapple juice to equal $1\frac{3}{4}$ cups. ✒ Dissolve gelatins in juice mixture in a medium saucepan over low heat. Pour into a greased 13 x 9 x 2-inch baking dish or gelatin mold. Refrigerate. ✒ When gelatin begins to set, add cranberries, pineapple, oranges, and pecans. ✒ Refrigerate until congealed. Cut into squares or unmold, and serve on crisp lettuce leaves. Garnish with mayonnaise and paprika, if desired.

[BETTS PATTON DRENNEN]

This beautiful salad is a favorite for Thanksgiving and Christmas.

SERVES 12

1 (8-ounce) can crushed
    pineapple, undrained
2 envelopes unflavored gelatin
2 cups cottage cheese, drained
3/4 cup mayonnaise
1 tablespoon sugar
1 cup coarsely chopped walnuts
1 small green pepper, chopped
    except for 1 pepper ring
1 (4-ounce) jar chopped pimien-
    to, drained
1 cup whipping cream, whipped

HOLIDAY MOLD

Drain pineapple, reserving liquid. Set aside 2 tablespoons pineapple. ✒ Dissolve gelatin in reserved liquid. Heat gelatin mixture in saucepan, stirring constantly, until gelatin completely dissolves. ✒ Combine cottage cheese and next 6 ingredients. Stir in pineapple. Pour into a greased 10 x 5 x 3-inch loafpan or gelatin mold. Refrigerate until firm or at least 8 hours. Garnish with pepper ring filled with reserved 2 tablespoons pineapple.

[CAROLYN RITCHEY KING]

SERVES 4

4 ears corn
1 shallot, minced
2 teaspoons finely chopped mixed
    fresh herbs (thyme, parsley,
    chives)
1½ teaspoons fresh lemon juice
1½ teaspoons Sherry vinegar
1½ teaspoons honey
    Salt and pepper
3 tablespoons extra-virgin
    olive oil
2 bunches arugula
½ cup peeled mango, diced

CORN AND ARUGULA SALAD

Pull back husks from corn but do not detach. Remove silk, then rewrap husk around corn. ✒ Cook corn in boiling water 6 minutes; drain. Grill corn about 5 to 6 inches over coals for 8 to 12 minutes, or until husks are lightly charred. ✒ Remove husks and cut corn kernels from cobs. ✒ To prepare vinaigrette, combine shallot and next 5 ingredients. Add oil slowly, whisking until blended. ✒ Toss arugula with vinaigrette. Sprinkle with corn and mango.

[FRANK STITT, CHEF/OWNER]
HIGHLANDS BAR & GRILL

ROQUEFORT DRESSING

Combine all ingredients. Chill at least 24 hours prior to serving.

[CATHERINE SMITH STYSLINGER]

2 cups sour cream

2 cups mayonnaise

3 to 4 ounces Roquefort cheese, crumbled

1 clove garlic, minced

1/2 teaspoon dried chives

2 teaspoons sugar

1 teaspoon salt

1 teaspoon lemon juice

POPPY SEED DRESSING

Combine first 7 ingredients. Stir well. Using mixer, add oil slowly until mixture thickens. Chill.

[LAURA HALSEY WOOD]

MAKES 1 CUP

1/2 cup sugar

1 teaspoon poppy seeds

1 teaspoon salt

1 teaspoon paprika

1 teaspoon dry mustard

1 teaspoon grated onion

4 tablespoons red wine vinegar

1/2 cup vegetable oil

CELERY SEED DRESSING

Place first 6 ingredients in a mixer or blender with 1 tablespoon vinegar. With machine running, slowly add oil and remaining vinegar. Mix until thickened. ✐ This is perfect for a fruit salad. Or try a Greek salad with avocado, grapefruit, and oranges.

[LELLA CLAYTON BROMBERG]
PAST PRESIDENT

MAKES 1 CUP

1 teaspoon celery seeds

1 teaspoon paprika

1 teaspoon salt

1 teaspoon dry mustard

1 teaspoon grated onion

1/3 cup sugar

4 tablespoons cider vinegar, divided

1 cup vegetable oil

MAKES ABOUT
1 1/4 CUPS

1/2 cup sugar

1/4 cup white vinegar

1 tablespoon lemon juice

2 tablespoons finely chopped
 onion

1/3 cup ketchup

1 teaspoon salt

1 teaspoon paprika

1/2 cup vegetable oil

MAKES 1 1/2 CUPS

1 cup vegetable oil

5 tablespoons red wine vinegar

4 tablespoons sour cream

1 1/2 teaspoons salt

1/2 teaspoon dry mustard

2 tablespoons sugar
 Pepper

2 teaspoons chopped, fresh
 parsley

2 cloves garlic, crushed

MAKES 2 CUPS

1 cup mayonnaise

1/2 cup chili sauce

3 tablespoons finely chopped
 fresh parsley

1 tablespoon minced onion

1 tablespoon snipped chives
 Dash of cayenne pepper

1 (3-ounce) bottle capers,
 drained

1/4 cup whipping cream, whipped

BIRMINGHAM'S FAVORITE SLAW DRESSING

Combine first 7 ingredients in electric blender. Blend well. With blender on high, gradually add oil in a slow, steady stream, blending until thick. Chill. Serve over thinly shredded cabbage.

[ANNE STARNES FINCH]

SPINACH SALAD DRESSING

Combine all ingredients. Chill at least 6 hours.

[MARION HUNT NEWTON]

LOUIS DRESSING

Mix all ingredients. Chill. Serve dressing over crabmeat on a bed of shredded lettuce.

[CARL MARTIN HAMES]

BLUE CHEESE VINAIGRETTE

Whisk together mustard, salt, sugar, and vinegar. Whisk in oil. Add blue cheese, and chill.

[PAT SHADOIN WILLIAMSON]

MAKES 1 1/2 CUPS

1 tablespoon Dijon mustard
Pinch of salt
Pinch of sugar
1/3 cup balsamic vinegar
2/3 cup olive oil
4 ounces crumbled blue cheese

BALSAMIC VINAIGRETTE

Combine all ingredients except olive oil in a blender until smooth. While blender is running, pour in oil. The dressing is best if flavors are allowed to mellow for a day or two before serving.

[JANE CAMPBELL ESTES]

MAKES 1 1/2 CUPS

2 tablespoons rice wine vinegar
2 teaspoons Dijon mustard
4 dashes Tabasco Sauce
3 teaspoons sugar
1 teaspoon dried oregano
6 tablespoons balsamic vinegar
5 cloves garlic, peeled
1 teaspoon freshly ground black pepper
1 teaspoon Worcestershire sauce
1 1/2 teaspoons salt
1 cup extra-virgin olive oil

GREEN GODDESS MAYONNAISE

Puree spinach and herbs with 3 tablespoons mayonnaise. Dice shallot and cook in 2 tablespoons wine until all wine is absorbed. Combine spinach mixture, shallot mixture, and remaining 1 cup mayonnaise. Season with garlic, lemon juice, and salt and pepper to taste.

[MARY-CLAYTON ENDERLEIN]

MAKES 2 CUPS

2 1/2 cups loosely packed spinach leaves, blanched
3 tablespoons chopped fresh parsley
1 tablespoon each fresh chervil, tarragon, dill, chives
2 cups mayonnaise, divided
1/2 shallot
2 tablespoons white wine
2 cloves garlic, minced
lemon juice
Salt and pepper

Fettuccine Primavera à la Mer, page 145

The Traveler

-VICKI COVINGTON-

MY FAMILY'S OLD HOMEPLACE is for sale. It's been on the commercial market for years. Someday it will be demolished. That's sad. That's life. After my grandmother died, we were rummaging through a toolshed that stands behind the homeplace. In it were old chests, quilts, trinkets, and documents dating back to 1929.

It was a winter, Saturday morning. Sub-freezing temp. My hands were cold, numb. I was frenzied. Like I'd lost something irreplaceable. I kept digging in a mess of pastel hankies, dusty newspapers, and Christmas lights—miles of them. These were the final items nobody wanted, a collection of family fetish and idiosyncrasy. Who'd save a hundred issues of The Alabama Baptist, empty spools of thread, soap?

I felt like a deranged archaeologist. My hands were dirty. That's always a good sign. I've heard that the reason women like to dig in the dirt is that they're digging for bones. They're digging for their ancestors.

And, sure enough, under a pile of aprons, I at last uncovered the jewel: family recipes. Some were in my grandmother's handwriting, some in her sister's.

It was wonderful. Anybody who's ever eaten dinner with me has had Aunt Weeby's chocolate pie. And here it was, the original. And the squash casserole we had every Christmas Eve. And the Lane cake.

Here I was, standing in the toolshed holding in my hands the recipe for the Lane cake. All those ingredients—coconut, raisins, cherries, pecans, eight egg whites. It must have taken her hours. And I never knew, because you can't know until you're grown, until you're the cook, what went into the preparation of your -CONTINUED-

VICKI COVINGTON

VICKI COVINGTON WAS BORN
AND RAISED IN BIRMINGHAM.
SHE IS THE AUTHOR OF 3
NOVELS: *GATHERING HOME*,
BIRD OF PARADISE, AND *NIGHT
RIDE HOME*. SEVERAL SHORT
WORKS OF FICTION HAVE
APPEARED IN THE NEW
YORKER. HER WEEKLY COLUMN,
"SOUTHERN EXPOSURE"
APPEARS WEEKLY IN THE
BIRMINGHAM NEWS.
SHE IS PRESENTLY UNDER
CONTRACT WITH SIMON &
SCHUSTER FOR A 4TH NOVEL.
MRS. COVINGTON LIVES IN
BIRMINGHAM WITH
HUSBAND DENNIS, ALSO
A NOVELIST AND JOURNALIST,
AND TWO DAUGHTERS.

childhood bliss. It's a Southern thing, this marriage of dying and feeding. All those day-of-the-funeral casseroles, Decoration Day where we clean the graves then have dinner on the grounds, the way we remember friends by their recipes.

My mother has a recipe called Betty Pifer's maid's blueberry pie. Betty Pifer was a neighbor. I didn't know her maid, but I always wonder about her when my mother makes her pie. I have a recipe called Dennis's daddy's Avalon Slade's butterscotch pound cake. Dennis's daddy is dead. Avalon isn't.

Since that day of discovering the recipes, I've been acutely aware of my own recipe box. There is a recipe for bread, called Unadulterated Loaves. It is in the handwriting of my friend, Diane, who died at 41 with ovarian cancer. Her words are precise, printed; and under how many the recipe will serve, she's written, "Multitudes."

I've got a recipe for chess pie, in the handwriting of another friend, Cathy. In 1985, she gave me a baby shower. A year later, she was dead—melanoma, at age 27.

We have one photograph of Cathy. It was taken at a Halloween party. In it, she is dressed as a martian but resembles a funky Peter Pan—green face, tam haircut, and curlicue antennae. We used to tell our daughters, "This is Cathy. She died." I wonder how they interpreted this, in retrospect. Did they think this is how you look once you're gone? She died the day Challenger exploded. So I associate my friend's dying with astronauts and sky and travel.

Three days before my grandmother died, I had a

dream. My grandmother was clutching her black purse, standing in line at a terminal. There were planes, trains, and buses. Hers for the choosing. A mauve light surrounded her. I asked somebody, "Who is she?" and was told that she was The Traveler.

The Traveler's recipes are scribbled in a tiny, blue spiral notebook. Her handwriting was always kind of messy, slanting backwards, with lots of languid commentary: Stir awhile, beat it real good, cook a minute or so, let it set a bit, don't overdo it.

This is the talk of Southerners. It's the inexact science of life. The pinch of salt. The way we give directions: just go up the road a piece. And where's my thingamajig, you know, that do-hicky?

In time, of course, we lose all our thingamajigs and do-hickies. The land, the homeplace, the word, "homeplace." We rummage, as a culture, in the toolshed—where the final remnants of Southern life are tossed. Under it all is simply this: friends of the family, and how they were always wanting to give us the recipe for something good. THE END

THERE IS NO SUBSTITUTE FOR FRESH HERBS in any cuisine. Whether perennials or annuals, most are grown easily in our Southern climate. Where winters are colder, they can be planted in containers for use all year. Try growing and cooking with a few, then experiment with different ones. You will find they enliven and enhance all dishes.

CARE OF FRESH HERBS

Once picked or purchased, use herbs within a day or prepare them for storage. Do not wash herbs before refrigerating. If there are no roots attached, wrap a damp paper towel around the stem ends, pull off wilted or discolored leaves, and place in an airtight plastic bag. If the leaves are very moist, place a dry paper towel in the bag to help absorb excess moisture. Parsley, cilantro, and basil may be placed in a glass with a couple of inches of water. Place a plastic bag over the top as a tent.

Herbs can be dried by hanging, or dried in the microwave. Once dry, cover tightly and store in a cool place.

The flavor of herbs is actually more concentrated in dried than in fresh, so remember when substituting, **1 tablespoon minced fresh herbs equals 1 teaspoon dried.**

"Test and toss" commercial ground herbs often. If they are no longer aromatic, discard them.

HERBS FOR COOKING

BASIL is a very fragrant herb with a mildly spicy-mint flavor. It goes well with tomatoes, vegetables, pasta, salad dressings, and stews. It, like so many herbs, does not with-stand long cooking, so add at the end. Opal basil tastes like the green leaf variety, and lemon basil has a subtle hint of citrus. If you're making pesto, don't worry if some of the stem gets into the food processor; lots of flavor is in the stem.

BAY LEAF is the pungent leaf of the laurel tree. Use it sparingly in soups, stews, jambalaya, and one-dish grain meals. It should be removed immediately after cooking; if left in a dish while cooling or chilling, the bay leaf will impart a bitterly strong flavor.

CHERVIL is not easily found fresh. It is a delicate cousin to parsley and compliments mild vegetable, egg, and rice dishes.

CHIVES have a mild onion/garlic flavor. Stir in cooked dishes at the end of cooking. Sprinkle on potatoes, salads, in soups, or use as a garnish.

CILANTRO is the leaf of the coriander plant, with a distinctive taste that is added to Oriental and Mexican/Spanish dishes.

DILL leaves have a subtle licorice taste and are used in soups and vinaigrettes, with potatoes, cucumbers and fish.

FENNEL has a strong licorice flavor in its leaves and edible bulb. Seeds are used to season sausages and richly flavored meats. Cook the sliced bulb or eat raw as you would celery.

MARJORAM is a mild cousin of oregano, used in Italian dishes, with creamed vegetable soups, poultry, and stuffings.

MINT with its cool refreshing flavor, is used in beverages, jellies, sauces, and desserts. Delicately flavored peas, lettuce and potatoes are enhanced with a small amount of mint.

OREGANO has a more pronounced flavor than marjoram, and is used for foods such as pizza, stews, and full-flavored dishes.

PARSLEY is a mild tasting herb. Curly parsley is most often used as a garnish. Italian flat-leaf parsley has a more pronounced flavor and will enhance the flavor of other herbs in many foods. It has tons of Vitamin A and is a great addition to salads; add by the handful.

ROSEMARY has a pinelike scent that can be overpowering if overused. Crush in the palm of your hand or with a mortar and pestle before adding to richly flavored dishes such as lamb, beef, veal and game. A little bit of cinnamon added to the dish compliments rosemary.

SAGE is a strong herb that can easily dominate a dish. Use with game, poultry, cheese and sausage.

TARRAGON is a sweet herb with an anise-like taste, often used in French cooking to enhance delicate fish, chicken, veal, and egg dishes, as well as sauces.

THYME is popular in strongly flavored stuffings, soups, fish and poultry dishes. Add a little to basil in making pesto, and use in salad dressings with white wine vinegar.

P A S T A S

SERVES 6

Sauce:

8 tablespoons butter, divided
3 cloves garlic, minced
1 ounce Knorr Newburg sauce mix
32 ounces canned crushed tomatoes
1½ tablespoons fresh lemon juice
½ teaspoon dried basil
½ teaspoon pepper
¼ teaspoon dried crushed red pepper
¼ teaspoon dried marjoram
½ pound fresh mushrooms, sliced
1 cup finely chopped green pepper
1 cup finely chopped sweet red pepper
½ cup finely chopped onion

16 ounces angel hair pasta or linguine
1½ pounds medium fresh shrimp, peeled and deveined
Grated Parmesan cheese

SERVES 4 TO 6

1 cup packed fresh basil leaves
½ teaspoon salt
3 tablespoons grated Parmesan cheese
2 tablespoons grated Romano cheese
3 tablespoons pine nuts
2 cloves garlic
½ cup extra-virgin olive oil
1 pound linguine

SHRIMP AND VEGETABLE MARINARA

Melt 6 tablespoons butter in large saucepan over medium heat. Sauté garlic 1 minute. Add sauce mix and next 6 ingredients. Stir well and simmer 10 minutes; set aside. Melt remaining 2 tablespoons butter in large skillet. Sauté vegetables 3 minutes or until crisp-tender. Stir in sauce and simmer 5 additional minutes. Cook pasta according to package directions; set aside. Add shrimp to sauce and cook until shrimp turn pink and mixture is thoroughly heated. Spoon sauce over pasta. Serve with Parmesan cheese.

[LEIGH ANNE PHILIPS]

LINGUINE WITH BASIL SAUCE

Combine basil and salt in food processor. Process until chopped (just a few seconds). Add cheeses and next 3 ingredients. Process until smooth. Cook linguine according to package directions. Drain linguine, reserving 1 tablespoon water. Add reserved water to basil mixture, and process just until blended. Toss basil mixture with linguine.

[DEBORAH FIORAVANTE WHITE]

LINGUINE WITH OLIVADA VINAIGRETTE

Cook linguine according to package directions, and drain; set aside. Combine olives, onion, tomatoes, and zucchini. Place linguine in a large bowl. Spoon olive mixture over pasta. ✒ Whisk together garlic and remaining ingredients. Pour over pasta and toss. Serve warm or cold.

[KATHY G. MEZRANO]
KATHY G'S CATERING

SERVES 6 TO 8

1 pound fresh linguine
1 cup sliced green olives
½ cup sliced or whole ripe olives
1 medium purple onion, finely chopped
1 to 2 tomatoes, chopped, or 1 pint cherry tomatoes
1 medium zucchini, diced

Vinaigrette:
2 cloves garlic, minced
½ teaspoon salt
¼ teaspoon ground black pepper
¼ cup white wine vinegar
1½ teaspoons dried Italian seasoning
⅔ cup olive oil
1 tablespoon Olivada paste

LINGUINE WITH SARDINIAN CLAM SAUCE

Heat oil over medium heat in a large skillet. Sauté garlic and red pepper 1 to 2 minutes. Add chopped tomatoes, olives, oregano, and 1 tablespoon chopped parsley. Cover and cook 3 to 5 minutes or until tomatoes begin to break down. ✒ Add clams in juice, additional clam juice, and wine. Cover. Increase heat to medium-high. ✒ Cook linguine according to package directions and drain. Add linguine to sauce. Toss mixture over high heat 1 minute, allowing pasta to absorb sauce. Top with freshly grated Parmesan cheese, if desired, and sprinkle with remaining parsley.

[SALLY PELTON MATHIS]

SERVES 6

½ cup olive oil
3 cloves garlic, minced
½ teaspoon dried crushed red pepper
1 (28-ounce) can red Italian-style tomatoes, drained and chopped
¼ cup pimiento-stuffed olives, quartered
2 tablespoons chopped fresh oregano, or 1 teaspoon dried
2 tablespoons chopped fresh parsley, divided
2 (10-ounce) cans whole baby clams, undrained
¾ cup bottled clam juice
¼ cup dry white wine
1 pound fresh linguine (can substitute other pastas)
Freshly grated Parmesan cheese (optional)

SERVES 4 TO 6

1 clove garlic, minced

1 medium onion, chopped

2 tablespoons fresh chopped parsley

6 tablespoons olive oil

28 ounces canned whole tomatoes, drained and chopped

6 ounces canned tomato sauce

1½ teaspoon salt

½ teaspoon dried basil

16 ounces cottage cheese

2 cups (8 ounces) grated mozzarella cheese

3 tablespoons grated Cheddar cheese

1 tablespoon chopped fresh parsley

½ teaspoon salt

1 egg, beaten

12 ounces uncooked manicotti noodles

¼ cup grated Cheddar, mozzarella, or Parmesan cheese (optional)

SERVES 6 TO 8

¼ cup olive oil

¾ cup chopped onions

2 cloves garlic, minced

1½ pounds medium shrimp, peeled and deveined

1½ pounds fresh tomatoes, peeled and chopped

1 pound angel hair pasta

½ cup grated fresh Parmesan cheese

8 to 12 fresh basil leaves, julienned

MANICOTTI

Sauté garlic, onion, and parsley in oil 3 to 4 minutes. Add tomatoes, tomato sauce, 1½ teaspoons salt, and dried basil. Simmer sauce 20 minutes. ✍ Combine cottage cheese and next 5 ingredients. Stuff uncooked manicotti noodles with cheese mixture. Place in a greased baking dish. Pour sauce over noodles. ✍ Cover and bake at 400° for 40 minutes. ✍ Sprinkle with additional cheese, if desired, and bake 10 additional minutes.

[ANNE WALTON LILES]

SHRIMP AND ANGEL HAIR PASTA

Heat oil in heavy skillet over medium heat. Add onions and garlic; cook until golden brown, stirring frequently. Reduce heat to low and add shrimp and tomatoes. Cook until almost all liquid evaporates, stirring occasionally. Add basil. ✍ Cook pasta al dente. Drain thoroughly. Add pasta to shrimp mixture, and toss well. Sprinkle liberally with Parmesan cheese. Garnish with fresh chopped basil.

[JAYNE HOCK]
AMSOUTH EXECUTIVE DINING ROOM

FETTUCCINE PRIMAVERA À LA MER

Combine first 4 ingredients of dressing in food processor. Process until smooth. With processor on low, gradually add oil in steady stream. Add sour cream, whipping cream, and parsley. Puree until smooth. Add salt and pepper to taste. Refrigerate until serving. Cook fettuccine. Toss with ⅓ cup olive oil and vinegars. Add salt and pepper to taste. Chill. Steam asparagus, broccoli, and peas until bright and tender. Chill. Poach scallops 2 minutes. Poach shrimp just until pink. Rinse with cold water. Peel shrimp, and devein, if desired. Toss seafood with ⅓ cup olive oil, vinegars, and 1 clove garlic. To serve, arrange spinach leaves around edge of platter. Toss pasta with vegetables, scallions, and seafood. Place on platter and spoon sauce over top. Serve any extra sauce on the side. Serve at room temperature for best flavor.

[ALYSON LUTZ BUTTS]

SERVES 8 TO 10

Basil Cream Dressing:
- ⅓ *cup white wine vinegar*
- ½ *cup tightly packed fresh basil*
- 2 *tablespoons Dijon mustard*
- 2 *cloves garlic*
- ⅓ *cup olive oil*
- 1 *cup sour cream*
- ½ *cup whipping cream*
- 3 *tablespoons minced fresh parsley*
- *Salt and pepper*

Pasta:
- 16 *ounces fettuccine (lemon or basil flavored are excellent)*
- ⅓ *cup olive oil*
- ¼ *cup white wine vinegar*
- 1 *tablespoon sherry wine vinegar*
- *Salt and pepper*
- 16 *asparagus spears, cut into 1½-inch pieces*
- 2 to 3 *cups broccoli florets*
- 2 to 3 *cups fresh green peas or sugar snap peas*
- 2 *pounds bay scallops*
- 2 *pounds unpeeled, medium fresh shrimp*
- ⅓ *cup olive oil*
- 3 *tablespoons white wine vinegar*
- 3 *tablespoons sherry vinegar*
- 1 *clove garlic, minced*
- 1 *pound fresh spinach*
- 6 *scallions*

A N G E L H A I R P A S T A
W I T H S P I N A C H

Sauté pine nuts in olive oil until golden brown. Remove nuts and set aside. In same oil, sauté garlic and red pepper for 1 minute; set aside. Cook pasta according to package directions until tender; drain. Reheat oil containing garlic and peppers; add spinach and sauté until wilted (about 3 minutes). Stir in butter. In large bowl, toss pasta, spinach, pine nuts, and cheese. Add salt and pepper, and serve.

[CAMERON DALEY CROWE]

F R E S H T O M A T O E S
O N F E T T U C C I N E

Toss tomatoes with next 5 ingredients. Add salt and pepper to taste. Cover and leave at room temperature until ready to serve. Cook pasta according to package directions; drain. Serve tomato mixture on fettuccine. Sprinkle with fresh Parmesan.

[MARGARET McKINNON MUSSELMAN]

L I N G U I N E WITH S A U S A G E AND P E P P E R S

Brown sausage in a large skillet; drain. Cut into ½-inch slices. Set aside. Add olive oil to skillet. Sauté garlic, onions, and peppers until soft. Remove from pan.   In same skillet, bring wine and chicken broth to boil. Cook, stirring constantly, until reduced by half. Add sausage and pepper mixture, then fresh oregano. Cook linguine according to package directions; drain. Add linguine to sausage-pepper mixture along with parsley, fresh pepper to taste, and cheeses. Toss well.

[C A R R I E C A I N M c M A H O N]

8 ounces Italian sausage
   (2 to 3 links)
3 tablespoons olive oil
3 cloves garlic, minced
2 medium onions, chopped
2 sweet red peppers, sliced
   into 1-inch pieces
1 green pepper, sliced into
   1-inch pieces
½ cup dry white wine
½ cup chicken broth
2 tablespoons chopped fresh
   oregano
12 ounces linguine
½ cup chopped fresh parsley
   Fresh ground pepper
4 ounces feta cheese, crumbled
⅓ cup grated fresh Parmesan
   cheese

T H R E E - C H E E S E M A C A R O N I

Melt butter in a saucepan over low heat. Add flour, stirring to make white sauce. Add milk gradually, stirring constantly until thickened (about 10 minutes). Remove from heat.   Add cheeses and spices. Stir until cheeses melt. Combine cheese sauce with macaroni. Spoon into a greased 2-quart baking dish. Top with breadcrumbs.   Bake at 350° for 30 minutes.

6 tablespoons butter
4 tablespoons all-purpose flour
2 cups milk
3 cups grated sharp Cheddar
   cheese
⅓ cup grated fresh Parmesan
   cheese
3 tablespoons ricotta cheese
1 teaspoon salt
½ teaspoon dry mustard
¼ teaspoon cayenne pepper
¼ teaspoon ground white pepper
1 pound macaroni, cooked and
   drained
½ cup breadcrumbs

SERVES 8

1/2 pound bacon, chopped
2 1/2 pounds ground beef
6 cloves garlic, minced
2 cups finely chopped onion
1 cup finely chopped green pepper
3 (2-pound, 3-ounce) cans Italian plum tomatoes
3 (6-ounce) cans tomato paste
1 1/2 cups dry red wine, divided
5 teaspoons dried oregano, divided
5 teaspoons dried basil, divided
1 1/2 cups water
1/2 cup chopped fresh parsley
2 teaspoons dried thyme
1 bay leaf
2 tablespoons salt
Freshly ground pepper
Hot cooked spaghettini

SERVES 6

2 to 3 tablespoons butter
2 to 3 tablespoons olive oil
4 cloves garlic, minced
2 large onions, finely chopped
1 medium sweet red or yellow pepper
1 medium green pepper
15 medium to large ripe tomatoes, peeled, seeded, and chopped
20 to 25 fresh basil leaves, shredded
1 teaspoon salt
Freshly ground black pepper

BACON BEEF SPAGHETTINI

Cook bacon in a large skillet until crisp. Drain bacon, reserving drippings. Set drippings and bacon aside. Brown ground beef in same skillet. Add garlic, onion, and green pepper. Cook 10 minutes, adding reserved bacon drippings if needed to moisten. ⚜ Crush tomatoes with spoon. Stir into beef and peppers. Add tomato paste, bacon, 1 cup wine, 4 teaspoons oregano, 4 teaspoons basil, and next 6 ingredients. Bring to a boil. ⚜ Reduce heat and simmer, uncovered, 3 hours, stirring occasionally. Adjust seasonings to taste after 1 hour. Blend in remaining wine, oregano, and basil 15 minutes before serving. ⚜ Serve sauce over hot cooked spaghettini.

[CATHY CRISS ADAMS]

FROM-YOUR-GARDEN PASTA SAUCE

Heat butter and olive oil in saucepan. Sauté garlic, onion, and peppers until translucent (about 10 minutes). Transfer to a large saucepan or Dutch oven. Add tomatoes and basil. Cook over low heat for 1 hour. ⚜ Season to taste.

[BETH OLIVER LEHNER]

B A K E D   V E R M I C E L L I   A N D   S P I N A C H

Sauté mushrooms and green onions in 3 tablespoons butter; set aside. ✒ Make a white sauce by cooking 2 tablespoons butter and flour in a saucepan over low heat. Add milk, juice from mushrooms, and sherry, if desired. Add salt, pepper, basil, and nutmeg. ✒ Cook vermicelli al dente. ✒ Assemble casserole in a lightly greased 8 x 12-inch baking dish. Layer half vermicelli, half mushrooms and onions, half cheese, and all of spinach. Repeat process ending with cheese. Pour white sauce over all. Bake, uncovered, at 350° for 30 minutes.

[S H I R L E Y   A N N E   S T R I N G F E L L O W]

May assemble day ahead.
Bring to room temperature and bake until hot.

1 pound fresh mushrooms, sliced
5 green onions, sliced
5 tablespoons butter, divided
2 tablespoons flour
2 cups milk
2 tablespoons sherry (optional)
1 teaspoon salt
1/8 teaspoon pepper
1/4 teaspoon dried basil
  Dash nutmeg
1 (8-ounce) package vermicelli
2 cups grated mozzarella
2 cups cooked fresh or frozen spinach, drained well

T H E   O N L Y   M A R I N A R A

Sauté garlic in olive oil over medium heat. Drain 2 cans tomatoes; add tomatoes to pan. Add third can of tomatoes (in juice) to pan; crush tomatoes with a spoon. Add oregano, crushed red pepper, and parsley. Add salt and pepper, if desired. ✒ Simmer, uncovered, 15 to 20 minutes.

[R O B E R T   A .   B U R L E S O N]

Try this delightful marinara over an Italian sausage ravioli for
hearty fare or your favorite pasta for a light, quick meal!

2 cloves garlic, minced
1 1/2 tablespoons olive oil
3 (14.5-ounce) cans whole tomatoes, undrained
1 teaspoon dried oregano
1 teaspoon dried crushed red pepper
3 tablespoons chopped fresh parsley or 1 tablespoon dried parsley flakes
Salt and pepper

FRESH VEGETABLE SPAGHETTI SAUCE

Low Fat

Steam or sauté vegetables until crisp-tender. Stir vegetables into tomato sauce. Cook over high heat 5 minutes. Serve over spaghetti.

[CINDY KEENUM BROWN]

SIMPLE TOMATO SAUCE

Low Fat

Heat oil in a large saucepan. Sauté onion until soft, about 7 minutes. Add tomatoes and salt. Cook over medium heat for 20 minutes or until sauce thickens. Pour into a food processor or blender, and puree but do not liquefy. Return puree to heat, and continue cooking until desired consistency. (Thin with white wine or water, if necessary). Remove from heat. Stir in basil and pepper.

[EVELYN BRITTON STUTTS]

PECAN PESTO

Combine first 4 ingredients in food processor. Process until blended. With motor running, add cream, and process until smooth paste forms. Serve pesto over hot cooked pasta.

[DAVID KERN STALLWORTH]

S U N - D R I E D   T O M A T O   S A U C E

Combine first 8 ingredients, stirring well. Add oil, and mix well.
Serve over hot cooked pasta.

[K A T E   G I L M E R   P H I L L I P S]

MAKES 3 CUPS

2 cups chopped and seeded ripe tomatoes
1/2 cup sliced scallions
1/4 cup sun-dried tomatoes packed in oil, drained and chopped
1/4 cup chopped fresh basil
1/4 cup chopped fresh Italian parsley
2 cloves garlic, crushed
1/2 teaspoon salt
1/8 teaspoon ground black pepper
1/2 cup olive oil

M U S H R O O M   P A S T A   S A U C E

Sauté mushrooms in wine; set mushrooms aside. In same skillet, sauté garlic and shallots in butter. Add flour, then slowly add half-and-half. Add salt, pepper, and mushrooms. Add additional half-and-half, if necessary. Serve over hot cooked pasta.

Try shiitake, oyster, Cremini, or morels for a new mushroom sauce.

SERVES 4

1/2 pound fresh mushrooms, diced
1/2 cup white wine
1 clove garlic, minced
2 tablespoons chopped shallots
2 tablespoons butter
2 tablespoons all-purpose flour
3/4 to 1 cup half-and-half
1/4 teaspoon salt
1/8 teaspoon ground white pepper

A L F R E D O   S A U C E

Melt butter over low heat in large saucepan. Add sour cream, and stir to blend. Heat slowly 1 to 2 minutes. Turn heat to medium. Gradually add whipping cream then cheese. Stir in chives, salt, pepper, and nutmeg to taste. Cook, stirring constantly, 3 to 5 additional minutes. Serve immediately over hot pasta.

[C A M I L L E   A D A M S]

SERVES 4 TO 6

6 tablespoons unsalted butter
8 ounces sour cream
1 cup whipping cream
1/2 cup grated fresh Parmesan cheese
2 tablespoons chopped fresh or frozen chives
Salt and pepper
Freshly grated nutmeg

Char-Grilled Vegetables, page 174

Like Corn, Like Me

- LOIS TRIGG CHAPLIN -

LOIS TRIGG CHAPLIN

LOIS LIVES IN BIRMINGHAM, WHERE SHE GARDENS BETWEEN DEADLINES AND CARPOOLS. HER CAREER BEGAN WITH DEGREES IN HORTICULTURE AND ENTOMOLOGY FROM THE UNIVERSITY OF FLORIDA, WHICH LED TO A JOB AS GARDEN EDITOR OF *SOUTHERN LIVING* MAGAZINE. TODAY SHE WRITES BOOKS, MAGAZINE ARTICLES, AND COMMERCIAL COMMUNICATIONS FOR THE GREEN INDUSTRY. LOIS'S TRAINING BEGAN BY FOLLOWING HER FATHER AND UNCLE AROUND THE GARDEN AT AGE SIX WHEN SHE LEFT HER NATIVE HAVANA, CUBA, AND MOVED TO JACKSONVILLE, FLORIDA.

Reprinted from A GARDEN'S BLESSINGS by Lois Trigg Chaplin, copyright c 1993 Lois Trigg Chaplin. Used by permission of Augsburg Fortress.

ON ONE OF MANY OCCASIONS my uncle Raymond and I shucked corn together, he said to me: "You know, Lois, if you count the silks and kernels on that ear, their number will be the same." Well, to a nine-year-old that was tantamount to learning of the sparkle emitted from Wintergreen Life Savers when you bite down on them in a dark closet. Immediately I picked up a new ear of corn and began to dissect it, one tassel at a time.

When you're only nine, it's no easy task to keep up with each tassel and the count in your head, too. Corn silks are very fine and hard to handle, and more than once I had to start over with the pile of silks I carefully laid out on the picnic table. Next I counted kernels, marking each with a poke of my nail as I worked first up and then down the ear. In about two hours I finished (with my uncle's help), and the count, which I don't remember exactly, was so close that I knew he must be right. Suddenly I thought of the many ears of corn I'd shucked or eaten in ignorance of such fabulous knowledge.

Many years later I read in Matthew and Luke where a reassuring Christ told his anxious disciples that even the hairs on their heads were numbered. That line sprang off the page at me. After years of studying biology, zoology, botany, genetics, and other sciences in school, I now have no doubt that every hair in the universe is numbered. Yet the ear of corn from the garden had showed me the same thing long ago. THE END

Ode to Southern Vegetables

- CHARLES GAINES -

Oh vegetables, oh Southern Vegetables,
Arrayed on Heights Cafe Steam Tables -
Long may you live in songs and fables
That celebrate the great cuisines.

Mashed potatoes, corn and butterbeans,
Squash, peas and turnip greens,
Red, green and pinto beans,
Cabbage, okra, green tomatoes fried -

With sweet iced-tea and corn bread on the side,
You link the country club and double-wide
In loud hosannas undenied
Wherever Southern people eat.

Here where barbeque is hard to beat,
And all desserts are extra sweet,
No meal is ever half complete
(Or half as palatable) without you, noble vegetable.

CHARLES GAINES

BEST KNOWN FOR HIS PORTRAYAL OF THE WORLD OF BODY-BUILDING IN THE 1972 NOVEL *STAY HUNGRY*, CHARLES GAINES IS ALSO THE AUTHOR OF THE CRITICALLY ACCLAIMED *A FAMILY PLACE*. IN THAT RECENTLY PUBLISHED NONFICTION BOOK HE RECOUNTS HIS FAMILY'S REDEMPTION THROUGH BUILDING A HOUSE BY HAND IN NOVA SCOTIA. HE IS A GRADUATE OF BIRMINGHAM-SOUTHERN COLLEGE AND LIVES IN NEW HAMPSHIRE AND NOVA SCOTIA WITH HIS WIFE, PATRICIA. THEY HAVE THREE GROWN CHILDREN.

V E G E T A B L E S

SERVES 6

1 pound fresh asparagus, blanched and drained
1 cup chopped cooked chicken
1 ounce dried morels
2 tablespoons brandy or white wine
½ cup grated Swiss cheese
¼ cup grated Parmesan cheese
1 cup sour cream
1 cup chicken broth
2 eggs, beaten
1 teaspoon dried thyme
1 teaspoon dried marjoram
Salt and pepper

ASPARAGUS AND MORELS

Place asparagus in a single layer in a greased 2-quart baking dish. Sprinkle chopped chicken over top. Place morels in a measuring cup with brandy or wine. Cover with plastic wrap, and microwave 2 minutes to rehydrate. When softened, add to casserole, reserving any liquid. Combine cheeses. Add ¼ cup cheese mixture to sour cream. Stir in chicken broth, eggs, thyme, marjoram, and salt and pepper to taste. Pour over casserole, and top with remaining cheese. Bake, uncovered, at 350° for 45 minutes or until bubbly.

[SPENCE LEE STALLWORTH]

SERVES 4

1 pound fresh asparagus
¼ cup olive oil
1 to 2 tablespoons fresh lemon juice
1 clove garlic, minced
2 to 3 tablespoons fresh chopped basil
½ teaspoon dried oregano, crumbled
½ teaspoon salt
Freshly ground pepper
4 tablespoons pine nuts, toasted

ASPARAGUS WITH LEMON HERB SAUCE

Remove ends and any tough scales from asparagus. Cut spears into thirds (bite-size pieces). Steam asparagus until crisp-tender. Drain and rinse with cold water. Whisk together olive oil and next 6 ingredients. Microwave on HIGH 45 seconds. Toss asparagus with olive oil mixture. Arrange on a serving dish; sprinkle with pine nuts. Cool to room temperature, and serve.

[ANSLEY PITTS KRAMER]

B L A C K   B E A N
P H Y L L O   B U R R I T O S

1½ cups dried black beans or
    2 (15-ounce) cans, drained
1 small onion, minced (½ cup)
2 cloves garlic, minced
1 tablespoon chili powder
2 teaspoons paprika
1 teaspoon cumin
    Salt
1 small sweet red pepper,
    seeded and diced
2 teaspoons barbecue sauce
1 cup grated smoked Gouda
    cheese
1 tablespoon chopped jalapeño
    peppers (optional)
16 sheets phyllo dough
½ cup butter or vegetable oil

Soak dried beans overnight. Drain. Put in large pot with just enough water to cover. Cook for 1 to 2 hours, until beans are soft. Drain. Add onion and next 4 ingredients. Cook 15 minutes. Add salt. ✍ Add red pepper, barbecue sauce, grated cheese, and, if desired, chopped jalapeños. Remove from heat and cool. ✍ Lay out one sheet of phyllo with short side facing you. Lightly brush with melted butter. Lay another sheet on top and brush with melted butter. Repeat with 2 more sheets (4 total). ✍ Cut phyllo in half crosswise. Place ⅓ cup bean mixture on bottom of each strip. Roll one-fourth of the way up. Tuck in sides and continue rolling to end. Repeat procedure with remaining phyllo. ✍ Brush burritos with melted butter, and place seam side down on lightly greased baking sheet. ✍ Can make ahead to this point and store, covered, in refrigerator. ✍ Bake at 375° for 15 to 20 minutes or until golden. Serve with salsa or guacamole and sour cream.

[K E L L Y   S C O T T   S T Y S L I N G E R   ]

SERVES 6 TO 8

4 cups water
12 ounces dried black beans
1 chopped green pepper
1 chopped onion
1½ cloves garlic
2 tablespoons olive oil
1 bay leaf
1½ teaspoons dried oregano
1 teaspoon ground cumin
1½ teaspoons salt
½ teaspoon black pepper

BASIC BLACK BEANS

Heat water and beans to boiling in a large Dutch oven. Boil 2 minutes, remove from heat, and let stand for 1 hour. Sauté green pepper, onion, and garlic in oil until tender. Stir into beans. Add more water if needed to cover beans. Stir in seasonings. Cover and simmer until beans are tender, approximately 2 hours.

[ANNE BROYLES PROCTOR]

Wonderful with seafood, especially crab cakes.

SERVES 10

2½ pounds fresh green beans
3 cups water
⅓ cup olive oil
1 cup sliced fresh mushrooms
⅓ cup chopped onions
3 cloves garlic, crushed
1 (8-ounce) can sliced water
    chestnuts, drained
½ teaspoon salt
½ teaspoon freshly ground pepper
½ teaspoon dried basil
½ teaspoon dried Italian
    seasoning
Grated Parmesan cheese

FANTASTIC GREEN BEANS

Wash, trim, and string beans. Break in half. Place in water in large saucepan. Bring to a boil; reduce heat and simmer 6 to 8 minutes or until crisp-tender. Drain. Plunge into ice water to stop cooking process. Set aside. In same saucepan heat oil. Sauté mushrooms and next 7 ingredients until tender. Stir in green beans and cook until thoroughly heated. Sprinkle with grated Parmesan before serving.

[CAROLINE MCDONNELL FARWELL]

G R E E N   B E A N S   W I T H   B A L S A M I C   V I N A I G R E T T E

SERVES 4 TO 6

1 pound fresh green beans
1 tablespoon minced shallots
1½ tablespoons Dijon mustard
1½ tablespoons balsamic vinegar
¼ cup olive oil
½ teaspoon lemon juice
  Salt and pepper
2 tablespoons chopped fresh dill

Cook green beans in boiling salted water until crisp-tender. Drain and keep warm. Combine shallots and next 4 ingredients in small saucepan or microwavable dish. Add salt and pepper to taste. Whisk together. Heat mixture. Pour vinaigrette over green beans and toss to coat. Sprinkle with dill. Serve immediately.

[S H I R L E Y   S Y N D E R   G R E E N   ]

H A R I C O T   V E R T S

SERVES 4

16 ounces slender green beans
½ cup dry white wine
3 tablespoons sugar
3 tablespoons tarragon vinegar
2 tablespoons butter
1 small purple onion, thinly sliced
½ teaspoon salt
  Coarsely ground pepper

Blanch green beans. Set aside. Combine wine, sugar, and vinegar in a medium saucepan. Stir and cook over low heat until sugar melts. Raise heat; add butter and cook 2 to 3 minutes or until butter is melted. (Do not bring to a full boil.) Arrange beans and onions in baking dish. Add salt and pepper to taste. Pour sauce over beans. Cover and bake at 350° for 30 minutes.

SERVES 16

4 pounds brussels sprouts
10 tablespoons unsalted butter
3 medium leeks, cut into
    1/4-inch pieces
6 ounces thinly sliced prosciutto,
    julienned
    Salt and pepper

BRUSSELS SPROUTS WITH PROSCIUTTO

Remove outer leaves from brussels sprouts; cut in half lengthwise. Cook in boiling salted water 5 minutes or just until tender. Rinse in cold water; drain. (These may be prepared 1 day ahead. Wrap in towel, and place in a plastic bag and refrigerate.) Melt butter in a heavy large deep skillet over medium heat. Add leeks and sauté until softened (about 5 minutes). Add brussels sprouts; sauté another 5 minutes. Add prosciutto and toss to combine. Season with salt and pepper to taste.

[REBECCA OLIVER HAINES]

SERVES 4

4 to 6 slices bacon
1 small cabbage, coarsely
    chopped
1 medium onion, coarsely
    chopped
1/3 cup sugar
    Salt and pepper
2/3 cup white vinegar

GERMAN SWEET AND SOUR CABBAGE

Fry bacon until crisp; drain, reserving drippings. Crumble bacon. Place cabbage in a large saucepan; cover with water. Bring to a boil. Reduce heat to medium, and cook 10 to 12 minutes or until crisp-tender. Drain and return to saucepan. While cabbage is hot, stir in onion, sugar, and salt and pepper to taste. Let stand over low heat, tightly covered, for several minutes. Reheat reserved dripping in a small saucepan. Stir in vinegar, and bring to a boil. Pour over cabbage, stir and let stand 2 to 3 minutes. Top with crumbled bacon.

[EMILY HASSINGER MCCALL]

CAULIFLOWER WITH CAPER SAUCE

Wash cauliflower; remove outside leaves. Place whole cauliflower in saucepan with 1 inch water and 1 teaspoon salt. Bring to a boil. Cook, uncovered, 5 minutes. Cover and continue cooking 20 minutes or until tender, turning head once. Drain and measure liquid. (There will be about 1 cup, depending upon diameter of saucepan.) Blend in 1 teaspoon cornstarch for every $1/2$ cup liquid. Add butter, lemon juice, onion, salt, pepper, and turmeric. Cook, stirring often, until sauce has thickened. Add capers and pour over cauliflower head. Garnish with chopped fresh parsley.

[MELANIE DRAKE PARKER]

SERVES 8 TO 10

1 large head cauliflower
1 teaspoon salt
  Cornstarch
3 tablespoons butter
3 teaspoons fresh lemon juice
1 tablespoon grated onion
$1/2$ teaspoon salt
$1/4$ teaspoon black or lemon
  pepper
$1/2$ teaspoon turmeric
2 tablespoons capers
  Chopped fresh parsley

CAULIFLOWER SOUFFLÉ

Wash cauliflower; break into florets. Cook florets covered, in a small amount of boiling water for 10 minutes. Puree in a food processor. Add milk, egg yolks, flour, butter, salt, and pepper. Process until smooth. Beat egg whites until stiff peaks form. Fold egg whites and grated Parmesan into cauliflower mixture. Pour into a buttered $1^{1}/2$-quart soufflé dish. Sprinkle cracker crumbs over top. Bake at 350° for 1 hour.

[LYNN OTEY TUTWILER]

SERVES 6

1 large cauliflower
$1/2$ cup milk
4 eggs, separated
$1/4$ cup all-purpose flour
$1/4$ cup butter, softened
$1/2$ teaspoon seasoned salt
$1/2$ teaspoon pepper
$1/2$ cup grated Parmesan cheese
$1/2$ cup cracker crumbs

C A R R O T S   C O I N T R E A U

Low Fat

SERVES 8

2 pounds carrots, scraped and julienned

3 to 4 cups water

1 tablespoon grated orange rind

$1/4$ cup sugar

$1^1/2$ tablespoon frozen orange juice concentrate, thawed and undiluted

$1/4$ teaspoon salt

2 tablespoons butter

1 tablespoon cornstarch

4 tablespoons Cointreau
Chopped fresh parsley

Cook carrots in 3 to 4 cups boiling water 15 minutes or until tender. Drain carrots, reserving liquid. Set carrots aside. Combine $3/4$ cup carrot liquid, orange rind, sugar, orange juice concentrate, salt, and butter. Bring mixture to a boil; reduce heat, and simmer 5 minutes. Dissolve cornstarch in $1/4$ cup cold carrot liquid, and stir in orange mixture. Add cooked carrots and Cointreau. Garnish with chopped parsley, if desired.

G R E E N   C H I L I   C O R N

SERVES 6

4 (10-ounce) packages frozen shoe peg corn with butter

2 (8-ounce) packages cream cheese, softened

4.5 ounces chopped green chilies

$1/2$ teaspoon garlic salt

Defrost corn in large mixing bowl. Combine cream cheese and green chilies in food processor or beat with an electric mixer until well blended. Stir in garlic salt. Add cream mixture to corn, mixing well. Spoon into a greased 2-quart baking dish. Bake at 350° for 40 to 45 minutes or until golden brown.

[JANN TURNER BLITZ]

CORN CUSTARD

Remove corn kernels from cob by grating. Set aside. ✒ Melt butter in a saucepan over low heat. Stir in flour and salt until smooth. Whisk in milk and egg yolks. Stir in corn. ✒ Beat egg whites until stiff; fold into corn mixture. Pour into a greased round 1-quart baking dish. Place dish in a larger baking pan. Add water to pan to depth of 1 inch. Bake at 350° for 45 minutes or until set and lightly browned.

[ABBIE SEARCY RAU]

SERVES 6

6 ears white corn
2 tablespoons butter
2 tablespoons all-purpose flour
1 teaspoon salt
1 cup milk
3 eggs, separated

FIVE-STAR EGGPLANT

Cut eggplant in half lengthwise. Scoop out pulp, leaving a $1/2$-inch shell. Fill shell with ice water and set aside. ✒ Chop eggplant pulp and mushrooms. Sauté eggplant, mushrooms, and onion in butter 10 minutes. Add seasonings and ham. Drain eggplant shell and pat dry. Stuff shell with mixture. Top with bread crumbs. ✒ Bake at 400° for 25 minutes or until browned.

SERVES 4 TO 6

1 medium eggplant
1 cup fresh mushrooms
$1/2$ cup chopped onion
4 tablespoons butter
$1/4$ teaspoon salt
$1/8$ teaspoon pepper
1 cup minced baked ham
$1/2$ cup buttered fine bread crumbs

SERVES 8

4 cups chopped fresh tomatoes
2 tablespoons chopped fresh basil
1 teaspoon sugar
1 large eggplant, peeled and cubed
2 large onions, sliced
1 cup English peas
2 cups grated Parmesan cheese
1/2 teaspoon salt
1/2 teaspoon dried thyme
1/4 teaspoon pepper
1/2 cup olive oil
1 cup dry bread crumbs
Chopped fresh basil or parsley

EGGPLANT ITALIA

Sprinkle tomatoes with basil and sugar. In a 3-quart baking dish, layer tomatoes, eggplant, onions, and peas. Sprinkle with cheese, salt, thyme, and pepper. Pour olive oil over vegetables. Top with bread crumbs. Bake, covered, at 425° for 2 hours, removing from oven and stirring after 1 hour. Garnish with basil or parsley, if desired.

[AGNES EREGLER]

SERVES 8

2 tablespoons butter
2 large Bermuda onions, sliced into rings
2 cups grated Swiss cheese
1/4 teaspoon pepper
1 cup water
2 beef bouillon cubes
1 (10 1/2-ounce) can cream of chicken soup
2 cups cubed French bread
3 tablespoons butter, melted

ONIONS CELESTIAL

Melt butter in medium skillet; add onion rings, and cover. Cook over low heat 20 to 30 minutes, stirring often. Spoon into shallow 1 1/2-quart baking dish. Sprinkle cheese and pepper evenly over onions. In saucepan, heat water with bouillon cubes until dissolved. Stir in soup. Pour over cheese layer. Swirl to let sauce flow to bottom of dish. Top with bread cubes; drizzle with melted butter. Bake at 350° for 20 to 30 minutes or until lightly browned and bubbly.

[ANNIS IRA DALEY]

VIDALIA ONION PIE

Combine Ritz crackers and ¼ cup melted butter. Press into greased pieplate. Sauté onions in remaining 2 tablespoons butter. Pour into crust. Combine eggs, milk, salt, and pepper; pour over onions. Top with grated Cheddar cheese. Sprinkle with paprika. Bake at 350° for 30 minutes.

[MARTHA DELL STEPHENS STANCIK]

SERVES 6

1 cup crushed Ritz crackers
¼ cup plus 2 tablespoons melted butter, divided
3 cups chopped Vidalia onions
2 eggs
¾ cup milk
½ teaspoon salt
¼ teaspoon pepper
1 cup grated Cheddar cheese
⅛ teaspoon paprika

Just a Thought

*Vidalia onions from Georgia, or Texas "Sweets," are a mild, sweet yellow onion, with a delicate flavor.
To store, place in old nylon pantyhose, tying one knot between each onion. Hang up and cut one off as needed.*

BAKED PEPPERS

Wash and seed peppers. Cut into quarters. Combine olive oil and remaining ingredients, and stuff into pepper quarters. Bake at 450° for 15 minutes.

[PAT McCABE FORMAN]
PAST PRESIDENT

SERVES 6

4 sweet red or yellow peppers
2 tablespoons olive oil
1 cup (8-ounces) goat cheese
⅔ cup sour cream
2 egg yolks
2 teaspoons dried basil
Salt and pepper
Dash of Tabasco Sauce
Dash of Worcestershire sauce

SERVES 8 TO 10

4 cups red potatoes, peeled and
   sliced
1 cup milk
1/2 teaspoon ground nutmeg,
   divided
1/2 teaspoon pepper, divided
   Bouquet garni
1/4 teaspoon salt
1 cup grated Gruyère cheese
1/2 cup whipping cream

FRENCH POTATO GRATIN

Peel and slice potatoes. Rinse under cold water, and pat dry. Place in a Dutch oven; add enough water to cover potatoes. Add milk, 1/4 teaspoon nutmeg, 1/4 teaspoon pepper, and bouquet garni. Boil 15 minutes or until tender. ❧ Combine half of grated Gruyère cheese, cream, remaining nutmeg, 1/4 teaspoon salt, and remaining pepper. Arrange half of the potatoes in a buttered 3-quart baking dish. Spoon cheese mixture over. Arrange another layer of potatoes and top with remaining grated cheese. ❧ Cover and bake at 350° for 30 minutes. Uncover and bake 10 to 15 additional minutes. Allow to stand 5 to 10 minutes before serving.

[LYDIA LONGSHORE SLAUGHTER]

Just a Thought

To make a bouquet garni, simply combine assorted fresh herbs such as parsley, rosemary, thyme, and chives. Tie with a strip of fresh leek or place in cheesecloth and tie with a string.

SERVES 4 TO 6

1 to 2 pounds new potatoes,
   unpeeled
1/4 cup butter
1/2 teaspoon salt
1/4 teaspoon pepper
2 teaspoons lemon juice
1 tablespoon prepared
   horseradish
2 tablespoons chopped fresh
   parsley

NEW POTATOES WITH LEMON HORSERADISH

Peel 1/2 inch strip from around center of each potato. Melt butter in 2-quart baking dish. Add salt, pepper, lemon juice, and horse-radish. Stir in potatoes until well coated with mixture. ❧ Cover and bake at 350° for 1 hour or until potatoes are tender. Garnish with chopped fresh parsley.

[ELISABETH CROW BRANCH]

GARLIC STUFFED POTATO

Rub potatoes with 2 tablespoons olive oil. Bake at 400° for 1 hour or until done. Cut ¼ inch off top of head of garlic. Roast at 275° for 1 hour. Scoop out potato pulp, and reserve potato shells. In large bowl, combine potato pulp, feta, 3 tablespoons olive oil, and roasted garlic pulp. Mix well. Stuff potato shells with mixture. Bake at 350° for 20 minutes; broil until tops are brown.

[MARTIN WALKER JONES]

SERVES 4

2 medium baking potatoes
5 tablespoons olive oil, divided
1 head garlic
1 cup (4-ounces) crumbled feta cheese with tomato and basil

GERMAN POTATOES

Boil potatoes in water to cover, until tender. Drain, peel, and cut into ⅛-inch-thick slices. Arrange in bottom of a greased 2-quart baking dish. Cook bacon until crisp. Drain, reserving drippings, and crumble bacon. Sauté onion in drippings until soft. Stir in flour, sugar, vinegar, salt, pepper and water. Cook 8 to 10 minutes or until sauce thickens. Add celery seeds and parsley. Pour sauce over sliced potatoes. Bake at 350° for 40 minutes or until thoroughly heated.

[MARGARET S. DERRICK]

SERVES 8 TO 10

3 pounds small red potatoes
8 slices bacon
¼ cup minced onion
1 tablespoon all-purpose flour
1 tablespoon plus ½ teaspoon sugar
⅔ cup cider vinegar
½ cup water
  Salt and pepper to taste
½ teaspoon celery seeds
3 tablespoons chopped fresh parsley

SERVES 12

4 pounds sweet potatoes
2 cups fresh cranberries, rinsed
1 cup butter, melted
1 cup pure maple syrup

MAPLE ROASTED SWEET POTATOES AND CRANBERRIES

Peel sweet potatoes. Cut in quarters lengthwise; cut crosswise into ½-inch pieces. Combine sweet potatoes and cranberries in a bowl. In a separate bowl, combine butter and maple syrup. Pour over cranberry mixture, and mix well. Pour into a greased 3-quart baking dish. Cover tightly, and bake at 375° for 30 to 35 minutes or until potatoes are soft.

[EVELYN BRITTON STUTTS]

SERVES 4

2 tablespoons vegetable or olive oil
1 tablespoon butter, melted
2 pounds new potatoes
1½ teaspoons dried rosemary, crushed
½ teaspoon garlic salt
½ teaspoon pepper

ROSEMARY ROASTED POTATOES

Combine oil and butter in a 2-quart roasting pan. Add potatoes; stir to coat. Sprinkle with rosemary, garlic salt, and pepper. Stir well. Bake at 400° for 30 minutes, stirring often, until tender and brown.

[ANNE STARNES FINCH]

SERVES 12

6 large baking potatoes
Vegetable oil
1 cup sour cream
6 tablespoons butter, softened
3 tablespoons milk
4 ounces Gorgonzola cheese, crumbled
1 teaspoon salt

GORGONZOLA POTATOES

Wash potatoes and rub skins with oil. Bake at 450° for 45 minutes. Cut in half. Scoop out potato pulp, leaving potato shells. Mash potato pulp in a large bowl. Add sour cream, butter, milk, and cheese; blend well. Stir in salt. Mound in potato skins. Bake 10 more minutes to heat. (Can make ahead and freeze. Reheat at 350° for 30 minutes.)

[JEAN KINNETT OLIVER]

Mexican Spinach

Sauté onion and garlic in butter 2 to 3 minutes. Add tomato puree, lemon juice, and next 3 ingredients. Simmer 5 more minutes. Add spinach, and stir well. ✍ Pour mixture into a greased 1-quart baking dish. Top with cheese. Bake at 350° for 20 minutes.

[ANNALISA THOMPSON JAGER]

SERVES 6

½ cup chopped onion
1 clove garlic, minced
2 tablespoons butter, melted
2 cups tomato puree
2 tablespoons lemon juice
2 tablespoons chili powder
1 teaspoon salt
⅛ teaspoon pepper
8 ounces frozen chopped spinach, thawed and drained
½ to 1 cup grated Cheddar cheese

Spinach Strudel

Sauté mushrooms, onion, and garlic in butter until tender. Add drained spinach, and cook 2 minutes or until excess moisture is evaporated. Add cream cheese, and stir until well blended. Add salt, pepper, and nutmeg. ✍ Cut equally spaced ½-inch strips along both long edges of pastry, leaving strips attached at the center. Place cooked spinach mixture in center of pastry. Fold pastry strips over spinach mixture forming a Chevron pattern. Combine egg and 2 tablespoons water. Brush egg mixture over pastry. ✍ Bake at 350° for 20 to 30 minutes or until golden.

[SPENCE LEE STALLWORTH]

SERVES 4 TO 6

6 mushrooms, chopped
1 small onion, chopped
1 clove garlic, minced
2 tablespoons butter, melted
2 (10-ounce) packages frozen chopped spinach, thawed and well drained
1 (8-ounce) package cream cheese
½ teaspoon salt
¼ teaspoon pepper
¼ teaspoon ground nutmeg
1 sheet frozen puff pastry, thawed
1 egg
2 tablespoons water

SERVES 6

1 tablespoon olive oil
1/2 teaspoon minced garlic
1/4 cup pine nuts
10 ounces fresh spinach, trimmed
1/2 cup raisins

WILTED SPINACH WITH PINE NUTS

Heat olive oil in wok or large skillet. Sauté garlic and pine nuts 1 to 2 minutes. Add spinach and stir 2 minutes. ✍ Toss with raisins. Serve warm.

[MARTHA ROONEY WALDRUM]

SERVES 4

1 large spaghetti squash
8 slices bacon
1/4 cup butter
1/2 teaspoon salt
1/4 teaspoon pepper
3/4 cup grated Parmesan cheese

SPAGHETTI SQUASH PARMESAN

Score squash 1/2 inch deep in two places. Bake at 350° for 30 minutes. ✍ Fry bacon until crisp. Drain and crumble. ✍ Cut squash in half lengthwise; remove seeds. Scrape meat of the squash with fork tines until it looks like spaghetti. Add salt and pepper. ✍ Dot spaghetti squash with butter. Sprinkle with Parmesan cheese and crumbled bacon. Broil 5 minutes. Remove squash from shells to serve.

[BROOK MORRIS]

For a different presentation, halve the squash, steam, then remove squash from shell, forming a mound or "nest." Top with cheese and bacon.

S Q U A S H
S T U F F E D   W I T H
S W E E T   R E D   P E P P E R

Cut a thin slice from the top of each squash, reserving slices. Chop slices and set aside. ✐ Steam squash and chopped slices in microwave or steamer 5 minutes or until soft. Cool 5 minutes. Scoop out squash, and discard seeds. ✐ Sauté onion in olive oil for 3 to 4 minutes, until clear. Add red pepper. Sauté 3 additional minutes. Remove from heat. ✐ Stir in spinach and cook until wilted. Add chopped squash, and stir well. Add 1 tablespoon Parmesan cheese. Add salt and pepper to taste. ✐ Arrange the hollowed squash shells in a baking dish; sprinkle with remaining Parmesan cheese. ✐ Spoon vegetable mixture into squash shells. Bake at 375° for 5 minutes.

[A N N E   T H I E L E   B L A C K E R B Y]

SERVES 4

4 medium-size yellow squash
1/2 cup chopped sweet onion
2 tablespoons olive oil
1/3 cup finely diced sweet red pepper
1 cup chopped fresh spinach
2 tablespoons grated fresh Parmesan cheese, divided
Salt and pepper

T O M A T O E S   R O A S T E D
W I T H   S P I N A C H   A N D
R O M A N O

Melt butter in large saucepan. Sauté onion in butter 3 minutes or until tender. Add spinach, and sauté 3 minutes. Add salt and pepper to taste. ✐ Remove tops from tomatoes. Scoop out half of the flesh from each. Fill each with spinach mixture. Top with grated Romano cheese. ✐ Bake at 375° for 20 minutes.

[A L I S O N   B E R R Y]

SERVES 4

1/4 cup butter
1 medium onion, finely chopped
1/2 to 3/4 pound fresh spinach, trimmed
1/2 teaspoon salt
Freshly ground pepper
4 medium tomatoes
2/3 cup freshly grated Romano or pecorino cheese

BALSAMIC GRILLED TOMATOES

Cut tomatoes in half. Combine vinegar and remaining ingredients. Marinate tomatoes in half of vinegar mixture for 1 hour. Drain tomatoes. ✍ Grill over medium heat for 15 minutes or until done. Toss with remaining vinegar mixture, and serve.

[CHEF SCOTT BERG]
VINCENT'S MARKET

This would also work well with a variety of colorful sweet peppers, tossed with eggplant.

SERVES 10

20 Roma tomatoes
1 cup balsamic vinegar
2 cups olive oil
2 tablespoons minced garlic
1/4 cup chopped fresh basil
2 tablespoons kosher salt
2 tablespoons freshly
  ground pepper

ZUCCHINI BOATS

Remove top one-third of zucchini. Scoop out pulp, leaving hollow shells; chop pulp and set aside. ✍ In a large frying pan sauté onion, peppers, and garlic in butter or oil. Add zucchini pulp, salt, and pepper. Cook 5 minutes. ✍ Stuff zucchini shells with mixture. Combine Parmesan cheese and breadcrumbs. Sprinkle over mixture. Add crumbled bacon, if desired. ✍ Bake at 350° for 30 to 40 minutes.

SERVES 6

6 medium zucchini
1 cup chopped onion
1 medium sweet red pepper,
  chopped
2 cloves garlic, minced
2 tablespoons butter or oil
1/2 teaspoon salt
1/4 teaspoon pepper
3 tablespoons grated Parmesan
  cheese
1/4 cup dry breadcrumbs
3 slices bacon, cooked and
  crumbled (optional)

S O U T H E R N   S U C C O T A S H

SERVES 4 TO 6

Cook bacon in a large skillet until crisp. Remove bacon, and add corn and next 8 ingredients into skillet with bacon drippings. Stir well, and cook over low heat 30 minutes or until vegetables are cooked. Adjust spices to taste. Add water, if needed. Stir often. To serve, crumble bacon over top.

[D O R O T H Y   D E R A M U S   B O Y D   ]
P A S T   P R E S I D E N T

3 slices bacon
2 cups fresh corn kernels
2 cups sliced fresh okra
4 medium tomatoes, peeled and chopped
1 medium sweet onion, chopped
1/2 teaspoon salt
1/4 teaspoon celery salt
1/4 teaspoon garlic salt
1/4 teaspoon dried oregano
1/8 teaspoon pepper
1/4 cup water (optional)

R A G O U T   O F   V E G E T A B L E S

SERVES 6

Coat a 2-quart baking dish with 1 tablespoon olive oil. Add potatoes and next 7 ingredients in order listed. Season each layer with salt and pepper to taste. Combine oil, chicken broth, and garlic. Pour over vegetables. Cover baking dish, and cook at 325° for 1 hour. Remove vegetables to a warm platter. Sprinkle with chopped fresh parsley.

[E V E L Y N   B R I T T O N   S T U T T S   ]

1 tablespoon olive oil
2 baking potatoes, peeled and cubed
2 medium onions, sliced
1 eggplant, sliced
1 red or yellow pepper, seeded and cubed
1 stalk celery, sliced
2 carrots, scraped and sliced
4 Roma tomatoes, sliced
2 tablespoons green peas
Salt and pepper
1/3 cup olive oil
1/2 cup chicken broth
2 cloves garlic, minced
2 tablespoons chopped fresh parsley

SERVES 8 TO 10

2 medium zucchini
2 medium yellow squash
1 eggplant
2 medium tomatoes
2 medium sweet red peppers
1 sweet yellow pepper
1 green pepper
1 small purple onion
1 pound mushrooms
1 stalk leeks
3/4 cup balsamic vinegar
3/4 cup honey
3/4 cup vegetable oil
1 tablespoon salt
1 teaspoon pepper
1/4 cup chopped fresh basil

CHAR-GRILLED VEGETABLES

Low Fat

Cut zucchini, squash, and eggplant in half lengthwise. Cut tomatoes into thick slices. Quarter peppers. Slice purple onion. Leave mushrooms whole. Cut leeks in half. Combine vinegar and next 4 ingredients. Pour over vegetables. Chill 2 hours. Grill vegetables over low heat on skewers or in a grill basket. Toss with basil. Adjust seasonings to taste.

[CHEF SCOTT BERG]
VINCENT'S MARKET

SERVES 6

1 quart milk
1 teaspoon salt
1 cup regular grits
8 tablespoons butter, divided
1/4 teaspoon ground white pepper
1 cup grated mozzarella cheese

BAKED GRITS WITH MOZZARELLA

Heat milk over medium-high heat in a large heavy saucepan. Bring to a boil. Add salt and gradually add grits, stirring constantly. Reduce heat to low. Add 6 tablespoons butter, and cook slowly for 10 minutes. Pour into a large mixing bowl, stir in white pepper, and beat at low speed for 5 minutes. Grease a 2-quart casserole with 2 tablespoons melted butter; pour grits into casserole. Set aside until cool and firm. (Do not refrigerate.) Before baking, sprinkle cheese over grits. Bake at 350° for 30 minutes.

[JANN TURNER BLITZ]

POLENTA WITH FRESH HERBS

Combine 1 quart milk and sea salt in large saucepan over medium-high heat. Bring to a boil, slowly adding cornmeal and whisking often. (If mixture is too thick, add additional milk.) Reduce heat, and simmer 25 minutes. ✸ Remove from heat; add butter and herbs. Pour into a 15 x 10 x 2-inch baking dish. Cool until firm. ✸ Cut into 4-inch squares, and cut in half diagonally. To serve, sprinkle with grated Parmesan. Broil until golden. Garnish with chopped fresh herbs.

[CAMERON DALEY CROWE]

SERVES 12

1 to 1 1/2 quarts milk
1/2 teaspoon sea salt
1 1/2 cups yellow cornmeal
1/3 cup butter
1/4 to 1/2 cup combined fresh herbs (thyme, oregano, parsley) plus chopped fresh herbs
1/3 cup grated Parmesan cheese

FRUITED RICE MIX

Combine all ingredients. Store in airtight container until needed (up to 2 months). ✸ To prepare, combine 1 cup rice mix with 2 cups water and 2 tablespoons butter or margarine. Place in saucepan; bring to a boil. Reduce heat, cover, and simmer for 25 to 30 minutes or until all water is absorbed. ✸ Makes 5 cups dry mix. (Each cup makes 4 to 6 servings.)

[MARCIE GROVER MATTE]

4 SERVINGS

3 cups uncooked long-grain rice
1 cup chopped dried apples
1/3 cup golden raisins
1/3 cup slivered almonds
1/4 cup instant chicken bouillon granules
3 tablespoons dried minced onion
4 1/2 teaspoons curry powder

Just a Thought

Fill mason jars with Fruited Rice Mix and tie with a festive bow—makes a great gift!

SERVES 6

1 cup uncooked couscous
Chicken broth
1 small purple onion, finely
chopped
1 small green pepper, finely
chopped
2 ounces ripe olives, sliced
(optional)
3 tablespoons pine nuts
(optional)
1/3 cup red wine vinegar
1/4 cup olive oil

ROSS'S COUSCOUS

Prepare couscous according to package directions, substituting chicken broth for water. Add chopped vegetables. Cover and let stand 5 minutes. Stir in pine nuts, if desired, vinegar, and oil.

[ELLISON JONES GRAY]

For a variation, use green onion, red pepper, and Roma tomatoes. This is a nice accompaniment to any simple meat dinner.

SERVES 4

1 tablespoon butter
1 medium onion, chopped
1 clove garlic, minced
1 cup chicken broth
1 cup uncooked rice
1 cup dry white wine
1/2 cup grated Parmesan cheese

PARMESAN WINE RICE

Melt butter in heavy medium skillet over medium heat. Add onion and garlic; cook 8 minutes or until translucent. Stir in broth, rice, and wine. Bring to a boil. Reduce heat to low; cover and cook 25 minutes or until liquid is absorbed. Stir in grated Parmesan, and serve warm.

[CATHY CRISS ADAMS]

A R M E N I A N   R I C E

Sauté garlic in butter in a large skillet over medium-low heat. Remove garlic and add vermicelli. Stir and cook until dark brown being careful not to burn. 🌾 In greased 2-quart baking dish, spread rice, vermicelli mixture, green pepper, and next 3 ingredients. Pour chicken broth over all. Season with salt to taste. 🌾 Cover with foil, and bake at 350° for 1 hour or until rice in center is done. (May bake ahead and reheat next day with additional ¼ cup broth, covered, at 325° for 30 minutes.)

[SHIRLEY ANNE STRINGFELLOW]

SERVES 10 TO 12

2 to 4 cloves garlic, minced
8 tablespoons butter
1 cup 1-inch vermicelli pieces
1 cup uncooked white rice
1 green pepper, chopped
1 (8-ounce) can sliced water chestnuts, drained
1 (2½-ounce) can sliced ripe olives, drained
1 (4-ounce) can chopped mushrooms, drained
2 cups chicken broth
Salt

B A R L E Y   C A S S E R O L E

In a large skillet, sauté onions and mushrooms in butter until tender. Add barley, and cook until lightly browned. 🌾 Place mixture into a greased 2-quart casserole dish. Add pimientos and chicken broth; salt and pepper to taste. 🌾 Cover tightly and bake at 350° for 50 to 60 minutes. 🌾 Great with wild game or other meat, as alternative to rice.

[KELLY PRIDE HARGROVE]

SERVES 8

½ cup butter
2 medium onions, coarsely chopped
¾ pounds fresh mushrooms, sliced
1½ cups barley
3 pimientos, coarsely chopped
2 cups chicken broth
Salt and pepper

A BASIC STUFFING

SERVES 4

1/2 cup fine dry breadcrumbs
1/4 cup olive oil
3 tablespoons chopped green
   onions
1 clove garlic, minced
1/4 teaspoon dried thyme
1/4 teaspoon salt
1/4 teaspoon sugar
   Juice of 1 lemon
1 teaspoon Worcestershire
   sauce
3 tablespoons fresh parsley

Combine first 10 ingredients, mixing well. Mound stuffing into hollowed-out tomatoes, squash, or sweet peppers; or use for stuffing snapper or Cornish hens. In dish, bake at 325° for 1 hour. Sprinkle chopped fresh parsley on top before serving.

[MELANIE DRAKE PARKER]

CHESTNUT-PISTACHIO STUFFING

SERVES 8 TO 10

1/2 pound fresh chestnuts
1 cup pistachio nuts, unshelled
1 1/2 pounds ground pork sausage
1 cup chopped onion
1/2 cup chopped celery
1 clove garlic, minced
6 cups dry white bread, cubed
1/4 cup chopped fresh parsley
1 1/2 teaspoons poultry seasoning
1/2 teaspoon dried thyme, crushed
1/4 teaspoon pepper
1 to 1 1/4 cups half-and-half

Score chestnuts and roast at 400° for 15 minutes. Shell and coarsely chop chestnuts and pistachio nuts. Brown sausage; drain and reserve 1 tablespoon drippings. In same skillet, cook onion, celery and garlic in drippings until tender. Combine nuts, sausage, onion mixture, bread cubes, parsley, and seasonings. Toss until well blended. Drizzle with half-and-half until mixture holds together. Pack into a 1 1/2 to 2-quart baking dish. Bake, covered, at 325° for 1 hour, adding half-and-half as necessary to moisten.

[DOUG RICHEY]

ROASTED CHESTNUTS

MAKE 2 TO 3 CUPS

Score chestnuts with cross on flat side. Place in a single layer on baking sheet. ✒ Roast at 325° for 1 hour. Shell and remove inner brown skin. Toss with butter and salt, if desired.

2 pounds unshelled chestnuts
¼ cup melted butter (optional)
1 teaspoon salt (optional)

BLUE CHEESE SOUFFLÉS

SERVES 8

Grease 8 (6-ounce) ramekins, and sprinkle evenly with 3 table-spoons Parmesan. ✒ Melt butter over low heat; add flour, and stir 2 minutes. Add milk gradually, whisking until smooth. Add pepper. Remove from heat, and add crumbled blue cheese and ¼ cup Parmesan. Stir until smooth. Cool 10 minutes. ✒ Stir 4 egg yolks in a large bowl, and add several tablespoons of warm cheese mixture. Stir until blended. Fold in remaining cheese mixture. Stir in fresh herbs. ✒ Beat egg whites with salt until stiff peaks form. Stir one-third of beaten whites into cheese mixture; gently fold in remaining whites. ✒ Fill ramekins three-fourths full and place in a large baking dish. Pour boiling water into pan, filling to halfway up sides of ramekins. ✒ Bake at 350° for 15 to 20 minutes or until soufflés rise and are slightly brown. Serve immediately.

[DEEDEE TOMKINS BLOOM]

Cheese mixture may be made a day ahead.
Add egg yolks and beaten whites before baking.

3 tablespoons Parmesan cheese
2 tablespoons unsalted butter
3 tablespoons all-purpose flour
⅔ cup milk
¼ teaspoon ground pepper
8 ounces blue cheese, crumbled
¼ cup grated Parmesan cheese
4 large eggs, separated
2½ tablespoons chopped mixed fresh herbs (thyme, parsley, chives)
Pinch of salt

SERVES 4

2 eggs, beaten
3/4 cup whipping cream
1/2 teaspoon salt
1/8 teaspoon ground nutmeg
1/8 teaspoon cayenne pepper
1/2 teaspoon pepper
2 tablespoons chopped fresh
  flat-leaf parsley
1/4 cup chopped fresh basil
3/4 cup goat cheese (plain or herb)
1/2 cup freshly grated Parmesan
  cheese
Garnish: freshly grated
  nutmeg or chopped fresh
  parsley

SAVORY FLAN

Combine eggs and cream in bowl. Add salt and next 7 ingredients, stirring to combine. ✍ Pour into 4 greased individual soufflé dishes. Place dishes in shallow pan; pour water in pan so that it comes halfway up sides of soufflé dishes. ✍ Bake at 400° for 20 minutes or until set and lightly browned. ✍ Garnish each with freshly grated nutmeg or chopped fresh parsley, if desired.

[ALYSON LUTZ BUTTS]

SERVES 4 TO 6

1/4 pound of bacon, diced
1 medium onion, julienned
1 serrano pepper, diced
1 clove garlic, minced
1 1/2 pound kale, julienned
  Pinch of sugar
1 cup chicken stock
  Salt and pepper
  Whole okra, cooked

KENYA GREENS

Cook diced bacon in a large skillet. Remove bacon, reserving drippings; drain. ✍ Add onion, serrano pepper, and garlic to pan drippings. Cook 1 minute. Add kale and sugar. Cook down, adding chicken stock as needed. Salt and pepper to taste. Garnish with cooked whole okra and crisp bacon.

[CHEF CLAYTON SHERROD]

APRICOT CASSEROLE

SERVES 6

Layer half of apricots in a greased 2-quart baking dish. Combine crackers, sugar, cinnamon. Sprinkle half of sugar mixture over apricots. Repeat layers. ✍ Pour melted butter over top. Bake at 350° for 30 minutes.

[J A N E   C R O W]

3 (16-ounce) cans apricot halves, well-drained
20 to 30 Ritz Crackers, crushed
1½ cups firmly packed brown sugar
1 teaspoon ground cinnamon
½ cup butter, melted

AUTUMN VEGETABLE PUREE

SERVES 3 TO 4

Rub vegetables with olive oil. Place in a large roasting pan and sprinkle with thyme. Roast at 425° until vegetables are tender, removing smaller vegetables as they are done. (Squash will require longest roasting time, 1 to 1½ hours.) ✍ Peel vegetables; puree in food processor with butter; add salt and pepper to taste. Serve immediately.

[F R A N K   S T I T T , C H E F / O W N E R]
B O T T E G A   I T A L I A N   R E S T A U R A N T

This may be prepared in advance.
Reheat in a large saucepan over low heat,
adding additional butter if necessary, and stirring often.

2 parsnips, scraped
2 carrots, scraped
1 rutabaga
1 butternut squash
2 sweet potatoes
¼ cup olive oil
2 tablespoons fresh thyme, crumbled
3 tablespoons butter (or more)
Salt and pepper

Garlic Roasted Chicken, page 192

A Chicken in Every Yard

BY PAUL HEMPHILL

NOWADAYS, OF COURSE, HOMEMAKERS under a certain age hardly know what a real live chicken looks like. They go to the grocery store and head for the Poultry Section and pick over the array of selections neatly wrapped in cellophane–Chicken Strips, Boneless Chicken Breasts, Drumsticks, Miscellaneous Chicken Parts–all of them neatly mass-produced at the "poultry plants," the horrors of which humans are spared. Then they take them home and drag them through some flour and drop them in oil and announce that fried chicken is on the table.

This was not so during the hard times of the Depression and Second World War when many folks in the blue-collar neighborhoods of Birmingham had little vegetable gardens in the backyard and, in the case of my Aunt and Uncle Lacey in East Lake, a goat for milk and some chickens for meat and eggs.

My cousin Jim and I had some times with those chickens, I tell you. "Shoot, you can't hypnotize no chicken," I said to him one day. He lured the rooster, Henry, with a palmful of corn kernels, grabbed him with both hands, forced his beak into the hard-scrabble dirt, and directed me to slowly scratch a line in the dirt away from Henry's beak. When I had drawn the line about three feet, Jim slowly took his hands off of the bird and–lo–Henry squatted, motionless and transfixed, until the spell was broken by the backfiring of a car.

In retrospect, I can say Jim and I probably gave those chickens what little joy ever came into their brief lives. Because in the late afternoon, my sweet Aunt Ethel would come out into the yard with the cold smile of an ·CONTINUED·

PAUL HEMPHILL

AUTHOR OF THE ACCLAIMED
1993 MEMOIR, *LEAVING
BIRMINGHAM*, PAUL HEMPHILL
HAS DISTINGUISHED HIMSELF
AS A WRITER FOR NEWSPAPERS
AND MAGAZINES, INCLUDING
THE NEW YORK TIMES MAGAZINE
AND AS AN AUTHOR OF
SEVERAL BOOKS: *THE
NASHVILLE SOUND, MAYOR:
NOTES ON THE SIXTIES, THE
GOOD OLD BOYS, LONG GONE,
TOO OLD TO CRY, THE
SIXKILLER CHRONICLES,
ME AND THE BOY,*
AND *KING OF THE ROAD.*
A BIRMINGHAM NATIVE, HE
NOW LIVES IN ATLANTA WITH
HIS WIFE, SUSAN PERCY,
SENIOR EDITOR OF *ATLANTA
MAGAZINE.* HE IS THE FATHER
OF FOUR CHILDREN.

assassin on her face, a hank of twine in one hand and a huge gleaming cleaver in the pocket of her apron. Clucking serenely, she would pounce on a plump unsuspecting hen, grab her by the neck, throw her to the ground, and wrap the twine around her legs four times. It was like a rodeo cowboy roping a dogie. Then Aunt Ethel would tie the twine to the clothesline, stretch the chicken by its beak, fish the cleaver from her apron and zip briskly. Two hours later we were eating fried chicken.

But, hey, that was fairly humane compared to the technique used by Louvenia. She was our maid, a couple of years later when we had moved to Woodlawn. We didn't keep chickens in the yard, like the Laceys, but bought ours from a truck farmer named Mister Amberson. No cleaver for Louvenia. She would go out to the truck and pick a chicken and haul her straight to the backyard, without any ceremony, then grab the chicken firmly by the neck and begin twirling her in the air until the neck was in Louvenia's hand and the body was flopping all over the yard in a silent dance of death. "Go get her, Paul Jr.," she would say. "I'm 'on fry you up some chicken." THE END

POULTRY

H O N E Y   R U M   C H I C K E N

S E R V E S   4

1 carrot, diced
2 onions, diced
1 stalk celery, diced
4 tablespoons butter
1 (3¹/2-pound) broiler-fryer,
  or 3¹/2-pounds chicken pieces
¹/2 cup honey
¹/4 to ¹/2 cup dark rum
1 tablespoon paprika
1¹/2 teaspoons salt

Sauté carrot, onion, and celery in butter. Place chicken in a shallow baking dish, and top with vegetables. Combine honey, rum, paprika, and salt, and pour over chicken. Bake at 350° for 1 hour and 15 minutes, turning chicken and basting with sauce every 20 minutes.

[K A T E   G I L M E R   P H I L L I P S   ]

C H I C K E N   I N   R I E S L I N G

S E R V E S   6   T O   8

2 (2 to 3-pound) broiler-fryers,
  quartered
Salt and ground white pepper
6 tablespoons butter
2 tablespoons vegetable oil
2 tablespoons finely
  chopped shallots
¹/4 cup brandy, warm
¹/4 pound mushrooms,
  thinly sliced
1 cup Riesling wine
¹/3 cup whipping cream
2 tablespoons all-purpose flour
Hot cooked noodles or rice

Sprinkle chicken with salt and white pepper to taste. In a large skillet, sauté chicken quarters, skin side down in butter and oil for 2 to 3 minutes on each side. Add shallots, and cook 2 minutes. Add heated brandy and ignite. Shake until flames go out. Add mushrooms and Riesling wine. Cover and cook over medium heat 20 to 25 minutes or until tender. Transfer chicken to serving platter and keep warm. Skim fat from juices. Combine cream and flour, and add to pan juices. Cook, stirring constantly, until thick and smooth. Add salt and white pepper to taste, and pour sauce over chicken. Serve with noodles or rice.

[A N N E   S T A R N E S   F I N C H   ]

CHICKEN PROVENÇAL

SERVES 6 TO 8

Cut chicken into large pieces. Combine flour, tarragon, thyme, salt, and pepper. Add chicken pieces and shake to coat on all sides. ✍ In a large skillet, heat 1 tablespoon butter and 1 tablespoon olive oil. Add half the chicken, and cook until lightly browned. Remove to a baking dish. Heat remaining butter and olive oil, and brown remaining chicken. Add to baking dish. ✍ Sauté garlic briefly in skillet. Add wine to skillet to deglaze. Add tomatoes, mushrooms, and olives to garlic, and stir gently to combine. Pour tomato mixture over chicken. ✍ Cover and bake at 350° for 45 minutes to 1 hour. ✍ Garnish with chopped parsley and serve with hot cooked rice.

[MARY BARNUM COLGIN]

6 boneless, skinless chicken breast halves
½ cup all-purpose flour
1 teaspoon dried tarragon, crushed
½ teaspoon dried thyme, crushed
½ teaspoon salt
½ teaspoon ground white pepper
2 tablespoons butter, divided
4 tablespoons olive oil, divided
2 cloves garlic, minced
½ cup dry white wine
1 (28-ounce) can Italian plum tomatoes, undrained and chopped
½ pound mushrooms, quartered
1 (4-ounce) can ripe olives, drained
Chopped fresh parsley
4 cups hot, cooked rice

ROSEMARY CHICKEN

SERVES 6

Combine first 6 ingredients. Pour over chicken and marinate overnight. Drain, reserving marinade. ✍ Arrange chicken on an aluminum foil-lined baking pan. Bake at 325° for 45 minutes.

[LOUISE OBERMEYER]

May serve hot or cold on a sandwich bun.

4 tablespoons lemon juice
¾ cup olive oil
½ cup white wine
1½ teaspoons pepper
1½ teaspoons rosemary
2 cloves garlic, minced
6 boneless, skinless chicken breasts

SERVES 4

4 cups self-rising flour, divided
2 cups buttermilk
1 teaspoon salt
  Pepper
4 boneless, skinless chicken
  breast halves
  Shortening

Sauce:
1/2 cup white wine
1/2 cup whipping cream
  Salt and ground white pepper
4 fresh basil leaves, sliced
4 tablespoons butter, melted
  Juice of 1/4 lemon

BUTTERMILK FRIED CHICKEN

Combine 2 cups flour and buttermilk. Stir until paste-like consistency. ✒ In a paper bag, combine remaining flour, salt, and pepper to taste. ✒ Shake chicken in flour mixture, then dredge in buttermilk mixture, and shake in flour mixture again. ✒ Heat shortening in iron skillet to 350°. Fry chicken approximately 20 to 25 minutes or until golden brown. ✒ Sauce: Heat wine in a small saucepan until it's reduced by two-thirds. Add cream and boil for 20 seconds. Simmer 2 minutes. Remove from heat. ✒ Add salt and white pepper to taste, and stir in basil. Add butter slowly, whisking constantly. Stir in lemon juice. Serve sauce over each chicken.

[CHRIS DuPONT]
CAFÉ DuPONT

SERVES 4

3/4 cup butter, melted and
  divided
1/2 cup fine dry breadcrumbs
2 tablespoons grated Parmesan
  cheese
1 teaspoon dried basil
1 teaspoon dried oregano
1/2 teaspoon garlic salt
1/4 teaspoon salt
4 boneless, skinless chicken
  breast halves
1/4 cup dry white wine
1/4 cup chopped green onion
1/4 cup chopped fresh parsley

CHICKEN KIEV WITH PARSLEY WINE BUTTER

Pour 1/4 cup butter in large bowl. Combine breadcrumbs and next 5 ingredients. Dip chicken breasts in melted butter, then coat with crumb mixture. ✒ Place chicken in an ungreased 2-quart baking dish. Bake at 375° for 50 to 60 minutes or until chicken is tender. Add wine, green onions, and parsley to remaining 1/2 cup butter. When chicken is golden brown, pour butter sauce over. Continue baking for 3 to 5 more minutes.

[KATHERINE LIVINGSTON ARD]

CHICKEN BREASTS WITH LIME BEURRE BLANC

Pat chicken breasts dry. Season with salt and pepper to taste. Heat oil. Cook chicken in oil 4 to 5 minutes or until lightly browned. Cover chicken, reduce heat, and cook 10 more minutes or until tender. Remove chicken to a warm platter. Drain oil and discard. In same skillet, add lime juice, and cook over low heat until juice begins to boil. Scrape sides of skillet to loosen browned particles. Add butter, stirring constantly until butter melts and sauce begins to thicken. Stir in chives and dillweed. Spoon sauce over chicken. Serve immediately.

[CINDY COMPTON TAYLOR]

SERVES 6

6 boneless, skinless chicken
    breast halves
  Salt and pepper
1/3 cup vegetable oil
  Juice of two limes
1/2 cup butter (no substitutes),
    softened
  1 teaspoon chopped fresh chives
  1 teaspoon fresh dillweed

CHICKEN CILANTRO

Sauté onion and garlic in oil and butter until onion is translucent. Add chicken, salt, and pepper; cook over medium heat about 20 minutes or until done. Stir in tomatoes and cilantro. Cook 1 more minute, and serve. Garnish with lemon slices, if desired.

[JANE CAMPBELL ESTES]

SERVES 6

1/2 cup chopped onion
  1 clove garlic, minced
  2 tablespoons vegetable oil
  2 tablespoons butter
  6 skinless, boneless chicken
    breast halves, quartered
  1 teaspoon salt
1/4 teaspoon pepper
  2 medium tomatoes, chopped
  2 tablespoons chopped fresh
    cilantro
  Lemon slices

Y O G U R T   C H I C K E N   *Low Fat*

SERVES 6 TO 8

1½ cups plain yogurt or light
    sour cream
¼ cup lemon juice
1 teaspoon onion salt
1 teaspoon paprika
1 teaspoon celery salt
1 teaspoon Worcestershire sauce
1 (16-ounce) package herb
    stuffing mix
8 skinless, boneless chicken
    breast halves
    Vegetable cooking spray
    Liquid Butter Buds
    (optional)

Combine yogurt and next 5 ingredients. Marinate chicken breasts in yogurt mixture overnight or at least 4 hours. ✎ Remove chicken and coat with herb stuffing mix. Place in shallow baking dish that has been sprayed with a nonstick cooking spray. Bake at 350° for 40 minutes. Just prior to serving, drizzle each piece of chicken with liquid Butter Buds, if desired.

[B E R N A D I N E   R U S H I N G   F A U L K N E R]

C H I C K E N   C R E M I N I

SERVES 6

6 skinless, boneless chicken
    breast halves
    Salt and pepper
1 clove garlic, minced
½ pound Cremini mushrooms,
    finely chopped
3 tablespoons butter
6 ounces light cream cheese,
    softened
¼ teaspoon garlic salt
¼ cup chopped fresh marjoram
    Marjoram sprigs

Pound chicken breasts between 2 sheets of wax paper until thin. ✎ Salt and pepper each breast to taste. ✎ In a large skillet, sauté garlic and mushrooms in butter. ✎ Mix cream cheese, garlic salt, and marjoram. Spread 1 ounce on each breast. Layer mushrooms on top of cream cheese. (You will have some extra.) Roll up breasts and secure with a wooden pick. ✎ Bake at 400° for 45 minutes. Garnish each roll with marjoram sprig and the reserved extra mushrooms.

[J E A N   K I N N E T T   O L I V E R]

BRANDIED CHICKEN AND SPINACH STRUDELS

SERVES 4

Arrange chicken in shallow baking pan. Sprinkle with ½ cup brandy, and bake at 400° for 20 to 30 minutes, basting frequently. (More brandy may be added as necessary.) Remove chicken from pan, reserving drippings. Cool and julienne chicken. Sauté mushrooms in butter. Add chicken, reserved drippings, spinach, and any remaining brandy. Stir in tarragon, cheeses, salt, and pepper. Adjust seasonings and use to fill strudel. Strudel may be made as 1 or 2 large strudels using 10 sheets of phyllo and generously brushing each sheet with melted butter as it is stacked. Add filling and roll up. Seal edges of pastry. For individual strudels, use 2 sheets of phyllo brushed with melted butter. Bake at 350° for 30 to 40 minutes or until crisp.

[CHEF SCOTT BERG]
VINCENT'S MARKET

A fine sprinkling of dry breadcrumbs between the phyllo will make pastry crispier and flakier.

2 pounds skinless, boneless chicken breast halves, trimmed
1 cup brandy, divided
8 ounces shiitake mushrooms
2 tablespoons butter
2 (10-ounce) packages frozen chopped spinach, thawed and well drained
½ bunch fresh tarragon, trimmed and chopped
½ pound whole-milk ricotta cheese
¼ pound grated fresh Parmesan cheese
1 tablespoon Kosher salt
1½ teaspoon pepper
1 pound fresh phyllo dough
Melted butter

SERVES 6 TO 8

1 (3-pound) broiler-fryer
1 carrot, scraped and sliced
1 medium onion, sliced
2 green, sweet red, or sweet
   yellow peppers, seeded and
   diced
5 tablespoons butter
1/4 cup all-purpose flour
1/4 cup whipping cream
1 teaspoon dried thyme
1 small bunch fresh parsley,
   chopped
1/2 teaspoon ground pepper
1 cup sliced fresh mushrooms
1 sheet frozen puff pastry,
   thawed, or 1 (9-inch)
   prepared pastry shell

NEW SOUTHERN CHICKEN POT PIE

Cook chicken in water to cover until done. Drain, reserving 1 cup stock. Skin and bone chicken; cut meat into bite-size pieces, and set aside. Blanch vegetables in a small amount of boiling water. Drain and set aside. In a heavy skillet or saucepan, melt butter over low heat. Whisk in flour, stirring until golden brown. Add 1 cup reserved chicken stock and whipping cream. Bring to a boil, whisking constantly; cook until thickened and bubbly. Stir in herbs, pepper, and mushrooms. Combine sauce, vegetables, and chicken. Spoon into a deep-dish pieplate or casserole dish. Roll out puff pastry or pastry shell, and place over top. Crimp edges. Cut slits in top for steam to escape. Bake at 350° for 40 minutes.

[ANNALISA THOMPSON JAGER]

SERVES 4

1 (4 to 5-pound) broiler-fryer
6 cloves garlic, peeled
1 bay leaf
1 tablespoon dried rosemary
   or 1 branch fresh
   Salt and pepper
1 lemon, cut into wedges

GARLIC ROASTED CHICKEN

Wash chicken and pat dry. Stuff cavity with remaining ingredients. Tie legs together, and place bird in roasting pan. Roast chicken at 400° for 20 minutes per pound (about 2 hours) or until skin is golden. Baste frequently with juices.

[LYDIA LONGSHORE SLAUGHTER]

T U R K E Y   C H E E S E   P U F F S

Beat cream cheese and butter with an electric mixer until smooth. ✎ Add milk and Tabasco Sauce, if desired. Stir in turkey and pepper. Add celery or water chestnuts, if desired. ✎ Unroll crescent roll dough, and separate into 4 rectangles. Press out perforations to seal. ✎ Spoon $\frac{1}{2}$ cup turkey mixture in center of each rectangle. Moisten edges of rectangle with water. Bring four corners to the center of filling. Pinch edges to seal. Brush with egg white. Place on an ungreased baking sheet. Bake at 350° for 20 to 25 minutes.

[F R A N C E S   P.   L Y O N S]

T U R K E Y   B R E A S T   W I T H   H E R B   R U B

Skin turkey breast; wash and pat dry. Rub with lemon juice. ✎ Melt 3 tablespoons butter. Add salt, paprika, thyme, basil, pepper, and 1 packet instant broth, forming a paste. Rub turkey breast inside and out with paste. ✎ Place turkey breast on a rack in a roasting pan. Combine remaining packet of instant broth and white wine. Pour in bottom of roasting pan. Make an aluminum foil tent over turkey breast. ✎ Roast at 300° for 3 hours, basting occasionally with drippings.

[S U E   E L L E N   L U C A S]

SERVES 4

3 ounces cream cheese, softened
2 tablespoons butter, softened
2 tablespoons milk
  Dash of Tabasco Sauce (optional)
2 cups cooked chopped turkey
$\frac{1}{8}$ teaspoon pepper
$\frac{1}{4}$ cup chopped celery or water chestnuts (optional)
1 (8-ounce) can crescent dinner rolls or 1 package frozen puff pastry
1 egg white

SERVES 4 TO 6

1 (2-pound) turkey breast
  Juice of 1 lemon
3 tablespoons butter
$\frac{1}{2}$ teaspoon salt
$\frac{1}{4}$ teaspoon paprika
$\frac{1}{8}$ teaspoon dried thyme
$\frac{1}{8}$ teaspoon dried basil
$\frac{1}{8}$ teaspoon pepper
2 packets instant chicken broth or 1 tablespoon chicken bouillon granules
1 cup dry white wine

SERVES 6

1 pound skinless, boneless
   chicken breasts
1 (10³/4-ounce) can chicken
   broth
2 cups couscous
1 (10¹/2-ounce) can chick peas,
   drained
¹/2 cup sliced almonds
¹/2 cup currants
1 orange, peeled and sectioned
3 scallions, chopped
8 ounces plain yogurt
¹/4 cup lemon juice
3 tablespoons olive oil
2 cloves garlic, minced
1 teaspoon curry powder
¹/2 teaspoon ground cumin
   Salt and pepper

CHICKEN WITH ALMOND CURRANT COUSCOUS

Poach chicken in broth 10 to 15 minutes. Cool in broth. Drain, reserving broth. ✿ Pour broth into saucepan. Bring to a boil. Add couscous and cook according to package directions. (You may have to add water to meet liquid requirements.) Drain and cool. ✿ Combine chicken and couscous in a bowl. Stir in chick peas, almonds, currants, orange, and scallions. ✿ Combine yogurt and next 5 ingredients in a small bowl. Toss yogurt mixture with couscous mixture, and stir in salt and pepper to taste.

[ALYSON LUTZ BUTTS]

SERVES 4

2 tablespoons vegetable oil
2 tablespoons Thai curry paste
1¹/2 cups sliced chicken breast,
   uncooked
2 tablespoons Nampla fish
   sauce
1 (14-ounce) can coconut milk
2 green chile peppers, cut in
   half lengthwise
1 cup frozen or canned peas
1 (5-ounce) can bamboo shoots,
   drained (optional)
   Hot cooked rice

THAI CHICKEN CURRY

Heat oil over medium heat in a saucepan. Stir-fry curry paste 1 to 2 minutes. Add chicken slices and fish sauce. Add coconut milk, and bring to a boil. Stir in chile peppers. At this point you can turn heat off and let stand until ready to serve. ✿ Just before serving, stir in peas and, if desired, bamboo shoots. Heat, if necessary, and serve over rice. Warning: very spicy!

[LYN WEAVER GIVENS]

Curry paste is available in East Indian markets or gourmet markets.

SAN FRANCISCO STIR-FRY

SERVES 6

Combine marinade ingredients. Pour over chicken or steak, and marinate at least 1 hour. ❧ Put 3 tablespoons vegetable oil in a wok or large skillet, and heat until very hot. Add meat, and sauté until done. Add vegetables and cook, stirring constantly, until vegetables are crisp-tender. ❧ Serve immediately.

[BARBARA BANKHEAD OLIVER]

Marinade:
- ⅓ cup soy sauce
- 6 tablespoons vegetable oil
- ⅛ teaspoon garlic powder

- 4 skinless boneless, chicken breasts, cubed, or 2 pounds sirloin steak, cut into strips
- 3 tablespoons vegetable oil
- 1 head broccoli, cut up
- 1 pound fresh mushrooms, sliced
- 6 green onions, chopped
- 1 green pepper, chopped
- 1 small head Chinese cabbage, chopped
- 4 to 5 stalks celery, chopped

Just a Thought

Olive and peanut oils can be heated to a higher temperature than any other oils without smoking, which makes them perfect for stir-frying.

MOO GOO GAI PAN

SERVES 6

Cut chicken into ¼-inch slices. Sauté in hot oil for 3 minutes. ❧ Add onions and celery. Cook 5 minutes. Add water chestnuts and next 4 ingredients. ❧ Blend cornstarch and water. Add to chicken mixture. Cook until sauce thickens. Add salt and pepper to taste. Serve chicken mixture over hot cooked rice.

[MARILYN MCGUIRE]

- 2 skinless, boneless chicken breasts
- 3 tablespoons vegetable oil
- ½ cup finely diced onions
- 1 cup thinly sliced celery
- 1 (5-ounce) can whole water chestnuts, drained and sliced
- 1 (5-ounce) can bamboo shoots, drained and sliced
- 2 cups chicken broth
- 2 tablespoons soy sauce
- 1 (8-ounce) package frozen snow pea pods
- 1 tablespoon cornstarch
- ¼ cup cold water
  Salt and pepper
  Hot cooked rice

SERVES 6 TO 8

6 to 8 skinless, boneless chicken
    breasts, cut into strips
2 tablespoons Creole seasoning
4 tablespoons olive oil
1 sweet red pepper, sliced
1 green pepper, sliced
1 large white onion, thinly sliced
2 (14 1/2-ounce) cans Mexican-
    style stewed tomatoes
1/2 can water
3 bay leaves
1 (10-ounce) package yellow rice
1 small box frozen tiny green
    peas

SERVES 4

4 (8-inch) soft flour tortillas
3 cups chopped cooked chicken,
    warm
2 cups shredded Monterey Jack
    cheese
Shredded lettuce
Sour cream
Guacamole
Chopped tomatoes
Sliced jalapeños

ARROZ CON POLLO

Sprinkle chicken strips with Creole seasoning. Sauté chicken in olive oil about 20 minutes. Remove chicken from pan, reserving the drippings. In the same pan, sauté the peppers and onion, adding a little water if necessary. ✐ Add tomatoes, water, bay leaves, and chicken to onion and peppers, and let simmer for 30 minutes. ✐ Prepare rice and peas according to package directions. ✐ Remove bay leaves from chicken mixture, and serve chicken over yellow rice. Garnish with green peas.

[PAULA PERKINSON KENNEDY]

CHICKEN QUESADILLAS

Heat griddle to 140°. When hot, place 2 tortillas on griddle. Lightly cover tortillas with cheese. After cheese melts, add chopped chicken. Heat 2 other tortillas in skillet. Place 2 empty tortillas on top of those with chicken. Close like a sandwich and remove from heat; cut into six triangular pieces. Serve with lettuce, sour cream, guacamole, tomatoes, or jalapeños.

[LA PAZ RESTAURANT]

Just a Thought

Experiment with a new type of chile pepper.
From mild to hot, try Anaheim, poblano, Guero, serrano, or Habanero.
Go as hot as you'd like!

CREAMY CHICKEN ENCHILADAS

Cook chicken (poach or grill) until done, and cube. In a saucepan, melt butter. Add onion and sauté until translucent. Add green chiles and cream cheese, and stir constantly until blended. Remove from heat and stir in chicken. Soften tortillas according to package directions. Place 3 tablespoons of chicken in center of each tortilla. Top evenly with cheeses and salsa. Roll up tortillas and place, seam side down, in a greased, 2-quart casserole dish. Pour whipping cream over enchiladas. Top with any remaining cheese. Bake at 350° for 25 minutes or until hot and bubbly.

[KELLY SCOTT STYSLINGER]

SERVES 4 TO 6

4 skinless, boneless chicken breast halves
1 tablespoon butter
2 tablespoons chopped onion
2 tablespoons chopped green chiles
3 ounces cream cheese, diced
1 cup whipping cream
10 corn tortillas
1 cup grated Cheddar cheese
1 cup grated Monterey Jack cheese with jalapeño peppers
1 cup salsa

SOUTHWESTERN GRILLED CHICKEN

For marinade, combine first 7 ingredients, and mix well. Place chicken in heavy-duty zip-top plastic bag. Pour marinade over chicken. Squeeze out air and seal bag. Refrigerate at least 30 minutes. Remove chicken from bag, discarding marinade. Grill chicken over medium coals until done, turning once. Arrange chicken on a baking sheet. Top each breast with slice of avocado and grated Monterey Jack cheese. Broil until cheese is melted. Top with salsa. Garnish each serving with lime slice. Serve with refried beans, brown rice, and a salad.

[SANDY JENKINS BOWRON]

SERVES 4

1/8 cup apple cider vinegar
1/8 cup olive oil
1 tablespoon Dijon mustard
1/4 teaspoon onion salt
1/2 teaspoon coarsely ground pepper
1/2 teaspoon dried dillweed
1/2 teaspoon dried basil

4 skinless, boneless chicken breasts
1 ripe avocado, sliced
1 cup grated Monterey Jack cheese
Salsa
Lime slices

CHICKEN WITH SPICY PEANUT SAUCE

SERVES 4

Sauce:
1½ tablespoons creamy peanut butter
2½ tablespoons vegetable oil
2 tablespoons soy sauce
2 tablespoons sugar
2 teaspoons white vinegar
½ teaspoon sesame oil
¼ to ½ teaspoon ground red pepper

4 boneless chicken breasts
1½ tablespoons canola oil
3 or 4 hot red peppers
1 clove garlic, minced
1 (1-inch) piece fresh ginger, minced
1 tablespoon soy sauce
1½ tablespoons sherry
1 teaspoon sugar
5 green onions, chopped
1 (5½-ounce) can bamboo shoots, drained
⅓ cup crushed peanuts
Hot cooked rice
Chopped fresh cilantro

Prepare sauce by stirring together all ingredients. ✎ Pound breasts and slice thinly. ✎ Heat oil in wok. Stir-fry peppers until dark red (about 10 seconds). ✎ Add garlic and ginger, and stir-fry 10 seconds. Add chicken and cook until tender. Add soy sauce, next 5 ingredients, and sauce. Stir until thoroughly heated. ✎ Serve over rice, and sprinkle with cilantro.

Just a Thought

Store unpeeled ginger root tightly wrapped in refrigerator.
Slice and peel as needed.

CHICKEN FLORENTINE WITH SHERRY ARTICHOKE SAUCE

Cook spaghetti; drain. Sauté garlic in 2 tablespoons butter. Toss spaghetti with garlic butter, and place in a well-greased 3-quart baking dish. Drain spinach well and put on top of spaghetti. Layer chopped cooked chicken over spinach. Sauté mushrooms in 3 tablespoons butter and set aside. To make sauce, melt remaining 5 tablespoons butter in a large skillet. Add green onions and cook several minutes. Stir in flour, parsley, salt, and pepper; remove from heat. Add milk gradually; return to heat and stir until thickened. Add cheese and stir until melted. Cool slightly. Add lemon juice, wine, sherry, artichokes, and mushrooms. Pour sauce over chicken. Bake at 350° for 30 to 40 minutes.

[JANE SELLERS JOHNSON]

SERVES 6 TO 8

8 ounces spaghetti
1 clove garlic
10 tablespoons butter, divided
2 (10-ounce) packages chopped frozen spinach, thawed and drained
4 cups chopped cooked chicken
1 pound fresh mushrooms, sliced
1/4 cup sliced green onions
1/2 cup all-purpose flour
1/8 cup chopped fresh parsley
2 1/2 teaspoons salt
1/2 teaspoon white pepper
2 cups milk
3 ounces Swiss cheese
2 tablespoons lemon juice
3/4 cup dry white wine
1/4 cup sherry
2 (8-ounce) cans artichoke hearts, drained and chopped

CREAMY CHICKEN AND SHRIMP

Melt butter in a large skillet over low heat. Sauté green onions and parsley for 3 to 5 minutes. Blend in flour with a wire whisk. Raise heat to medium-low and blend in cream a little at a time. Add cheese and stir until melted. Add seasonings and cook 5 more minutes. Add shrimp and chicken; cook gently until shrimp turn pink. Stir in sherry. Serve in puff pastry shells, or on Holland rusk. Garnish with sprig of fresh parsley.

[ADELE WILLIAMSON SCIELZO]

For a cocktail buffet, substitute 1 pound of fresh crabmeat for the shrimp and chicken and serve in a chafing dish, with melba toast or toast points.

SERVES 4

1/2 cup butter
1/4 cup chopped green onions
1 cup chopped fresh parsley
3 tablespoons flour
2 cups half-and-half
8 ounces sharp Cheddar cheese, grated
1/4 teaspoon oregano
1 teaspoon basil
1 teaspoon garlic salt
1 teaspoon seasoning salt
2 cups shrimp, peeled
3 cups chopped cooked chicken
4 to 5 tablespoons sherry
Puff pastry shells or Holland rusk
Fresh parsley sprigs

SERVES 4

Mustard Butter:
1/2 cup butter
2 tablespoons chopped fresh shallots
1/2 teaspoon ground white pepper
1 1/2 tablespoons crushed fresh thyme leaves
2 tablespoons coarse-grained mustard
2 tablespoons Dijon mustard
3/4 teaspoon salt

Herb mixture:
1 teaspoon dried sage leaves, crushed
1 teaspoon dried oregano leaves, crushed
1 teaspoon ground ginger
1 teaspoon dried rosemary, crushed
1 teaspoon dried marjoram
1 teaspoon dried thyme
1 teaspoon celery seeds
1 teaspoon ground white pepper
2 teaspoons salt

4 skinless chicken breasts, bone in

GRILLED HERB CHICKEN WITH MUSTARD BUTTER

MUSTARD BUTTER:

Mix all ingredients. Form into a 6 to 8-inch log on wax paper. Chill.

HERB MIXTURE:

Mix all ingredients and pour onto a doubled piece of wax paper. Coat chicken breasts with herb mixture. Grill chicken over medium coals 4 to 5 minutes on each side or until browned. Transfer chicken to a baking dish, and roast at 400° for 30 minutes or until done. Top chicken with 1/2-inch slices of Mustard Butter.

[JOY SEALS MAGRUDER]

Mustard Butter enhances beef and lamb as well.

LEMONY CHICKEN KABOBS

SERVES 6 TO 8

Combine first 7 ingredients to make marinade. (Reserve some marinade for basting while grilling.) Pour over chicken and zucchini. Marinate in refrigerator 6 to 12 hours, stirring occasionally. Add mushrooms to marinade 1 hour before cooking. ⌇ Drain chicken mixture. Alternate chicken, zucchini, and mushrooms on skewers. Grill over medium coals until chicken is tender (approx. 15 minutes). Brush kabobs frequently with reserved marinade. ⌇ Prepare Lemon Butter, and keep warm. ⌇ Serve kabobs over hot rice with Lemon Butter.

[KAY WATT CLARK]

2 tablespoons grated lemon peel
2/3 cup lemon juice
1/2 cup olive oil
2 tablespoons sugar
2 tablespoons vinegar
4 teaspoons salt
1/2 teaspoon ground red pepper
8 skinless, boneless chicken breast halves, cubed
1 1/2 pounds small zucchini, sliced
1 pound medium mushrooms, stems trimmed
Hot cooked rice

Lemon Butter:
1/2 cup melted butter
2 tablespoons lemon juice
2 tablespoons chopped fresh parsley
1 teaspoon salt
Pinch ground red pepper

Just a Thought

One medium lemon yields 3 tablespoons of juice.
About 5 are needed for 1 cup.

SERVES 6

Purple Onion Marmalade:
- 3 large purple onions, thinly sliced
- 1/3 cup brown sugar
- 1 1/4 cup dry red wine
- 1/3 cup balsamic vinegar (no substitutes)
- 1/4 teaspoon salt

- 1/3 cup Dijon mustard
- 1 tablespoon fresh lime juice
- 1/4 teaspoon Tabasco Sauce
- 2 teaspoons Worcestershire sauce
- 1 clove garlic, crushed
- 1 tablespoon vinegar
- 6 skinless, boneless chicken breast halves, pounded flat

GRILLED CHICKEN WITH PURPLE ONION MARMALADE

Low Fat

To prepare Purple Onion Marmalade, cook onions and brown sugar in a large skillet over medium-high heat, stirring frequently. Watch carefully so it doesn't burn. Reduce heat, if necessary. Cook onions about 20 minutes or until caramelized. Add wine, vinegar, and salt, stirring constantly. Bring mixture to a boil, reduce heat to medium-low, and cook about 15 minutes, stirring frequently, until most of the liquid evaporates. Remove from heat, and cool. Marmalade may be made up to a week ahead and refrigerated until ready to use. To prepare chicken, preheat grill. Whisk together mustard and next 5 ingredients. Dredge chicken in mustard mixture. Grill chicken about 4 minutes on each side or until cooked, brushing occasionally with mustard mixture. Serve chicken with purple onion marmalade (chilled or room temperature).

[MELANIE BERRY McCRANEY]

A colorful relish adds flavor and interest to grilled chicken.

GRILLED CHICKEN WITH TARRAGON-RED PEPPER SAUCE

To prepare sauce, wash and seed red pepper. Chop into 1-inch chunks. Simmer red pepper in chicken broth 15 to 20 minutes or until tender. Place warm pepper in blender or food processor. Puree. With blender running, add melted butter in a slow, steady stream. Add sour cream slowly. Add tarragon. Continue processing. Add 1½ teaspoons lemon juice, and salt and pepper to taste. (Sauce may be prepared up to 1 hour before serving.) Sprinkle chicken with salt, pepper, and lemon juice to taste. Grill chicken over medium coals until done, turning once. Serve sauce over grilled chicken. This sauce is also excellent on grilled fish or shrimp.

[MOLLY PEARCE CLARK]

SERVES 4

Sauce:
- 1 medium sweet red pepper
- 3 tablespoons chicken broth
- 6 tablespoons butter, melted
- ½ cup sour cream, room temperature
- 1 to 1½ tablespoons chopped fresh tarragon
- 1½ teaspoons lemon juice
- Salt and white pepper to taste
- 4 skinless, boneless chicken breast halves
- Salt and pepper
- Lemon juice

OREGANO LEMON MARINADE

MAKES 1 CUP

1/3 cup olive oil
1/2 cup fresh lemon juice
2 cloves garlic, minced
1 tablespoon chopped fresh oregano
1/4 teaspoon salt
1/8 teaspoon pepper

Combine all ingredients, and pour over chicken or turkey tenderloin. (Reserve some marinade for basting while grilling.) Marinate several hours or overnight, turning occasionally. Drain meat, discarding marinade. Grill meat, basting with reserved marinade.

[KIM MOFFET WILLIAMS]

PECAN FRANGELICO SAUCE FOR GRILLED CHICKEN

SERVES 4

1 quart whipping cream
1 cup brown sugar
1 cup chopped pecans
1 1/2 cups Frangelico liqueur

Heat and reduce whipping cream and brown sugar. Stir in pecans and Frangelico liqueur. Continue reducing to desired thickness. Serve over grilled chicken.

ISLAND MARINADE

Combine all ingredients. Use to marinate chicken overnight or at least 5 hours for best flavor.

[LAURI GASKELL JORDAN]

MAKES 3 CUPS

1¾ cups pineapple juice
½ cup soy sauce
1 cup Sauterne
½ teaspoon garlic salt
¼ cup sugar

DAVIS'S BBQ SAUCE FOR CHICKEN

Melt butter in medium saucepan. Add remaining ingredients. Simmer 5 minutes. Delicious for barbecueing chicken. Baste during last 10 minutes of cooking.

[REBECCA OLIVER HAINES]

MAKES ¾ CUP

½ cup butter
3 tablespoons lemon juice
1 tablespoon Beau Monde seasoning
2 tablespoons soy sauce
2 teaspoons Worcestershire sauce
1 tablespoon ground ginger

MUSTARD BBQ SAUCE

Combine all ingredients. Whisk over low heat until smooth. Brush over chicken while grilling.

MAKES ¾ CUP

½ cup butter, melted
1 (6-ounce) jar prepared mustard
3 tablespoons vinegar
2 tablespoons Worcestershire Sauce
½ teaspoon salt
Tabasco Sauce (optional)

Grilled Tuna With Ginger and Provençal Sauce, page 213

The Bass Fisherman

He is the silent type, the mute scholar
reading the sky instead of his books,
wasting no words above the still waters,
searching instead for shades of detail,
for the sharp, deep shadows of silver,
for the subtle moves that only seers see.

He is the careful type, the peaceful brave
wrapping his weapon with string, down
and prayer, warming his sight with colors
of sunset, waiting for sunrise to show him
the way, watching the depth of each cloud
that floats on the lake of his eyes.

He is the simple type, the timeless boy
flipping and testing his first flying rod,
urging it on past limits of hand and arm
to the other side of vision and dreams,
using all of that first moment to cast
the perfect balance of boy and boat.

He is the cautious type, the prize bass
with the broken hook still in his mouth,
staring up at the lake's final surface of man,
following the drag of the feather's taunt,
waiting, waiting, learning at last
the only reward of patience, is patience.

CHARLES GHIGNA

CHARLES IS AN ACCLAIMED
POET AND CHILDREN'S AUTHOR
WHOSE WORK HAS APPEARED IN
MAGAZINES, NEWSPAPERS, BOOKS
AND LITERARY JOURNALS.
HIS BOOKS INCLUDE THE
PULITZER PRIZE NOMINEE
RETURNING TO EARTH,
SPEAKING IN TONGUES,
GOOD CATS, BAD CATS,
GOOD DOGS, BAD DOGS,
AND MOST RECENTLY
THE CHILDREN'S
BOOKS *TICKLE DAY: POEMS
FROM FATHER GOOSE* AND
RIDDLE RHYMES. HE LIVES
IN BIRMINGHAM.

With the push toward healthier eating, many food manufacturers have provided reformulated foodstuffs which help consumers have a better idea of the nutritional content of foods they are purchasing. The Food and Drug Administration (FDA) has standardized these and now requires product labeling. Below is an explanation for some of the more common terms and suggestions for low-fat substitutes to your menus:

STANDARD F.D.A. TERMS

Sugar-free: no more than 0.5 grams of sugar of any type per serving.

Calorie-free: no more than 5 calories per serving

Low-calorie: no more than 40 calories per serving

Low-sodium: no more than 140 milligrams of sodium per serving and per 100 grams

Cholesterol-free: no more than 2 milligrams of cholesterol and 2 grams of saturated fat per serving

Low-cholesterol: no more than 20 milligrams of cholesterol per serving and per 100 grams and no more than 2 grams of saturated fat per serving

Fat-free: no more than 0.5 grams of fat per serving, providing it has no added fat or oil. This may be called no-fat or zero-fat

Low-fat: no more than 3 grams of fat per serving and per 100 grams

Low saturated fat: no more than 1 gram of saturated fatty acids per serving and no more than 15 percent of the calories from saturated fatty acids

Reduced fat: no more than half the fat of an identified comparison and the reduction must be greater than 3 grams of fat per serving

Light or lite: at least one-third a reduction in calories with a minimum 40 calorie reduction and a reduction of more than 3 grams of fat. If 50 percent or more of calories are from fat, fat must be reduced by 50 percent compared to the reference food

Lean and extra-lean: these terms may describe fat content of meat, chicken and seafood. A meat labeled lean must have less than 10 grams of fat, less than 4 grams saturated fat and less than 95 milligrams of cholesterol per serving. Extra-lean products must have less than 5 grams of fat, less than 2 grams saturated fat, and less than 95 milligrams cholesterol per serving

LOW-FAT SUBSTITUTIONS

Fats and Oils

Butter:	Reduced-calorie margarine
Margarine:	Reduced-calorie margarine
Mayonnaise:	Nonfat or reduced-calorie mayonnaise
Oil:	Polyunsaturate or monounsaturated oil in reduced amount
Salad dressing:	Nonfat or oil-free salad dressing
Shortening:	Polyunsaturate or monounsaturated oil in amount reduced by one-third

Dairy Products

Sour Cream:	Nonfat sour cream alternative, light sour cream, low-fat or non-fat yogurt
Whipping Cream:	Chilled evaporated skimmed milk, whipped
American, Cheddar, colby, edam, Monterey Jack, mozzarella, and Swiss cheeses:	Cheeses with 5 grams of fat or less per pound
Cottage Cheese:	Nonfat or 1% low-fat cottage cheese
Cream Cheese:	Nonfat or light process cream cheese product, Neufchatel cheese
Ricotta Cheese:	Nonfat, lite, or part-skim ricotta cheese
Milk, whole or 2%:	Skim milk, ½% milk, 1% milk, evaporated skimmed milk diluted equally
Ice Cream:	Nonfat or low-fat frozen yogurt, low-fat frozen dairy dessert, ice milk, sherbet, sorbet

Meats, Poultry, and Eggs

Bacon:	Canadian bacon, turkey bacon, lean ham
Beef, veal, lamb, pork, high-fat cuts:	Chicken, turkey, or lean cuts of meat trimmed of all visible fat
Luncheon meat:	Skinned, sliced turkey or chicken breast, lean cooked ham, lean roast beef
Poultry:	Skinned poultry
Tuna packed in oil:	Tuna packed in spring water
Turkey, self basting:	Turkey basted with fat-free broth
Egg, whole:	2 egg whites or ¼ cup egg substitute

Miscellaneous

Soups, canned, condensed cream:	99% fat-free condensed cream soups
Chocolate, unsweetened:	3 tablespoons unsweetened cocoa plus 1 tablespoon polyunsaturated oil or margarine
Fudge sauce:	Chocolate syrup

SEAFOOD

SALMON FILLET BATHED IN SOY AND LEMON

Quick & easy

Rinse salmon, and pat dry. Combine basil and next 6 ingredients in a small bowl. Place salmon in broiler pan. Pour half of sauce over salmon. Broil 5 to 6 minutes. Pour remaining sauce over salmon. Broil 4 to 5 additional minutes until salmon flakes easily when tested with a fork. Serve with lime wedges.

[LAIDE LONG KARPELES]

POACHED SALMON WITH HORSERADISH SAUCE

To prepare sauce, combine all sauce ingredients, mixing well. Chill until ready to serve. Combine water, lemon, carrot, celery, and peppercorns in a large skillet. Bring to a boil over medium-high heat. Cover and reduce heat to low; simmer 10 minutes. Add salmon steaks. Cover and simmer 10 minutes.

Remove skillet from heat, and let stand 8 minutes. Remove salmon to serving plate, and spoon Horseradish Sauce over top. Garnish with lemon slices and sprigs of fresh dill.

[BETH OLIVER LEHNER]

Just a Thought

To make your own horseradish, simply peel then grate fresh horseradish. Add fresh lemon juice to taste. Can be stored indefinitely in the refrigerator, but it gets hotter with age!

B R O I L E D   G R O U P E R W I T H   M U S T A R D - H E R B S A U C E

SERVES 2 TO 4

1 tablespoon olive oil
1 to 1½ pounds grouper fillet
    (2 to 2½ inches thick)
1¼ cups dry white wine, divided
    Juice of 1 lemon
2 tablespoons chopped
    fresh parsley
2 teaspoons Dijon mustard

Pour olive oil into a large ovenproof skillet. Place grouper in skillet, turning to coat both sides and place fillet pretty side up. Pour ¾ cup wine around fish; broil in oven 10 minutes or until fish flakes easily when tested with a fork. (Be careful not to overcook.) If fish is not done, bake at 450° for 3 to 5 minutes. Do not turn fish over. Do not let the liquid cook away; add more wine, if necessary. Remove fish to a platter, and keep warm. Add remaining ½ cup of wine to cooking liquid in skillet. Bring to a boil, and boil down liquid rapidly. Scrape any browned bits in the skillet to deglaze. Add lemon juice and continue to boil liquid until it is reduced to 4 to 5 tablespoons. Whisk in chopped parsley and mustard. Drain any liquid that may have accumulated on the platter with the fish, and pour the sauce over the grouper. Serve immediately.

[S A L L Y   S C H R O E D E R   P R I C E]

B R O I L E D   F I S H W I T H   P A R M E S A N B U T T E R

Quick & easy

SERVES 6

½ cup grated Parmesan cheese
¼ cup butter, softened
3 tablespoons chopped green
    onions
3 tablespoons mayonnaise
2 tablespoons lemon juice
¼ teaspoon salt
    Dash of Tabasco Sauce
    Fish for 6 (grouper, dolphin,
    snapper)

Combine first 7 ingredients. Spoon mixture evenly over fish, and broil fish until golden brown and flakes easily when tested with a fork.

[C A M E R O N   D A L E Y   C R O W E]

S N A P P E R   A L   G R É C O

Combine first 6 ingredients and beat with a fork. Wash snapper fillets in cold water, and pat dry. Place in a 2-quart baking dish; pour three-fourths of the marinade over fish and refrigerate 1 hour. Drain, discarding marinade. ✧ Bake fish at 350° for 25 minutes, or broil for 15 minutes until fish flakes easily when tested with a fork. Baste occasionally with reserved marinade. Heat remaining marinade, and pour over fish on plate or serving platter.

[E U G E N I A   J E M I S O N   M A T T H E W S]

Just a Thought

*Make an easy sauce for baked fish by spreading
equal parts mayonnaise and sour cream over the fish.
Sprinkle with fresh dill and bake as usual.*

*For cold fish, such as salmon, substitute finely chopped cucumbers
and green onions for dill. Garnish with slices of purple onion,
chopped tomatoes, and capers.*

S H R I M P   É T O U F F É E

Prepare roux by heating oil or drippings in a heavy skillet. Add flour, and stir. Add garlic, and cook until medium brown. Remove garlic, and stir in shrimp and next 6 ingredients. Season with salt and cayenne to taste. ✧ Cover skillet, and cook over very low heat for 30 to 40 minutes or until shrimp is done and there is sufficient gravy. Stir occasionally. (Since no water is added this dish must be cooked slowly to avoid sticking.) Serve over hot cooked rice.

[S H I R L E Y   A N N E   S T R I N G F E L L O W]

SERVES 6

1 cup vegetable oil or ¹/₂ cup each of vegetable oil and olive oil

1¹/₂ teaspoons prepared mustard

5 ounces lemon juice

1 teaspoon salt

¹/₂ teaspoon pepper

2 teaspoons oregano

6 snapper fillets

SERVES 3 TO 4

¹/₄ cup vegetable oil or bacon drippings

¹/₂ cup all-purpose flour

2 cloves garlic, chopped

1¹/₂ pounds medium fresh shrimp, peeled and deveined

1 medium onion, chopped

¹/₂ cup chopped green onion

1 stalk celery, chopped

¹/₂ green pepper, seeded and chopped

¹/₈ cup chopped fresh parsley

2 large tomatoes, chopped

Salt

Cayenne pepper

S E A B A S S R O A S T E D W I T H C A P E R S

SERVES 2 TO 4

1 tablespoon olive oil
2 tablespoons lemon juice
2 tablespoons capers
2 tablespoons golden raisins
1/4 teaspoon salt
1/4 teaspoon pepper
1 (1/2-pound) sea bass fillet
1 tablespoon chopped fresh basil
1/3 cup breadcrumbs
1/4 cup pine nuts (optional)

Combine first 6 ingredients in a bowl. Dip sea bass fillets in mixture, turning to coat both sides, and sprinkle with basil, breadcrumbs, and pine nuts, if desired. Reserve olive oil mixture. Place fish in roasting pan, pour olive oil mixture over fillets. Roast at 400° for 20 minutes. (Raisins will become quite brown.) Sprinkle with pine nuts, if desired.

[L Y D I A L O N G S H O R E S L A U G H T E R]

G R I L L E D T U N A W I T H G I N G E R A N D P R O V E N Ç A L S A U C E

SERVES 4

4 tuna steaks, 1 inch thick
Salt
Freshly ground pepper
1 tablespoon grated fresh ginger
1 tablespoon lemon juice
1 tablespoon olive oil

Sauce:
1 large tomato (about 1/2 pound)
2 tablespoons red wine vinegar
1/4 cup olive oil
1/4 cup finely chopped shallots
1 teaspoon finely minced garlic
1/4 cup freshly chopped basil or parsley
1/2 teaspoon lemon rind, grated
Salt and freshly ground pepper

Tuna: Place tuna steaks on a plate, and season with salt and pepper to taste. Rub ginger on both sides of steaks, and sprinkle each with lemon juice and olive oil. Cover with foil, and let stand until ready to cook. *To grill,* place tuna on hot grill and cover. Cook 5 minutes. Turn tuna, cover, and cook an additional 5 minutes. *To broil,* place tuna on rack and broil about 6 inches from heat for 5 minutes with oven door slightly open. Turn and broil for an additional 5 minutes.

Provençal Sauce: Boil tomato for 9 seconds. Drain and pull off skin; cut out and discard core. Cut tomato in half crosswise. Remove and discard seeds. Cut tomato into 1/4-inch cubes (about 1/2 cup). In a mixing bowl, combine tomato, vinegar, and next 4 ingredients. Add lemon rind and salt and pepper to taste. Blend well with whisk. Serve tuna steaks with provençal sauce.

[M A R Y L A U R A S T A G N O]

SERVES 4 TO 6

2 *ounces brandy*
1 *ounce Kahlúa*
1 *ounce chopped shallots*
1 *ounce Bailey's Irish Creme*
1 *cup whipping cream*
1/2 *cup butter*
Salt
2 *to 3 pounds pan-fried or grilled lean white fish*
Garnish: chopped fresh parsley

BAILEY'S AND KAHLÚA BUTTER

In a heavy saucepan over medium heat, cook brandy, Kahlúa, and shallots until reduced by one-half. Add Bailey's and whipping cream to mixture and cook until reduced by three-fourths. Add butter and salt to taste.   To serve, ladle 1/8 cup warm sauce onto a plate and top with a piece of pan-fried or grilled fish. Garnish with chopped fresh parsley, if desired.

[ANNALISA THOMPSON JAGER]

SERVES 2 TO 3

1 *to 2 tablespoons butter*
1/4 *pound fresh mushrooms, thinly sliced*
1 *small onion, minced*
1 *pound light white fish (orange roughy, sole, etc.)*
1/4 *cup dry white wine*
1 *teaspoon dried tarragon*
Salt and pepper
Juice of 1/2 lemon

Low Fat

BAKED FISH WITH TARRAGON WINE SAUCE

Melt butter in skillet; add mushrooms and onion. Sauté 5 minutes or until soft.   Spray a 2-quart baking dish with vegetable cooking spray. Arrange fish in dish. Pour wine over top. Sprinkle with tarragon; season with salt and pepper to taste, and add lemon juice. Spoon mushroom mixture over top.   Cover with foil and bake at 350° for 30 minutes or until fish flakes easily when tested with a fork.

[CINDY SMITH SPEAKE]

P E C A N - C R U S T E D C A T F I S H

S E R V E S 4

1 cup pecan pieces
1 cup unseasoned breadcrumbs
3 eggs
1/2 cup milk
4 catfish, tuna or trout fillets
Creole seasoning
3 tablespoons butter

Quickly roast pecans under broiler 30 seconds to 1 minute to release flavor. Do not burn. ✿ Put pecans in a food processor, and chop just until coarse. Mix chopped pecans with breadcrumbs, and set aside. ✿ Beat eggs in a medium bowl, add milk, and set aside. ✿ Wash fish, and pat dry. Sprinkle generously with Creole seasoning on both sides. Dip each fillet in egg mixture, and roll in pecan mixture to coat. ✿ Melt butter in a skillet over medium heat. Cook each pecan-crusted fillet 3 minutes on each side to secure the crust. Place fish in a 15 x 10 x 1-inch jellyroll pan. (At this point, fish can be covered with plastic wrap and kept in the refrigerator until ready to cook.) To cook, bake at 350° for 35 minutes.

[K E L L Y S C O T T S T Y S L I N G E R]

For a great variation, omit Creole seasoning and use with
Bailey's and Kahlúa Butter (page 214).

G R I L L E D S W O R D F I S H S T E A K S

Quick & easy

S E R V E S 6

1 cup olive oil
Juice of 1 lemon
3 cloves garlic, finely chopped
1 tablespoon dried oregano
1 tablespoon crushed bay leaves
1 teaspoon celery salt
1 teaspoon coarsely ground pepper
6 swordfish steaks
Melted butter
Chopped fresh parsley (optional)

Combine first 7 ingredients, mixing thoroughly. ✿ Place steaks in marinade, turning to coat both sides. Cover and refrigerate 2 to 3 hours. ✿ Drain fish, reserving marinade. ✿ With the grill rack 6 inches from coals, grill steaks, uncovered, for 5 minutes. Turn, baste with reserved marinade, and grill 6 additional minutes. Remove from grill, and top with melted butter. Garnish with parsley, if desired.

[C A R O L I N E M C D O N N E L L F A R W E L L]

SERVES 2

2 flounder fillets
1 tablespoon lemon
1 tablespoon dry white wine
1/2 cup sliced fresh mushrooms
4 tablespoons butter, divided
2 tablespoons all-purpose flour
3/4 cup milk
1/4 teaspoon dried tarragon
1 teaspoon chopped fresh parsley
2 tablespoons dry white wine
1/4 teaspoon Worcestershire sauce
   Salt and pepper
1/4 pound small to medium fresh
   shrimp, peeled

FLOUNDER FILLETS IN TARRAGON SHRIMP SAUCE

Place flounder in a flat glass baking dish. Combine lemon juice and 1 tablespoon wine. Pour over flounder. Marinate in refrigerator 1 hour. ✒ Sauté mushrooms in 2 tablespoons butter. Drain and set aside. ✒ In a saucepan over medium-low heat, melt remaining butter. Stir in flour, and gradually add milk. Cook, stirring constantly, until thickened. Add tarragon and remaining ingredients. Stir in mushrooms, and cook 2 minutes. Set sauce aside. ✒ Remove fish from refrigerator. Loosely roll each fillet, jelly-roll fashion. Place in a shallow baking dish. Pour sauce over the top. Bake, uncovered, at 350° for 30 minutes, basting occasionally.

[LAURA WORTHINGTON BERRY]

SERVES 6

3 tablespoons butter, melted
   Juice of 2 limes
2 tablespoons Creole seasoning
   Fresh fish (enough for 6
   servings)
1 (16-ounce) can black beans,
   drained
   Salt
2 tablespoons sour cream
1 medium ripe tomato, chopped
1/2 cup hot salsa
   Garnishes: sour cream,
   4 chopped green onions

Quick & easy

LIME-MARINATED FISH WITH BLACK BEAN SAUCE

Combine first 3 ingredients. Marinate fish in butter mixture. ✒ Process black beans 5 seconds, just until chopped. Add salt to taste. Stir in 2 tablespoons sour cream. ✒ Combine tomato and salsa. Set aside. ✒ Broil fish until white and flaky. ✒ To serve, layer black bean sauce, broiled fish, and salsa mixture on a plate. Garnish with sour cream and chopped green onions, if desired.

[CAMERON DALEY CROWE]

SAUTÉED FISH WITH VERMOUTH CREAM AND ALMONDS

Quick & easy

SERVES 4

Combine eggs and buttermilk. Soak fish in buttermilk mixture. Combine flour and next 4 ingredients in plastic bag. Shake each fillet in flour mixture. In a large, heavy skillet, heat butter and olive oil just until steaming. Sauté fish fillets in butter mixture until golden on each side. Do not crowd in skillet. When golden, remove onto a warmed glass dish or individual serving plates. Combine cornstarch and water, and add to skillet. Stir in over low heat, scraping sides and bottom of skillet. Add vermouth and sour cream. If necessary, add more vermouth or water. Pour over fish. Sprinkle with toasted almonds. Garnish with parsley and lemon slices, if desired.

[MELANIE DRAKE PARKER]

2 eggs, beaten
1 cup buttermilk
4 fish fillets
3/4 cup all-purpose flour
3/4 cup cornmeal
1/2 teaspoon dried tarragon
1/2 teaspoon salt
  Pinch of pepper
4 tablespoons butter
1/2 cup olive oil
1 tablespoon cornstarch
2 teaspoons water
2/3 cup vermouth or dry white wine
1/3 cup light sour cream
1/3 cup sliced toasted almonds
  Garnishes: chopped fresh parsley, lemon slices

ISLAND AMBERJACK

SERVES 4

Rub fish fillets lightly with olive oil; spread sparingly with ginger. Broil approximately 10 minutes on each side or until fish flakes easily when tested with a fork. Sauté bananas in butter over medium-low heat 3 to 4 minutes or until thoroughly warmed. Add almonds, and cook 2 additional minutes, stirring occasionally. (Do not mash bananas.) Stir in pepper jelly. Cook 1 to 2 minutes. Serve banana sauce over fillets or to the side of fish. Serve with rice and a green salad.

[ANNE THIELE BLACKERBY]

2 pounds amberjack fillets
  Olive oil
1 to 1 1/2 teaspoons ground or minced ginger
3 ripe bananas, peeled and sliced diagonally
1 1/2 tablespoons butter, melted
1/3 cup sliced almonds
2 tablespoons hot pepper jelly

SERVES 4

1 pound salmon, poached and flaked

1 cup breadcrumbs

2 tablespoons lemon juice

4 tablespoons soy sauce

1/2 cup mayonnaise

1/2 teaspoon salt

1/2 sweet red pepper, diced

1/2 onion, finely chopped

2 tablespoons finely chopped fresh parsley

2 tablespoons chopped fresh basil

2 tablespoons Old Bay seasoning

1 egg
Vegetable oil or shortening

Sauce:

1/2 cup sugar

3 egg yolks

2 tablespoons lemon juice

1 cup mango vinegar*

2 tablespoons Dijon mustard

3 cups vegetable oil

*Mango vinegar is available at specialty foods stores.

MAKES 2 CUPS

1 1/2 cups butter, melted

2 teaspoons minced garlic

1 tablespoon Worcestershire sauce

1/4 cup dry white wine

1 drop Tabasco Sauce

1/2 (1-ounce) envelope Italian dressing
Juice of 2 to 3 lemons

SALMON CAKES WITH MANGO VINEGAR SAUCE

Combine first 12 ingredients in a large bowl. Form mixture into 4 cakes weighing about 5 ounces each. (Makes 6 smaller cakes for appetizers.) Fry in hot oil or shortening until golden, turning once.

To prepare sauce, combine sugar and next 4 ingredients. Add oil in a slow, steady stream, whisking constantly until combined.

Serve salmon cakes with sauce.

[CHEF ANTHONY DEXTER AVERY]
CIAO RESTAURANT

SIMPLE SEAFOOD MARINADE

Combine all ingredients. Pour over fish, and refrigerate for at least 2 hours. Perfect for snapper or grouper to be grilled.

[ALISON BRYANT]

CURRY-CRUSTED OYSTERS WITH LEMON CREAM

Combine flour, salt, pepper, and curry powder in a dish. Mix milk and egg in a separate bowl. ❧ Dip oysters in flour mixture and then in egg mixture. Dredge in flour mixture again. ❧ Fry oysters in hot oil until golden. ❧ To prepare sauce, sauté garlic in olive oil until golden. Add salt, curry powder, lemon juice, and cream. Serve oysters with sauce.

[CHEF ANTHONY DEXTER AVERY]
CIAO RESTAURANT

SERVES 3

2 cups all-purpose flour
1 teaspoon salt
½ teaspoon pepper
1½ teaspoons curry powder
2 cups milk
1 egg
1 pint fresh oysters, drained
Vegetable oil or shortening

Sauce:
1 teaspoon minced garlic
3 ounces olive oil
Pinch of salt
¼ teaspoon curry powder
Juice of ¼ lemon
½ cup whipping cream

FRESH CRABMEAT SANDWICH

Quick & easy

Combine first 6 ingredients, and set aside. ❧ Place 1 tomato slice on each piece of Holland rusk toast. Top each with cream cheese mixture and a slice of cheese. Bake at 350° for 20 minutes.

[JANET SMITH LUCAS]

SERVES 6 TO 8

1 (8-ounce) package cream cheese, softened
1 egg yolk
1¼ teaspoons onion juice
½ teaspoon Worcestershire sauce
½ pound fresh crabmeat, flaked
Salt to taste
2 tomatoes, sliced
1 package Holland rusks, toasted and slightly buttered
6 to 8 slices Cheddar cheese

S C A L L O P S G R A N D M A R N I E R

SERVES 4

1 pound scallops, halved if large
Salt and pepper
3 tablespoons unsalted butter, divided
1/2 cup minced shallots
1 1/2 cups chicken broth
1/2 cup dry white wine
1/3 cup orange juice
1/4 cup Grand Marnier
1 cup whipping cream
1 teaspoon grated orange rind
3 tablespoons lemon juice

Season scallops with salt and pepper to taste. In a large skillet, cook scallops in 1 1/2 tablespoons butter over medium-high heat for 1 minute, stirring frequently. Cover the skillet, and cook for 2 minutes or until they are opaque and just firm, stirring occasionally. With a slotted spoon, transfer scallops to a large plate and keep warm. Add shallots to skillet, and cook for 1 minute, stirring constantly. Add broth and next 3 ingredients, and bring to a boil. Boil mixture until it is reduced to 2/3 cup. Add cream, and simmer until lightly thickened. ✑ Whisk in remaining butter, orange rind, and lemon juice. Add salt and pepper to taste. ✑ Pour any accumulated juices from the scallops into the sauce. Divide scallops among 4 coquille shells, and spoon sauce over scallops.

[CATHY CRISS ADAMS]

S C A L L O P E D O Y S T E R S

SERVES 5

2 cups cracker crumbs
1 quart medium to large oysters, drained, reserving liquid
4 tablespoons butter, cut into pieces
1/4 cup chopped fresh or frozen chives
1/4 teaspoon salt
1/4 teaspoon pepper
1 tablespoon Worcestershire sauce
1/4 cup sherry
1 cup milk, room temperature

Layer cracker crumbs, oysters, butter pieces, chives, salt, pepper, oyster liquid, Worcestershire sauce, and sherry, ending with cracker crumbs in a greased 1 1/2-quart baking dish. Pour milk over cracker crumbs. ✑ If possible, let stand 1 hour before baking. ✑ Bake at 350° for 25 to 30 minutes. Let stand 15 minutes before serving.

[ELEANOR SIBLEY HASSINGER]

OYSTERS ODETTE

Wash oysters, and drain well. Chop. Melt butter in a skillet, and sauté onions until tender. Add flour, and cook, stirring constantly, until browned. Reduce heat, stir in nutmeg, ground red pepper to taste, next 5 ingredients, and oysters.   Remove from heat and add egg yolk. If it does not thicken, return to heat for 2 minutes.   Put in shells or ramekins, and cover with buttered cracker crumbs.   Bake at 350° for 15 minutes, or bake at 150° for 1 hour. If oysters are too liquid, add additional cracker crumbs.

[MANDY HAMEL ROGERS]

SERVES 6 TO 8

3 dozen oysters
2 tablespoons butter
5 green onions, chopped
2 tablespoons all-purpose flour
1/8 teaspoon ground nutmeg
    Ground red pepper
1/2 teaspoon salt
2 tablespoons Worcestershire sauce
1 (2½-ounce) can chopped mushrooms, drained
1/2 teaspoon mustard
2 tablespoons dried parsley flakes
1 egg yolk
    Buttered cracker crumbs

EASY CRAWFISH ÉTOUFFÉE

Melt margarine in a 2-quart baking dish. Add onion and next 3 ingredients.   Cover and microwave on HIGH 3 to 5 minutes, stirring occasionally. Cook just until vegetables are translucent. Stir in flour and chicken broth. Microwave on HIGH for 4 minutes. Add crawfish and remaining ingredients. Cover and microwave on HIGH for 4 additional minutes.   Serve over rice.

[JANE GLENNON FEAGIN]

SERVES 4

4 tablespoons margarine
1 cup chopped onion
1/4 cup chopped green pepper
1/4 cup chopped celery
1 clove garlic, minced
2 tablespoons all-purpose flour
3/4 cup chicken broth (may use bouillon cube)
1 pound crawfish tails, cleaned
    Salt and pepper
    Dash of Creole seasoning
    Dash of Tabasco Sauce
    Dash of lemon juice
    Hot cooked rice

SERVES 4

2 quarts water
2 lobster tails
4 tablespoons butter
2 tablespoons whipping cream
2 tablespoons lemon juice
1 tablespoon chopped chives
1 clove garlic, minced
   Fresh chives

LOBSTER MEDAILLONS IN GARLIC-CHIVE SAUCE

Quick & easy

Bring water to a boil in a stockpot. Add lobster tails. Cover, reduce heat, and simmer for 12 minutes. Drain. Rinse with cold water. Split and clean tails. Cut lobster into $1/2$-inch slices. Cover and chill. Melt butter in medium saucepan. Add whipping cream, and cook over low heat for 1 minute, stirring constantly. Stir in lemon juice, chopped chives, and garlic, and remove from heat. To serve, arrange lobster slices on plate, and spoon sauce over lobster. (If butter starts to settle, whisk sauce.) Garnish with fresh chives, and serve immediately.

[PATRICIA SCHAEFER MIREE]

SERVES 6 TO 8

1 (4-pound) lobster or
   equivalent
4 tablespoons butter
2 teaspoons salt
$1/4$ teaspoon ground red pepper
$1/4$ teaspoon ground nutmeg
1 cup whipping cream
4 egg yolks, beaten
2 tablespoons brandy
2 tablespoons sherry
   Puff pastry shells

LOBSTER NEWBURG

Remove meat from lobster and cut into small pieces. Heat butter in a large skillet and add lobster. Cook slowly for 5 minutes. Add salt, pepper, and nutmeg. While stirring constantly, add cream and egg yolks. Cook slowly until thickened. Add brandy and sherry, and stir just until blended. Serve in puff pastry shells or on toast points. (Variation: shrimp or crabmeat may be substituted for lobster.)

[LOUISE RHETT OREM]

G R E E K   B A K E D   P R A W N S   W I T H   F E T A   C H E E S E

Heat 1/3 cup olive oil in heavy, medium-size saucepan over medium heat. Add chopped onion, and sauté 12 minutes or until golden brown. Add tomatoes, 3 tablespoons parsley, garlic, and red pepper. Add salt and black pepper to taste. Bring to a boil. Reduce heat, cover, and simmer for 20 minutes or until sauce thickens, stirring occasionally. (This can be made 1 day ahead. Cover and refrigerate. Rewarm sauce before continuing.) Heat 2 to 3 tablespoons olive oil in a large, heavy skillet over medium-high heat. Add shrimp, and sauté 1 minute. Remove skillet from heat. Add ouzo, and ignite with match. Return to heat and cook until flames subside. Add tomato mixture. Transfer shrimp mixture and sauce to a 9-inch pieplate. Sprinkle cheese over top. Bake at 400° for 10 minutes. Sprinkle remaining parsley over shrimp. Serve immediately over rice.

[S H E I L A   S H E A N   B L A I R]

SERVES 8

1/3 cup olive oil
4 medium onions, chopped
4 pounds tomatoes, peeled, seeded, and chopped
1/4 cup chopped fresh parsley, divided
4 large cloves garlic, minced
Pinch of ground red pepper
Salt and freshly ground pepper
2 to 3 tablespoons olive oil
4 pounds extra-large or jumbo shrimp, peeled
1 cup ouzo (liqueur)
16 ounces feta cheese, crumbled
Cooked rice

B A K E D   S H R I M P

Combine first 6 ingredients. Stir in pepper to taste. Marinate shrimp in butter mixture overnight or several hours. Bake shrimp mixture in a glass baking dish at 400° for 20 minutes.

SERVES 4

1 cup butter, melted
2 cloves garlic, minced
1 teaspoon dried rosemary
2 tablespoons Worcestershire sauce
1 tablespoon Tabasco Sauce
Juice of 2 lemons
Pepper
1 1/2 pounds large fresh shrimp, unpeeled

S H R I M P   A N D   G R I T S   B O U R S I N

SERVES 4

6 servings grits, prepared according to package instructions

6 to 8-ounce container Boursin cheese

1½ pounds fresh shrimp, peeled and deveined

1 tablespoon olive oil

2 tablespoons dry white wine

2 tablespoons fresh thyme, chopped

Salt and pepper

4 tablespoons butter

⅔ cup dry white wine

Fresh thyme sprigs

Prepare grits, and after thickened add Boursin cheese. Spray gelatin molds or coffee mugs with cooking spray. Spoon grits into molds or mugs. Set aside. Sauté shrimp in olive oil, 2 tablespoons wine, chopped thyme, and salt and pepper to taste, until shrimp turn pink and wine evaporates. Remove shrimp from pan, reserving liquids. Keep shrimp warm. Add ⅔ cup wine to drippings, and simmer over medium-high heat until reduced by one-half. Remove from heat and slowly whisk in butter, 1 tablespoon at a time until sauce thickens. Warm grits in microwave for 20 seconds. Unmold grits. If using coffee mugs, shake grits loose, and slice into ½-inch rounds. To serve, place grits on individual serving plates, mound with shrimp, and drizzle with sauce. Garnish with fresh thyme sprigs.

[ELLISON JONES GRAY]

Note: sauce can be easily doubled.

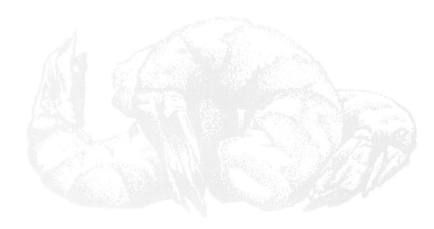

KUNG PAO SHRIMP

Combine first 3 ingredients in a medium mixing bowl, stirring well. Stir in cornstarch mixture. Add shrimp to mixture, and stir well. Cover and refrigerate for 1 to 2 hours. Combine sauce ingredients in a small bowl. Set aside. Heat wok on high until hot. Add oil, and coat wok. Add onion, and cook until limp and translucent. Add nuts and shrimp mixture. Stir-fry until shrimp turn pink. Add peppers and bamboo shoots. Toss gently for 1 minute. Stir in sauce. Cook, stirring constantly, until sauce boils and thickens. Serve over rice.

[DR. SCOTT ARNOLD]

2 tablespoons soy sauce
2 tablespoons chicken broth
2 teaspoons sesame oil
1 teaspoon cornstarch, mixed with 2 teaspoons water
3/4 pound fresh medium shrimp, peeled and deveined
2 tablespoons peanut or vegetable oil
1/2 medium onion, sliced
2 ounces peanuts or cashews
8 to 12 (1-inch) dried hot chile peppers, chopped
1 (8-ounce) can sliced bamboo shoots, drained
Hot cooked rice

Kung Pao Sauce:
2 teaspoons sugar
1 teaspoon cornstarch
1/3 cup chicken broth
2 tablespoons rice vinegar or red wine vinegar
1 tablespoon soy sauce
1 tablespoon dark soy sauce
2 teaspoons sweet bean paste
1 1/2 teaspoons sesame oil

MARINATED SHRIMP

Combine all ingredients. Cover and refrigerate overnight. Serve with toothpicks.

[ADRIENNE LANGE BURROUGHS]

2 to 3 pounds large fresh shrimp, cooked and peeled
2 small onions, thinly sliced
1 1/2 cups vegetable oil
1 cup white vinegar
1 1/2 teaspoons celery seeds
1 teaspoon salt
Capers or mushrooms (optional)

SERVES 4

3 *cloves garlic, minced*

4 *tablespoons butter, softened*

1 *tablespoon fresh or frozen chives, chopped*

Salt

2 *tablespoons oregano*

1 *tablespoon dry mustard*

2 *teaspoons dried basil*

1 *teaspoon dried rosemary*

2 *bay leaves, crumbled*

4 *eggs, lightly beaten*

2 *tablespoons vegetables oil*

2 *pounds shrimp, peeled and deveined*

1/4 *cup all-purpose flour*

3 *tablespoons butter, melted*

2 *tablespoons lemon juice*

1/4 *teaspoon Worcestershire sauce*

1/2 *pound fresh crabmeat, flaked*

HERBED SHRIMP

Cream garlic and butter in a small bowl. Add chives and salt to taste; cover and let stand at room temperature for 1 hour. Process oregano and next 4 ingredients in an electric blender for 5 seconds, and transfer herb mixture to a small dish. In a separate bowl, beat eggs with vegetable oil. Sprinkle shrimp with salt, and toss in herb mixture. Dredge shrimp in flour, and coat with egg mixture. In a skillet, sauté shrimp in butter for 2 to 3 minutes on each side or until golden brown. Using a slotted spoon, transfer shrimp to a warm serving platter. Pour off excess butter, and add the garlic butter mixture to skillet; melt mixture over moderate heat. Add lemon juice, Worcestershire sauce, and pinch of salt. Stir in crabmeat and cook until heated thoroughly. Spoon over shrimp, and serve immediately.

[PATRICIA SCHAEFER MIREE]

To peel garlic easily, hit the cloves with the flat side of a knife blade.

G R I L L E D   S H R I M P
W I T H   R O S E M A R Y

SERVES 6

3 pounds large fresh shrimp
1 bunch fresh rosemary, crushed
6 cloves garlic, minced
1/2 cup olive oil
  Juice of 2 lemons
  Salt and freshly ground pepper
1 lemon, sliced

To prepare shrimp, remove legs, but do not peel. Using a small knife, cut several slits lengthwise along the inner curve of each shrimp. Insert 2 to 3 small sprigs of rosemary into each slit. ✍ In a large bowl, whisk together garlic, olive oil, lemon juice, and salt and pepper to taste. ✍ Toss shrimp in olive oil mixture, coating well. Add more rosemary sprigs and lemon slices. Cover and marinate in refrigerator for 1 to 2 hours. ✍ Drain shrimp, and grill on skewers over medium heat for 3 to 5 minutes on each side or until shrimp begin to curl and are opaque.

[A N N A L I S A   T H O M P S O N   J A G E R]
Serve with lots of napkins.

E L E G A N T   S H R I M P
A N D   A R T I C H O K E

SERVES 8

1 1/2 pounds medium shrimp
1 (10-ounce) package frozen artichoke hearts
6 1/2 tablespoons butter
4 1/2 tablespoons flour
3/4 cup whole milk
1 cup whipping cream
1 teaspoon Worcestershire sauce
1/4 cup dry sherry
1/4 teaspoon salt
1/4 teaspoon cayenne pepper
  Pepper to taste
1/4 pound mushrooms, sliced thick
1 cup grated fresh Parmesan cheese
  Paprika

Cook shrimp just until pink. Peel and devein. Steam, drain, and coarsely chop artichoke hearts. ✍ Make a white sauce by melting butter in a saucepan over low heat. Add flour and stir. Slowly add milk then cream, stirring constantly until thickened. Remove from heat. Bring to room temperature. Add Worcestershire sauce, sherry, salt, and peppers; stir until well combined. ✍ Layer artichoke hearts, shrimp, and mushrooms in a greased 3-quart casserole. Sprinkle with Parmesan cheese; then pour white sauce over all. Sprinkle paprika. Bake at 350° for 20 to 30 minutes or until hot and bubbly. Serve over wild rice.

[C A R O L I N E   R A T H E R   C L A R K]

SERVES 8

3 pounds fresh shrimp, peeled
  and rinsed well
1/3 cup fresh lime juice
2 teaspoons garlic, minced
2 teaspoons fresh minced ginger
1/2 cup plain yogurt
4 teaspoons ground cumin
4 teaspoons ground coriander
1 teaspoon paprika
1 teaspoon freshly ground
  pepper
1/2 teaspoon ground red pepper
1/2 teaspoon salt
  Olive oil

CARIBBEAN GRILLED SHRIMP

Combine first 4 ingredients in a large mixing bowl, and cover. Marinate at room temperature for 30 to 45 minutes. Drain. ✍ Combine yogurt and next 6 ingredients in a small bowl. Pour half of yogurt mixture over shrimp; stir well. Cover and chill for 1 to 3 hours. Drain and skewer shrimp. Brush with olive oil. ✍ Grill until shrimp are just firm, turning once. Toss with reserved yogurt sauce, and serve.

[ALYSON LUTZ BUTTS]

SERVES 4

1 cup orzo, uncooked
2 tablespoons olive oil, divided
  Salt and pepper
2 cloves garlic, minced
1 to 1 1/2 pounds large fresh
  shrimp, peeled and deveined
1/2 teaspoon salt
1/4 teaspoon pepper
1/4 cup chopped fresh parsley,
  divided
1/2 cup diced sweet red pepper
  Juice and rind of 1 to 2
  lemons
1 cup dry white wine
5 tablespoons butter
1 tablespoon capers

LEMON SHRIMP SAUTÉ

Cook orzo in boiling salted water until tender; drain. Toss with 1 tablespoon olive oil; add salt and pepper to taste. Set orzo aside. ✍ In large skillet, heat remaining 1 tablespoon olive oil. Add garlic, and sauté 1 minute. Add shrimp, salt, pepper, and 2 tablespoons parsley. Cook 3 minutes. Turn shrimp and add red pepper; cook 3 additional minutes. Remove from pan, and keep warm, reserving drippings in skillet. ✍ Add lemon juice and wine to skillet. Bring to a boil, reduce heat, and simmer until mixture is reduced by one-third (about 2 minutes). Remove from heat. Add remaining parsley, and stir in butter, lemon rind, and capers. Add salt and pepper to taste. ✍ Pour sauce over shrimp, and serve on a bed of orzo.

[ANNALISA THOMPSON JAGER]

SHRIMP AND CRAB MORNAY

Melt butter in a 2-quart saucepan. Stir in flour, and cook over medium heat for 5 minutes, stirring often. Add onion and green onions, and cook 2 to 3 minutes without browning. Stir in parsley. Gradually add cream, and cook, stirring constantly, until hot. Add wine and next 3 ingredients, and mix well. Simmer, stirring occasionally. Stir in Swiss cheese, and cover. Remove from heat, and let cool. When sauce has cooled to lukewarm, stir in lemon juice. In a 3-quart baking dish, layer shrimp, crabmeat, quartered artichoke, and mushrooms, using sauce between each layer, and on top. Sprinkle Romano cheese over top. Cover and refrigerate until ready to cook. Before cooking, uncover and bring to room temperature. Bake at 350° for 30 to 45 minutes or until thoroughly heated.

[ANN L. MOORE & SUSAN W. NADING]

SERVES 8

1/2 cup butter
1/2 cup all-purpose flour
1/4 cup grated onion
1/2 cup chopped green onion
1/8 cup fresh parsley
2 cups whipping cream
1 cup dry white wine
2 1/2 teaspoons salt
1/2 teaspoon ground white pepper
1/4 teaspoon ground red pepper
2 1/2 ounces Swiss cheese, diced
2 tablespoons lemon juice
2 pounds fresh shrimp, cooked and peeled
1 pound fresh lump crabmeat, flaked
8 artichoke bottoms, quartered
1/2 pound fresh mushrooms, sliced thick
3 tablespoons Romano cheese

Just a Thought

When wine is added to a sauce, the alcohol evaporates within a few minutes of cooking, leaving only the flavor.

SERVES 6 TO 8

1 pound spiced or garlic sausage
1¹/₂ pounds fresh shrimp
1 (2 to 3-pound) broiler-fryer
1 (16-ounce) can chopped tomatoes
1 (6-ounce) can tomato paste
2 cups finely chopped onion
1 cup chopped green pepper
1 cup finely chopped green onion
¹/₄ cup chopped fresh parsley
2 tablespoons garlic, minced
2 bay leaves
¹/₂ cup celery, chopped
2 teaspoons salt
³/₄ teaspoon fresh ground black pepper
³/₄ teaspoon ground red pepper
¹/₂ teaspoon mild chili powder
1 cup uncooked rice

CHICKEN, SHRIMP & SAUSAGE JAMBALAYA

Cook sausage; drain and slice. Steam and peel shrimp. Boil chicken in 4 quarts water until tender. Drain, bone, and cube chicken; reserve 2 cups broth. In a large saucepan, combine reserved broth, tomatoes, and tomato paste. Cook 8 minutes over medium heat, stirring often. Add onion and next 6 ingredients. Cook 15 minutes or until vegetables are tender. Stir in salt and next 4 ingredients. Add sausage, shrimp, and chicken. Cover and simmer 30 minutes.

[BURT CHANDLER]

SERVES 4

Lake Place Rice:
1 cup tomato orzo
1 cup basmati rice
1 cup long-grain rice
8 plum tomatoes, cubed
3 cloves garlic, minced
1 tablespoon chopped scallions
¹/₄ cup ripe olives, pitted and sliced
2 pounds fresh shrimp, peeled and deveined
2 tablespoons butter
¹/₄ cup feta cheese, crumbled
Freshly ground pepper

Quick & easy

LAKE PLACE SHRIMP ATHENIAN

Separately cook orzo and rices according to package directions. Combine. Set rice mixture aside. Sauté tomatoes and next 4 ingredients in butter in a skillet until shrimp turn pink. Serve over rice mixture, and top with feta cheese and freshly ground pepper.

[LAKE PLACE RESTAURANT]
SEA GROVE, FLORIDA

HIGHLANDS CRAB CAKES

SERVES 8

Toss together the first 11 ingredients. Taste and adjust seasonings if necessary. Form mixture into eight equally portioned patties, being sure not to press too firmly. ✎ Dip patties in egg-water mixture, then in remaining breadcrumbs. Let stand a few minutes. Heat clarified butter almost to smoking point. Add crab cakes, being sure not to crowd sauté pan. ✎ Cook over medium-high heat until golden brown, about 3 to 4 minutes; turn and cook until just done. Remove to serving plates and pour Beurre Blanc around. ✎ Garnish with plenty of lemon wedges.

Beurre Blanc:

Combine wine, vinegar, and shallots. Simmer to reduce to a syrupy glaze. Remove saucepan from heat, and stir in cream. Return to low heat to reduce volume slightly. Begin adding butter, bit by bit, stirring constantly. When all butter is incorporated, add lemon juice, salt and pepper to taste, and strain. Hold at warm room temperature until needed.

[FRANK STITT, CHEF/OWNER]
HIGHLANDS BAR & GRILL

2 pounds fresh blue crabmeat
3 cups bread crumbs from day-old French bread
6 tablespoons unsalted butter, melted and cooled
2 eggs, beaten
2 tablespoons chopped shallots
2 tablespoons chopped green onions
2 tablespoons chopped parsley
2 tablespoons fresh lemon juice
Pinch of freshly grated nutmeg
Pinch of cayenne pepper
Salt and pepper to taste
2 eggs, beaten with 2 tablespoons water
1 cup breadcrumbs
3 tablespoons clarified butter
Lemon wedges

Beurre Blanc:
1 cup white wine
¼ cup white wine vinegar
2 tablespoons chopped shallots
1 tablespoon cream
½ cup unsalted butter at room temperature
Lemon juice
Salt and pepper

Just a Thought

To clarify butter, melt in a heavy saucepan over low heat until foamy. Remove from heat and skim foam from top. Strain through a fine mesh sieve and discard residue on bottom of pan. Refrigerate in a tightly sealed container for up to 2 weeks.

Mustard-Crusted Rack of Lamb, page 238

A Memory of Spring Lamb

-JOHN LOGUE-

CONNIE KANAKIS SAT IN A BOOTH just off the kitchen in the restaurant of his own name. Not for long. He was up in a panic. Key was lost to the wine room. Now he was back, sitting in a warm, lively chaos of plates passing in the hands of waiters, customers eating, laughing, a rare few silent as stones, an old friend, slinging some irreverence in his direction, provoking a very Greek response.

"Sure, I grew up in Birmingham," said Connie, glad to remember those years, "at 821 16th Place, Southwest. Right across the street from Harrison Park. A big old wooden house, nice front porch with a swing on it, a big shade tree. I still have that house. A couple of cooks who work with me live there."

Subject of the conversation was to be lamb. Spring lamb. But not yet. Connie swung the last of his coffee in his cup and looked back on his early life. "My grand-daddy was in the restaurant business. My daddy...he died when he was 38 years old...had the original L&N Cafe. Started it on Morris Avenue across from the train station, then moved it to First Avenue and 19th Street. The month that he died, he was opening L&N Cafe No. 2. It would have been catty-cornered from the Trailway Bus Station down on 19th Street and Fourth Avenue.

"My granddaddy, John Balabanos, and my Uncle Nick took over the L&N Cafe and operated it until they died. They called my grandfather 'Papa John.' He had a big handle-bar mustache. Cold black, curly hair, parted in the middle. A good man. Summers I'd sweep up, bus tables, and ride home on the -CONTINUED-

JOHN LOGUE

JOHN LOGUE WAS BORN IN
BAY MINETTE, ALABAMA, AND
GRADUATED FROM AUBURN
UNIVERSITY IN 1955.
AS A YOUNG SPORTSWRITER,
HE WROTE FOR THE
MONTGOMERY ADVERTISER AND
*THE ATLANTA JOURNAL-
CONSTITUTION*. HE CAME TO
SOUTHERN LIVING MAGAZINE IN
1967, WHERE HE SERVED AS
FEATURES EDITOR, MANAGING
EDITOR, AND EXECUTIVE
EDITOR. FROM 1982 TO 1991
HE SERVED AS CREATIVE
DIRECTOR OF SOUTHERN
PROGRESS CORPORATION.
NOW RETIRED, JOHN IS THE
AUTHOR OF SEVERAL NOVELS
AND MYSTERIES. HE AND
HIS WIFE, HELEN,
HAVE THREE SONS.

trolley with my granddaddy at midnight. The L&N stayed open 24 hours a day."

What was the Greek community like in Birmingham in those years, during and just after World War II?

"I think at that time there were about 500 or 600 Greek people. Maybe 90 families," said Connie. "They started a little church on the Southside: Holy Trinity, Holy Cross, which is now The Cathedral. We must have a membership today of about 4,000, over 50 percent of them Orthodox, but non-Greeks.

"When I grew up there were three Greek families that lived in Blessed Sacrament. The rest of the Greek community lived on Norwood Circle and Norwood Boulevard. As a kid I went to West Second Academy, a Catholic school about a block and a half from my house. But on Mondays, Wednesdays, and Fridays we all went to Greek school, to learn the language. We had a little schoolhouse next door to the church. On Sundays, we'd all be either in the choir, or serving on the alter, or ushering. The old guys, who worked 12, 15-hour days, would sit around, play checkers, a little casino. The kids would run. We all knew each other. I called men 'Uncle John' until they died, and we were not related at all. We just felt related. Now we are spread out all over the city. But we do see each other. But it's not the same."

A stranger stopped at the table to say she came to the restaurant because she "recognized the name." Kanakis welcomed her like a lost member of the family.

"The Greeks had a great tradition," he said, taking up the conversation, "of celebrating your Name Day. My Name

Day is May 21, the day of Constantine and Helen. On Sunday before your Name Day, your mama, or your wife, would leave church five minutes early to go home and get ready. The congregation that day, after they had their lunch, would come by your house to wish you a happy Name Day. They'd give you a little shot of bourbon, and a little Greek liqueur they'd make from grapefruit rinds or orange rinds. No invitations. You just knew they were coming. It gave us all such a strong identity...of being part of a community."

And who was the great cook in his family?

"Oh, my grandmother. Her name was Angelina Balabanos. She was an immigrant. Came over at age 16 from a little village on the Mediterranean. She could cook in the great Greek tradition. Or she could cook black-eyed peas and butter beans and ham hock. She was once asked to cook for a big family wedding here in Birmingham and the daughter of that bride, born seven years later, is my wife."

And now we come to the lamb.

"It was a tradition," said Connie, "to buy a spring lamb before the 40 days of Lent. And fatten it. And at the end of Lent, Papa John would slaughter it. And my grandmother would skin it and cut it up and cook it. Nobody ever cooked it better.

"Here's how she did it: You get a fresh leg of lamb. The best lambs come from Tennessee. I can't tell you why that's true. You trim the fat, get it all off. You salt and pepper it good. You make four little slits, two on each side. And you take a fresh garlic bud and cut it into fours and put a piece in each slit. And you put the lemon to it. You squeeze a fresh lemon over the lamb and you rub it into it. You can't use too much lemon. We Greeks believe in the magic of lemon. You add just enough water to cover the bottom of a roasting pan...and set the oven at 375° and let that sucker cook for about 3^1/2 to 4 hours, or until you can take a fork and put it in and easily slide it out. I promise you will have the best piece of lamb you ever tasted." T H E   E N D

THERE'S MORE TO BURGERS THAN BEEF. Variations of ground turkey, lamb, pork—even grains—will spice up your cookouts. These ideas will each make 4 servings; just mix the ingredients, form 4 patties, slightly less than 1 inch thick. Grill or pan-fry, being careful not to overcook them.

Oriental Burger: mix 1 1/2 pounds ground beef, 1/3 cup minced water chestnuts, 1/3 cup minced green onion, 2 tablespoons hoisin sauce, and 1 teaspoon ground ginger. Serve in buns with alfalfa or bean sprouts and thinly sliced cucumber.

Mexican Burger: mix 1 1/2 pounds ground beef, 2 cloves crushed garlic, 1 1/2 teaspoons ground cumin, 2 tablespoons minced pickled jalapeño pepper, 1/2 teaspoon salt, and 1/2 teaspoon red pepper. Form into 4 (1 1/4-inch-thick) oval patties. Serve rolled in flour tortillas with sour cream, salsa, shredded lettuce, sliced avocado, and ripe olives.

French Burger: mix 1 1/2 pounds ground beef, 1 tablespoon Dijon mustard, 2 tablespoons minced shallot, 1 teaspoon dried tarragon, 1/2 teaspoon freshly ground pepper. Form into oval patties, wrapping each portion around 1 ounce blue or Roquefort cheese and sealing well. Serve in French bread rolls with Dijon mustard and arugula.

Asian Turkey Burger: mix 1 1/2 pounds ground turkey, 1 tablespoon soy sauce, 1 tablespoon grated fresh ginger, 1 clove crushed garlic, 2 teaspoons sesame oil. Serve in sesame buns with spinach leaves and alfalfa sprouts, chutney, and plain yogurt.

Bistro Turkey Burger: mix 1 pound ground turkey, 1 cup dried Italian breadcrumbs, 2 teaspoons dried thyme, 1 clove crushed garlic, 1 cup finely shredded carrot, 2 tablespoons Italian salad dressing. Serve in 5-inch lengths toasted, split French bread with marinated mushrooms and watercress.

Greek Lamb Burger: mix 1 1/2 pounds ground lamb, 1 (10-ounce) package frozen chopped spinach, thawed and squeezed dry, 1/2 cup minced onion, 1/2 cup dried breadcrumbs, 2 teaspoons dried oregano. Serve in whole-grain deli rolls, such as rye or wheat, with fresh spinach leaves and crumbled feta cheese.

Italian Pesto Burger: mix 3/4 pound lean ground beef, 3/4 pound ground veal, 1 tablespoon olive oil, 1 cup freshly grated Parmesan cheese, 1/2 cup minced fresh basil, 1/4 cup toasted pine nuts, 1 or 2 cloves crushed garlic. Serve between thick slices toasted Italian bread, brushed with olive oil, with sliced plum tomatoes and fresh basil slices or arugula.

California Burger: mix 1 1/2 pounds lean ground beef, 1/2 cup minced green onion, 1/4 cup finely chopped, drained sundried tomatoes packed in oil, 1 teaspoon crushed dried rosemary. Serve topped with goat cheese, between wedges of foccacia.

MEATS

SERVES 6

1½ cups fresh breadcrumbs
1½ teaspoons dried, crumbled
    thyme
    Salt and pepper
2 well-trimmed racks of lamb
    (7 ribs each)
1 clove garlic, halved
½ cup minced shallots
¼ cup unsalted butter
½ cup minced fresh parsley
3 to 4 tablespoons Dijon
    mustard

MUSTARD-CRUSTED RACK OF LAMB

Season breadcrumbs with thyme and salt and pepper to taste. Season lamb with salt and pepper to taste. Rub with garlic halves. ✿ In large skillet sauté shallots in butter for 2 minutes. Remove from heat. Stir in breadcrumb mixture. Cool. Add parsley; mix well. ✿ Spread mustard evenly over lamb. Pat crumb mixture generously onto mustard. Chill 2 to 3 hours. Bring to room temperature. ✿ Bake at 450° for 30 minutes or until lamb registers 130° to 135° on meat thermometer for rare. Let stand 10 minutes. Remove to platter. Carve into chops, and serve 2 ribs per person.

SERVES 6 TO 8

Marinade:
1 tablespoon salt
2 tablespoons chopped fresh onion
    or 1 tablespoon instant minced
    onion
3 tablespoons lemon juice
1 tablespoon red wine vinegar
¼ cup olive oil
2 teaspoons ground coriander
1 tablespoon minced fresh ginger
    or 1 teaspoon ground ginger
1½ teaspoons curry powder
1 teaspoon ground black pepper
1 teaspoon minced fresh garlic or
    ¼ teaspoon instant minced garlic

2 pounds lean leg of lamb
18 mushroom caps
3 green peppers, seeded and chopped
3 to 4 medium tomatoes, quartered

GRILLED LAMB KABOBS

Combine first 10 ingredients and place marinade in a large bowl with lid. Add lamb; cover and marinate 3 to 4 hours or overnight. ✿ Drain lamb, reserving marinade for basting. ✿ String lamb on skewers with mushrooms caps and pieces of green pepper. ✿ Grill or broil 10 to 15 minutes or until done, basting with reserved marinade. Add tomatoes during last 5 minutes of grilling or broiling time.

[CATHY CRISS ADAMS]

L A M B   S H A N K S   P R O V E N Ç A L

Insert cloves of garlic into fat of lamb (1 per shank). ✿ Heat olive oil in a large skillet over medium-low heat. Add chopped onion, and sauté until tender. Remove onion. Increase heat and add lamb shanks. Cook until browned. Return onion to skillet, and stir in salt and pepper to taste and remaining ingredients. Bring to a boil. Reduce heat. ✿ Cover and simmer approximately 1$\frac{1}{2}$ hours. Transfer shanks to a warm platter, reserving liquid in skillet. ✿ Transfer reserved liquid to saucepan and bring to a boil. Discard lemon and bouquet garni. Puree liquid in blender. Pour half of sauce over shanks, and bake at 425° for 15 to 20 minutes. Serve with remaining sauce.

SERVES 4

4 cloves garlic
4 lamb shanks
$\frac{1}{3}$ cup olive oil
2 medium onions, chopped
    Salt and pepper
4 carrots
2 stalks celery
2 cups plum tomatoes,
    fresh or canned
1 cup dry red wine
1 cup beef bouillon
1 lemon, halved and seeded
    Bouquet garni

L E G   O F   L A M B   W I T H   H E R B S

Rub both surfaces of flattened meat with garlic, and place it in a marinating container or a glass dish. ✿ Combine red wine, vinegar, oil, juice of $\frac{1}{2}$ lemon, and leaves stripped from 1 rosemary stalk. Add thyme and oregano, crushed to release flavor. Pour over meat. Squeeze remaining lemon half on top, slice lemon halves, and scatter over and under meat. Distribute remaining rosemary in the same way. Sprinkle cracked pepper to taste. Marinate in refrigerator several hours, turning occasionally. ✿ Remove lemon slices. Combine marinated rosemary stalks and fresh mint and insert into crevices of meat. Grill over hot fire about 25 minutes for medium-rare. Garnish with fresh herbs.

[A N N E   T H I E L E   B L A C K E R B Y]

SERVES 6 TO 8

1 (4 to 5-pound) leg of lamb,
    boned, butterflied, and
    well trimmed
1 to 2 cloves garlic, minced
$\frac{1}{4}$ cup red wine
$\frac{1}{4}$ cup red wine vinegar
$\frac{1}{2}$ cup olive or canola oil
1 lemon, halved and divided
3 to 4 stalks of fresh rosemary
    (approximately 6 to 8 inches)
4 sprigs fresh thyme
    (approximately 3 to 4 inches)
3 to 4 short sprigs of oregano
    or $\frac{1}{4}$ teaspoon dried
    Cracked pepper
    Approximately 6 sprigs of
    fresh mint, 6 inches long

LEG OF LAMB WITH WHITE BEANS

Soak beans overnight in water to cover. Drain beans. Add water to cover and bring to a boil. Reduce heat, and simmer 1 hour or until beans are tender but not mushy. Drain and set aside. Sauté onion and garlic in olive oil until tender. Combine beans, onion mixture, 2 teaspoons salt, 1/2 teaspoon rosemary, 1/2 teaspoon thyme, pepper, and tomatoes in a roasting pan, stirring to combine. Trim fat from lamb. Make slits in lamb, and insert garlic slivers. Sprinkle lamb with remaining salt, rosemary, and thyme. Place lamb in roasting pan, and bake, uncovered, at 325° for 2 1/2 to 3 hours. Let stand 20 minutes before carving. Garnish with parsley, if desired.

[ALYSON LUTZ BUTTS]

LAMB CHOPS STUFFED WITH FETA CHEESE

Quick & easy

Cut a deep slit down the fatty side of each lamb chop. Rub chops with garlic halves. Squeeze lemon juice over chops. Brush chops with olive oil. Sprinkle with salt and pepper to taste. Stuff feta cheese into the slit in each chop. Close slits in chops with wooden picks. Broil 5 to 6 minutes per side for medium-rare.

[MELANIE BERRY McCRANEY]

H E R B E D   R O A S T   B E E F

In a small bowl, combine first 6 ingredients; mix well. Rub meat with olive oil, lemon juice, and seasoning mixture until well coated. Place roast on rack in a shallow roasting pan.   Bake at 500° for 15 minutes. Reduce temperature to 350° and bake an additional 45 minutes (or until a meat thermometer inserted into thickest portion of meat registers 140°, rare).

[N A N C Y   M A T T H E W S   M A S O N   ]

SERVES 6 TO 8

2 teaspoons coarsely ground
  black pepper
1 teaspoon garlic powder
1 teaspoon fresh rosemary or
  1/2 teaspoon dried rosemary
1 teaspoon fresh thyme or 1/4
  teaspoon ground thyme
1 teaspoon fresh oregano or
  1/2 teaspoon dried oregano
1/2 teaspoon poultry seasoning
1 (3-pound) eye of round beef
  roast or tenderloin
1 tablespoon olive oil
2 tablespoons lemon juice

R I B   R O A S T   R O Y A L E

Season rib roast with salt, pepper, and lemon-pepper. Broil in a broiler pan 15 minutes on each side.   In a saucepan melt butter. Add lemon juice, Worcestershire sauce, beef bouillon cubes, and mushrooms; stir until bouillon has dissolved.   Pour sauce over meat. Bake at 350° for 20 minutes each side.

[W A R R E N   B A I L E S   C A I N   ]

SERVES 2 TO 4

1 (4-rib) standing rib roast
1/2 teaspoon salt
1/2 teaspoon pepper
1 teaspoon lemon-pepper
1/2 cup butter
  (reduced-calorie may be used)
1 tablespoon lemon juice
1 tablespoon Worcestershire
  sauce
2 beef bouillon cubes
8 ounces fresh mushrooms,
  sliced

Just a Thought

To make a savory Orange Butter, melt 1/2 cup butter in a saucepan. Add
2 tablespoons orange juice, 2 tablespoons orange rind, and
1 tablespoon chopped fresh mint. Mold, chill, and use with lamb or beef.
Served warm, the butter becomes a marinade for lamb kabobs.

POT ROAST WITH MAPLE PAN SAUCE

SERVES 4 TO 6

4 to 5 pounds pot roast
(eye of round, top or
bottom round)
2 tablespoons vegetable oil
1 teaspoon salt
1 teaspoon seasoned salt
1/2 teaspoon ground allspice
1 bay leaf
20 peppercorns
2 large onions, chopped
3 tablespoons maple syrup
3 tablespoons cider vinegar
2 cups beef consommé
2 tablespoons all-purpose flour

In a Dutch oven, sear meat on all sides in oil; remove roast and wipe Dutch oven clean. Return meat to Dutch oven, and add salt and next 7 ingredients. Heat consommé to boiling, and add to meat mixture. Cover and cook slowly for 3 to 3½ hours. Refrigerate overnight. Make a paste with flour and ¼ cup gravy from meat. Heat in a skillet and stir until thickened. Reheat meat. Slice and serve with gravy.

CHINESE PEPPER STEAK

Quick & easy

SERVES 4 TO 6

2 beef bouillon cubes
2 cups hot water
1 to 2 pounds beef steak,
cut into bite-size pieces
2 ounces vegetable oil
1/4 cup chopped green onion
2 cloves garlic, minced
1 cup chopped celery
1/2 cup soy sauce
1/8 teaspoon black pepper
3 green peppers, cubed
1 (4-ounce) can sliced
water chestnuts, drained
2 tablespoons cornstarch
1/2 cup cold water
Hot cooked rice

Dissolve bouillon cubes in hot water. Brown meat in oil. Add bouillon mixture, green onion, and next 4 ingredients to meat. Cook several minutes until meat is done. Add green pepper and water chestnuts; simmer for 3 minutes. Combine cornstarch and cold water. Add cornstarch mixture, and simmer until slightly thickened. (More soy sauce may be added if needed.) Serve over hot cooked rice.

[MANDY HAMEL ROGERS]

T E X A S - S T Y L E
F L A N K   S T E A K

3 tablespoons liquid smoke
1 teaspoon garlic powder
1 teaspoon onion salt
1 teaspoon celery salt
3 to 3 1/2 pounds flank steak
  Pepper
  Worcestershire sauce
  Commercial barbecue sauce
  (optional)

Combine liquid smoke, garlic powder, onion salt, and celery salt. Pour over steak; seal in foil. Marinate overnight. ✍ Unwrap steak and add pepper to taste. Add a generous amount of Worcestershire sauce on top. Reseal foil pack. Bake at 275° for 5 hours. Remove meat; slice across grain and serve. For a different flavor, pour barbecue sauce over meat, if desired. Reseal. Bake 1 additional hour.

[J A N E   B .   C O M A N]

F L A N K   S T E A K
P A U P I E T T E

1 1/2 pounds flank steak
  Dijon mustard
3 tablespoons soy sauce
3 tablespoons Worcestershire
  sauce
3 tablespoons lemon juice
3 tablespoons red wine

Score steak on diagonal grain. Spread one side of steak with Dijon mustard. Roll up steak, and place, seam side down, in marinating container. ✍ Combine soy sauce, Worcestershire sauce, lemon juice, and red wine. Pour marinade over steak. Chill several hours, turning occasionally. ✍ Unroll and grill 25 minutes on low heat, or cook quickly until meat thermometer registers medium-rare. Slice across grain to serve.

[C A R O L I N E   M C D O N N E L L   F A R W E L L]

ELEGANT BEEF TENDERLOIN

Sauté mushrooms and onions in butter. Drain, and stir in parsley; set aside. ✒ Cut tenderloin lengthwise, cutting to, but not through, bottom. Sprinkle meat with salt and pepper. Spoon mushroom mixture into opening. Place tenderloin in baking dish. ✒ Combine remaining ingredients. Pour over meat; cover and refrigerate overnight. ✒ Place tenderloin on rack in a roasting pan; insert meat thermometer below stuffing. ✒ Bake at 425° for 30 to 45 minutes or until meat thermometer registers 140° (rare) or 150° (medium).

[JEANNE REID SHEARER]

ROAST TENDERLOIN OF BEEF

Combine first 10 ingredients in a saucepan. Bring to a boil and stir. Remove from heat. Tie small end of tenderloin so it will cook evenly. Make a "boat" from 2 to 3 layers of heavy-duty aluminum foil to fit the length of roast. Pour sauce over meat, and bake, uncovered, at 350° for 45 to 55 minutes for rare to medium meat. Let stand 10 minutes before slicing.

[ELLISON JONES GRAY]

CHILLED BEEF TENDERLOIN WITH CAPER HORSERADISH CREAM

SERVES 10 TO 12

Combine first 5 ingredients to make a paste. Rub paste on all sides of beef. Refrigerate 1 to 2 hours. ✿ Place meat in roasting pan, and place in a 500° oven. Reduce heat to 400° immediately. Cook approximately 40 minutes. (Meat thermometer will register 140° for rare.) Let beef cool, refrigerate until well-chilled before slicing. (May be served warm if desired.) ✿ Sauce: Combine mayonnaise and next 4 ingredients. Chill. Serve with sliced beef tenderloin.

[MIKE McCRANEY]

Beef:
- *2 tablespoons dried rosemary, crumbled*
- *3 tablespoons cracked black pepper*
- *1/4 cup soy sauce*
- *4 tablespoons butter, softened*
- *1 small clove garlic, crushed*
- *2 beef tenderloins (3 to 4 pounds when trimmed)*

Sauce:
- *1 1/4 cups mayonnaise*
- *1 1/2 cups sour cream*
- *1/4 cup horseradish*
- *1/4 cup capers, drained*
- *Freshly ground pepper*

VEAL CHOP WITH PORT WINE REDUCTION

SERVES 4

Salt and pepper veal. Grill over hot coals until browned well on both sides (3 to 4 minutes per side for medium-rare). ✿ Roast entire head of garlic. (See page 14 for how to roast garlic.) ✿ In a sauté pan over high heat, cook port wine until reduced by one-half. Add roasted garlic and demiglace to pan and reduce again until 1/2 cup of liquid remains. ✿ Place veal chops on warm plates. Quickly whisk 1 tablespoon butter into hot sauce and pour over veal chops.

[BONGIORNO ITALIAN RESTAURANT]

- *2 (12 to 14-ounce) veal chops*
  Salt and pepper
- *1 cup port wine*
- *1 head of garlic*
- *1/4 cup demiglace**
- *1 tablespoon butter, room temperature*

*Available at specialty food stores.

SERVES 2

1/2 tablespoon freshly ground pepper

2 (1 1/4-inch-thick) filet mignon steaks

1 tablespoon butter, divided

1/2 tablespoon vegetable oil

2 teaspoons salt, divided

1 clove garlic, minced

3 green onions, minced

1 tablespoon brandy

1/3 cup whipping cream or half-and-half

1 tablespoon Dijon mustard

SERVES 4

1 (3 to 4-pound) eye of round, room temperature

1 clove garlic, crushed

Fresh rosemary leaves

1/4 cup Dijon mustard with seeds

PAN-SEARED FILET WITH MUSTARD CREAM SAUCE

Sprinkle pepper evenly over both sides of steaks, and press into meat. Melt 1/2 tablespoon butter with oil in heavy 12-inch skillet over high heat. Salt steaks on one side, and add to skillet, salted side down. Cook 2 minutes or until browned. Salt tops, and turn; cook second sides until browned. Reduce heat to medium, and cook to desired degree of doneness, turning every 2 minutes (6 minutes for rare, 8 minutes for medium-rare). Transfer steaks to heated plates, and set aside. ✍ Add remaining 1/2 tablespoon butter to same skillet, and melt over medium heat. Add garlic and green onions; sauté 1 minute. Remove from heat and add brandy. Return to heat, and bring to a boil, scraping bits. Boil until reduced to a glaze. Add cream and boil 1 minute or until thickened. Stir in mustard and juices from steaks. Spoon sauce over steaks.

[BETH OLIVER LEHNER]

EYE OF ROUND DIJON

Rub meat with garlic, and place in a baking dish, fat side up. ✍ Press rosemary into surface of meat and spread mustard over roast, covering all exposed surfaces. Insert meat thermometer. ✍ Put roast in a 500° oven, and immediately reduce heat to 350°. Roast 18 to 20 minutes per pound or to desired degree of doneness, using a meat thermometer.

[ANNE THIELE BLACKERBY]

REUBEN CASSEROLE

In a 2-quart baking dish, layer sauerkraut, corned beef, and Swiss cheese. Add dressing and tomato slices, and dot with 3 tablespoons butter. ✼ Spread remaining 3 tablespoons butter on bread. Toast and crumble bread on top of casserole. Sprinkle with seeds, if desired. Bake at 400° for 30 minutes or until bubbly.

SERVES 6

1 can sauerkraut, drained
½ pound corned beef, sliced
2 cups grated Swiss cheese
3 tablespoons Thousand
    Island salad dressing
2 medium tomatoes, thinly
    sliced
6 tablespoons butter, divided
6 to 8 pieces rye bread
¼ teaspoon caraway seeds
    (optional)

CAJUN MEATLOAF

Sauté onion and garlic in butter. ✼ Combine onion mixture and next 15 ingredients in large bowl. Stir in salt and pepper to taste. Mix well and place in a loafpan. ✼ Combine ketchup and molasses, and pour over loaf. Bake at 350° for 50 minutes.

[BARBARA BANKHEAD OLIVER]

SERVES 6 TO 8

1 cup finely chopped onion
2 cloves garlic, minced
2 tablespoons butter
¼ cup chopped fresh parsley
½ cup chopped green onion
½ cup chopped carrot
½ cup chopped celery
¼ cup chopped green pepper
¼ cup chopped sweet red pepper
1 teaspoon ground cumin
½ teaspoon ground red pepper
½ teaspoon dried thyme
½ teaspoon paprika
1½ pounds ground beef
½ pound ground pork or turkey
¾ cup breadcrumbs
¼ cup milk
2 eggs, beaten
    Salt and pepper
¼ cup ketchup
¼ cup molasses

SERVES 4

SERVES 4

2 tablespoons Dijon mustard
2 tablespoons vegetable oil
1 tablespoon soy sauce
1 clove garlic, minced
1/4 teaspoon ground pepper
1 1/2 pounds pork tenderloin, scored 1/4 inch deep every 2 inches

SERVES 6 TO 8

1 (3 to 4-pound) pork loin roast
1 teaspoon dried thyme
1/4 teaspoon pepper
1/4 teaspoon salt
2/3 cup apple cider
3 tablespoons dry white vermouth
1 1/2 cups chicken broth
1 1/2 cups whipping cream
3 tablespoons butter, divided
3 cooking apples, peeled, cored, and sliced
3/4 to 1 pound fresh mushrooms, sliced

MUSTARD-GLAZED PORK TENDERLOIN

Quick & easy

In a bowl, blend first 5 ingredients. Brush half of marinade on pork; let stand for 10 minutes. ✎ Place pork on a rack in a preheated broiler pan. Broil pork 4 inches from heat source for 8 minutes. Remove from heat, turn, and brush remainder of marinade over pork; return to oven. Broil 8 to 10 minutes. Slice thin and serve immediately.

[SUSAN JONES DRIGGERS]
Great on grill. Cook 10 minutes on each side.

PORK LOIN ROAST WITH APPLES AND MUSHROOMS

Sprinkle roast with thyme, pepper, and salt to taste. Place in a greased roasting pan. Bake at 450° for 15 minutes; reduce heat to 325°, and bake 30 minutes per pound. Remove roast and set aside. ✎ Place dish over medium heat, add apple cider, stirring to scrape up any drippings. Add vermouth, chicken broth, and whipping cream. Bring to a boil; cook 15 minutes or until thickened, stirring often. Remove from heat. ✎ Melt 1 1/2 tablespoons butter in a large skillet; add apples, and cook until golden. Remove apples from skillet, keeping warm. ✎ Melt remaining butter in skillet; add mushrooms, and cook until tender. Stir in cream mixture, and cook over low heat until thoroughly heated. Serve slices of pork with mushroom sauce on top and apples on the side.

[JANET GOODMAN STEVENSON]

APPLE CIDER PORK CHOPS

Combine first 6 ingredients; add pork chops. Marinate at least 2 hours. Drain pork chops, discarding marinade. Bake pork chops at 350° for 40 minutes. Garnish with chopped fresh parsley or baked apple slices, if desired.

[MARTHA ROONEY WALDRUM]

SERVES 6 TO 8

1/2 cup apple cider
2 cloves garlic, minced
1 tablespoon dry mustard
1 teaspoon ground ginger
1 teaspoon dried thyme
1/2 cup soy sauce
8 pork chops
Chopped fresh parsley or baked apple slices

PORK CHOPS IN CAPER SAUCE

Combine flour and salt and pepper to taste. Dredge pork chops in flour mixture, and sauté in skillet over medium-high heat until browned on both sides (approximately 2 minutes per side). Remove chops from skillet, and turn heat to medium-low. Add beef broth, and stir in mustard and capers. Cook 5 minutes. Return chops to pan, cover, and cook 45 minutes. Before serving, stir sour cream into sauce.

[LYDIA LONGSHORE SLAUGHTER]

SERVES 4

1 tablespoon all-purpose flour
Salt and pepper
4 large pork chops
1 (16-ounce) can beef broth
1 tablespoon Dijon mustard
3 tablespoons capers
1 tablespoon sour cream

P O R K   C H O P S   I N   B E E R

Quick & easy

SERVES 4

1 cup all-purpose flour
Salt and pepper
4 pork chops
2 tablespoons butter
2 tablespoons vegetable oil
12 ounces light beer
1/3 cup soy sauce
1/2 teaspoon ground ginger
1 teaspoon minced garlic

Combine flour and salt and pepper to taste. Coat pork chops with seasoned flour. In a large covered frying pan, brown chops in butter and oil. ✻ Combine beer and remaining ingredients in saucepan; bring to boil. Pour over chops. Cook, covered, for 15 to 20 minutes over low heat.

[J E A N   K I N N E T T   O L I V E R   ]

A N D O U I L L E   S A U S A G E   A N D   B L A C K - E Y E D   P E A S

SERVES 6 TO 8

1 1/2 pounds andouille sausage
  (no substitutes), sliced
1 pound fresh or frozen
  black-eyed peas
2 slices bacon
1 1/2 cups chopped onion
1 large green pepper, chopped
1/4 cup chopped fresh parsley
2 cloves garlic, minced
  Salt
1 teaspoon pepper
2 tablespoons Allegro
  (or soy-based meat marinade)
1 (16-ounce) can tomatoes,
  drained and chopped
1/4 teaspoon dried oregano
1/4 teaspoon dried thyme
1/2 teaspoon ground red pepper
2 to 3 drops Tabasco Sauce
  (optional)
  Hot cooked rice

Sauté sausage in a large skillet until done. Remove from pan; drain. ✻ Cook peas in water to cover with bacon, onion, and pepper. ✻ Stir in sausage, parsley, garlic, salt to taste, and next 6 ingredients. Add Tabasco Sauce, if desired. ✻ Simmer 30 minutes. ✻ Serve over hot cooked rice.

[C E C E   E L L I O T T   M A R T I N   ]

ITALIAN SAUSAGE PIE

Combine Monterey Jack and mayonnaise. Place half of mixture in bottom of pastry shell. ✒ Layer sausage, remaining cheese mixture, and tomato slices in pastry shell. Sprinkle with salt, pepper, basil, oregano, and Parmesan cheese. ✒ Bake at 375° for 25 minutes.

[LUCIE HOWISON MILLER]

SERVES 6

1 pound grated Monterey
  Jack cheese
½ cup mayonnaise
1 (9-inch) pastry shell, baked
  and cooled
½ pound sweet Italian sausage,
  cooked and crumbled
1 large ripe tomato, peeled
  and thinly sliced
½ teaspoon salt
¼ teaspoon pepper
1 teaspoon dried basil
½ teaspoon dried oregano
¼ cup grated fresh
  Parmesan cheese

VEAL PICCATA

Pound veal to ¼-inch thickness. Season with salt and pepper to taste. Dredge veal in flour. Pan-fry in 3 tablespoons butter until brown. Remove veal from pan. ✒ In same skillet, sauté garlic and mushrooms in additional 2 tablespoons butter. Return meat to skillet. Add lemon juice and wine. Simmer 15 to 20 minutes. Add capers. ✒ Garnish with parsley, if desired, and lemon slices.

[ELIZABETH MCDONALD DUNN]

SERVES 4

1½ pounds veal
  Salt and pepper
¼ cup all-purpose flour
5 tablespoons butter, divided
2 cloves garlic, minced
½ pound fresh mushrooms, sliced
4 tablespoons lemon juice
½ cup dry white wine
2 tablespoons capers
3 tablespoons chopped fresh
  parsley (optional)
1 lemon, sliced

Just a Thought

When buying veal, look for a creamy-white to pale-pink color. This indicates a younger calf and is therefore a more tender selection.

SERVES 4

1 pound veal scallops
¼ cup all-purpose flour
½ teaspoon salt
½ teaspoon freshly ground pepper
2 tablespoons butter, divided
1 tablespoon olive oil
½ cup dry white wine
½ cup sliced mushrooms
1 cup artichoke hearts
1 cup whipping cream
2 tablespoons Dijon mustard
3 cups hot cooked rice
   (preferably basmati)
   or hot cooked fettuccine

VEAL SCALLOPS WITH MUSHROOMS AND ARTICHOKE HEARTS

Pound veal between 2 sheets of wax paper until thin. ✍ Combine flour and salt and pepper; coat veal in flour mixture. Melt 1 tablespoon butter with olive oil over medium heat. Add veal, and sauté 2 to 3 minutes or until golden brown. Transfer veal to a plate, reserving drippings in skillet. Keep veal warm. Stir wine into skillet drippings. Add remaining 1 tablespoon butter. Stir in mushrooms, and sauté until tender. Blend in artichokes, cream, and mustard. Cook until thoroughly heated. Pour mixture over veal, and serve over rice or pasta.

[ALYSON LUTZ BUTTS]

SERVES 4

¼ cup butter
1 sweet yellow or red pepper,
   sliced
   Juice of ½ fresh lime
2 tablespoons peanut butter
3 cloves garlic, chopped
¼ cup sliced almonds
4 (1 to 1½-inch-thick) large
   veal chops

CHAR-GRILLED VEAL CHOPS

Melt butter in a 12-inch sauté pan. Add pepper and next 4 ingredients. Heat to medium-high; cook 5 minutes, stirring constantly. Cool to room temperature. ✍ Marinate veal chops in sauce for 1 hour. ✍ Heat grill to 500° or hotter, with grate 8 to 10 inches above coals. Remove chops from marinade. Grill chops 3 to 4 minutes; turn over. After turning, pour three-fourths of marinade over chops. This will make fire flame, but do not extinguish. Cook another 3 to 4 minutes. (This will be cooked about medium.) Remove and enjoy!

[KEITH FIERMAN]

THE BEST OSSO BUCCO

Season flour with salt and pepper to taste. Heat oil and butter in ovenproof Dutch oven. Dredge veal in flour mixture and brown well on all sides in heated oil mixture. Transfer veal to plate. Add onions, garlic, basil, and oregano to Dutch oven, and cook 10 minutes. Add tomatoes and salt and pepper to taste, and cook another 10 minutes. Skim off excess fat. Add wine. Bring to a boil, and reduce heat. Simmer, uncovered, for 15 minutes.   Return shanks to Dutch oven and add enough beef broth to just cover. Bake, covered, at 350° for 1½ hours. Uncover and bake another 30 minutes. Sprinkle with chopped fresh parsley and lemon zest, if desired.

[ELLISON JONES GRAY]

Serve with saffron rice or polenta and Merlot.
Truly Italian, elegant, and delicious.

SERVES 6 TO 8

1 cup all-purpose flour
Salt and pepper
½ cup extra-virgin olive oil
¼ to ½ cup butter
Veal shanks for 6 to 8, usually one each, 2 inches thick
2 medium-size yellow onions, coarsely chopped
6 large cloves garlic, peeled and chopped
½ teaspoon dried basil
½ teaspoon dried oregano
1 (28-ounce) can peeled tomatoes, drained
2 cups dry white wine
2 cups beef broth
¾ cup chopped fresh Italian parsley
Grated zest of 1 lemon (optional)

FLANK STEAK MARINADE

Combine all ingredients. Use to marinate flank steak before grilling and to baste during grilling.

[MARY REID REYNOLDS FISHER]

SERVES 4

¼ cup soy sauce
3 tablespoons honey
2 tablespoons white vinegar
1½ teaspoons garlic powder
1½ teaspoons ground ginger
¾ cup vegetable oil
1 small green onion, chopped

MAKES 1/2 CUP

1/4 cup soy sauce
2 tablespoons chili sauce
2 tablespoons honey
1 tablespoon vegetable oil
1 tablespoon minced green onion
2 teaspoons curry powder

PORK TENDERLOIN MARINADE

Combine all ingredients. Use to marinate pork tenderloins before cooking.

[MARY REID REYNOLDS FISHER]

MAKES 1 CUP

2 tablespoons honey
2 tablespoons soy sauce
1/2 cup lemon juice
1 tablespoon grated lemon rind
1/3 cup olive oil
1 teaspoon Worcestershire sauce
1 teaspoon prepared mustard
1 clove garlic, minced
2 green onions, chopped

STEAK MARINADE

Combine all ingredients. Use to marinate steaks several hours or overnight.

[ALICE DERRICK REYNOLDS]

MAKES 1/2 CUP

1/4 cup olive oil
1/4 cup balsamic vinegar
2 cloves garlic, minced
2 tablespoons fresh thyme
or 1/2 teaspoon dried thyme
1 tablespoon seasoned salt
1 teaspoon paprika
1/2 teaspoon cumin
3 green onions, sliced

LAMB MARINADE

Combine all ingredients and mix well. Excellent when used to marinate lamb chops or boned and butterflied leg of lamb.

[PEGGY LANNING BYRD]

BURGUNDY MARINADE FOR BEEF TENDERLOIN

Combine Burgundy, lemon juice, and olive oil. Sprinkle tenderloin with tarragon and steak salt. Cover and marinate in refrigerator 24 hours. ✒ Grill over medium heat for 45 to 50 minutes for medium-rare. (Can be slightly undercooked, wrapped in foil, and held in warm oven up to 2 hours without becoming overcooked.)

[ANNE TERRY JOHNSON]

MAKES 2 1/2 CUPS

2 cups Burgundy
1/4 cup lemon juice
1/4 cup olive oil
7 to 8 pounds beef tenderloin
2 tablespoons tarragon
2 tablespoons steak salt

MARINADE FOR KABOBS

Combine all ingredients, and mix well. ✒ Excellent for marinating beef, chicken, pork, or shrimp.

[LINDA McMEANS BYRNE]

MAKES 3 CUPS

1 1/2 cups olive oil
3/4 cup soy sauce
1/4 cup Worcestershire sauce
2 tablespoons dry mustard
2 1/4 teaspoons salt
1 tablespoon pepper
1/4 cup red wine vinegar
1 1/2 teaspoons dried parsley flakes
2 cloves garlic, crushed
1/3 cup lemon juice

BRINE FOR BASTING PORK

Combine all ingredients in a large saucepan. Bring to a boil. Reduce heat, and simmer 30 minutes. Use for basting pork ribs, chops, shoulder, or Boston butt.

[ANNE TERRY JOHNSON]

MAKES 1 GALLON

2 cups cider vinegar
2 cups water
2 cups lemon juice
1 cup Worcestershire sauce
1/4 cup pepper
1/4 cup dehydrated minced onion
1/4 cup dehydrated minced garlic
1/2 teaspoon Tabasco Sauce

Deep-Dish Pheasant Pie, page 265

The Metaphysics of Canned Meat

-Robert Reeves-

THAT I SHOULD REMEMBER A SANDWICH my father prepared for me over three decades ago is in itself unusual. Over the years, my brain had distinguished itself chiefly as an organ of suppression, not memory. But this particular sandwich, and the small sack of groceries from which it emerged, lingers in my mind. I have yet to digest it.

I was six, maybe seven years old, and my father and I had escaped Birmingham for the weekend, escaped the women in our family for the masculine pleasures of the modest cabin he had built on Smith Lake. We stopped at a small country store for provisions: sardines, potted meat, pork and beans, saltines, white bread, a jar of pig's feet for him, Moon Pies for me, Budweiser for him, Grapico for me.

The grocery sack held, too, a can of Vienna sausages, the featured ingredient of the sandwich I am recalling. My requirements for Viennas were very precise even then. My father knew that I liked them fried. So he took a metal cup from a rack above the stove, poured a spot of grease into our ancient iron skillet, then laid in the pinkish cylinders of processed meat. It soon became apparent to him, though not to me, that the small weenies were bubbling queerly. They gurgled. They began to spit violently. But they were soon brown, and they found their way between two slices of white bread. I positioned them just so. No doubt generous quantities of mayonnaise were involved.

So, while my father opened his can of beer and his jar of pig's feet, I feasted happily: the warm blandness of the soft meat, the cool blandness of the mayonnaise, the doughy blandness of the white bread.

Later my father returned to the stove. His mind must ·CONTINUED·

ROBERT REEVES

NOVELIST ROBERT REEVES
WAS BORN IN BIRMINGHAM.
HE TAUGHT AT HARVARD
UNIVERSITY FOR 15 YEARS,
WHERE HE WROTE
*THE RIDICULOUS TO THE
DELIGHTFUL*, A COMPENDIUM OF
LITERARY CRITICISM, AND *THE
LANGUAGE OF INSECTS*. HIS
FIRST WIDELY ACCLAIMED
FICTIONAL WORK WAS
DOUBTING THOMAS, WHICH
RECEIVED RAVE REVIEWS UPON
ITS PUBLISHING IN 1990.
PEEPING THOMAS, IN 1991,
WAS THE SECOND IN HIS SERIES
FEATURING DETECTIVE
THOMAS THERON. THE THIRD,
*THOMAS SOLVES THE MYSTERY
OF LIFE*, IS CURRENTLY
UNDERWAY. ROBERT REEVES
NOW RESIDES IN NEW YORK.

have been working on the mystery of the gurgling and spitting in the skillet. I watched him retrieve the metal cup from which he'd poured the grease. For some moments he peered into it. I still remember the quality of his laugh, weighted with adult irony.

My father had prepared the skillet not with grease, but dishwashing liquid. I had feasted happily on Vienna sausages à la Lux Liquid.

I here confess that we were both curiously proud of the mistake. We must have reasoned thus:

A man will eat anything.

I had eaten processed meat sautéed in liquid detergent.

Therefore, I was a man.

If you resist the notion that our adult lives are merely the exfoliation of the minutiae of childhood, then consider that sandwich, consider that small sack of groceries. Those tins of meat are imprinted on my psyche; they surface unbeckoned as the secret cravings of my life. In the evening in Cambridge, Massachusetts, I have strolled past elegant French bistros, charming Italian trattorias, in order to buy a can of potted meat. In Manhattan, I have walked among the wafted fragrances of innumerable delicacies—oblivious to exotic victuals of the very world itself—in search of a can of pork and beans. And to this day, there is only one aisle in the supermarket where I linger, where my eyes glaze and I am transported. It is where the shelves are laden with canned meat. And when the groceries get unpacked at home, one or two of these tins of meat appear, as if with the inevitability of fate. I don't remember putting them there, but there they are.

My wife lifts them out of the sack, regarding them as if they were the dark, totemic emblems of a dream. And she is right, of course. What I have slipped into the grocery bag is a subterranean history of myself, the icons of a Southern past alien and somehow incommunicable. A part of me still prepares for a weekend at Smith Lake.

And so, when my wife and son are sleeping, when the middle of the night finds me at my kitchen counter in New York, I nearly swoon with the thrill of conspiracy. I dress the small cracker with potted meat, swirled deft and neat. I take it carefully into my mouth and commune with my former self.

To know the public man, observe him among friends at a meal. To know the private man—naked, unadorned, bereft of the masks that he presents to the world—learn what he snacks on. Learn what he fixes himself to eat when no one is looking. Learn what he puts into his mouth when he has no one to account to but himself. THE END

WHEN YOU WANT TO ADD A HOMEMADE TASTE to plain grilled or roasted meats, poultry, or fish, mix one of these sauces right from your pantry and refrigerator.

• Heat 1/2 cup apricot jam, 3 tablespoons teriyaki sauce, 1 tablespoon rice or white wine vinegar, and 1 teaspoon crushed dried rosemary. Serve with lamb, chicken, or pork.

• Mix 1/4 cup orange juice concentrate, 1/4 cup Dijon mustard, and 1 to 2 teaspoons lime juice. Use as a baste and sauce for poultry or fish.

• Mix 1 cup diced fresh orange sections, 1/4 cup minced sundried tomatoes packed in oil, 2 tablespoons minced fresh cilantro, 2 teaspoons grated ginger, and Tabasco Sauce. Use with grilled meats.

• Mix 1 snack-size can diced pears, undrained, 2/3 cup chutney, 2 tablespoons minced crystallized ginger; serve with grilled pork tenderloin.

• Heat 2/3 cup apple jelly, 1 cup diced seeded tomato, 1/2 cup minced chives or green onion, 1/2 cup minced sweet red pepper, and 1/2 teaspoon ground allspice; serve with chicken or pork.

• Mix 3/4 cup honey mustard barbecue sauce and 1/2 cup orange marmalade. Serve with ham, ribs, and hamburgers.

• Mix seeded and diced plums, 2 tablespoons orange juice concentrate, 1 teaspoon lemon juice, 1 tablespoon minced jalapeño, 1/4 teaspoon ground ginger, and 1/4 teaspoon ground cinnamon. Serve with chicken, pork, ham slices.

• Mix 1 cup mayonnaise, 2 tablespoons barbecue sauce, 2 tablespoons balsamic vinegar, 1 tablespoon Worcestershire sauce, 1/2 teaspoon each garlic powder, dry mustard, and freshly ground pepper. Serve with smoked or grilled meats, as a dipping sauce, or sandwich sauce.

• Heat 2/3 cup commercial cranberry-orange sauce, 1/4 cup Amaretto, 1/4 cup minced shallots or green onion, 1/2 teaspoon dried thyme, and 1/3 cup toasted slivered almonds, if desired. Serve with poultry or lamb.

• Heat 1 cup pepper jelly, 1 drained (8-ounce) can unsweetened crushed pineapple, 1/2 cup minced sweet red pepper, 1/4 teaspoon ground ginger, and minced jalapeño, if desired. Serve with roasted meats.

• Puree 1 drained (17-ounce) can apricots, 1/2 cup Heinz 57 Sauce, 1/4 cup packed brown sugar, and 1 teaspoon chili powder. Serve hot or cold with ribs, ham, and roasted meats.

• Mix 1 cup mayonnaise, 1 tablespoon molasses, 1 tablespoon lemon juice, 1/4 cup minced green onion, 2 cloves crushed garlic, 1 teaspoon dry mustard, 1 teaspoon freshly ground pepper, 1/2 teaspoon red pepper, 1/2 teaspoon oregano for homemade jerk sauce. Serve chilled with roasted meats, seafood, or as sandwich spread.

G A M E

SERVES 4

12 doves, dressed
4 tablespoons olive oil
½ teaspoon celery salt
½ teaspoon garlic salt
¼ teaspoon curry powder
¼ teaspoon dry mustard
   Salt and pepper
1 cup water
2 tablespoons Worcestershire
   sauce
   Juice of 1 orange
   Juice of 1 lemon

CITRUS BAKED DOVES

Roll doves in olive oil to coat. Combine seasonings and salt and pepper to taste; sprinkle each bird with mixture. Place birds in a covered casserole dish. Add 1 cup water to dish, until sides of dove are covered. Bake, covered, at 250° for 1½ hours. Add Worcestershire, orange juice, and lemon juice, and cook 10 more minutes. Serve with baked polenta.

[MARTHA SULZBY CLARK]

SERVES 4

3 tablespoons butter
1 teaspoon celery salt
1 teaspoon salt
1 teaspoon paprika
½ teaspoon curry powder
½ teaspoon pepper
½ teaspoon dried oregano
4 boneless pheasant breast
   halves, 6 to 8 partridge
   breasts, 10 dove breasts,
   or 6 quail breasts
2 cups half-and-half
½ cup sliced fresh mushrooms
½ cup sliced almonds
1 cup sour cream
1 cup fine dry breadcrumbs

GAME BIRDS IN CREAM SAUCE

Melt butter and add next 6 ingredients in a large skillet. Brown breasts quickly in mixture, and transfer breasts to a baking dish. Reserve sauce mixture in skillet. Cover birds with half-and-half, mushrooms, and almonds. Bake, covered, at 375° for 45 minutes. Add sour cream to reserved sauce in skillet, stirring well. After the birds have baked 45 minutes, top with sour cream mixture; sprinkle with breadcrumbs. Return birds to oven, and bake, uncovered, at 375° for 15 more minutes. Serve breasts with wild rice.

[BONNY AND DAVID CHISHOLM]

D O V E - S A U S A G E   G U M B O

Place dove breasts in a Dutch oven, and cover with water. Boil 10 minutes. Cool and remove meat from bones. Reserve 2 1/4 cups liquid; add consommé and bouillon cube.   Brown dove meat in oil, and drain off all but 1/4 cup oil. Remove meat. Add flour to oil, and cook over medium heat until roux is the color of a copper penny (10 to 15 minutes).   Gradually add 1 1/2 cups of consommé mixture, stirring constantly until thick. Stir in onion and celery. Cook 5 minutes. Add remaining consommé mixture to roux, and stir well. Stir in Worcestershire, garlic, and seasonings. Brown sausage, and drain well. Stir sausage and dove into roux mixture. Simmer 1 1/2 hours. Add wine and Tabasco Sauce. Remove bay leaves, and serve over hot cooked rice.

[S U S A N   S M I T H   B L A I R   ]

MAKES 1 3/4 QUARTS

15 *dove breasts*
1 *(10 1/2-ounce) can beef consommé*
1 *beef bouillon cube*
1/2 *cup vegetable oil*
1/2 *cup all-purpose flour*
1 1/2 *cups finely chopped onion*
1 *cup finely chopped celery*
2 *tablespoons Worcestershire sauce*
2 *cloves garlic, minced*
2 *bay leaves*
1/2 *teaspoon dried basil*
1/4 *teaspoon poultry seasoning*
1/4 *teaspoon ground black pepper*
1/4 *teaspoon ground red pepper*
1/8 *teaspoon ground allspice*
1/8 *teaspoon ground cloves*
3/4 *pound smoked sausage, sliced*
1/4 *cup dry red wine*
1/8 *teaspoon Tabasco Sauce*

L I M E   G R I L L E D   D U C K

Quick & easy

Soak duck breasts in lime juice for about 1 hour. Dip each breast in melted butter.   Grill over hot flame, 2 to 3 minutes on each side.   Delicious and so easy!

[B A Y A R D   S H I E L D S   T Y N E S   ]

SERVES 4

4 *breasts wood duck or teal*
4 *cups lime juice*
1/2 *cup butter, melted*

SERVES 8

1 cup chopped yellow onion
1 cup chopped green onion
4 tablespoons all-purpose flour
1 teaspoon peanut oil
12 ounces bacon,
    cooked and crumbled
4 cups hot water
1 teaspoon seasoned salt
3 teaspoons chili powder
1 teaspoon dry mustard
1 teaspoon ground white pepper
1/2 teaspoon dried crushed
    red pepper
1 cup chopped parsley
1 large or 2 small duck, dressed
1 pound smoked link sausage,
    sliced
1 (16-ounce) can tomatoes,
    drained and chopped
1/2 pound medium fresh shrimp,
    peeled and deveined

D U C K   G U M B O

In large saucepan or stockpot, sauté yellow and green onions and flour in peanut oil. Add crumbled bacon, water, and seasonings. Add duck; bring to a boil. Reduce heat, and cook 1 hour. Remove duck, debone, and cut into bite-size pieces. Return to stockpot. Add sausage, tomatoes, and shrimp. Simmer $1\frac{1}{2}$ additional hours. Serve over brown rice.

[LEIGH LEACY BROMBERG]

This is spicy! It's great for a cold midwinter night with homemade sourdough bread and a crisp green salad.

4 SERVINGS

2 wood ducks
1 teaspoon salt
1 cup chopped celery
1 cup chopped onion
2 tablespoons bouquet garni
1/2 cup butter or bacon drippings
1/2 cup all-purpose flour
    Salt and pepper
1 cup red wine

C R E O L E   W I L D   D U C K

Barely cover ducks with salted water in a large Dutch oven. Add celery, onion, and bouquet garni. Boil until meat falls from bone. Remove from heat and debone. Reserve and strain liquid. Make a roux with butter or bacon drippings and flour. Cook over low heat, stirring until brown. Add reserved liquid to roux. Stir in duck, salt and pepper to taste, and simmer 3 hours. Add red wine and simmer 1 hour. Serve over brown rice.

[ELLISON GRAY HUGHES]

PAN-ROASTED DUCK

Wash duck and pat dry. Salt and pepper bird inside and out. Stuff breast and neck cavities with celery, onion, and if desired, green pepper. Place duck in a Dutch oven along with giblets. Slice 4 garlic cloves. Mince remaining cloves. Stir sliced garlic into Dutch oven. Cover top of duck with minced garlic. Sprinkle duck sparingly with Cajun seasoning. Add chicken stock. Cook, covered, at 175° for 5 to 6½ hours. Remove duck and keep warm, reserving broth. Freeze broth 30 minutes and remove solidified fat. Make gravy out of broth, flour, and if desired, bourbon. Serve duck and gravy with Barley Casserole (page 177). Wood duck–5 hours–serves 2 Mallard–6 hours–serves 4 Domestic (4 pounds)–6½ hours–serves 4

[MELANIE DRAKE PARKER]

1 wood duck or mallard, dressed
Salt and pepper
1 stalk celery, sliced
1 small onion, sliced
1 small green pepper, sliced (optional)
Giblets, sliced
2 heads garlic
Cajun blackened seasoning
1½ cups chicken stock
2 tablespoons all-purpose flour
⅛ cup bourbon (optional)

DEEP-DISH PHEASANT PIE

Line a deep casserole dish with 1 piecrust. Melt 3 tablespoons butter in a heavy saucepan. Stir in flour and next 5 ingredients until smooth and combined. Cook, stirring often, over medium heat until thickened. Set white sauce aside. Sauté onion, celery, and mushrooms in remaining 1 tablespoon butter. Fold vegetables into white sauce. Fold in eggs and meat. Pour into pastry-lined dish. Cover with remaining piecrust. Crimp edges to seal. Cut slits in top for steam to escape. Brush with half-and-half, and bake at 350° for 25 minutes or until crust is done.

[RAYMOND J. HARBERT]

1 (15-ounce) package refrigerated piecrusts
4 tablespoons butter, divided
¼ cup all-purpose flour
1½ cups half-and-half
1½ cups chicken broth
1 teaspoon salt
½ teaspoon ground white pepper
¼ teaspoon grated nutmeg
1 medium onion, chopped
1 stalk celery, sliced
½ pound fresh mushrooms, sliced
4 hard-cooked eggs, coarsely chopped
4 cups pheasant or quail, cooked and cubed (may substitute chicken)
Half-and-half

SERVES 4

1 (2 to 3-pound) pheasant, dressed
2 teaspoons chopped fresh parsley
1 teaspoon chopped fresh chives
1 teaspoon chervil
1 teaspoon rosemary, crumbled
1/4 teaspoon dried sage
2 to 3 tablespoons finely chopped onion
2 cloves garlic, chopped
2 tablespoons sunflower oil
2 1/2 tablespoons butter, divided
1 cup white wine
1 cup chicken broth
Salt and pepper

SERVES 4 TO 6

8 quail, dressed
3 1/2 cups milk, divided
Salt and pepper
1 cup all-purpose flour
1/2 cup butter
1 medium onion, chopped
1 medium green pepper, seeded and chopped
1 (10 3/4-ounce) can condensed cream of chicken soup or 1 cup chicken broth
1/2 cup sherry

HERB-ROASTED PHEASANT

Cut a 2-inch slit in the breast skin and leg skin of pheasant. Combine parsley and next 6 ingredients, and blend together to make a paste. Stuff the paste under the skin at the leg and breast incisions until you cover the flesh with the herb spread. Roast pheasant, covered, in a roasting pan at 420° for about 40 minutes, basting frequently with sunflower oil and half of the butter. Remove bird when done, and keep warm. Discard fat from the pan, and deglaze pan with wine and broth. Cook over low heat until liquid is reduced to 1 cup, and stir in remaining butter. Season with salt and pepper to taste. Simmer and reduce until sauce thickens (will coat back of spoon). Pour through a wire-mesh strainer, and serve with the pheasant.

[BONNY AND DAVID CHISHOLM]

BAKED QUAIL WITH SHERRY SAUCE

Soak quail in 3 cups milk overnight. The next day, drain and salt and pepper the quail to taste. Dredge in flour. Melt butter in a large skillet, and brown quail in butter. Remove quail to a baking dish, reserving half of the drippings in skillet. Sauté onion and green pepper in reserved drippings. Stir in soup, sherry, and 1/2 cup milk. Stir well, and pour over quail. Bake, covered, at 300° for 30 to 40 minutes.

[SELWOOD FARM AND HUNTING PRESERVE]

QUAIL WITH 7-GRAIN STUFFING

Crumble bread, and soak in chicken broth. Sauté shallots and mushrooms in butter. Remove and combine with bread. Spread into a greased 3-quart baking dish. ✍ Wash and dry quail; brown in same skillet, and reserve drippings. Arrange on stuffing mixture. Salt and pepper to taste; dot with butter, and sprinkle with wine. ✍ Roast at 400° for 30 to 45 minutes. Deglaze skillet with sherry. Add cream and adjust seasonings to taste. Pour sauce over birds.

SERVES 6

4 to 6 slices 7-grain bread
1 cup chicken broth
2 shallots, chopped
8 ounces fresh mushrooms, sliced
2 tablespoons butter
12 quail, dressed
    Salt and pepper
2 tablespoons butter, cut into pieces
2 tablespoons port wine
1/4 cup sherry
1/2 cup whipping cream

ORANGE CURRANT GAME SAUCE

Combine all ingredients in a saucepan. Simmer for 10 minutes or until jelly is dissolved. ✍ Serve with cooked game birds.

For an alternative, cook birds in the sauce. Cover 8 doves, 4 to 6 quail, or 6 whole chicken breasts. Roast at 325° for an hour. This makes a delicious gravy!

MAKES 1 1/2 CUPS

1/2 teaspoon grated orange rind
1 cup orange juice
1/4 cup port wine
1/4 cup currant jelly
3 tablespoons lemon juice
1/4 teaspoon ground ginger
    Salt and pepper

1 to 2 pounds venison stew meat
2 cups buttermilk
1 cup all-purpose flour
3 tablespoons vegetable oil
1½ cups beef broth
½ cup dry red wine
1 cup chopped onion
1 bay leaf
2 carrots, sliced (optional)
2 potatoes, chopped
Salt and pepper
1 to 2 tablespoons Worcestershire sauce

Marinade:
½ cup Burgundy
1 cup red wine vinegar
1½ cups vegetable oil
¼ cup lemon juice
1 teaspoon salt
3 tablespoons Worcestershire sauce
1 clove garlic, minced
1 small onion, grated

1 (3 to 5-pound) venison tenderloin

VENISON STEW

Soak stew meat in buttermilk overnight. Drain. Dredge meat in flour, and brown in oil. Put meat in a large Dutch oven. Add broth and next 5 ingredients. Stir in salt, pepper, and Worcestershire sauce to taste. Cook over low heat, covered, 7 to 10 hours, stirring occasionally and adding water, if necessary. About 30 minutes before serving, increase heat to medium high to soften vegetables.

[JOHN THOMASON OLIVER]

Venison is a term for the meat of deer, elk, or caribou. It is very lean. The tenderloin and steaks may be broiled. Other less tender cuts benefit from overnight marination (which tenderizes them) and are better cooked in a liquid.

VENISON TENDERLOIN

Combine marinade ingredients. Marinate tenderloin at least 3 hours. Grill over medium-hot coals 15 to 20 minutes or until an instant-read thermometer measures medium-rare. Slice into steaks, and serve with béarnaise sauce.

[ANNE TERRY JOHNSON]

GRILLED QUAIL WITH MOLASSES GLAZE

SERVES 4

3 tablespoons olive oil
2 tablespoons molasses
6 sprigs mixed herbs
   (thyme, rosemary,
   marjoram), crushed
4 juniper berries, crushed
2 large cloves garlic, crushed
   Salt and pepper
4 quail

Combine olive oil and next 4 ingredients to make marinade. Season with salt and pepper to taste. ✒ Remove backbone from each quail with kitchen shears. Cut each bird in half lengthwise. ✒ Marinate quail at least 3 hours or overnight. Bring to room temperature. Remove from marinade. Grill 4 to 5 inches over medium heat for 3 to 4 minutes on each side. (Meat will be pink.) Let stand 5 minutes. ✒ Serve with grits and spinach salad for dinner, or Corn and Arugula Salad (page 132) for a light lunch.

[FRANK STITT, CHEF/OWNER]
HIGHLANDS BAR & GRILL

Fresh Fruit Salsa, page 281

Desperately Seeking Sauces

·JOHN FORNEY·

IT WAS FLATTERING TO BE INCLUDED among the flower of Alabama *belle letters* and contribute to this most worthy gastronomic compendium. My inclusion was likely occasioned more by my well-merited reputation as a trencherman of some renown than by my skill as a crafter of polished pearl-like prose. So be it.

The subject is sauces, my own choice for this disquisition—not "on the sauce" (which I am not) or "in the sauce" (which I admittedly have been at times) but just sauces generally.

Over a lifetime of dining out not necessarily wisely but certainly too well, it is my gut feeling (that pun deserves no pardon) that the care and preparation of sauces are a significant yardstick by which to measure a chef's ability. And this can be from the simplest sort of red sauce for seafoods to something truly Lucullan for lamb or veal or other meats. It's amazing that something like a red sauce can vary so, with the tomato base, perhaps a bit of oil and lemon and the proper degree of horseradish.

Two old friends of mine, Joe Daole and Jake Levine, joined together right after World War II and established Dale's Cellar, a restaurant in an old building which faced Linn Park (where Park Place office building is now). Conventional Birmingham wisdom consigned them to failure: "Nobody will go to a basement to eat." They were extraordinarily successful, eventually branching out here as well as Atlanta, Huntsville, and Montgomery. In my opinion, their creative abilities with sauces was a key part of their success. They are gone but their steak sauce thrives and is a basic part of marinades for thousands of backyard cookouts throughout ·CONTINUED·

J O H N F O R N E Y

A NATIVE OF TUSCALOOSA,
ALABAMA, JOHN FORNEY
SPENT 36 YEARS IN THE
ADVERTISING BUSINESS
IN BIRMINGHAM
AND NEW YORK CITY.
HE WAS FOR FOUR DECADES
A RADIO SPORTSCASTER.
JOHN FORNEY PUBLISHED
CRIMSON MEMORIES,
GOLDEN DAYS IN 1980,
ABOVE THE NOISE OF THE
CROWD IN 1986, AND
TALK OF THE TIDE IN 1993.
HE RESIDES IN BIRMINGHAM
WITH HIS WIFE AND FAMILY.

the South. (They also had a soy-based dark salad dressing I thought was wonderful and just wish it, too, was on the market. I'm an anchovy freak and it blended superbly with the controversial little fishes.) All their sauces were truly distinctive.

Mentioning cookouts brings to mind one of my many character flaws, to wit: I am terrible at cooking steaks or hamburgers on outdoor grills, always misjudging cooking times assuring the meat is either rawish or godawfully overdone. But my faults start before this. I usually spill the charcoal, get my clothes dirty and certainly struggle with lighting the fire even with the new easy-blaze surefire briquets.

Therefore, I have never been able to share a wondrous macho moment with other men by saying in a hopefully deep and manly voice, "You'll have to come over to our place sometime and I'll cook you a steak." When such an invitation is extended to me, I always reply, "That'd be great," adding wimpily, "and I'll toss us a really super salad."

It is a super salad and if the aphorism "what's sauce for the goose is sauce for the gander" is correct then we have reached gender-equity with the sauce. Or more specifically, with the red Roquefort dressing which I have shamelessly copied from the Birmingham Country Club, adding just a dash of non-creamy Italian and a bit more Roquefort (or bleu if that's your preference) to give it firm consistency. White, watery Roquefort dressing is not only bad, it's depressing.

A head of lettuce should be torn apart by hand, placed

in a bowl and the following items added: a well-diced fresh tomato (never tomato wedges or little cherry tomatoes) and a couple of medium onions, chopped artichoke hearts, and well-diced black and green olives, ditto for a small jar of mushrooms, generous quantity of pepper (salt should be added after the serving), crumbled crisp bacon bits and croutons lightly marinated in the non-creamy Italian. Topping it with a sprinkling of Parmesan cheese or adding a few anchovies is optional.

You will note that no cucumbers are called for and will never be by me because a "cuke" just serves to "nuke" my otherwise stellar digestion.

Add the dressing and toss, toss, toss. It is a salad with no pretense of being "calorically correct" but it is good. And, hopefully, somewhat manly to earn justly the name I have decided to give it: Forney's Macho-Gander Super Salad. THE END

SONNET FOR A SAUCY MEAL

To begin the repast I'd give the nod
To a crab imperial or shrimp remoulade.
Then a savory salad would be a pleaser –
A Waldorf maybe, or Greek or Caesar.

A superb beef tender with a delicate béarnaise
Or simply au jus or sauce bordelaise
But if red meat you chose to bar,
Just have fruits de mer with a sauce tartare.

Expand the meal and make it better
With a baked potato topped with aged Cheddar.
Then come dessert... now don't you budge
Till you revel in a Sundae laden with thick hot fudge!

Then stand – toast the meal and shout hooray
With a dollop or two of Grand Marnier!

TODAY IT IS EASIER THAN EVER TO CREATE YOUR OWN fabulous salad dressings and marinades. With the wide abundance of fresh herbs, oils, and vinegars available, it is simply a matter of choosing the ones you like and combining them in a variety of different ways.

A Survey of Vinegars

The word "vinegar" comes from the French words "vin" and "aigre," meaning "soured wine." When wine or any other naturally fermented alcohol (such as beer or hard cider) is exposed to air, it gradually turns to vinegar. In Japan and China, vinegar is made from rice wine. In the United States, the primary ingredient is apple cider, and throughout Europe, wine and sherry are preferred.

Apple Cider Vinegar: When properly aged, apple cider vinegar has an amber color and a fresh, tart, apple taste. A variety of apples are ground into a sauce and pressed to extract cider. Cider is placed in wooden casks and the natural sugars ferment into alcohol. Use in potato salads and coleslaw; stir into vegetable soups or stews at the end of cooking; use in homemade pickles and chutneys.

Balsamic Vinegar: Unlike any other vinegar, aceto balsamico is a rich, dark-brown vinegar that is so intensely aromatic and naturally sweet that it can be used alone on a salad or splashed on strawberries. To be called aceto balsamico, the vinegar, made from the must of wine grapes that contain a high sugar content, has to age a minimum of 3 years in wooden barrels. However, the finest, and most expensive, varieties can age for 50 to 100 years. Balsamic is stronger than most vinegars, so use less. Use to marinate meats and poultry, or to deglaze pan juices from chicken, meat, or fish dishes. Mix with fresh wild mushrooms and toss with a little olive oil. Add a half-teaspoon to an oyster on the half-shell.

Japanese Rice Vinegar: A mild, slightly sweet condiment made from rice wine, it is more delicate than American and European vinegars with a low acidity. The light flavor is compatible with mild foods, and is great to cook with — especially chicken, fish, and vegetables. Mix with grated ginger and soy sauce for a dipping sauce, and sprinkle on seafood salads.

Wine Vinegar: Wine vinegars are the most versatile. They are made from red and white wine, Spanish sherry wine, and champagne vinegar. Use white or red wine vinegars in vinaigrettes, add to chicken salad, rub on beef or lamb roasts before cooking, add to gazpacho, deglaze a chicken, veal, or pork sauté.

Sherry Vinegar: Rich and intensely flavored, it is good served with artichokes, seafood and vegetables, salads. Marinate lamb in sherry vinegar and garlic, then baste occasionally while grilling or roasting. Use in potato salads with capers, olive oil, and chopped pickles.

Champagne Vinegar: This is made from dry white wine (not champagne) from the Champagne region of France. Use as you would any other wine vinegar.

Herb and Fruit Vinegars: Herb and fruit-flavored vinegars are made by steeping fresh herbs or fruit in white wine or apple cider vinegar. They can be made inexpensively and easily from herbs and fruits of your garden. However, some commercially made types are distinguished by the addition of an herb or fruit "extract," making them more pronounced in flavor.

Roasted Red Pepper Vinegar: Roast a red and yellow sweet pepper. Use one-fourth of each for vinegar, saving remainder for another use. Cut each fourth into strips. Heat 4 ounces Champagne vinegar and 8 ounces distilled white vinegar in saucepan. Combine all ingredients in quart jar. Cover and store in a cool, dark place for 2 weeks. Strain and pour into decorative 12-ounce bottles.

ACCOMPANIMENTS, ETC.

MAKES
APPROXIMATELY
2 CUPS

6 egg yolks
1 cup butter, room temperature
2 shallots, sliced
6 sprigs fresh parsley
2 tablespoons lemon juice
1 cup boiling water
Salt and pepper

LEMON SAUCE
FOR VEGETABLES

Combine first 5 ingredients in blender. Add water. Blend until smooth. Pour mixture into the top of a double boiler. Cook for 20 minutes, stirring occasionally. Stir in salt and pepper to taste. Leftover sauce can be refrigerated then brought back to room temperature. Spoon over hot vegetables.

[JOHN FORNEY]

MAKES ³/4 CUP

2 egg yolks
Juice of 1 large lemon
Pinch of salt
2 drops Tabasco Sauce
(optional)
½ cup butter, melted

BLENDER
HOLLANDAISE

Place egg yolks in an electric blender. Add lemon juice, and blend. Add salt and, if desired, Tabasco Sauce. Add butter in a slow, steady stream while blender is running. Pour mixture into saucepan. Cook over low heat, stirring constantly, until thick.

*Sauce works best if egg yolks are at room temperature
and melted butter has cooled.*

MAKES ABOUT ½ CUP

⅔ cup sugar
6 tablespoons water
1 tablespoon white vinegar
⅓ cup fresh mint leaves, chopped

MINT SAUCE

Combine sugar and water in medium saucepan. Stir slowly over low heat until sugar dissolves. Increase heat and bring to a slow rolling boil. Boil 2 minutes. Remove from heat. Add vinegar. Stir mint into syrup mixture. Serve with lamb.

RÉMOULADE SAUCE

Combine all ingredients. Chill. Great over broiled, chilled shrimp.

[BETTY BLACKMON KINNETT]

MAKES 1 1/2 CUPS

2 tablespoons olive oil
1/2 teaspoon pepper
1/2 teaspoon prepared horseradish
1 cup finely chopped celery
2 tablespoons red wine vinegar
4 teaspoons prepared mustard
1/2 cup chopped onion
1/2 teaspoon dried parsley flakes

WHITE RÉMOULADE SAUCE

Combine first 10 ingredients. Add green onion, if desired. Chill 2 to 3 hours. Pour over fresh crabmeat.

[PAT McCABE FORMAN]
PAST PRESIDENT

MAKES 3 CUPS

2 cups mayonnaise
1/4 to 1/2 cup diced sour pickles (not dill pickles)
2 tablespoons capers, drained and dried
1 tablespoon Creole mustard
1 tablespoon chopped fresh parsley
1 teaspoon dried tarragon
1 teaspoon dried chervil
1/4 to 1/2 cup finely chopped celery
Juice of 1 lemon
1 tablespoon chopped chives
Chopped green onions (optional)

SHERRIED MUSHROOM GRAVY

Sauté mushrooms in butter. Set aside. Combine milk, flour, and whipping cream. Add to mushrooms. Cook over low heat, stirring constantly, until sauce thickens. Add sherry, paprika, and salt to taste just before serving. Great with baked chicken and rice.

[BEBE OGLETREE BURKETT]

MAKES 2 CUPS

1 pound fresh mushrooms, sliced
1/2 cup butter, melted
1/2 cup milk
2 tablespoons all-purpose flour
1 cup whipping cream
1 tablespoon cooking sherry
Paprika
Salt

MAKES 1^1/2 CUPS

2 tablespoons butter, divided
3 tablespoons chopped onion
2 teaspoons paprika
1 tablespoon all-purpose flour
½ teaspoon dried thyme
½ cup chicken broth
½ cup whipping cream
2 teaspoons lemon juice
   Salt and pepper
1 teaspoon cognac
¼ cup sour cream

SERVES 8

4 green onions, chopped
2 tablespoons vinegar
6 tablespoons white wine
2 tablespoons chopped
   fresh tarragon
2 teaspoons Worcestershire sauce
4 egg yolks
1 cup butter, melted

PAPRIKA SAUCE

Melt 1 tablespoon butter in a small saucepan, and cook onion until clear. Sprinkle with paprika, flour, and thyme. Stir to mix. Stir in chicken broth with a wire whisk. Simmer 3 minutes. Add cream, and bring to a boil. Add lemon juice, salt and pepper to taste, and cognac. Pour through a wire-mesh strainer. Return to heat, and stir, adding remaining butter and sour cream. Reheat. Do not boil.

[VIRGINIA FLYNN HOLLINGER]

BÉARNAISE SAUCE

Combine first 5 ingredients in saucepan, and cook liquid down a little. Set aside to cool. Mix onion mixture in blender. With blender on high, add egg yolks (best if at room temperature) and slowly add butter. Return to saucepan, and cook, stirring constantly, over very low heat until thick. A special treat on any red meat. You can make this before company comes and leave in pan. Just as good at room temperature.

[MARY REID REYNOLDS FISHER]

Just a Thought

If not planning to use a sauce immediately,
cover the sauce surface entirely with plastic wrap or wax paper.
This will prevent a skin from forming.

H O T   P E P P E R   J E L L Y

Grind peppers in a blender with ½ cup vinegar. Put peppers with sugar and remaining vinegar in a large pot. Cook for 45 minutes over low heat. Increase heat and bring to a full boil. Immediately remove pot from burner. Let stand for 5 minutes. Add Certo, and stir well. Add green or red food coloring (sparingly). The jelly will be green without the food coloring because of the peppers.

[J A N E   G E L Z E R   M E N E N D E Z]

MAKES 6 (8-OUNCE) JARS

½ cup hot jalapeño peppers, finely cut
1½ cups cider vinegar, divided
1 cup bell pepper, finely cut
6½ cups sugar
1 (6-ounce) bottle liquid Certo Green or red food coloring

J E Z E B E L   S A U C E

Combine all ingredients. Chill. A good alternative to cream cheese and pepper jelly. Also good on ham, turkey, shrimp or as a dip for raw vegetables.

[C L A I R E   K I N N E T T   T A T E]

MAKES 2 PINTS

4 ounces prepared horseradish
8 ounces Dijon mustard
10 ounces red plum jelly
10 ounces pineapple preserves

S W E E T   &   H O T   M U S T A R D

In medium saucepan, whisk sugar and mustard. Add eggs and vinegar. Cook over low heat, stirring constantly, for 10 minutes. ✍ Cool and store in refrigerator. Will keep about 1 month. ✍ Wonderful with ham or to add to stuffed eggs.

[J O A N N E   M I L L E R   G A E D E]

MAKES 1½ CUPS

1 cup sugar
⅔ cup dry mustard
3 eggs, beaten
⅔ cup white vinegar

MAKES 1 CUP

1/2 cup sugar
3 heaping tablespoons
   dry mustard
1 egg
1/4 cup butter
1 1/2 tablespoons vinegar

MAKES ABOUT
1 1/2 CUPS

6 tablespoons vegetable oil
3 tablespoons vinegar
1/2 cup sugar
1/2 cup prepared mustard
   Pinch of salt
1/8 teaspoon cayenne pepper
1/8 teaspoon paprika

MAKES 6 PINTS

3 quarts figs
3 quarts sugar
   Scant 1 1/4 cups
   (9 ounces) water

HOT MUSTARD

Mix all ingredients. Cook in top of double boiler until desired consistency.

[CATHY CRISS ADAMS]

MUSTARD SAUCE

Combine all ingredients in a jar, and shake well. Delicious over ham.

[MARTHA SULZBY CLARK]

FIG PRESERVES

Wash and trim stems from figs. Chop in large pieces. Combine sugar and water in large saucepan. Cook over medium heat until mixture comes to a boil. Add figs. Lower heat and cook 15 to 20 minutes or until thickened. Pour into sterilized jars and seal.

CRANBERRY WINE JELLY

Combine first 4 ingredients. Bring to a boil, and stir until sugar is dissolved. Remove from heat. Stir in wine and pectin. Skim off all foam. Quickly pour into sterilized jars and seal.

[CORNELIA FOX CRUMBAUGH]

MAKES 4 PINTS

7 cups sugar
3 cups cranberry juice
1/4 teaspoon ground cloves
1/4 teaspoon ground cinnamon
1 cup port wine
2 (3-ounce) packages liquid fruit pectin

FRESH FRUIT SALSA

Combine all ingredients. Serve chilled or at room temperature with grilled chicken or fish.

[BETH JOHNSON]

Just a Thought

Tomatillos look like small, hard green tomatoes. Blanch them in boiling water for 1 minute before using.

MAKES 1 QUART

1/2 cup diced cantaloupe
1/2 cup diced pineapple
1/2 cup diced kiwi
1/2 cup diced purple onion
1 cup diced tomatillos
1 cup diced tomatoes
1/4 cup seeded chopped jalapeño pepper
Juice of 1 lime
Juice of 1 lemon
1/4 to 1/2 cup chopped fresh cilantro

ORANGE-BOURBON CRANBERRY SAUCE

Bring first 4 ingredients to a boil. Cook until mixture is reduced to a syrupy glaze (about 10 minutes). Add cranberries and sugar and cook, stirring constantly, until sugar is dissolved. Reduce heat, and simmer, uncovered, for 10 minutes or until most of the cranberries have burst. Remove from heat, and stir in pepper. Let cool, then refrigerate. Very good with pork or chicken.

[TRICIA JENKINS NOBLE]
PAST PRESIDENT

MAKES 2 CUPS

1/2 cup bourbon
1/2 cup orange juice
Grated peel of 1/2 orange
1/2 cup shallots minced
1 (12-ounce) package fresh cranberries
1 cup sugar
1 teaspoon freshly ground pepper

MAKES 1 1/2 QUARTS

5 *to 6 large Bosc or other pears,*
  cored
3 *apples, peeled and cored*
3 *peaches, peeled and pitted*
2 *ripe tomatoes, peeled*
2 *lemons, seeded*
1 *lime, seeded*
1 1/2 *cups golden raisins*
2 *to 3 tablespoons finely chopped*
  ripe red jalapeño or other hot
  pepper (or 3 tablespoons dried
  crushed red pepper)
1/2 *cup crystallized ginger, chopped*
1 *large clove garlic, minced*
2 *cups cider vinegar*
1 *tablespoon salt*
1 1/2 *teaspoons ground cinnamon*
1 *teaspoon ground cloves*
1/4 *teaspoon ground nutmeg*
1/4 *teaspoon ground allspice*

MAKES 17 PINTS

10 *pounds cabbage*
2 1/2 *pounds cucumber*
8 *yellow onions*
2 *tablespoons ground black pep-*
  per
1 *teaspoon ground red pepper*
1/2 *cup salt*
2 1/2 *quarts cider vinegar*
1/3 *cup turmeric*
1/3 *cup celery seed*
1/2 *cup dry mustard*
1 *cup all-purpose flour*
5 *cups sugar*
1/2 *pound white mustard seeds*

LABOR DAY CHUTNEY

Chop first 6 ingredients. Combine all ingredients in large stock-pot. Simmer for 2 1/2 hours. ✎   Spoon into sterilized jars and seal.

[ANNE THIELE BLACKERBY]

Delicious with pork, delightful served over cream cheese
as an appetizer–delectable gift!

CABBAGE PICKLE

Grind cabbage, cucumber, and onions. Add remaining ingredients. Place in a large Dutch oven. Cook slowly 1 to 2 hours over low heat, stirring often, until thick. Seal in canning jars.

[ALICE DERRICK REYNOLDS]

Great in sandwiches or as an accompaniment to vegetables
(especially black-eyed peas).

CRANBERRY CHUTNEY

MAKES 6 CUPS

In large stockpot combine first 8 ingredients. Bring to a boil; stir until sugar is dissolved. Reduce heat. ✒ Add lemon rind and sections, orange rind and sections, and chopped apples. Simmer 10 minutes. ✒ Add 3 cups of cranberries, raisins, and apricots. Simmer 30 to 40 minutes, stirring occasionally. Stir in 2 cups of cranberries; simmer 10 minutes. Add remaining 1 cup of cranberries and walnuts and simmer 15 minutes, stirring occasionally. Transfer to a bowl or jars.

[CAROL S. RICHARD]

Spread over cream cheese and top with chopped green onions and sesame seeds.

1/2 cup vinegar
2 1/4 cups firmly packed light brown sugar
3/4 teaspoon curry powder
1/2 teaspoon ground ginger
1/4 teaspoon ground cloves
1/4 teaspoon ground allspice
1/2 teaspoon ground cinnamon
1 1/2 cups water
2 lemons, rinds grated, pith discarded, and fruit cut into sections
2 navel oranges, rinds grated, pith discarded, and fruit cut into sections
1 apple, cored, peeled, and coarsely chopped
6 cups cranberries, divided
1/2 cup golden raisins
1/2 cup dried apricots, chopped
1/2 cup chopped walnuts

CANDIED BRANDIED CRANBERRIES

MAKES 2 CUPS

Place cranberries in a shallow layer in 15 x 10 x 2-inch baking pan. Sprinkle 2 cups sugar over berries. Cover tightly, and bake at 350° for 1 hour. Cool. ✒ Mix in brandy or cognac, and sprinkle lightly with remaining sugar. Spoon into sterile jars. Chill.

[BEVERLY PENFIELD WESTFALL]

This will knock the socks off your turkey!

4 cups (1 pound) fresh cranberries
2 1/4 cups sugar, divided
4 tablespoons brandy or cognac

Lemon Soufflé Cake with Raspberry Sauce, page 311

Charlotte Russe

- Ellen Tarry -

WHENEVER I AM ASKED ABOUT MY FAVORITE DESSERT I remember the only time I ever had enough Charlotte Russe.

My mother was a member of the St. Paul Methodist Episcopal Missionary Society. I looked forward to the times Mama entertained the Missionary Society because of the fancy sandwiches or salads and wonderful Charlotte Russe she served.

After the sandwiches or salads were placed on beds of lettuce they were garnished with sweet pickles and olives. Though I sometimes helped myself to the olives and pickles, I watched the ladies as they helped themselves to the Charlotte Russe, always hoping there was plenty left.

I would have already watched Mama as she mixed then whipped the Charlotte Russe. I would cross my fingers when she poured the mixture over the crisp ladyfingers, hoping she did not scrape all of the mixture off the sides of the bowl. If I was in her good graces that day she would hand me the bowl to wash. But before water touched the bowl I used a finger to make sure there was none of the Charlotte Russe floating around. The number of bowls I cleaned depended on the number of ladies expected at the meetings.

This particular day was bright and sunny. So all day ladies had been calling to say they would attend. I had already told myself that the bowl of Charlotte Russe that Mama usually put aside for the family might have to be used for the ladies when I heard a loud noise.

I ran to the front of the house in time to see the driver · CONTINUED ·

ELLEN TARRY

ELLEN TARRY WAS BORN IN 1906
IN BIRMINGHAM, ALABAMA.
SHE ATTENDED ALABAMA STATE
NORMAL SCHOOL FOR COLORED IN
MONTGOMERY AND MOVED
TO NEW YORK TO PURSUE HER
DREAM OF BECOMING A WRITER.
AFTER WORLD WAR II,
WHICH SHE SPENT IN ANNISTON,
ALABAMA, DIRECTING A USO FOR
AFRICAN AMERICAN SOLDIERS
STATIONED AT FORT MCCLELLAN,
SHE WROTE SEVERAL BOOKS FOR
YOUNG READERS, INCLUDING
BIOGRAPHIES OF JAMES WELDEN
JOHNSON AND PIERRE TOUSSAINT.
SHE WROTE *THE THIRD DOOR*
IN 1955 TO TELL AMERICA ABOUT
THE PLIGHT OF HER PEOPLE.
SHE NOW LIVES IN NEW YORK.

of a hack manage to stop his raring horses at our door. (This all happened before automobiles crowded the streets of Birmingham.) Then I saw a tall man who I recognized as a Mr. Black from LaFayette down in Chambers County get out of the hack. But Mr. Black was mad and he was cussing. He only had on a bathrobe and I could not imagine what had happened. But I did remember Mama had said Mr. Black was at St. Vincent's Hospital "for the cure."

Mama had known Mr. Black all of her life. When he and his older brother came to Birmingham they always went to the barber shop where my father worked and left their bags there for the shoe shine boys to take to their hotel while they came to our house to eat the good dinners Mama always fixed for them.

But this day Mr. Black was mad and he was doing some loud cussing. Out of the corner of my eye I could see the ladies peeping out of the living room door. I was not sure of whether I should try to help Mr. Black up the steps or go and get my mother. Then I looked up and saw my father running down the street.

I later learned that a young nurse at the hospital who had been calling my father to cut Mr. Black's hair and shave him had called Papa after the fire broke out and Mr. Black was listed as missing.

Mama finally ran out on the front porch by the time Papa helped Mr. Black up the steps. She was telling him to be quiet, but he kept cussing. And the ladies from the Missionary Society were all crowded around the door of the living room urging Papa to "get that man out of the house."

Mama managed to steer Mr. Black to the dining room at the rear of the house where the table was all set for the ladies of the Missionary Society. Then the ladies moved in on Papa and told him it was a shame and a disgrace for that man to be at our house.

My father explained that Mama had known Mr. Black all of her life and told them the man was ill and when a fire broke out at the hospital he came to the only person he knew in Birmingham.

The ladies kept yelling about "that man in his bathrobe" until Papa ordered them to shut up. But they told him that Mr. Black had to leave the house or they would.

Papa held the front door open as he faced the ladies and said Mr. Black was his friend and he would be staying as long as necessary. He then tipped his hat to the ladies as they filed out one by one.

I was the only one in the house who could still smile. I was smiling because I knew I would have as much Charlotte Russe as I wanted. I was still eating when the nurse from the hospital came for Mr. Black. I stopped eating to join Mama and Papa on the front porch when they waved to Mr. Black as the hack drove away.

Though I ate more Charlotte Russe than I had ever eaten before, I learned an important lesson in integrity and loyalty that day. Mr. Black was white and my father was Black and this all happened in Birmingham of yesteryear. THE END

CHARLOTTE RUSSE

1 package cherry
  or strawberry gelatin
1 cup boiling water
1 pint whipping cream
6 Ladyfingers

Line bowl or mold with ladyfingers. To 1 package of strawberry or cherry gelatin add 1 cup boiling water. Sir until gelatin is dissolved. Add 1/2 pint whipping cream and stir this mixture vigorously. Whip if necessary. Pour this mixture over 6 ladyfingers arranged in the bowl or mold. Decorate with fresh fruit according to flavor used. Refrigerate. Serve and enjoy.

WITH TODAY'S BUSY LIFESTYLE, it is difficult to entertain and prepare every part of a full meal from scratch. Often we must forgo home-baked bread for something we've picked up from our local bakery. If there's no time for creating a divine but complicated dessert for friends, we still can concoct a little something for that "sweet ending." Use fruits in season, keep some simple staples in the pantry, and the rest is up to your imagination!

FOR SPRING AND SUMMER:

• Scoop fresh cantaloupe, honeydew, or watermelon into balls. Sprinkle with lemon juice and a little honey. Present in a clear glass bowl; garnish with a sprig of mint.

• Scoop melon balls; return to melon shell; cover with Blueberry Sauce.

• Cut a kiwifruit in half, scoop out the fruit. Mix with fresh sliced strawberries. Return to shell. Garnish with strawberry.

• Slice angel food or pound cake; serve with fresh berries and cream, or with lemon curd (page 301) spooned over top.

• Make an instant sorbet by mixing 4 cups fresh berries, slightly smashed, with 1/2 cup super-fine sugar and 1/4 water; freeze for 1 1/2 hours, stir and serve.

• For a quick parfait, layer in a pretty tall glass: fresh fruit, commercial whipped cream, and your favorite cookie crumbs.

FOR FALL AND WINTER:

• A hot fruit compote is easy to make: crumble cookies into individual ramekins; top with fresh or canned fruit, honey or brown sugar, and butter; bake until warm.

• Use puff pastry sheets or canned crescent rolls, fill with sliced fruit and nuts, or fruit and cheese; bake, and sprinkle with cinnamon or powdered sugar.

• Crisps and buckles require only sliced fruit (preferably fresh or canned), a topping of oatmeal and brown sugar, or with Bisquick and butter; bake.

• Dress up a coffee drink. Keep on hand whole cinnamon sticks and chocolate "straws." Stir in a liqueur, cinnamon, cocoa powder, ice cream, or whipping cream.

ORANGE CUSTARD SAUCE

Whisk 4 egg yolks and 1/2 cup sugar. Scald 1 cup whipping cream and 1/3 cup milk. Gradually add yolk mixture to cream mixture, stirring constantly. Add 1/4 cup orange juice and 1 teaspoon grated orange rind. Cook slowly until thick. Delicious over fruit dumplings.

BLUEBERRY SAUCE

Cook 1 pint fresh blueberries, 1/2 to 3/4 cup sugar, 1 teaspoon lemon juice, and 1/4 cup water over low heat for 15 minutes.

DESSERTS

SERVES 15 TO 20

2 cups sugar
1 1/4 cups vegetable oil
3 eggs
3 cups all-purpose flour
1/2 teaspoon salt
1 teaspoon baking soda
2 teaspoons ground cinnamon
1 teaspoon vanilla extract
1 cup chopped pecans
2 large Red Delicious apples, diced

Icing:
1/4 cup butter, melted
1/2 cup firmly packed light brown sugar
2 tablespoons milk
1 1/2 cups powdered sugar
1/4 teaspoon vanilla extract

CARAMEL-GLAZED APPLE CAKE

Beat sugar, oil, and eggs together. Add flour, salt, soda, and cinnamon. (Batter will be very stiff.) Add vanilla, pecans, and apples. Pour into a greased 10-inch tube pan. Bake at 350° for 1 hour. Icing: Combine butter and brown sugar, and cook over low heat for 2 minutes, stirring constantly. Add milk, and continue cooking and stirring until mixture comes to a boil. Remove from heat, and add powdered sugar and vanilla. Thin with additional milk if necessary. Pour over warm cake.

[POLLY PRATT LONG]

SERVES 12

1 1/2 cups butter
1 1/2 cups sugar
1 dozen eggs, separated
1 1/2 cups all-purpose flour
18 to 20 ounces semisweet chocolate morsels, finely chopped
12 ounces almonds, chopped
Whipping cream, whipped
Chocolate shavings

CHOCOLATE ALMOND DECADENCE

Mix butter and sugar. Add egg yolks, then flour. Add chocolate morsels and almonds. Whip egg whites until stiff. Fold into batter. Pour batter into a well-greased 9-inch springform pan. Bake at 350° for 1 hour and 15 minutes. Cake should be moist but not soupy when done. Chill 2 to 3 hours. Serve with whipped cream and chocolate shavings.

[MARILYN MCGUIRE]

ANNUAL BIRTHDAY CAKE FOR DR. KENNEDY

Stir together soda and buttermilk, and set aside. ✍ Cream butter and sugar. Add eggs, one at a time, beating well after each addition. ✍ Sift together flour and next 4 ingredients. Add flour mixture to butter mixture, alternately with buttermilk mixture and oil, adding a third at a time. ✍ Mix in vanilla, fig preserves, and pecans. ✍ Pour into well-greased and floured 10-inch tube pan or Bundt pan. Bake at 350° for 45 to 60 minutes in tube pan or 1 hour and 15 minutes in Bundt pan. ✍ Optional topping: 8 ounces light cream cheese whipped with 1 tablespoon honey or liquid drained from homemade preserves. (For preserves, see page 280.)

[KYTHA W. HODGENS]

SERVES 12 TO 15

1 teaspoon baking soda
1 cup buttermilk
1 cup butter
2 cups sugar
4 eggs
3 cups all-purpose flour
1/4 teaspoon salt
1 teaspoon ground cinnamon
1/2 teaspoon ground allspice
1/2 teaspoon ground nutmeg
1/2 cup vegetable oil
1 teaspoon vanilla extract
1 1/2 cups fig preserves
1 cup chopped pecans

LEMON TORTE

To prepare cake layers, cream butter and sugar until light and fluffy. Sift together flour and baking powder, and add to butter mixture alternately with milk. ✍ Beat egg whites until stiff; fold into mixture. Grease 3 (9-inch) cakepans and divide mixture evenly between them. ✍ Bake at 350° for 25 minutes. Cool layers. To prepare filling, combine all filling ingredients in the top of a double boiler, and heat over boiling water, stirring constantly until mixture thickens. Remove from heat, cool, and spread between layers. ✍ Frost top and sides with White Icing (page 292), if desired.

[ALICE HIGDON PRATER]

SERVES 10 TO 12

Cake Layers:
1 cup butter
2 cups sugar
3 cups all-purpose flour
2 tablespoons baking powder
1 cup milk
8 egg whites

Filling:
2 cups powdered sugar
8 egg yolks
1 tablespoon butter
Grated rind of 1 lemon
Juice of 2 lemons

MAKES ENOUGH
TO FROST 1 CAKE

1³/4 cups sugar
2 egg whites
1 tablespoon light corn syrup
1 teaspoon vanilla extract
¹/2 cup water
¹/2 cup chopped marshmallows

WHITE ICING

Beat first 5 ingredients at high speed for 1 to 2 minutes. Pour into top of a double boiler. Add marshmallows, and cook over rapidly boiling water for 5 to 8 minutes. Pour into a bowl and beat until spreading consistency.

SERVES 12

1¹/3 cups boiling water
1 cup quick-cooking oats
¹/2 cup butter
1 cup sugar
1 cup brown sugar
1¹/3 cups sifted all-purpose flour
1 teaspoon baking soda
1 teaspoon salt
1 teaspoon ground cinnamon
1 teaspoon vanilla extract
2 eggs, well beaten

Icing:
1 (16-ounce) package powdered sugar
1 (8-ounce) package cream cheese
Dash of milk
¹/2 cup chopped pecans

OATMEAL CAKE WITH CREAM CHEESE-PECAN ICING

Pour boiling water over oats, and let stand for 20 minutes. Cream butter with sugars, and set aside. Add flour and remaining ingredients to oats. Combine butter mixture and oat mixture, and pour into lightly greased loafpan. Bake at 300° for 1 hour. Remove from pan, and cool completely before icing. To prepare icing, cream sugar and cream cheese together, and stir in milk and nuts.

[AMY GEORGE COX]

R E D   V E L V E T   C A K E

Sift together first 4 ingredients. Add remaining ingredients in order listed. Mix thoroughly. ❧ Spread batter into 2 greased and floured 9-inch cakepans, and bake at 350° for 25 minutes or until done. ❧ Remove from pans, and let cool. ❧ To prepare frosting, soften butter and cream cheese; mix together. Add sugar, and beat until creamy. Add vanilla and nuts, and spread over cooled cake.

[J E A N   R O S S   S M A L L W O O D   ]

SERVES 12

2½ cups all-purpose flour
1½ cups sugar
1 teaspoon baking soda
1 teaspoon cocoa
1 cup buttermilk
1½ cups vegetable oil
1 teaspoon vinegar
2 eggs
1 to 2 ounces liquid red food coloring
2 teaspoons vanilla extract

Frosting:
½ cup butter
1 (8-ounce) package cream cheese
1 (16-ounce) package powdered sugar
½ teaspoon vanilla extract
1 cup chopped nuts

B L U E B E R R Y - B U T T E R M I L K
S P I C E   C A K E

Cream butter and sugar, and beat thoroughly. Add eggs, one at a time, beating well. ❧ Sift together flour and next 5 ingredients; add to butter mixture alternately with buttermilk. Fold in blueberries. Smooth batter into a greased and floured 13-cup Bundt pan. Sprinkle batter with 3 teaspoons sugar, and bake at 350° for 40 to 50 minutes.

[C O N N I E   S I M P S O N   L A N K F O R D   ]

*When buttermilk is unavailable,
simply use ½ cup milk with 1 teaspoon white vinegar.*

SERVES 12

⅔ cup butter or shortening
1½ cups sugar
2 eggs
2½ cups all-purpose flour
½ teaspoon salt
2 teaspoons ground cinnamon
1 teaspoon ground cloves
1 teaspoon baking soda
1 teaspoon ground nutmeg
½ cup buttermilk
1 pint fresh or 2 (16-ounce) cans blueberries, drained
3 teaspoons sugar

4 SERVINGS

1 cup unsalted butter
2 cups sugar
4 eggs, separated
1/2 cup cocoa
1/2 cup strong coffee, cooled
1 teaspoon vanilla extract
2 cups all-purpose flour
1 1/2 teaspoons baking soda
1 cup sour cream

Icing:
5 (1-ounce) squares
    unsweetened chocolate
4 tablespoons butter, melted
2 cups powdered sugar, divided
1 tablespoon brandy
1 egg white, lightly beaten
    Apricot or peach jam
    (optional)

SERVES 12

1/4 cup shortening or butter
1/2 cup sugar
1/2 teaspoon vanilla extract
2 eggs, separated
1 cup sifted cake flour
1 1/2 teaspoons baking powder
1/4 teaspoon salt
1/2 cup milk
2 egg whites
1/2 cup sugar
    Sweetened strawberries
    Whipped cream

CHOCOLATE BIRTHDAY CAKE

Cream butter and sugar. Add egg yolks, one at a time. Mix cocoa and coffee to form a paste. Add to batter, and stir in vanilla. Combine flour and soda; add to butter mixture alternately with sour cream. Beat egg whites until stiff, and fold into batter. Pour into 3 greased and floured 8-inch cakepans. Bake at 350° for 30 minutes. Cool 10 minutes on wire racks. Remove from pans. Frost cakes with icing when cool. ✍ For icing, melt chocolate and stir in melted butter. Add 1 cup sugar and brandy. Stir in remaining sugar and beaten egg white. Beat until spreading consistency. ✍ Spread layers with apricot or peach jam, if desired. Frost top and sides of cake with chocolate icing.

[ANNE THIELE BLACKERBY]

STRAWBERRY MERINGUE SHORTCAKE

Cream shortening. Gradually add 1/2 cup sugar and vanilla. Beat in yolks. ✍ Sift together flour, baking powder, and salt. Add flour mixture to cream mixture alternately with milk. Pour into 2 greased or wax paper-lined 8 1/2-inch cakepans. ✍ Beat egg whites until frothy. Gradually add 1/2 cup sugar, and beat until stiff peaks form. Spread evenly over batter. ✍ Bake at 350° for 30 to 35 minutes. ✍ Cut into pieces, and top with sweetened strawberries and whipped cream.

[JANET SMITH LUCAS]

C H O C O L A T E   S H O R T C A K E   W I T H   S T R A W B E R R I E S ,   I C E   C R E A M ,   A N D   H O T   F U D G E

SERVES 8 TO 10

1⅔ cups all-purpose flour
1½ teaspoons baking powder
½ teaspoon baking soda
3 tablespoons cocoa
¼ teaspoon salt
⅓ cup granulated sugar
¼ cup chilled unsalted butter, cut into 4 pieces
½ cup semisweet chocolate morsels
¾ cup buttermilk

Filling:
1 quart fresh strawberries
½ cup granulated sugar
2 cups whipping cream
3 tablespoons powdered sugar
Vanilla ice cream
Hot fudge or chocolate sauce

Position knife blade in food processor; combine first 6 ingredients in processor. Add butter, and pulse until mixture is consistency of coarse meal. Add chocolate morsels and buttermilk, and mix until dry ingredients are moistened and dough begins to hold together. Turn dough out onto well-floured board. (Dough will be sticky.) Knead about 10 minutes, and pat into a 7-inch circle (³/4 inch thick). Cut out 7 to 8 biscuit rounds with a floured 2-inch cutter. Combine leftover pieces of dough and pat them into a circle, then cut out about 4 more rounds. Bake at 450° on an ungreased cookie sheet for 10 to 12 minutes. Quarter strawberries. Toss with ½ cup sugar, and let stand for 30 minutes. Whip cream until thick; add powdered sugar and beat until soft peaks form. To serve, split each round, and top each with ice cream, strawberry mixture, and sweetened whipped cream; drizzle with hot fudge sauce.

[C A M E R O N   D A L E Y   C R O W E]

F A N T A S T I C   C H O C O L A T E   S A U C E

MAKES 1½ CUPS

¼ cup butter
2 ounces unsweetened chocolate
1 (5-ounce) can evaporated milk
1 cup sugar
1 teaspoon vanilla extract
1 teaspoon instant coffee granules

Melt butter and chocolate in a medium saucepan. Stir in evaporated milk, sugar, vanilla, and coffee granules. Stir until well blended. Cook over medium heat, stirring constantly, until thick and smooth (about 10 to 15 minutes).

SERVES 10

Cake:
- 1 cup butter
- $1/2$ cup shortening
- 3 cups sugar
- 5 eggs
- $1^1/4$ cups milk
- 3 cups all-purpose flour
- $1/2$ cup cocoa
- $1/2$ teaspoon salt
- $1/2$ teaspoon baking powder
- 1 teaspoon vanilla extract

Icing:
- $2/3$ cup evaporated milk (5-ounce can)
- 2 cups sugar
- $1/4$ cup cocoa
- $1/4$ teaspoon salt
- $1/2$ cup butter
- 1 teaspoon vanilla extract
- Garnish: semisweet chocolate mini-morsels

MAKES $1^1/2$ CUPS

- 2 cups fresh peaches, peeled and sliced
- 1 teaspoon lemon juice
- 4 tablespoons sugar
- 1 tablespoon flour
- 2 tablespoons butter
- $1/2$ teaspoon cinnamon
- $1/4$ teaspoon nutmeg
- 1 teaspoon vanilla

CHOCOLATE POUND CAKE

To prepare cake, cream together first 3 ingredients. Add eggs, one at a time, beating after each. Add milk. Mix together flour and next 3 ingredients. Add dry ingredients and vanilla to creamed mixture. Spoon into a greased and floured 13-cup Bundt pan. Bake at 300° for $1^1/2$ hours. Do not open oven door until after $1^1/2$ hours.

To prepare icing, mix first 4 ingredients in a saucepan, and boil rapidly for 2 minutes. Remove from heat, and add butter and vanilla. Beat with wooden spoon until creamy. After icing cake, garnish with mini-morsels.

[BINGHAM HARDIE CARLSON]

FRESH PEACH SAUCE

Combine peaches with remaining ingredients. Heat over low heat in saucepan for 5 to 10 minutes stirring often, or bake in a small greased casserole dish at 350° for 20 minutes. Serve over pound cake with vanilla ice cream, or over angel food cake for a lighter dessert.

F O U R T H   O F   J U L Y   P O U N D   C A K E

To prepare cake, cream butter and cream cheese in mixture until fluffy. Mix in sugar. Add 3 eggs, then alternate remaining eggs and flour, beginning and ending with flour. Add vanilla. Pour into a greased and floured 13 x 9 x 2-inch cakepan. Bake at 300° for 1 hour. 🍃 To prepare icing, cream butter and cream cheese until fluffy. Add powdered sugar and vanilla. Frost cake and place fruit in a "stars and stripes" pattern to look like the American flag.

[K A Y E   W I N N   M A T T H E W S]

B R O W N   S U G A R   P O U N D   C A K E

Grease and flour a 15-cup Bundt pan or 10-inch tube pan. Sprinkle pecan pieces on bottom of pan. 🍃 In a large mixing bowl, cream butter and sugars, mixing well. Add eggs. 🍃 In a small bowl, combine flour and baking powder. In another small bowl, combine milk and vanilla. Add flour mixture and milk mixture alternately to the creamed mixture. 🍃 Pour into prepared pan and bake at 325° for 1½ to 2 hours or until a toothpick inserted in center comes out clean. Allow to cool in pan about 30 minutes, then remove. Tip: Milk and eggs should be at room temperature.

[E L E A N O R   H A S S I N G E R   B U R D E T T E]

SERVES 15

Cake:
1½ cups butter
1 (8-ounce) package cream cheese
3 cups sugar
6 eggs
3 cups all-purpose flour
2 teaspoons vanilla extract

Icing:
½ cup butter
1 (8-ounce) package cream cheese, softened
1 (16-ounce) package powdered sugar
1 teaspoon vanilla extract
Strawberries, hulled and halved
Blueberries

SERVES 16

½ cup coarsely chopped pecans
1½ cups butter, softened
2 cups brown sugar
1 cup sugar
5 large eggs
3 cups all-purpose flour
½ teaspoon baking powder
1 cup milk
1 teaspoon vanilla extract

WHIPPING CREAM POUND CAKE

Beat egg whites with $3/4$ cup sugar, and set aside. Cream together remaining $2^1\!/4$ cups sugar and butter. Add egg yolks, one at a time, beating well. Add flour, alternating with whipping cream. Add vanilla and lemon juice. Fold in egg white mixture. Pour into a greased and floured 10-inch tube pan. Place in cold oven, and bake at 325° for $1^1\!/4$ to $1^1\!/2$ hours. *Lemon variation:* add 1 teaspoon lemon extract; glaze with $1/2$ cup milk, juice of 1 lemon, $1^1\!/4$ cups sugar. *Almond variation:* add 1 teaspoon almond extract; glaze with $1/2$ cup powdered sugar, $1/3$ cup water, $1/2$ teaspoon almond extract.

[CAROLE PINCKARD HAMM]

WALNUT-PUMPKIN CHEESECAKE

Combine crust ingredients, and press into bottom and up sides of lightly greased 10-inch springform pan. Beat cream cheese and sugars in electric mixer. Add eggs, one at a time, blending well. Add cream, cinnamon, nutmeg, and pumpkin. Pour into prepared crust. Bake at 350° for 1 hour. Combine topping ingredients. Sprinkle over cheesecake. Cook an additional 15 minutes. Chill.

[ELLEN MCELVAIN RHETT]

GUILTLESS CHOCOLATE KAHLÚA CHEESECAKE

Combine cream cheese and sour cream (or cottage cheese) until creamy. Add sugar and Equal, blending well. Add eggs and next 3 ingredients, and mix well. ✍ Combine cookie crumbs and margarine. Press into bottom and up sides of a 10-inch springform pan, lightly sprayed with vegetable cooking spray. ✍ Pour batter into pan. Wrap outside of pan with aluminum foil. ✍ Place in a shallow baking dish and fill with water up to the top of the spring-form pan. ✍ (This allows the cheesecake to cook evenly, and the foil prevents water from seeping into the cheesecake pan.) Bake at 325° for 30 minutes. Lower temperature to 300° and bake 40 additional minutes or until a wooden pick inserted in center comes out clean.

[BOMBAY CAFE]

FRENCH SILK PIE

Cream butter. Gradually add sugar and beat until mixture is smooth. Beat in melted chocolate and vanilla. Add eggs, one at a time, beating 5 minutes after each addition. ✍ Pour into baked pastry shell. Chill several hours. Garnish with whipped cream and grated chocolate, if desired.

[SUSAN SMITH BLAIR]

SERVES 8 TO 10

3 (8-ounce) packages light cream cheese, softened

1 cup light sour cream or cottage cheese

1 cup powdered sugar

1/2 cup or 15 packets Equal sweetener

3 large eggs

1 teaspoon vanilla extract

2 tablespoons Kahlúa

1 cup melted chocolate or Hershey's Syrup

3 cups reduced-fat cookie crumbs or graham cracker crumbs

1 cup margarine, melted

SERVES 8

1/2 cup butter, softened

3/4 cup sugar

1 (1-ounce) square unsweetened chocolate, melted

1 teaspoon vanilla extract

2 eggs*

1 (9-inch) baked pastry shell
Garnishes: sweetened whipped cream, 3 tablespoons grated chocolate

* See Just a Thought, page 305.

SERVES 8 TO 10

Crust:

1¼ cups graham cracker crumbs

¼ cup sugar

⅓ cup butter, melted

¼ teaspoon cinnamon

Filling:

3 (8-ounce) packages cream cheese, softened

1 cup dark brown sugar

⅔ cup evaporated milk

2 tablespoons all-purpose flour

2 teaspoons vanilla extract

3 large eggs

Sauce:

1 (12-ounce) can evaporated milk

1 (16-ounce) box dark brown sugar

½ cup butter

1 teaspoon vanilla extract

1 cup chopped pecans (optional)

SERVES 8

Crust:

2½ dozen coconut macaroons

½ cup butter, melted

Cheesecake:

4 (8-ounce) packages cream cheese

½ cup whipping cream

1¾ cups sugar

4 eggs

1 cup finely ground blanched almonds, divided

⅓ cup amaretto

PRALINE CHEESECAKE

Combine cracker crumbs, sugar, melted butter, and cinnamon. Press into bottom and up sides of a 9-inch springform pan. Bake at 300° for 10 minutes. ✎ Combine cream cheese and next 4 ingredients and blend well. Add eggs, one at a time, beating well after each addition. Pour into prepared crust. Bake at 325° for 50 minutes. Refrigerate. ✎ To prepare sauce, mix together evaporated milk and next 3 ingredients in top of a double boiler. Cook over boiling water for 1 hour; remove from heat. Beat with an electric beater for 3 minutes. Add pecans, if desired. ✎ Serve cheesecake with sauce drizzled on individual slices, or passed separately.

[ALICE DERRICK REYNOLDS]

AMARETTO CHEESECAKE

To prepare crust, coarsely chop macaroons in a food processor. Mix with butter. Press into bottom and up sides of a 9-inch springform pan. Bake at 375° for 5 minutes or until golden brown. ✎ To prepare cheesecake, beat cream cheese and whipping cream until smooth and light. Beat in sugar, a little at a time. Beat in eggs, and fold in ¾ cup ground nuts and amaretto. Pour into crust, and bake at 350° for 1½ hours. ✎ After cooking, sprinkle with remaining ground nuts.

[BETH WALKER WILLIAMS]

New York-Style Cheesecake

To prepare crust, blend all crust ingredients together. Put half the mixture on the bottom of a greased 8-inch springform pan. Put the remaining mixture on the sides of the greased pan. Bake at 400° for 6 to 8 minutes. ✒ To prepare filling, beat the softened cream cheese, vanilla, and whipping cream together. Add eggs and egg yolks, one at a time, beating well after each addition. Slowly add the remaining filling ingredients, and blend well. Pour into prepared pan. Bake at 475° for 10 to 15 minutes; reduce temperature to 200° and bake for 1½ hours. Remove from oven and cool. Place cheesecake in refrigerator for 10 hours. When ready to serve, remove sides of the springform pan.

[THERESA HUNTINGTON ARNOLD]

SERVES 10 TO 15

Crust:
- ½ cup butter, softened
- 1 egg yolk
- ¼ cup sugar
- 1 cup sifted all-purpose flour
- 1 teaspoon vanilla extract
- ½ teaspoon grated lemon rind

Filling:
- 5 (8-ounce) packages softened cream cheese
- 1½ teaspoons vanilla extract
- ¼ cup whipping cream
- 5 eggs
- 2 egg yolks
- 2 cups sugar
- 3 tablespoons all-purpose flour
- ½ teaspoon salt

Lemon Tartlets

To prepare tart shells, combine butter and next 3 ingredients. Mix well. Roll into small balls. Press into lightly greased miniature muffin pans. Bake at 325° for 25 minutes. ✒ To prepare lemon filling, combine lemon juice, rind, and sugar in top of a double boiler. Add butter, and heat over boiling water until butter is melted. Add eggs, and continue cooking about 15 minutes or until thick. Chill and fill tart shells. ✒ Lemon filling may be kept refrigerated for several weeks. (Makes a great gift.)

[BETTY BLACKMON KINNETT]

MAKES 36

Tart Shells:
- 6 tablespoons butter
- 1 (8-ounce) package cream cheese
- 1 cup all-purpose flour
- Dash of salt

Filling:
- ½ cup fresh lemon juice
- Grated rind of 2 lemons
- 2 cups sugar
- 1 cup butter
- 4 eggs, beaten

SERVES 10 TO 12

1½ cups chocolate wafer crumbs
¼ teaspoon ground nutmeg
½ cup butter, melted
2 (8-ounce) packages cream
   cheese, softened
¾ cup sugar
3 eggs
8 ounces sour cream
6 (1-ounce) squares semisweet
   chocolate, melted
1 tablespoon plus ¾ teaspoon
   cocoa
1 teaspoon vanilla extract
½ cup whipping cream,
   whipped
   Garnishes: additional
   whipped cream, sliced
   almonds, chocolate curls,
   maraschino cherries

SERVES 8

2 (1-ounce) squares
   unsweetened chocolate, melted
3 tablespoons butter, melted
¾ cup sugar
1 cup light corn syrup
3 eggs, beaten
1 tablespoon vanilla extract
1 cup chopped pecans
1 (9-inch) unbaked pastry shell
   Vanilla ice cream or sweetened
   whipped cream

RICH CHOCOLATE CHEESECAKE

Combine first 3 ingredients, mixing well. Press mixture into bottom of a 9-inch springform pan; chill. ✿ Beat cream cheese until light and fluffy; gradually add sugar, mixing well. Add eggs, one at a time, beating well after each addition. Stir in sour cream, melted chocolate, cocoa, and vanilla; mix well. Gently fold in whipped cream; spoon into prepared pan. ✿ Bake at 300° for 1 hour. Turn off oven; allow cheesecake to cool in oven 30 minutes. Open door, and allow cheesecake to cool in oven an additional 30 minutes. Refrigerate 8 hours. Remove sides of springform pan, and garnish, if desired. Can be frozen.

[CATHY CRISS ADAMS]

CHOCOLATE PECAN PIE

Melt chocolate and butter in a small saucepan. ✿ In a separate saucepan, combine sugar and syrup, and bring to a boil. Reduce heat and simmer 2 minutes. Remove from heat. Add chocolate mixture. Add beaten eggs, stirring frequently. Add vanilla and pecans. Pour into pastry shell. ✿ Bake at 375° for 40 to 45 minutes. ✿ Serve with ice cream or whipped cream.

[ELLISON GRAY HUGHES]

S O U T H E R N
S T R A W B E R R Y   P I E

S E R V E S   6   T O   8

Combine sugar, water, cornstarch, and salt in a large saucepan. Cook over low heat until thickened. Add pureed green strawberries and several drops of red food coloring. Cool 10 to 15 minutes. ✍ Combine glaze with sliced strawberries and pour into pastry shell. Chill. Garnish with whipped cream sweetened with sugar to taste and extra whole strawberries.

[S U S A N   J O N E S   D R I G G E R S]

1 cup sugar

1 cup water

2 tablespoons plus 1 teaspoon cornstarch

Pinch of salt

1 cup green unripened strawberries, pureed

Red liquid food coloring

2 pints fresh strawberries, hulled and sliced

1 9-inch deep-dish pastry shell, baked

1 pint whipping cream, whipped

1/8 to 1/4 cup sugar

Whole strawberries

D A T E - P E C A N   P I E

S E R V E S   6   T O   8

Combine first 8 ingredients in order listed. Pour into an unbaked pastry shell. ✍ Bake at 325° until pie is set in middle and crust is golden brown (about 1 1/2 hours). Do not refrigerate.

[C A T H Y   C R I S S   A D A M S]

4 eggs

2 cups sugar

1 tablespoon vanilla extract

1/2 cup butter

1 cup dates or raisins

1 cup pecan halves

1 tablespoon white vinegar

Pinch of salt

1 (9-inch) unbaked deep-dish pastry shell

SERVES 8

Pastry:
1²/3 *cups sifted all-purpose flour*
½ *teaspoon salt*
3 *ounces cream cheese, softened*
²/3 *cup butter*
Pie Filling:
2 *cups milk*
1 *cup sugar*
¹/3 *cup cornstarch*
¼ *teaspoon salt*
2 *tablespoons butter*
3 *egg yolks, beaten*
¹/3 *cup fresh lemon juice*
1 *teaspoon lemon rind*
1 *egg white, beaten*
Meringue:
2 *egg whites*
¼ *cup sugar*
¼ *teaspoon salt*
¼ *teaspoon lemon extract*

LEMON MERINGUE PIE

To prepare pastry, combine all pastry ingredients until well blended. Roll into ball. Chill until pie filling is cooked. Roll out, and press into a greased 9-inch pieplate.   To prepare pie filling, scald milk by heating until almost boiling (until bubbles begin at edge of pan). Gradually stir in sugar and next 7 ingredients in a 2½-quart saucepan. Cook until thick (about 10 minutes), stirring constantly. Cool slightly, and pour into pastry crust.   To prepare meringue, beat egg whites, gradually adding sugar and salt until stiff peaks form. Add lemon extract. Top pie with meringue. Bake at 400° for 5 to 7 minutes. Chill 4 to 6 hours before serving.

[SUSAN MEADOWS LEACH]

SERVES 8

3 *egg whites*
½ *teaspoon baking powder*
1 *cup sugar*
1 *cup graham cracker crumbs*
1 *cup chopped pecans*
1 *teaspoon vanilla extract*
1 *cup whipping cream*
3 *tablespoons sugar*
½ *teaspoon vanilla extract*
Graham cracker crumbs

PECAN CRUNCH PIE

Beat egg whites with baking powder until stiff. Add sugar gradually while beating. Beat until very stiff.   Combine crumbs and pecans, and fold into egg white mixture. Fold in vanilla. (Do not beat.)   Spread into well-greased 9-inch pieplate.   Bake at 350° for 30 minutes. Cool.   Whip cream with 3 tablespoons sugar and ½ teaspoon vanilla, and spread over top of pie. Sprinkle with additional graham cracker crumbs.   Chill 4 to 6 hours or overnight before serving.

[WINN COLE SHANNON]

PUMPKIN CHIFFON PIE

Combine first 9 ingredients in a saucepan and cook over medium heat until custard consistency. Remove from heat. Soften gelatin in cold water. Stir into pumpkin mixture, stirring until dissolved. Chill. Beat egg whites with 1/2 cup sugar until stiff. When pumpkin mixture begins to stiffen, remove from refrigerator and stir in egg white mixture. Pour into baked pastry shell. Chill well, and top with whipped cream and sprinkle with chopped nuts.

[CAROLYN RITCHEY KING]

SERVES 6 TO 7

1 cup pumpkin (canned or freshly cooked, mashed)
3 egg yolks
1/2 cup sugar
1 cup milk
1 teaspoon ground cinnamon
1/2 teaspoon salt
1/2 teaspoon ground ginger
1/4 teaspoon ground nutmeg
2 teaspoons butter, melted
1 tablespoon unflavored gelatin
1/4 cup cold water
3 egg whites
1/2 cup sugar
1 (8-inch) baked pastry shell
1 cup whipping cream, whipped
1/3 cup chopped nuts

FABULOUS FRESH PEACH PIE

Cream butter, sugar, and egg. Pour into crust. Chill 1 hour. Arrange sliced peaches over sugar mixture. Top with whipped cream and sprinkle with chopped nuts.

[TANYA MELTON COOPER]

SERVES 8

1/2 cup butter, softened
1 1/2 cups powdered sugar
1 egg, beaten
1 (9-inch) graham cracker crust
8 medium to large peaches, sliced
1/2 pint whipping cream, whipped
1/2 cup chopped pecans or almonds

Just a Thought

Health officials currently recommend that raw eggs should not be consumed by babies, pregnant women, the elderly, or anyone with health risks.

SERVES 6 TO 8

Piecrust:
  2 cups all-purpose flour, sifted
  2/3 teaspoon salt
  3/4 cups shortening, chilled
  6 tablespoons ice water

Apple Pie Filling:
  2 cups peeled and chopped
    apples
  3/4 cup sugar
  2 tablespoons all-purpose flour
  1/2 teaspoon salt
  1 cup sour cream
  1 egg, beaten
  1/2 teaspoon vanilla extract

Topping:
  1/3 cup sugar
  1/3 cup all-purpose flour
  1 teaspoon cinnamon
  1/4 cup butter, softened

SOUR CREAM APPLE PIE

To prepare piecrust, sift together flour and salt. Cut in chilled shortening. Add water. Form into ball, and chill. Roll out and fit into 2 or 3 (9-inch) pieplates. ✎ To prepare apple filling, mix together apples and next 6 ingredients in order listed. Pour into unbaked piecrust. ✎ Bake at 400° for 15 minutes. Reduce heat to 325°, and continue baking 30 to 40 minutes. ✎ Combine topping ingredients. Remove pie from oven, and gently spread with topping mixture. Bake at 325° for an additional 10 minutes. Cool and serve.

[LORA TUTTLE TERRY]

SERVES 8

  3 eggs
  1 1/2 cups sugar
  1/4 cup butter, melted
  1 cup buttermilk
  1 tablespoon vanilla extract
  1 (9-inch) unbaked pastry shell

BUTTERMILK CUSTARD PIE

Beat eggs well. Add sugar slowly, and beat well. Beat in butter. Add buttermilk and vanilla. Beat until all ingredients are well blended. ✎ Pour into pastry shell and bake at 350° for 45 minutes or until a knife inserted in center comes out clean. Chill and serve.

[CARL MARTIN HAMES]

THREE-BERRY TART

To prepare pastry, combine flour, nuts, and sugar. Cut in butter until mixture resembles coarse crumbs. Add water just until pastry can be shaped into ball. Chill. ✒ Roll out on a floured surface. Fold over bottom and sides of a 9-inch tart pan with removable bottom. (Reserve extra dough for garnishing top.) ✒ Rinse and drain all berries. Remove hulls from strawberries. ✒ Combine filling ingredients. Pour into pan. Top with pastry leaves or other pastry cutouts. ✒ Bake at 400° for 30 to 40 minutes.

[JEAN KINNETT OLIVER]

SERVES 6 TO 8

Pastry:
1¼ cups all-purpose flour
¼ cup ground macadamia nuts
2 tablespoons sugar
½ cup butter
3 to 4 tablespoons water

Filling:
1 cup fresh raspberries
1 cup fresh strawberries
1 cup fresh blackberries
¾ to 1 cup sugar
2 tablespoons all-purpose flour
½ teaspoon ground nutmeg
½ teaspoon ground ginger

HOMEMADE VANILLA ICE CREAM

Heat milk and sugar in a saucepan until hot and sugar is dissolved. (Do not boil.) ✒ Stir a little of the hot milk into beaten eggs. Add eggs to remaining hot milk in saucepan, and stir well. Remove from heat and cool. Add vanilla, and refrigerate. (Keeps for several days.) ✒ When ready to freeze, stir in half-and-half, whipping cream, and any optional ingredients. Pour into a hand-turned or electric ice-cream freezer. Freeze according to manufacturer's directions.

[NANCY STEWART PETERSON]

MAKES 1½ GALLONS

1 quart milk
3 cups sugar
5 eggs, beaten
1 tablespoon vanilla extract
3 cups half-and-half
3 cups whipping cream
Toasted coconut (optional)
Toasted almonds (optional)
Kahlúa (optional)

LEMON SHERBET

SERVES 4 TO 6

1 cup sugar
1/2 cup lemon juice
2 1/2 cups milk, very cold
1 cup whipping cream
2 egg whites
2 tablespoons sugar
Pinch of salt

Dissolve sugar in lemon juice. Pour cold milk and cream into a large bowl. Slowly stir in lemon juice. Pour into a 13 x 9 x 2-inch pan, and freeze about 20 minutes (until mixture begins to freeze). Meanwhile, beat egg whites until soft peaks form. Add 2 tablespoons sugar and salt. Continue beating until stiff peaks form. Fold egg whites into the lemon mixture, and freeze for at least 45 additional minutes.

[RUTH VAN BUREN]

FROZEN AMARETTO TORTE

SERVES 12 TO 15

1/3 cup butter, melted
2 cups chocolate wafer cookie crumbs (40 wafers)
1/2 cup slivered almonds, toasted
6 ounces semisweet chocolate morsels
1 (15-ounce) can sweetened condensed milk
2 cups sour cream
1/3 cup amaretto
1 cup whipping cream, whipped

Combine butter, cookie crumbs, and almonds. Reserve 1 1/2 cups crumb mixture. Press remainder firmly into bottom of a 9-inch springform pan. Heat chocolate and condensed milk in a small saucepan over medium heat. In a large bowl, combine sour cream and amaretto; mix well. Stir in chocolate mixture; fold in whipped cream. Pour half of amaretto mixture over prepared crust; top with 1 cup of reserved crumb mixture. Add remaining amaretto mixture. Top with remaining 1/2 cup crumb mixture. Cover and freeze 6 hours or until firm.

[KATE GILMER PHILLIPS]

GOURMET ICE CREAM

Heat half-and-half in top of a double boiler until bubbles form around edge of pan.   Beat egg yolks and sugar until thick and pale. Add ½ cup of hot half-and-half to yolk mixture. Stir well. Pour yolk mixture into top of double boiler. Cook, stirring constantly, until mixture coats the back of a spoon.   Remove from heat, and add your choice of flavorings. Stir in whipping cream. Cool to room temperature. Chill at least 4 hours. Pour into container of a hand-turned or electric ice-cream freezer. Freeze according to manufacturer's directions.

[DAVID KERN STALLWORTH]

SERVES 8 TO 10
MAKES 1½ QUARTS

2 cups half-and-half
6 egg yolks
⅔ cup sugar
   One of the following desired flavorings
1 cup whipping cream, chilled

Flavorings:
¼ cup brandy
2 teaspoons vanilla extract
8 ounces semisweet chocolate, melted; plus ¼ cup bourbon
¼ cup cream sherry; 2 ounces candied lemon peel; plus 3 ounces toasted almonds

CANDIED CITRUS PEEL

Use a citrus zester (or sharp paring knife) to remove the rind only from fruit. Do not remove the white part (pith).   In a small, heavy saucepan, combine the sugar with ¼ cup water. Bring to a slow rolling boil. Lower heat to simmer. Add the citrus strips, and simmer 40 minutes. Remove peelings from syrup, and let dry on wax paper.   Candied citrus peel can be stored indefinitely in the freezer in an airtight container.

[CAROLINE STEVENS BOLVIG]

Wonderful dipped in melted chocolate or grated as a zest in desserts.

SERVES 4

2 to 3 lemons (or other citrus fruit)
2 cups sugar
¼ cup water

ICE-CREAM BOMBE

SERVES 12

1 (5½-ounce) package
shortbread cookies, crumbled,
or 6 ounces homemade
shortbread
2 tablespoons crème de cacao
½ gallon vanilla ice cream
½ gallon coffee ice cream
1 pint chocolate chunk or
toffee ice cream

Chocolate Sauce:
2 tablespoons butter, divided
½ cup chopped pecans or
almonds
2 teaspoons salt
2 ounces unsweetened chocolate
½ cup sugar
½ to ¾ cup milk
1 teaspoon vanilla

Place a 9½-inch stainless steel bowl in freezer. Soak shortbread cookies in creme de cacao. To prepare chocolate sauce, melt 1 tablespoon butter in a small saucepan over medium heat. Add nuts and salt. Cook until nuts are brown. In medium saucepan, melt 1 tablespoon butter and chocolate over low heat. Add sugar. Add ½ cup milk slowly, stirring until smooth. Add vanilla. (Sauce should be creamy. If not, add a little milk to achieve correct consistency.) Stir in nuts. Set aside.

To assemble the bombe, make sure ice creams are well-frozen and chocolate sauce is room temperature. Remove bowl from freezer. Working quickly, with carving knife slice vanilla ice cream into layers. Press into bottom of bowl to form a ¼-inch-thick layer. Cover with chocolate sauce. Next add a ¼-inch-thick layer of coffee ice cream, then add shortbread mixture. Top with chocolate chunk ice cream. Finish with remaining vanilla ice cream so that the bowl is completely full. Cover with plastic wrap and freeze immediately. Freeze at least 24 hours before serving. To serve, remove bowl and place on serving platter. Soak dish towel in very hot water. Place towel on top of bowl. May have to repeat several times to loosen ice cream from bowl. Slice as you would a cake. Serve immediately.

[ASHLEY CARR SMITH]

Layered Mocha Mud Pie

Serves 12

12 ounces macaroon cookies or pecan sandies, crumbled
1 quart chocolate fudge ice cream, softened
1 recipe Fantastic Chocolate Sauce (page 295), warm
1 quart coffee ice cream
½ cup crushed toffee bits (Heath, Skor, or Bits of Brickle)

Lightly spray bottom of 9-inch springform pan. Pat half of crumbled cookies into the pan. Spread chocolate ice cream over cookies. Drizzle half of chocolate sauce over ice cream. Layer remaining cookies over chocolate sauce. Spread coffee ice cream over cookies. Drizzle remaining chocolate sauce. Top with crushed toffee bits. Freeze until firm (at least 1 hour).

[Jeanie Jemison Matthews]

Lemon Soufflé Cake with Raspberry Sauce

Serves 8

1 envelope unflavored gelatin
½ cup warm water
4 eggs, separated
1 cup sugar, divided
Cream of tartar (optional)
1 pint whipping cream
¼ to ⅓ cup lemon juice
1 tablespoon grated lemon rind
2 dozen ladyfingers (soft kind)
2 (10-ounce) packages frozen raspberries
¼ cup sugar

Soften gelatin in warm water. Beat whites until foamy, gradually adding ½ cup sugar. Beat until stiff (may need to add a pinch of cream of tartar if egg whites will not hold a peak). Whip cream. Beat egg yolks, and add ½ cup sugar, beating until light and thick (about 10 minutes). Add lemon juice, rind, and gelatin. Fold egg white mixture into yolk mixture; fold in whipped cream. Line sides and bottom of a 9-inch springform pan with ladyfingers. Add half of mixture, and layer with ladyfingers. Cover with remaining mixture. Refrigerate 24 hours. Thaw berries and puree with ¼ cup sugar. Pour through a wire-mesh strainer, and refrigerate. Slice dessert, and serve drizzled with raspberry mixture.

[Cameron Daley Crowe]

SERVES 8

3 eggs
1 cup sugar
3/4 cup canned pumpkin
1 teaspoon lemon juice
3/4 cup all-purpose flour
1 teaspoon baking powder
2 teaspoons ground cinnamon
1 teaspoon ground ginger
1/2 teaspoon ground nutmeg
1/2 teaspoon salt
1 cup chopped pecans, divided

Filling/Frosting:
8 ounces cream cheese, softened
1/2 cup butter, softened
1 cup powdered sugar
2 tablespoons bourbon

PUMPKIN-PECAN ROULAGE WITH BOURBON-CREAM CHEESE FILLING

Beat eggs on high speed of an electric mixer for 5 minutes, gradually adding sugar. Stir in pumpkin and lemon juice. ✺ In a separate bowl, combine flour and next 5 ingredients, and fold into egg mixture. ✺ Grease jellyroll pan or coat with vegetable cooking spray. Line with wax paper; grease again and flour. Pour mixture into pan, and bake at 375° for 15 minutes. Immediately turn out cake onto towel that has been dusted with powdered sugar and roll up together length or widthwise in towel, depending on how many people you will be serving. Cool on wire rack. ✺ Prepare filling/frosting while cake is baking. ✺ To prepare filling, combine cream cheese and butter. Sift powdered sugar over bowl, and then stir in bourbon. ✺ Once cake has thoroughly cooled, carefully unroll and place a small amount of cream cheese mixture in the center. Sprinkle with 3/4 cup nuts. Roll up, and transfer to a serving platter. Completely frost roll with remaining cream cheese mixture, and sprinkle top with remaining nuts. Refrigerate.

[NATALIE HICKS LEE]

E I G H T - L A Y E R C H O C O L A T E   T O R T E

SERVES 10

1 cup sifted all-purpose flour
1 teaspoon baking powder
3/4 cup sugar
4 eggs, separated
1/2 teaspoon salt
1/2 teaspoon cream of tartar
1/3 cup sugar
1/4 cup water
1 teaspoon vanilla extract
1 teaspoon orange extract
   Garnish: finely chopped
   almonds or pecans

Frosting:
1 1/4 cups butter, softened
2 1/2 (1-ounce) squares unsweetened
   chocolate, melted
1 1/4 teaspoons vanilla extract
3/4 teaspoon maple flavoring
2 1/2 cups sifted powdered sugar

Place sheet of aluminum foil or parchment on a 15 x 10-inch baking sheet. Grease bottom of foil or parchment. Repeat procedure with second sheet of foil and second baking sheet. ✐ Sift together flour, baking powder, and sugar in a small mixing bowl. ✐ In a large bowl, beat egg whites, salt, and cream of tartar until soft mounds form. Gradually add 1/3 cup sugar, beating until stiff peaks form. (Do not overbeat.) ✐ Combine egg yolks, water, vanilla, and orange extract. Add to flour mixture, and beat at medium speed with an electric mixer 1 minute. Fold batter into egg white mixture gently but thoroughly. ✐ Spoon batter into 2 foil pans, spreading batter evenly. Bake at 375° for 10 to 12 minutes. Cool in pan 10 minutes. Remove foil pans, and cut each cake into quarters. Wrap in foil and store, or frost immediately. ✐ To prepare frosting, cream butter until fluffy. Add chocolate, flavorings, and powdered sugar, beating until blended. Beat at high speed until mixture reaches spreading consistency. ✐ Stack all 8 layers, spreading frosting between each layer. Frost sides and top of cake. Garnish, if desired. Chill at least 2 hours.

[I R E N E   M O S E L E Y   S H I V E R I C K   ]

SERVES 6 TO 8

1 cup chopped pitted dates
1 cup black walnuts (pecans
  may be substituted)
1 egg
1 cup sugar
¼ teaspoon baking powder
1 cup milk
  Whipped cream

SERVES 12

Pudding:
  1 loaf French bread
  1 quart milk
  3 eggs
  2 cups sugar
  2 tablespoons vanilla extract
  1 cup chopped, unpeeled apple
  1 cup raisins
  3 tablespoons butter, melted

Whiskey Sauce:
  8 tablespoons butter
  1 cup sugar
  1 egg, beaten
    Whiskey to taste
    (2 tablespoons bourbon)

MAKES ABOUT
1 1/2 CUPS

1 teaspoon grated orange zest
1 cup apricot preserves
2 tablespoons water
3 tablespoons apricot brandy

CHRISTMAS DATE NUT PUDDING

Combine first 6 ingredients. Pour into a large lightly greased loafpan. Bake at 350° for 30 minutes. Serve warm with whipped cream.

[FLORENCE HARTSFIELD ANDERSON]

BREAD PUDDING WITH WHISKEY SAUCE

Tear bread into small pieces. Combine with milk in a large bowl, crushing pieces until well mixed. Combine eggs, sugar, vanilla, and fruits. Pour into bread mixture, and stir well. Pour melted butter into a 4-quart round baking dish. Add bread mixture. Bake at 350° until very firm and brown on top (1¼ to 1½ hours). Let cool at room temperature. Serve with whiskey sauce. For whiskey sauce, cook butter and sugar in top of double boiler until sugar is dissolved. Add egg and whisk so that it does not curdle. Add whiskey to taste. Serve over bread pudding. For a different sauce, try Warm Apricot Sauce.

[MARGARET McKINNON MUSSLEMAN]

WARM APRICOT SAUCE

In a small saucepan, combine orange zest, preserves, and 2 tablespoons water; cook over medium heat, stirring constantly, until boiling. Reduce heat and simmer until thick. Remove from heat, and stir in brandy. Serve warm over ice cream or bread pudding.

CHOCOLATE BREAD PUDDING

Combine bread, chocolate morsels, and milk in a large bowl; soak 15 minutes. ✢ Mix together egg yolks, sugar, cinnamon, salt, and vanilla. Add to soaked bread mixture. Stir lightly with fork until well blended. ✢ Pour into a greased 2-quart baking dish. Set dish into a larger pan of hot water. Bake at 350° for 45 minutes. ✢ Serve with whipped cream.

[FRANCES LLOYD SHEARER]

SERVES 6

5 cups diced white bread
6 ounces semisweet chocolate morsels
3 cups warm milk
3 egg yolks
1/3 cup sugar
1/2 teaspoon ground cinnamon
1/4 teaspoon salt
1 teaspoon vanilla extract
Whipped cream

RASPBERRY POACHED PEARS IN CHOCOLATE SAUCE

Combine water and sugar in saucepan. Cook until sugar dissolves. Reduce heat to low simmer, and add raspberry vinegar. ✢ Peel and core pears, and immediately place into hot sugar mixture. Simmer 30 minutes, turning pears several times. Do not overcook. Let cool in syrup. Serve cold as is, or reheat and serve with chocolate sauce. ✢ To prepare sauce, melt chocolate and butter in a saucepan, stirring often. Add sugar, salt, vanilla, and liqueur, and serve over pears.

[DOUG RICHEY]

SERVES 4

3 cups water
1 1/2 cups sugar
4 tablespoons raspberry vinegar (can use 1 vanilla bean instead)
4 pears (ripe, but firm)

Chocolate Sauce:
4 ounces semisweet chocolate
1/2 cup butter
3/4 cup sugar
Pinch of salt
1 teaspoon vanilla extract
2 tablespoons any flavor liqueur (optional)

SERVES 6 TO 8

1 tablespoon unflavored
   gelatin
¼ cup cold water
3 eggs, separated
1 cup sugar
⅓ cup lemon juice
   Grated rind of 1 lemon
1 teaspoon vanilla extract
2 cups whipping cream
   Garnishes: lemon slices,
   sprigs of mint

SERVES 6 TO 8

2 (1-ounce) squares
   unsweetened chocolate,
   melted
½ cup powdered sugar
1 cup hot milk
¾ cup granulated sugar
1 envelope unflavored gelatin
¼ teaspoon salt
½ cup water
1 teaspoon vanilla extract
2 cups whipping cream,
   whipped
¼ cup toasted slivered almonds

COLD LEMON SOUFFLÉ

Dissolve gelatin in cold water. Place container of gelatin mixture in a pan of hot water. Heat gelatin mixture until it becomes clear and liquid. Set aside. Beat egg yolks until lemon colored. Gradually add sugar, and heat until very light. Beat in lemon juice, grated lemon rind, and vanilla. Add gelatin. Allow mixture to cool until it starts to congeal. Beat cream until stiff. Fold into lemon mixture. Beat egg whites until stiff. Fold into lemon mixture. Pour mixture into medium soufflé dish, and chill several hours. Garnish with slices of lemon or sprigs of mint. Serve with cookies.

[LOUISA MACLEOD HAINES]

CHOCOLATE MOUSSE WITH RASPBERRY SAUCE

Combine chocolate and powdered sugar in saucepan. Gradually add hot milk, stirring constantly. Place over low heat, and stir until mixture almost reaches boiling point. (Do not boil.) Remove chocolate mixture from heat. Combine granulated sugar, gelatin, and salt in a small saucepan. Stir in water, and place over low heat until gelatin is dissolved, stirring constantly. Add gelatin mixture and vanilla to chocolate mixture. Chill until slightly thickened. Beat with a rotary beater until light and fluffy. Fold in whipped cream. Spoon into 2-quart mold or serving dish. Garnish with toasted almonds. Chill 2 to 3 hours. Serve with Raspberry Sauce.

[MARY EUGENIA BERRY]

R A S P B E R R Y   S A U C E

SERVES 6 TO 8

Puree raspberries in blender, and pour through a strainer into saucepan, discarding seeds and pulp. Combine cornstarch and water, and stir into puree. Cook until slightly thickened. Add lemon juice and crème de cassis. ✦ Serve hot. Add sugar if berries need sweetening.

1 (10-ounce) package frozen raspberries, thawed, or 1 pint fresh
1 tablespoon cornstarch
2 tablespoons water
Juice of 1/2 lemon
2 tablespoons crème de cassis
Sugar to taste

B I T T E R S W E E T
C H O C O L A T E   T R U F F L E
T A R T

SERVES 8

Combine butter and sugar in food processor. Add salt, vanilla, and cocoa. Process 1 minute. Add flour. Process until just blended. ✦ Between 2 sheets of wax paper, roll out mixture into an 11-ounce disk. Refrigerate several hours. Press into a 10-inch springform pan, and prick bottom of shell with fork. Bake at 375° for 5 minutes or until pastry is dry. Cool. ✦ Heat bittersweet chocolate and whipping cream over low heat until smooth. Pour chocolate cream mixture through a wire-mesh strainer into cooled tart shell. Refrigerate at least 3 hours. ✦ To serve: Lay a decorative stencil over center of tart. Using a fine wire-mesh strainer, sift remaining 1 tablespoon of cocoa over top. Lift off stencil to reveal chocolate pattern on tart. Unmold and remove from pan.

6 tablespoons butter, softened
1/2 cup sugar
1/8 teaspoon salt
3/4 teaspoon vanilla extract
1/4 cup plus 3 tablespoons Dutch processed cocoa
3/4 cup all-purpose flour
10 ounces bittersweet chocolate, chopped
1 1/4 cups whipping cream

[SPENCE LEE STALLWORTH]

S E R V E S 6 T O 8

1½ cups sugar
½ cup water
2¼ cups whipping cream
¾ cup cream of coconut
3 eggs plus
3 egg yolks
¾ cup sweetened flaked coconut
1 teaspoon almond extract
¼ cup sliced almonds, toasted
¼ cup sweetened flaked coconut, toasted

C O C O N U T   C A R A M E L   F L A N

Heat sugar and water in medium saucepan over low heat, stirring occasionally, until sugar is dissolved. Increase heat and boil until sugar caramelizes (about 10 minutes). Pour immediately into soufflé dish. Swirl in dish to cover bottom and part of sides. 🌿 Bring cream and cream of coconut to a boil in a heavy saucepan; remove from heat, and set aside. 🌿 Beat eggs and yolks until thick. Gradually add to hot cream mixture. Stir in ¾ cup coconut and almond extract. Pour into prepared soufflé dish. Place dish in a large roasting pan. Add enough water to roasting pan to reach halfway up sides of soufflé dish. Bake until a wooden pick comes out clean. Cool to room temperature; cover and chill. To serve, invert flan onto platter and sprinkle with toasted almonds and ¼ cup flaked coconut.

[A L Y S O N L U T Z B U T T S]

M A K E S 1 Q U A R T

4 eggs
4 cups whole milk
½ cup sugar
⅛ teaspoon salt
1½ teaspoons vanilla extract

B O I L E D   C U S T A R D

Bring eggs to room temperature. Heat milk in a heavy saucepan until scalding. 🌿 Beat eggs in bowl. Add sugar and whisk. Slowly add hot milk (drop by drop) to egg mixture, stirring constantly with a wire whisk. When completely blended, return to saucepan. 🌿 Cook over medium-low heat, stirring constantly until mixture is thick and coats a spoon. 🌿 Add salt and vanilla. Strain, if necessary. Chill or serve hot. Custard thickens as it cools.

[L U A N N E G R A V L E E C H A P M A N]

Z A B A G L I O N E

In a heatproof bowl, whisk eggs, sugar, and wine until thickened and light. ✒ Place bowl over simmering water until sauce thickens. ✒ Cool completely. Stir in cream. Serve chilled over fresh berries.

[B E T H   O L I V E R   L E H N E R]

SERVES 4

4 eggs
3/4 cups sugar
1/2 cup dry white wine
1 cup whipping cream
1 pint each blueberries and
 raspberries

M O C H A   M O U S S E
D E M I T A S S E

Blend chocolate chips 10 seconds on medium speed in blender. Add coffee; blend 5 seconds. Add egg yolks and flavoring; blend 15 seconds. ✒ In a separate bowl, beat egg whites and cream of tartar until soft peaks form. Add sugar 1 tablespoon at a time, until sugar is dissolved. Fold in chocolate mixture. Pour into demitasse cups and top with sweetened whipped cream.

[T H E   D A I L Y   C U P]

SERVES 6

6 ounces chocolate morsels
1/2 cup hot brewed coffee
4 eggs, separated
3/4 teaspoon rum, brandy or crème
 de cacao
1/4 teaspoon cream of tartar
3 tablespoons sugar
 Sweetened whipped cream

Just a Thought

For desserts such as this or the French Silk Pie (page 299),
or for meringues, use Superfine instant dissolving sugar.
It can be found at specialty stores and dissolves much faster
than regular granulated sugar.

B E R M U D A T R I F L E

SERVES 10

1 sponge or layercake
1/4 cup Jamaican rum (optional)
1 pint fresh strawberries or
  1 (16-ounce) package frozen
  strawberries, thawed
1 (3-ounce) package instant
  vanilla pudding mix
1 cup whipping cream
1/4 cup sugar
1/4 cup toasted slivered almonds
Garnishes: fresh whole
  strawberries and sliced
  kiwifruit

Slice cake and arrange over bottom and up sides of trifle bowl. Pour rum over cake, if desired. ✒ Spoon strawberries over cake. Prepare pudding according to package directions. Let stand 5 minutes, then pour over strawberries. ✒ Beat whipping cream and sugar until stiff. Spoon over pudding layer. Sprinkle top with almonds; garnish with fresh strawberries and kiwifruit, if desired.

[Y V O N N E C . W I L L I E]

G R A N D M A R N I E R S O U F F L É

SERVES 12

4 tablespoons butter
1/4 cup all-purpose flour
1 3/4 cups hot milk
1/2 cup sugar
5 egg yolks
3 tablespoons Grand Marnier
7 egg whites

Melt butter in small saucepan. Add flour, and whisk to make a roux. Add hot milk and sugar. Cook until thick. Remove from heat. Add egg yolks one at a time, and stir in Grand Marnier. ✒ Beat egg whites until stiff but moist. Fold them in. ✒ Pour into buttered 2-quart soufflé dish. Bake at 375° for 30 to 40 minutes.

[C H E F S T A N D E R E N C I N]
M O U N T A I N B R O O K C L U B

CRIOLLA'S COFFEE

Pour first 3 ingredients into a large mug. Add enough coffee so cup is three-fourths full, and stir. ✦ Top with whipped cream and chocolate shavings.

[ANNALISA THOMPSON JAGER]

SERVES 1

1 ounce Bailey's Irish Cream
1 ounce Kahlúa
1/2 to 1 ounce Frangelico
1 cup fresh brewed coffee
    Whipped cream
    Chocolate shavings

CREAMY COCONUT-PECAN SQUARES

Place layer of graham crackers across bottom of a 13 x 9 x 2-inch glass baking dish. ✦ In saucepan, heat butter, sugar, and milk until boiling. Remove from heat. ✦ Add coconut, pecans, and cracker crumbs. Pour evenly over layer of graham crackers. Combine first 3 icing ingredients. Stir in 4 tablespoons milk and beat until fluffy. (Add remaining 2 tablespoons milk, as needed, for easy spreading.) Spread over coconut mixture. Chill several hours. Cut into squares.

[KATHERINE LIVINGSTON ARD]

MAKES 2 1/2 DOZEN

1 (1-pound) box graham
    crackers
1/2 cup butter
1 cup sugar
1/2 cup milk
1 cup flaked coconut
1 cup chopped pecans
1 cup graham cracker crumbs
Icing:
1/2 cup melted butter
2 cups powdered sugar
1 teaspoon vanilla extract
4 to 6 tablespoons milk

SHORTBREAD

Soften butter. Cream butter and sugar. Add flour, mixing well. Press into a 13 x 9 x 2-inch baking dish for thick shortbread or 15 x 10 x 1-inch jellyroll pan for thin shortbread. Cut into 1-inch squares. Pierce each piece with fork. ✦ Bake at 325° for 35 to 40 minutes or until golden brown. Recut while hot. Cool on wire rack. Remove from pan.

[BESS RICE McCRORY]

MAKES 4 TO 5 DOZEN

2 cups butter (do not substitute)
1 cup sugar
5 cups all-purpose flour

MAKES 3 DOZEN

1 cup peanut butter
1 cup chopped dates
1 cup powdered sugar
1 cup chopped nuts
3 tablespoons butter, melted

Coating:
¼ block paraffin
12 ounces chocolate morsels

CHOCOLATE-DIPPED PEANUT BUTTER

Combine first 5 ingredients, and form into walnut-size balls.
Melt paraffin in top of a double boiler over hot water. Add chocolate, and stir until melted. Dip balls in chocolate mixture, and place on wax paper. Chill.

[CELENE EASSON]

MAKES 2½ DOZEN

1 (10-ounce) bar sweetened baking chocolate
4 tablespoons whipping cream
6 tablespoons butter
1 tablespoon Cointreau (optional)
¼ cup cocoa

PARTY TRUFFLES

Break chocolate into pieces. Microwave on HIGH for 2 minutes.
Stir until smooth. Stir in cream, butter, and if desired, Cointreau.
Chill 30 minutes. Form into small balls. Roll in cocoa.

[KAY CATHEY BROWN]

MAKES 2½ DOZEN

2 cups milk chocolate morsels
¼ cup sour cream
2 tablespoons amaretto
2 cups chopped almonds

CHOCOLATE AMARETTO TRUFFLES

Melt chocolate morsels in top of a double boiler over hot water; stir until smooth. Remove from heat, and blend in sour cream. Add amaretto, and mix well. Chill until firm. Drop by teaspoonfuls onto waxed paper. Shape into balls, and roll in almonds. Chill 30 minutes.

[CATHY CRISS ADAMS]

PRALINE BROWNIES

Combine first 4 ingredients in large mixing bowl; stir until well blended. Add salt, and gradually add sifted flour until blended. Stir in nuts. ✒ Bake in a 15$\frac{1}{2}$ x 10$\frac{1}{2}$ x1-inch pan at 350° for 25-30 minutes. Cool and cut into squares or bars.

[SUSAN EMACK ALISON]

MAKES 3$\frac{1}{2}$ DOZEN

1 (16-ounce) package light
    brown sugar
3 eggs, beaten
1 stick butter, melted
    Pinch of salt
1$\frac{1}{2}$ cups self-rising flour, sifted
1$\frac{1}{2}$ cups chopped pecans

FABULOUS BROWNIES

Cream butter and sugar. Add eggs, one at a time, mixing after each addition. Add flour, chocolate syrup, vanilla, and nuts. ✒ Pour into a greased and floured jellyroll pan, and bake at 350° for 15 to 20 minutes. ✒ To prepare frosting, place sugar, butter, and milk in a medium saucepan. Bring to a slow boil; boil 30 seconds. Add chocolate morsels, and stir until chocolate melts. Remove from heat, and pour immediately over brownies. (Frosting seems thin but will set.)

[EVELYN BLEVINS]

MAKES 3$\frac{1}{2}$ DOZEN

$\frac{1}{2}$ cup butter, softened
1 cup sugar
4 eggs
1 cup all-purpose flour
1 (16-ounce) can chocolate syrup
1 teaspoon vanilla extract
$\frac{1}{2}$ cup chopped nuts (optional)

Frosting:
1$\frac{1}{2}$ cups sugar
6 tablespoons butter
6 tablespoons milk
1 cup chocolate morsels

MAKES 1 1/2 DOZEN

1 1/4 cups all-purpose flour
1 cup firmly packed brown sugar
3/4 cup regular or quick-cooking oats
1/2 cup flaked coconut
1 tablespoon grated orange peel (optional)
1/2 teaspoon salt
3/4 cup butter, softened
3/4 cup real English marmalade (apricot jam may be substituted)

MAKES 4 DOZEN

2 cups brown sugar
2 tablespoons all-purpose flour
2/3 teaspoon salt
2 egg whites
2 teaspoons vanilla extract
2 cups chopped pecans

MAKES 2 DOZEN

2 egg whites
1/2 cup sugar
6 ounces chocolate morsels
1 (3.5-ounce) can moist coconut
2 drops peppermint oil

ENGLISH MATRIMONIALS

Combine first 6 ingredients; cut in butter with fork or pastry blender until mixture resembles coarse crumbs. Press half of mixture into an 8-inch square baking pan. Cover with marmalade, spreading gently. Top with remaining crumb mixture. Bake at 325° for 40 to 45 minutes. Cool. Cut into squares.

[MARGARET PETERSON CAMPBELL]

PRALINE COOKIES

Combine sugar, flour, and salt in large bowl. In small bowl, beat egg whites until peaks form. Add egg whites to sugar mixture, stirring until blended. Stir in vanilla and pecans. Drop by teaspoonfuls onto heavily greased baking sheets. Bake at 275° for 30 minutes. Remove to racks to cool.

[KATHY SKINNER]

CHOCOLATE MACAROONS

Beat egg whites until stiff peaks form. Add sugar slowly to egg whites. Melt chocolate, and add to egg whites. Fold in coconut. Put 2 drops of peppermint oil into a teaspoon; then pour back into bottle. Use spoon to stir mixture. Drop mixture by teaspoonfuls onto cookie sheet. Bake at 325° for 20 minutes.

[ASHLEY CARR SMITH]

P U M P K I N   C O O K I E S

Cream butter, sugar, and pumpkin. Add egg, and mix well. Combine flour and next 3 ingredients. Stir into creamed mixture, mixing well. Stir in raisins. ❧ Drop batter by teaspoonfuls onto greased cookie sheets. Bake at 375° for 10 to 12 minutes. ❧ To prepare frosting, heat butter, milk, and brown sugar until sugar is dissolved. Cool. Add powdered sugar and vanilla. Spread frosting on warm cookies.

[C A R O L   M A Y N E   B O U D R E A U X]

MAKES 4 DOZEN

1 cup butter
1 cup sugar
1 cup canned pumpkin
1 egg
2 cups all-purpose flour
1 teaspoon baking soda
1 teaspoon ground cinnamon
1/2 teaspoon salt
1 cup raisins

Frosting:
3 tablespoons butter
4 teaspoons milk
1/2 cup brown sugar
1 cup powdered sugar
3/4 teaspoon vanilla extract

O A T M E A L   C O O K I E S

Cream butter and sugars. Add egg. ❧ Combine flour, baking soda, and salt. Stir into creamed mixture, mixing until blended. Add oats and remaining ingredients. ❧ Drop by teaspoonfuls onto lightly greased cookie sheets. Bake at 350° for 8 to 10 minutes (will flatten to thin, crisp cookies).

[J E N N I F E R   J O H N S T O N   A D A M S]

MAKES 2 DOZEN

1/2 cup butter, softened
1/2 cup brown sugar
1/2 cup sugar
1 egg
1 cup all-purpose flour
1 teaspoon baking soda
1/2 teaspoon salt
1 cup quick-cooking oatmeal
1 cup Rice Krispies
1 cup flaked coconut (optional)
1 teaspoon vanilla extract
1 teaspoon ground cinnamon

MOLASSES SUGAR COOKIES

Combine first 4 ingredients, beating well. Add flour and next 5 ingredients; mix well. ✒ Form mixture into 1-inch balls. Roll in extra sugar. Place on ungreased cookie sheets. ✒ Bake at 375° for 8 to 10 minutes.

[TANYA MELTON COOPER]

WHITE CHOCOLATE MACADAMIA NUT COOKIES

Combine first 3 ingredients in small bowl, and set aside. ✒ Cream butter and sugars. Add eggs and vanilla. Add flour mixture, nuts, and white chocolate. ✒ Drop by teaspoonfuls onto cookie sheets. Bake at 350° for 15 to 20 minutes.

PRALINE SAUCE

Melt butter in small saucepan over low heat. Add pecans; cook, stirring, until lightly browned. Gradually add sugar, stirring until smooth. Stir in water. Bring to boiling; boil, stirring constantly, 1 minute. Serve warm.

BETTER-FOR-YOU BROWNIES

Coat a 13 x 9 x 2-inch baking dish with vegetable cooking spray. ✍ Melt chocolate, stirring often, in a small bowl or pan over a larger pan of hot water or in microwave at MEDIUM power. Set aside. ✍ In a medium bowl, stir together flour, cocoa, and salt. In a large bowl, whisk together egg whites and eggs. Add sugar, corn syrup, applesauce, oil, and vanilla. Whisk in melted chocolate. ✍ Add flour mixture to egg mixture, and stir with a spoon until blended. Pour into prepared pan, and sprinkle with walnuts. Bake at 350° for 35 minutes or until a wooden pick inserted in center comes out clean. Cool completely in pan. Cut into squares.

[DEE JAY'S BLUE & WHITE CAFE]

129 calories; 2 g. protein; 4 g. fat; 23 g. carbohydrate;
64 mg. sodium; 18 mg. cholesterol

MAKES 2 DOZEN

1 ounce unsweetened chocolate
1 cup sifted cake flour
3/4 cup unsweetened cocoa
1/2 teaspoon salt
3 egg whites
2 eggs
1 1/4 cups sugar
3/4 cup dark corn syrup
3/4 cup applesauce or prune puree
1/4 cup vegetable oil
1 tablespoon vanilla extract
1/2 cup toasted walnuts, chopped

TOO-EASY PEACH COBBLER

Place peaches in an 8-inch square baking dish coated with vegetable cooking spray. ✍ Cut each slice of bread into 5 long strips, and place evenly over fruit. ✍ In a bowl, combine sugar, flour, egg, and melted butter. Pour over fruit and bread. ✍ Bake at 350° for 35 minutes or until golden brown. (Butter and sugar caramelize over bread strips. You won't know it's bread!)

[NANCY BEAIRD BROMBERG]

SERVES 6

6 medium peaches, peeled and sliced
5 slices white bread, crusts removed
1 to 1 1/2 cups sugar
2 tablespoons all-purpose flour
1 egg
1/2 cup butter, melted

P E A R   C R I S P

Quick & easy

Place pears in a greased 2-quart baking dish. Toss pears with lemon juice, cinnamon, and nutmeg. In a bowl, combine flour and butter until mixture resembles crumbs. Add oats and brown sugar. Stir well; sprinkle over pears. Bake at 375° for 20 to 25 minutes or until browned and pears are tender. Serve with ice cream or whipped cream.

[A N D R E A   H U R T   S O M E R V I L L E   ]

S T R A W B E R R Y   C O B B L E R

Roll out pastry, and divide in half. Cut into 1-inch strips. Place half of strips on a baking sheet. Bake at 450° for 8 minutes. (Reserve other half for top of cobbler.) Combine strawberries, sugar, and water. Spoon half of berry mixture into a glass loafpan. Top with ⅛ cup butter, cut into pieces, and then baked pastry strips. Add remaining berry mixture and ⅛ cup butter. Top with unbaked pastry strips arranged in a lattice pattern. Bake at 425° for 15 minutes. Reduce heat to 250° and bake an additional 1½ hours.

[A N N E   T E R R Y   J O H N S O N   ]

SPECIAL THANKS

We would like to thank the many community members and businesses who have helped to make FOOD FOR THOUGHT what it is. Their generous contributions have increased the quality of our book, which will serve to increase the quality of life throughout the Birmingham community.

John Alex Floyd, Jr. , Editor, Southern Living *magazine*
Eleanor Griffin, Executive Editor, Southern Living *magazine*
Susan C. Payne, Senior Foods Editor, Oxmoor House
Judy Feagin, Home Economist, Southern Living *magazine*
Ashley Arthur, Foods Copy Editor, Southern Living *magazine*
Jean Liles
Bruce Akin, Oxmoor House
Barbara Finch, EBSCO Media
Terry G. Slaughter, SlaughterHanson Advertising
Ruth N. Bean, SlaughterHanson Advertising
Marion English, SlaughterHanson Advertising

Clyde Anderson, CEO, Books-a-Million
Kathleen Grasse, Color Unlimited, Inc.
Bonnie Bailey
Marjorie Johnston
Martin Hames
Scott Berg, Vincent's Market
Debby Maugans
Bridges Antiques
Bromberg and Co. Inc.
Charlotte & Company
The Chinaberry

We also wish to offer our appreciation to the numerous League members, families, and friends who so generously contributed their favorite recipes to FOOD FOR THOUGHT, as well as the volunteers who spent countless hours testing recipes to provide us with the quality entrées featured within. Lastly, we want to recognize those on the committee who enthusiastically joined in this project. It is our sincere hope that no one has been inadvertently overlooked.

Karen Jordan Askins
Jan Pittman Hunter
Frances Parker Faulconer
Allison Fitts Kearney
Harriet Pascoe McFadden
Marion Hunt Newton
Lee Foster Nix

Catherine Aubrey Pittman
Ellen MacElvain Rhett
Susan Ellis Thomas
Margaret Trechsel
Sharon Denise St. John
Kathy Russell
Amy Robertson Barr
Mary Manly McWilliams

Carol Collinsworth Hines
Jane Gelzer Menendez
Anne Straker Plosser
Susan Englund Gaskin
Alice Miller Ashton
Elizabeth Hightower Baker
Emily Lawson Wade

FOOD FOR THOUGHT

Please send ____ copies   @ $19.95 each $ _____

Postage and handling   @ $ 3.00 each $ _____

Alabama residents add 8% sales tax   @ $ 1.60 each $ _____

                                 TOTAL $ _____

Make checks payable to: JLB Publications
                                 Junior League of Birmingham
                                 2212 20th Avenue, South
                                 Birmingham, Alabama 35223

Phone orders welcome: (205) 879-9861 FAX: (205) 879-9868

Credit cards accepted: (Check one)   ❐ Visa   ❐ MasterCard

                                 No. _____ Exp. _____

Signature of cardholder: _____

Name:

_____

Mailing Address:

_____

_____

_____

City: _____ State: _____
Zip: _____
Phone: _____

FOOD FOR THOUGHT

Please send ____ copies   @ $19.95 each $ _____

Postage and handling   @ $ 3.00 each $ _____

Alabama residents add 8% sales tax   @ $ 1.60 each $ _____

                                 TOTAL $ _____

Make checks payable to: JLB Publications
                                 Junior League of Birmingham
                                 2212 20th Avenue, South
                                 Birmingham, Alabama 35223

Phone orders welcome: (205) 879-9861 FAX: (205) 879-9868

Credit cards accepted: (Check one)   ❐ Visa   ❐ MasterCard

                                 No. _____ Exp. _____

Signature of cardholder: _____

Name:

_____

Mailing Address:

_____

_____

_____

City: _____ State: _____
Zip: _____
Phone: _____

FOOD FOR THOUGHT

Please send ____ copies   @ $19.95 each $ _____

Postage and handling   @ $ 3.00 each $ _____

Alabama residents add 8% sales tax   @ $ 1.60 each $ _____

                                 TOTAL $ _____

Make checks payable to: JLB Publications
                                 Junior League of Birmingham
                                 2212 20th Avenue, South
                                 Birmingham, Alabama 35223

Phone orders welcome: (205) 879-9861 FAX: (205) 879-9868

Credit cards accepted: (Check one)   ❐ Visa   ❐ MasterCard

                                 No. _____ Exp. _____

Signature of cardholder: _____

Name:

_____

Mailing Address:

_____

_____

_____

City: _____ State: _____
Zip: _____
Phone: _____